PENGUIN BOOKS

HEIR OF STORMS

HEIR
OF
STORMS

LAURYN HAMILTON MURRAY

PENGUIN BOOKS

PENGUIN BOOKS

UK | USA | Canada | Ireland | Australia
India | New Zealand | South Africa

Penguin Books is part of the Penguin Random House group of companies
whose addresses can be found at global.penguinrandomhouse.com

www.penguin.co.uk   www.puffin.co.uk   www.ladybird.co.uk

Penguin
Random House
UK

First published 2025

001

Text copyright © Lauryn Hamilton Murray, 2025
Cover illustration copyright © Chris @ KJA-artists.com, 2025
Chapter head and map illustrations copyright © Tomislav Tomić, 2025

The moral right of the author and illustrators has been asserted

Set in 10.5/15pt Sabon LT Std
Typeset by Jouve (UK), Milton Keynes
Printed and bound in Great Britain by Clays Ltd, Elcograf S.p.A.

The authorized representative in the EEA is Penguin Random House Ireland,
Morrison Chambers, 32 Nassau Street, Dublin D02 YH68

A CIP catalogue record for this book is available from the British Library

ISBN: 978-0-241-68112-1

All correspondence to:
Penguin Books
Penguin Random House Children's
One Embassy Gardens, 8 Viaduct Gardens, London SW11 7BW

For anyone who has ever felt like drizzle

Prologue

For many, my birth meant death. It meant drowning in the rain I called with my first breath. Corpses were swept away in a ceaseless flood, left to bloat and rot, or devoured by sea creatures or wayward sirens. Their lives were stolen as mine was starting.

I was the beginning that brought the end, as the Fidra say.

When I was young, my mother used to tell me stories. She made *me* a story. She spoke of a girl with eyes like rainclouds and sea mist, a girl with the power to summon the greatest storm our people have ever known. She had this way of glossing over the ugliness, of making things beautiful. It was many years before I realized that this story, *my* story, is not beautiful, and that the girl, that *I*, must be twisted, wicked, cursed.

Blaze is my given name. My mother thought I was Flameborn, and of course she did. Every Harglade inherits fire flickering at their fingertips, searing through their veins, burning bright at their core. Harglade fire is ancient fire, rare and pure and uncontaminated, preserved down the generations by the careful crossing of Ignitia bloodlines. When I was born, she thought the prayers of her House answered. Only they weren't. Or at least, not by me.

The moment my twin brother was pulled from our mother's body, every candle, torch and hearth was set alight. Flint. Flameborn.

And then there was me. Small, scrawny, with strange eyes and a strong set of lungs. Yet still no one suspected a thing. Why would they? Who would have thought that I, my mother's daughter, a pure-blooded descendant of the Fire Goddess Vesta herself, could ever be anything other than a child of flame?

Then the storm came.

Rain pelted stained glass like an iron-tipped whip, streaming in great sheets, stirring up the sea which rose to meet it.

This wasn't any ordinary rain – it didn't stop.

The storm grew and grew, spreading across the realm, flooding each and every province, drowning Etheri and Fidra alike. The ocean began to rise. Rivers burst their banks. Lakes bled on to land. Still, the rain fell.

I sometimes wonder how long my mother was able to convince herself that it was impossible, that it was mere *coincidence* that a storm had been called down upon the earth the instant her daughter was placed upon her chest. I wonder at what point the doubt began to crawl up her spine.

After countless days, as the world was starving, drowning, dying, when she could stand it no longer, my mother turned to face the truth that loomed behind her like a shadow. She plucked me from my cradle in the dead of night and walked out into the storm. She conjured a flame to light her way, but no sooner had it unfurled in her palm than it was doused. She tried again and again. But it was no use.

My storm swallowed her fire.

My mother made it to the very top of the tallest cliff, the sea heaving beneath her, the sky weeping above. She told me that I held out a tiny hand and closed it into a fist, as if I were grasping a handful of the storm and keeping it, like a secret. And just as it had started, the rain stopped. She who called the storm quelled the storm.

Me.

The story begins and ends with me.

I have many names. Or rather, I am known by many. I don't think of them as mine. My names belong to the people who use them. Those who spit them in anger, whisper them in fear, sing them in prayer. Those who mouth them to one another, too afraid to speak them aloud, or mutter them softly during tales told by candlelight.

The last Rain Singer.

The Aquatori, Etheri with the power to manipulate water, have legends about the Rain Singers. They could turn the brightest days grey. They could end droughts, quench wildfires. But there was never a Singer who summoned a storm like mine.

Gods' damned.

That one's particularly uplifting.

Murderer.

I didn't mean to flood the empire. I was a newborn baby, after all. But those who died, died because of me. So I suppose I'll have to take that one on the chin.

Changeling.

The name given to a Rain Singer born into a House as pure as flame. The first Aquatori in generations of Ignitia.

Freak.

It drips like venom from the lips of those brave enough to say it. Sometimes I hear the attendants whisper it in the hallways when they think I'm not around.

Names have teeth. They bite right to the bone.

But there's this other name, one from which I can never escape, one that is seared on to my skin like the brandmark on the back of my hand.

Storm Weaver.

That is what they call me.

The girl who wove the storm that shook the world.

PART I

The Heirs

I stand, perfectly straight, in front of the mirror.

'Don't slouch, Blaze!' Grandmother barks, prodding me in the back with her stick. She circles me for a full minute, lips pursed. 'No. No, I think not. Next.'

The seamstress bows her head deferentially to hide the scowl on her face. Needles still clamped between her teeth, she helps me out of the cerulean dress and hands it to one of the attendants. Another gown is quickly produced, this one a pale seafoam. I raise my arms obediently and she eases it over my head, careful not to tousle my hair, which has been twisted into two braids and threaded with small pearls. The dress is huge. It bulges out around me in swathes of ruffled lace. I wrinkle my nose but say nothing. At this point, after a dozen vetoed dresses, I would wear a sack if it pleased Grandmother. She raises a thin dark eyebrow, looks me up and down, then motions with her finger for me to spin. I spin.

My twin pops his head round the door of the dressing room, a hand over his eyes.

'Are you decent?'

'Depends on who you ask,' I mutter.

Flint splays his fingers, lowers his hand and snorts loudly. 'You look like a meringue.'

I grab a hairbrush off the dresser and throw it at him, but he shuts the door before it can meet its mark. I hear him laughing to himself all the way down the corridor.

'Next,' Grandmother says with a sigh, settling herself comfortably on a red-silk chaise.

Her own gown is a rich scarlet. Rubies gleam at her throat, the same as those set into the golden hilt of her stick, which is shaped like the head of a cobra – the emblem of our House. Her hair, once darker than my own, is now greying slightly at the temples, and has been bound in crimson spiderweb netting at the back of her neck.

Families like mine always tend to wear their court colour. I have never seen Grandmother in a dress other than red, or adorned with jewels other than her rubies. She is the colour red, to me.

The room is uncomfortably warm, heady with the scent of incense and spiced candles.

'Could you open a window?' I ask an attendant, who flinches as if I've shouted at her. She does as I say, though not before first glancing at Grandmother for confirmation.

It's marginally better, but not much. Valburn, home province of House Harglade, is situated in the heart of the Firelands. Hot, dry and densely populated, it sprawls just to the right of the Rift, the great yawning chasm that splits Ostacre in half, straight down the middle.

The next dress is a light, iridescent turquoise.

'Well, my lady?' The seamstress does not direct this

question to me, and she is answered with a small, irritated shake of the head.

'*Grandmother*,' I implore. 'It's fine, they're all fine. Any will do. I don't mind, really.'

The seamstress bristles.

'Well, *I* mind, Blaze, and you should too,' Grandmother snaps. 'Do you have *any* appreciation for the planning that has gone into this evening? Have you forgotten exactly *who* will be in attendance? You must look perfect. You must *be* perfect.'

She glares at me with beady eyes, Harglade eyes, deep brown and flecked with gold. I swallow a sigh and nod, defeated.

Today marks seventeen years since the storm, which means that today is my seventeenth Name Day. Flint's and mine. Tonight Grandmother is throwing a ball, and soon the guests will begin to arrive in their thousands – Ignitia, Ventalla, Terrathian and Aquatori alike, Etheri from each of the four Crown Courts. I'm scared to look at them. To look into the faces of those who think me abhorrent, who perhaps lost loved ones at my hands. Some will have travelled for days – weeks, even – just to catch a glimpse of the girl they call the Storm Weaver. I am made of stories to them, not flesh. They come to put a face to the myth, to peer at me inside my prison as though I were a songbird in a cage. Because in a way, I am. Caged, I mean. I have spent seventeen years hidden away behind steel gates and stone walls. I'm told it's for my own protection, but really it's to protect others from me.

Only what they don't know is that I could not weave another storm, even if I tried. That ever since I was a child, my abilities have been entirely unremarkable. That whatever power I might have possessed, it's gone. And I am empty.

It's laughable, really. The last Rain Singer, incapable of summoning more than a weak flurry of drizzle.

There seems to be no explanation for it beyond some cruel twist of fate. My gift may have taken others' lives, but it defined mine. Losing it meant losing part of my identity. Without it I'm ... Well, that's the thing. I'm not quite sure what I am.

Perhaps if I were still able to wield my powers, my confinement might be a little easier to bear. Might help pass the time, too. But I can't. I'm stuck here, in Harglade Hall, hollowed out and useless. I've often wondered whether it's my punishment, retribution for a crime I have no memory of committing. A price placed upon my very existence.

Grandmother tells me not to worry, that one day my rain will return, but I've long suspected that this is a lie designed to comfort me. Best I cling on to hope than drown in the knowledge of my own emptiness. Best nobody discovers that the most hated girl in all the realm is utterly defenceless.

The turquoise gown is removed, a little less carefully this time, and I am once again left standing in my underclothes. I fold my arms over my chest as an attendant approaches nervously, laden with yet more dresses.

Grandmother jabs her stick at a bright cobalt silk embroidered with silver peacock feathers. 'That one,' she announces triumphantly.

The peacock is the emblem of House Bartell. Though it's common in several of our neighbouring kingdoms to take one's father's family name, in Ostacre Etheri take the name of the more powerful House, meaning that I am a Harglade, not a Bartell. Perhaps Grandmother feels my father should be represented today despite his absence. I don't have much of an affinity with the peacock, much less my father, who hasn't laid eyes on me since my mother died almost seven years ago. I wonder what she'd make of this, my first public appearance. I wonder what she'd make of me. Sometimes she comes to me in dreams, and I wake with my hand outstretched.

Grief changes people, but it changed my father beyond recognition. The man who once carried me around on his shoulders and brought me back exotic gifts from his every military posting, that calm, kind, steadying presence I had known and loved and leaned on, was suddenly gone, replaced by someone cold and distant, barely there at all. In many ways, it was as if he died, too. But unlike my mother, he couldn't pass on. He couldn't be anything for anyone, much less a father. And he couldn't bear to look at me any more, because I reminded him too much of *her*. So along came Grandmother, who whisked me and my brothers away to Harglade Hall, where we have remained ever since.

The seamstress fastens the last button with a flourish and steps back. Both of us wait for approval with bated breath. The dress is elegant, supple, the bodice closely fitted, the skirts cascading from my hips and pooling on the floor.

The girl in the mirror looks back at me, and I feel as though I hardly know her.

Grandmother nods slowly, satisfied. 'Yes,' she says. 'Good. Beautiful.'

Pearls are hung from my earlobes and looped round my neck, matching the ones woven through my hair. I slip my feet into blue-satin flats and sit patiently as one attendant stains my lips blush pink and another brushes some silvery powder along my cheekbones. Nerves begin to set in then, a series of red-hot pokers jabbing me in the chest. I take a few deep breaths, wiping my palms on my dress and then scowling when I'm scolded for it.

One more year, I tell myself. *Just one more year, and then I'll be free.*

Finally permitted to leave, I set off along the winding stone corridor in search of my brothers. Finding both their rooms empty, I head down the back staircase.

Steam and shouting fill the kitchens. Attendants dart about frantically, for once too busy to notice me. Almost every surface is covered in food. Gold platters groan under the weight of delicate canapés, cheeses, cold meats dusted with pepper and pomegranate seeds, mousses and pies, sugared nuts and iced cakes as tall as my younger brother and twice as wide. I help myself to a strawberry tart before slipping out again, deciding to try the library.

This is where I spend most of my time. I must have read every book in here twice over. I used to keep a log of sorts, scoring a line on the loose panel above the fireplace, but gave up after I ran out of space. Grandmother went mad when she found it, arranging for it to be concealed by a tapestry – a rather ugly thing depicting a Harglade cobra emerging from flames. There's a book in here somewhere about tapestries, another about the emblems of the Noble Houses of Ostacre. I'm not fussy. I'll read anything: storybooks, history books, picture books, thick anthologies filled with poetry and ballads, large leather-bound ledgers detailing anything from Valburn's trading district to the repairs on the roof of Harglade Hall.

But my favourite books of all are the ones about the Otherlands, the wild, mythical isles far across the Second Sea that were once ruled by the Magi. I have studied their ancient languages, pored over maps, dog-eared and yellowing with age. I've always been fascinated by them, ever since I was a child.

Books have been my way of exploring the world I've spent my life locked away from. It's only the idea of seeing the Otherlands for myself one day that keeps me from wallowing too much in self-pity.

Sure enough, Flint is waiting for me as I push open the door to the library.

'*Finally*,' he says in an accusatory way, as if I had gladly volunteered to spend all afternoon being dressed and undressed like one of Renly's dolls. '*There* you are.'

'Here I am.'

The moment I reach my brother he swipes the remainder of the tart from my hand.

As far as fraternal twins go, Flint and I are more or less identical. We have the same unruly dark curls, olive skin and pointed chins. The only real difference between us – if you exclude basic anatomy and the brandmarks on the backs of our hands – is our eyes. While my own are grey and currently wide with indignation, Flint blinks innocently back at me with the signature Harglade brown-gold. He's wearing a thick, heavily embroidered maroon doublet.

'You look like a carpet,' I tell him.

Suddenly there's a scuffle, and our younger brother swings into view, leaping off the sliding ladder attached to one of the towering bookshelves.

'Blaaaaaaaze!' Renly skids to a halt beside us before sweeping into a bow so low he almost topples over. 'I've been practising,' he announces proudly.

'Very impressive,' I say.

'Flawless,' Flint confirms. 'You'll put me to shame.'

Ren beams, his smile the spitting image of our mother's. He has no memory of her, since she died giving birth to him. Sometimes, though it hurts to admit it, I envy him. He doesn't miss her stories, or the musical cadence of her voice. He doesn't miss the smell of her perfume, the sweet scent of fig and orange blossom that would arrive in the room before she did and linger long after she'd left. He isn't haunted by her absence because he never felt her presence. He cannot miss what he never knew.

Willing away the drizzle that threatens to fall above my head, I busy myself fastening the top button of his crimson doublet, which is ever so slightly too big for him. Since House Harglade is one of the most renowned flame-wielding families in the realm, Ren is dressed in Ignitia red. Some Etheri are born with their gifts, like Flint and me, but it's more common for powers to emerge during infancy. Yet what is unusual, and troubling, is that at six years old, Ren remains giftless. Grandmother says he's a late bloomer, that we must be patient. But still, I worry. I often find myself watching the candles when he's nearby, waiting desperately for a sign. That he's inherited the gift of fire, not water. That he's like them, and not an anomaly like me. Or worse, that he's as empty as I've become.

'It's almost time,' says Flint. 'Shall we watch the arrivals?'

I hesitate, my insides twisting. Never, not once in seventeen years, have I had any contact with the outside world. And now, today, the outside world is coming to me.

It feels a bit like being thrown to the wolves. Only the wolves in question are under the false impression that I am the predator.

I glance at Ren, who nods eagerly.

'All right.' I wiggle my fingers so that he takes my hand. 'Come on, then.'

By the time we clamber out the trapdoor of the attic and on to the roof, the clouds are tinged pink and the sun is beginning its slow descent. Harglade Hall is a large stone fortress which sits upon a mound that was once a volcano. Up here, we can see for miles. Valburn stretches out beneath us, a city of slate and iron. The streets are cobbled and the buildings are tall, built high rather than wide. Twisting through the middle of it all is the Creek, the inland waterway which runs like a vein through every province. It glistens, as still as glass.

Flint stabs his finger into the air. 'There!'

Snaking along the western road is a long, trailing procession. I try to make out the colour on the banners. Grey, I think. Grey for the Ventalla. It seems the Court of Wind will be the first to arrive, led by King Balen, King of the Air, the emperor's younger brother. They say he rides a Threskan stallion, the fastest horse in the world. They say he can hear a whisper from a mile off. They say the wind listens for him, like a spy without eyes.

Far below us, the sentries are opening the gates. I dig my nails into my palms as guests begin to spill into the courtyard.

Beside me, Renly positively quivers with excitement. 'Look!'

I follow his gaze to where a sea of green is making its way down a rocky mountain pass. The Court of Leaves are rarely seen out of the Wildlands, preferring to remain in the Grove – the towering forest they call home. I've heard that Queen Aspen of the Terrathian refuses to travel on horseback, but rather walks barefoot upon the earth she protects.

Flint jerks his head. 'Right on cue.'

Crimson banners stream through the city. The Court of Flames travel in a cavalcade of solid-gold carriages pulled by red-maned, red-reined horses. Queen Yvainne of the Ignitia likes to make an entrance. Or rather, I should say, *Aunt* Yvainne. My mother's eldest sister elevated our family beyond measure when she was Chosen for the emperor's Crowned Council almost twenty-five years ago.

If I am a story, the Crowned Council are legend. For in Ostacre, kings and queens are not born to rule. Here, crowns are not inherited – they are *won*.

Around every quarter of a century there takes place a Choosing Rite, a deadly competition in which the most gifted young Etheri battle for each of the four thrones. This recurring transfer of power is designed to preserve one thing – youth. Unlike the frail, decrepit monarchs of some of our neighbouring kingdoms, Ostacre's rulers are forever sound of mind and able of body, for they are replaced by the next generation before they have the chance to grow old. And what with most of the current Crowned Council beginning to reach middle age, there are already murmurs about how soon the next eclipse will occur, signalling the Gods' call for new leadership. When the time comes, I know that it is my family's wish that Flint be branded an Heir to the Ignitia throne. Aunt Yvainne has been training him since he was younger than Renly. That's the one silver lining in all this. My lack of power, alongside the fact that my birth almost wiped out the empire, means that I will never be an Heir.

'We'd better get going,' Flint says, shielding his eyes from the setting sun.

I nod, but something stops me from rising to my feet.

I sense them before I see them, before Renly tugs at my dress and points. A fleet of boats with swirling blue banners is weaving its way along the Creek. With neither wind, nor sails, nor oarsmen, the vessels sail swiftly towards us on the shimmering water.

The Court of Waves.

And leading them is the largest boat of all, a gigantic beast carved from pale driftwood and curved at one end like a horn. Even from here I can make out the emblem engraved on its prow – a silver swordfish. My breath catches.

Queen Hydra of the Aquatori.

I wasn't sure she'd come. It must have taken weeks to travel to Valburn from the Lagoon, her court at the southernmost tip of the realm. But here she is. Here they are. All of them come to see me.

Unease pools in my throat. For while I will forever be the odd one out among my flame-wielding family as a Rain Singer, I don't belong entirely to the Aquatori either.

The Rain Singers were a group of Aquatori who possessed the power not only to manipulate water but also to summon the rain. Though they lived side by side with their Aquatori brothers and sisters for many years, their abilities could be unpredictable and often dangerous, and eventually led to a divide, with many of the Rain Singers breaking away, forming a colony of their own in the depths of the Waterlands. It's said they grew savage, cut off from civilization, driven mad by the rain's song.

The last known sighting of a Rain Singer was over half a century ago. They were believed to have died out, a species deemed extinct.

That is, until I was born.

The last Rain Singer – an aberration, a mystery, an ill-timed punchline to a joke that isn't funny.

Flint claps his hands impatiently, startling me. 'Time to go.'

'Yes,' I agree, gathering myself. 'Grandmother will be looking for us.'

And so she is. She's tapping her stick impatiently at the top of the grand staircase, barking at passing attendants.

'At *last*!' she exclaims. 'And *what*, exactly, have you been doing?'

'Oh, just making myself look pretty, Grandmother,' Flint tells her.

She fixes him with an icy glare, which rapidly melts into a fond smile. Renly tries to dart past her but she catches him by the shoulders. '*Best behaviour*,' she warns.

Guests are already swarming the entrance hall below. A cacophony of voices reverberates around the stone walls, and a tight knot coils itself inside my stomach like a fist.

'Stand up straight, Blaze,' Grandmother hisses as she motions for Flint to walk on her right side, me on her left.

I bite the inside of my cheek, hiding my trembling hands in the folds of my dress. The noise in the entrance hall is deafening now, and many Etheri have started glancing up at the staircase.

Grandmother grips her stick, inhaling sharply through her nose. 'Ready?'

I think it's supposed to be a question, but she says it like a command.

No, I think. *No, I'm not ready, Grandmother. Not now, maybe not ever.*

But I just swallow hard, forcing my feet to move as we begin the descent. The stairs swim in and out of focus. Faces blur. The world tilts.

Grandmother steadies me with a bony hand on my arm. 'Remember what I taught you,' she whispers. 'Grateful and graceful, my darling one. Grateful and graceful.'

I smile and smile and smile, as if I belong.

2

When I was young, a man tried to poison me.

He was one of Grandmother's guards, one of the few she trusted implicitly to safeguard her home and protect her family. After the storm, many of those sworn to House Harglade and House Bartell left their posts and renounced their oath of loyalty. But not him. He stayed, he obeyed, he put on the show of his life – all to get close enough to kill me.

He misjudged his first attempt. The poison was cheap and strong-smelling, and so the contaminated food, presumed spoiled, was thrown to the pigs, which died writhing around in their own filth.

The man was cleverer on his second attempt. This time, the poison was clear, colourless and completely unidentifiable. It was so strong, so corrosive, that it would take only a few drops to burn straight through the victim's throat.

Flint and I would often drink hot milk with honey before bed. And in this, the man saw his opportunity. To ensure my death, he poisoned both cups.

There was just one problem – the attendant instructed to take the tray up to our rooms never made it beyond the second flight of stairs. Just a sip, that was all it took. She was found in a pool of milk and vomit, blood leaking from the gaping hole in her oesophagus.

Rooms were searched, a pyre was built, and the man died screaming.

I found out years later that his entire family had drowned in the storm. He saw what he was doing as vengeance, not murder. He thought my death payment for the deaths of his loved ones. He looked at me and didn't see a child, but the bodies of his own children. Their flesh blue and bloated. His home flooded. His world empty.

I could never find it in me to hate him for what he tried to do. There were even times I wished he had succeeded – right now being one of them.

I can hear my heartbeat in my ears. Stares press in from all sides, suffocating me as I gaze down at the sea of upturned faces.

Fear. That's what greets me first. Then loathing. There's curiosity also, but devoid of any admiration. And in some eyes lies a commingling of the three. Masked by pleasantries, they bare their teeth at me and call it smiling. To these people I am not a girl, but a monster.

How easy it would be for one of them to make another attempt on my life. The pin of a brooch, a blade slid from beneath a ruffled sleeve – that's all it would take. And I have no way of defending myself.

I stay close to Grandmother as we reach the bottom of the staircase, pressing closer still as we are announced.

'Lady Harglade of Valburn, accompanied by her grandchildren, Flint, Renly and Blaze.'

As we make our way across the crowded entrance hall, many of the Etheri bow their heads. Some reach out and take Grandmother's hand, murmuring words of greeting. Formidable and head of one of the most powerful families in the realm, Grandmother was revered long before Aunt Yvainne was crowned Fire Queen. I've heard the stories. Leda Flameslinger, they called her. The most beautiful woman in all four kingdoms. Very skilled in combat, too. The Harglades have produced more Heirs than any other Noble House, and Grandmother was no exception. Though she didn't win the throne, she served as chief adviser to the old Ignitia King before the last Choosing brought his reign to an end, leaving all three of her daughters – and my father – to battle for the crown of golden flames.

As a Harglade and the son of two Heirs, Flint certainly has a lot to live up to when the next Choosing comes to pass, and I can't say I envy him.

The ballroom is made entirely from stone, from the gleaming dance floor to the long banquet table, which is heaped with golden platters of food and stacked with towers of champagne-filled glasses. A current of chatter begins to break apart the weighted silence, voices climbing over one another as they fill the cavernous hall.

Ren bounces excitedly on the balls of his feet. I take his hand, which I tell myself is to prevent him from running away rather than me.

Outside, dusk has fallen, dousing the ballroom in gloom. Grandmother raises her right hand, which is branded with the Ignitia fire sign, and in one sweeping gesture lights every candle in the hall, a thousand small flames sparking to life and banishing the encroaching darkness. There is a collective gasp and a smattering of applause.

I rub my thumb over the waxy scar where my first brandmark had been. I was branded at birth along with Flint, since they believed me to be Ignitia. They burned it away after the storm, replacing it with the waterdrop of the Aquatori on the other hand instead. All Etheri are branded on their right hands, yet my brand is on the left, serving as a constant, inescapable reminder both of who I was supposed to be, and of the anomaly that I am.

Flint catches my eye and raises an eyebrow – a question.

I don't tell him that I'm concentrating on keeping the contents of my stomach down, or that the stares feel as though they are burning holes into my flesh. Then someone calls his name and, with a squeeze of my arm and a rather exaggerated bow to Grandmother, Flint disappears into the throng. That's when I realize Renly has also vanished. I'm not happy about this, but I'm too much of a coward to charge through the crowd to hunt him down. Instead, I hover awkwardly at Grandmother's side, feeling like a child.

Countless guests approach to speak with her, although their eyes are fixed on me. Some introduce themselves and wish me a happy Name Day. Some even kiss my cheeks, admire my dress, tell me how like my mother I am. Others glower darkly, not bothering to conceal their hostility, while many appear flustered, their fear betrayed by the slight tremor in their voices or the clamminess of their palms. One ancient-looking woman, seemingly an old friend of Grandmother's, takes to flinching each time I blink. I attempt to stop blinking altogether in an effort to ease her alarm, but if anything this only adds to her distress. When she eventually totters away, a wrinkled hand pressed to her heart, I try to remember everything Grandmother taught me about court etiquette, but come up blank.

Turning my gaze towards the floor, I begin to nibble on the ragged skin around my cuticles.

'Stop eating your hands!' Grandmother hisses out the corner of her mouth.

After about an hour, when I've smiled so much my jaw seems to have locked in place, Grandmother tries to nudge me encouragingly into the crowd. I ignore her, planting my feet on the stone floor. This turns out to be a good thing, because the sudden gust of air that fills the hall is almost enough to knock me backwards.

The Court of Wind stride through the doors, dressed from head to foot in flowing robes of steel grey. I see King Balen at the forefront. Tall and striking, with pale skin and dark hair, he wears a billowing cloak that looks as though it's been cut from morning fog. On his head sits the Ventalla crown, a wreath of shining golden feathers.

Chatter slows, then stops entirely.

'King Balen of the Windlands,' a voice announces.

The king's raven eyes scan the crowd, snagging on Grandmother and coming to rest on me. There is no fear on his face, no loathing. I can't place his expression because I've never seen it worn before. I want to look away, but I don't. I force myself to hold his gaze, and when he speaks, his voice soft and silken, I know his words are meant only for me.

'Hello, little dove.'

King Balen does not speak loudly. In fact, from here, I would have hardly been able to hear him at all if it wasn't for the whistling streams of air that carry his words across the room. It's as though he's standing right next to me. As though he's whispering in my ear.

Another gust of wind fills the room as King Balen makes a casual, careless gesture. 'Go and play,' he tells his court.

The Ventalla courtiers disperse among the crowd, and before I can so much as blink, the king has crossed the floor in a few gliding strides. Grandmother leans heavily on her stick as we both curtsy deeply in unison. King Balen might not be the Ignitia or the Aquatori sovereign, but every member of the Crowned Council is Ostacrian royalty and must be afforded the same respect across each of the four kingdoms. His own kingdom, the Windlands, occupies the north of the empire. I've heard tales of his court, the Marble Palace, which sits at the very top of the tallest cliff, high above the clouds.

'Your Majesty, allow me to introduce my granddaughter, Blaze.'

King Balen angles his head, drinking me in. 'The last Rain Singer. What a privilege it is to meet you.'

My mouth has gone very dry. 'Your Majesty,' I mumble.

'How like Analiese she looks, don't you think, Lady Harglade?' muses King Balen.

Grandmother nods, her voice equal parts pain and pride as she says, 'Indeed, sire. Indeed she does.'

He's right. I do look like my mother, and it is because of this that my father cannot bring himself to look at me.

The king smiles, pressing the tips of his pale fingers together as if in prayer. 'Such a beautiful little thing. Tell me, how does one so pure sing a song of such destruction?'

I watch him notice my scar as he reaches for my hand. His lips are cold as he presses them to it.

My stomach feels as though it's been lined with lead. Is he taunting me? What does he want me to say? That I regret the storm? That I feel guilty? Well, I do. Every day.

Only what I will never admit, not to King Balen, not to anyone, is that there is another side to my guilt. For while I may mourn the loss of life, I mourn the loss of my gift, too. I can't help it, as selfish and soulless as it might be.

I can't help but wonder, *What was it all for?*

And I can't help but think, *What a waste.*

Grandmother lays a protective hand on my arm. 'Your Majesty,' she begins.

But King Balen only chuckles. 'Forgive me. Tonight we commemorate the past and celebrate the future. Tonight it is you we honour, little dove.'

The King of the Air bows low, and then he is gone, followed by a cold breeze.

Those around us who had clearly been hanging on to every word hurriedly strike up conversations with their neighbours. Suddenly I can breathe again. Grandmother pats me gently on the back, but her eyes are on the doors, a slow smile spreading across her face.

Over the din of hundreds of voices I can hear the loud clopping of hooves in the courtyard, hooves belonging to snow-white horses with scarlet manes and scarlet reins.

The Court of Flames spill into the ballroom. My aunt,

Queen Yvainne, sweeps towards us in a dress the colour of old blood. Perched upon her head is the Ignitia crown, a circlet of golden flames which reflects the flickering light of every candle in the room. Behind her is my mother's other sister, Hester, and Hester's daughter, my cousin Ember, each of them wearing tight rust-orange gowns.

Every guest in the hall bows their head as my aunt is announced. Grandmother opens her arms wide and I sink into another practised curtsy.

'Mother!' Yvainne calls, beaming.

'Mother,' Hester echoes stiffly.

Of the three Harglade sisters, Hester most resembles my late grandfather. She is short and wiry, her features sharp. Yvainne is taller, her beauty softer, her Harglade eyes brighter. My aunts have never been unkind to me, exactly, but I've always had the distinct impression that they regard me as some inconvenient pet of Grandmother's, one they cannot outwardly object to but would secretly prefer to see muzzled.

I smile at Ember. Her lip curls, but not in a smile. She is a slight girl of fifteen, with jet-black hair and heavy-lidded eyes. Her skin shimmers with gold powder, and dangling from her earlobes are long golden snakes studded with tiny garnets.

I thought we could be friends, once. Aside from a handful of the attendants, who do their best to avoid me, Ember is the only other girl I've ever come into contact with. But I learned from a very early age that my cousin has no interest in being my friend. Spoiled and spiteful, she has left me in little doubt as to her opinion of me and of my place in this family, from tugging on my braids when Grandmother's back was turned as children, to the snide comment about my dress whispered under her breath as she leans in to embrace me.

She knows I'll never tell. I'll never give her the satisfaction.

'Cousin.' Her girlish voice drips with honey-coated hatred.

Aunt Yvainne is peering round me. 'Where's your brother?'

She means Flint, her most treasured prodigy.

'Oh, around,' I say stupidly, shifting on my feet. 'With some friends, I think.'

Grandmother tucks a loose curl behind my ear. 'Why don't you see if you can find him for your aunt, Blaze? I'm sure Her Majesty would like to congratulate her nephew on welcoming his seventeenth Name Day just as much as she would like to congratulate her niece.'

Subtle, Grandmother.

'But of course,' says Yvainne, with a pointed smile.

Excuses form and die on my lips as I'm pushed gently into the sea of guests.

Alone, I am exposed. Chattering peters out, the crowd parting as I walk through it. Eyes follow me as I make my way across the ballroom.

Murderer.

Changeling.

Freak.

Whether whispered behind gloved hands or written across powdered faces, the words are there. They burrow beneath my skin.

After spending my life surrounded by the colour red, it's

28

strange seeing others dressed in blue. The Aquatori regard me with, if not direct hostility, then distrust, like I am some kind of wild animal draped in silk, playing at being domesticated. There's interest there, too. And maybe even a little envy – the kind that runs generations deep. Rain Singers are the most powerful Aquatori, after all, not only able to freeze, simmer and carve waves but also to summon the rain. For all they know, I could weave another storm tomorrow without so much as lifting a finger. I could drown the world, if I felt like it.

If only they knew how empty I truly am, I'd wager the resentful glances being shot in my direction would soon come to an end.

As I pass by a group of Ventalla courtiers, one of them blocks my path. He holds out a goblet of pale liquid. 'Would you care for some wine?'

I glance behind him at his friends. Most are smirking, while one snickers quietly into his hands. Something tells me that whatever is in that cup, it's not just wine. What have they laced it with, I wonder. Some awful substance which would cause me to appear ridiculous, or fall into a stupor? Or what if they're trying to poison me, just like that guard when I was young? Dread settles in my stomach. But surely they wouldn't dare, not with King Balen here. And it's not exactly discreet. Perhaps they just decided to spit in it. Or worse.

Mortified, I turn away, the courtiers erupting into laughter behind me. I spot Flint standing among a crowd of adoring disciples at the far end of the hall and start making my way towards him, but then a delicately pointed foot appears out of nowhere, tripping me up and sending me crashing to the ground. I lie on the stone floor, dazed and winded.

All of a sudden, the sound of sniggering dies down, replaced by gasps and murmurs. I look up just as a hand is held out in front of me, the smooth dark skin branded with the Aquatori waterdrop. I take it without thinking and let it pull me to my feet. The woman standing before me is dressed in a simple blue gown, her kind eyes the colour of deep water. Sitting atop her silvery-white hair is a crown of curling golden waves.

It takes me a moment to understand that I am looking into the face of Queen Hydra of the Aquatori.

I sink into a low, shaky curtsy. When I rise, I realize I'm still holding her hand.

'Blaze Harglade,' she says in a voice as light and warm as summer rain. 'I have long wondered when we would get the chance to meet.'

I open my mouth to speak and then close it again, completely overcome.

Concern creases her lovely face. 'Do you need to sit down?'

'Yes. No. No, thank you, Your Majesty,' I blurt out. 'I'm so sorry, I don't –'

'Calm, child,' she soothes. 'You have nothing to apologize for. All is well.'

I find myself returning her smile.

'Sometimes,' says Queen Hydra softly, leaning in closer to me, 'we must lose our footing in order to find our balance.'

She touches my cheek, once, lightly, before rejoining her court.

The Court of Waves are still trickling through the doors, dressed in innumerable shades of blue, the fabrics loose and flowing. To my astonishment, I notice that some are barely dressed at all, their bodies adorned with shells and shark teeth and sea flowers. One girl even wears a dress made from what looks like tiny silver fish scales.

I watch them, feeling a strange aching sensation take root inside my chest.

'What was all that about?' Flint asks, appearing at my side. 'What did Queen Hydra want?'

I smooth my skirts and clear my throat. 'Nothing. She was just being kind.'

'And you're all right? I'd imagine all this must be pretty overwhelming. Grandmother's really thrown you in the deep end.'

'I'm fine,' I tell him, hoping I sound firm.

My brother looks unconvinced. 'Sure?'

'Sure,' I say brightly. 'Surer than sure. The surest.'

Flint relents, satisfied, and offers me his arm. 'Where to?'

I let him smile for both of us as we walk through the crowd.

'Have you seen Ren?' I ask.

'I haven't. But I suspect he's under the table stuffing his face with cake.'

'I should go look for him.'

'No, leave him be. A little freedom is good for him. Let him have some fun. And the same goes for you.'

I roll my eyes. 'That's likely.'

'Tell you what, sister mine,' says Flint, ignoring Aunt Yvainne as she beckons to him, 'if you at least *try* to look as though you're not planning on bolting for the doors at any given moment, I will consider giving you your Name Day present.'

I bite my tongue. It's easy for him to say. My brother is adored by all who know him. He carries himself in a way only someone so assured of their place in the world can, and his outlook is unfailingly cheerful, choosing always to see the good. How could he even begin to understand what it feels like to have caused such devastation, to be so reviled?

Flint waves a hand in front of my face. '*Hello*? Blaze?'

I blink. 'Sorry.'

'As I was saying, if you continue to look miserable, not to mention nosediving in front of queens and such like, I will give your Name Day present to one of the attendants. Or throw it in the Creek. Or keep it for next year. I haven't decided yet.'

I conjure a smile from somewhere. 'Deal.'

Flint nods and walks away from me, towards the ring of Harglades. 'That includes dancing,' he calls over his shoulder. 'At least one dance. Non-negotiable.'

My smile becomes a scowl. I linger for a moment as our aunts kiss him in turn, then I circle back towards the banquet table in search of Renly.

Maybe I'm just tired, I tell myself, as Queen Aspen of the Terrathian and her Court of Leaves begin to filter into the ballroom, dressed in numerous shades of green, their gowns bedecked with foliage, their hair threaded with wildflowers. Maybe I just need to eat something. Maybe stuffing my own face with cake doesn't sound like such a bad idea.

I'm halfway through a slice of blueberry sponge when a thunderous sound fills the hall, reverberating off the stone walls.

I freeze. If they're blowing the horns, that can mean only one thing.

For a moment there is complete and utter silence.

Then, there is gold.

3

They walk into the hall, together and yet separately, each moving within their own sphere, commanding their own space. Their gowns are stiff with flakes of gold, their doublets embellished with gilded braid. Golden gloves conceal their brandmarks, and round their necks they wear gleaming chains, as thick and heavy as armour.

The Court of Eyes.

It's said they have eyes tattooed into the napes of their necks with needle and liquid gold, so they can watch you even when their backs are turned.

Through the centre of them, in a billowing golden cloak, strides the emperor himself, His Imperial Majesty, Alvar Castellion. He who is possessed of all four elemental gifts, and the one which only the firstborn Castellion sons have the ability to wield – light.

I recognize him immediately. Not just from his portrait, but because of how remarkably similar he and his younger brother look. Both King Balen and the emperor have that same unearthly paleness and those deep-set raven eyes.

My gaze lands on the Imperial Crown. It is an amalgamation of the crowns of the Crowned Council, an intricate melding of flames, feathers, leaves and waves. At the forefront sits a golden eye carved into the centre of a glimmering sun. While the Council must win their crowns, the Imperial Crown is inherited only by the firstborn son of House Castellion. The Castellions have ruled Ostacre since Dawnday, their line sired by the Maker himself. After the Choosing Rite, in exchange for their thrones, the new kings and queens bind their power with that of the new emperor. From that day forward, he draws from their gifts, thus possessing them all.

Behind the emperor walks a woman wearing a gown of golden silk, her mouth stretched into a glacial smile. That must be his wife, Empress Goneril. And at her side is a handsome dark-haired boy who can only be their son, Haldyn Castellion, the light-wielding Crown Prince of Ostacre.

As one, the Etheri sink to their knees. Only the four Council members remain standing, though each of them bows their head.

'Rise,' commands the emperor, holding out his arms as if to embrace the crowd before him. 'My lords, ladies and gentlemen. My subjects. My friends.'

I watch Grandmother move forward, her stick tapping on the stone floor. 'Your Imperial Majesty,' she says, sinking into a low curtsy. 'You honour us with your presence.'

'Lady Harglade, a pleasure, as always.' The emperor looks beyond her, scanning the room. 'She's here, I take it?'

Grandmother nods. 'Yes, sire. She and her brother both.'

I feel as though I've just swallowed a stone. No, a boulder.

'Well, then.' The ground trembles as the emperor clasps his hands together. 'Bring them forward. I wish to lay eyes upon the Storm Weaver.'

I take a small step back, panic roiling in my stomach. I can already see Flint making his way through the crowd, wearing his usual easy smile. The Etheri are beginning to glance around the ballroom. Next to me, a group of Ignitia courtiers are murmuring to one another, shooting pointed glances in my direction. Heat prickles at my cheeks. Before I know what I'm doing, I duck under a red tablecloth and crouch beneath the banquet table.

I listen as Flint graciously accepts the emperor's blessings and apologizes for his sister's temporary absence. After a few painful minutes, music starts up and the ballroom is once again filled with the sounds of string instruments and voices.

Underneath the table, I eat the rest of my cake and wallow in self-loathing. I keep expecting Grandmother's ruby-encrusted stick to poke through the tablecloth and jab me in the ribs. If it did, I'd deserve it.

It's difficult crawling in a dress. I bunch up the beautifully embroidered silk and throw it behind me, exposing my knees to the rough stone floor. If I can just make it to the far end of the ballroom, I can slip out of one of the concealed doors used by the attendants and escape down the back stairs. But then, out the corner of my eye, I spot a pair of slightly scuffed little shoes with carefully double-knotted laces.

Renly.

I grab his ankle and hear him yelp in surprise. A moment later he lifts the tablecloth, laughs with delight, and crawls under the table beside me.

'Blaze! What are you doing? Are we playing a game?'

'Where have you been?' I ask him peevishly, wiping chocolate from round his mouth with the sleeve of my dress.

He gestures wildly. '*Everywhere.*'

'No need to be so specific.'

Ren beams at me.

'What's happening out there?'

'Dancing,' he replies, pulling at the collar of his doublet. 'Lots and lots of dancing. Do you want to dance?'

'*No.*' That came out more harshly than I meant it to. I try again. 'No, thank you.'

'I'd dance with you,' Renly says earnestly.

I smile. 'That's very sweet of you, but I'm not hanging around.'

His face falls.

'Don't worry,' I say quickly. 'I've just had enough for tonight. I'm all smiled out.'

He points at my mouth. 'You just smiled at me.'

'That's because you're you,' I tell him, tapping his nose. 'And you can stay for a while, if you're sensible.'

He thinks this over. 'Blaze?'

'Yes?' I shift into a sitting position, knees aching.

'Please dance with me. Just one dance. *Please.*'

I shake my head firmly.

He pouts. 'Why not?'

'Renly,' I say sternly. 'Remember what Grandmother said?'

He lifts his chin high, looks down his nose at me and says, in a remarkably accurate impersonation of her voice, '*Best behaviour.*' Then, with an impish grin, he darts out from underneath the table before I can grab hold of him.

Brilliant.

For a moment I'm tempted to take Flint's advice and let Renly do as he pleases, but I'm not Flint, and if Renly's going to get up to mischief, it's best I find him before Grandmother does. And so, grinding my teeth, I give up on my bid for freedom and follow him.

Music swells around the hall as couples whirl across the dance floor. I bolt after Ren as he hurtles between them, weaving in and out of moving colours. I'm almost close enough to seize his shoulder when someone careens into me, causing me to stumble. When I glance back at where Ren was standing only seconds before, I see that he's already disappeared.

'What do you think you're *doing*?'

I turn to find a girl glowering at me. I remember her from earlier – the Aquatori courtier in the dress woven from silver fish scales. Her eyes and skin are a deep bronze and in her hair she wears tiny clips shaped like fish.

Her dance partner steps forward. His face is concerned, though a smile tugs at the corners of his mouth. 'Are you all right?'

I curse the star I was born under and curtsy low to the emperor's son. 'Your Imperial Highness. Forgive me.'

Intrigue gleams in Prince Haldyn's raven eyes. He's even more handsome up close. With his high cheekbones, chiselled jaw and porcelain skin, he looks as though he could have been carved from marble. I feel myself blush, which only makes his smile grow wider. He wears a fine gold doublet and a simple crown that he reaches up to straighten.

'No harm done,' he says warmly. 'Right, Marina?'

Marina looks as if she might throttle me, but when she turns back to the prince her face is all sweetness. 'Oh, absolutely. No harm done.'

I rub my throbbing side in disagreement. Couples are still dancing around us, making my head spin. I search desperately for the best route off the dance floor.

'Wait.'

I turn back to the prince, my heart sinking into my stomach.

'What's your name?'

'My name?' I repeat innocently, as if I've never heard of such a thing.

'Your name,' he confirms.

Which one? I think to myself.

I take a deep breath. 'My name is Blaze, Your Imperial Highness.'

The prince blinks in surprise. I wait for the hatred, the fear, but there is none. He just holds out a hand, branded with the Imperial sun and eye.

'Would you like to dance with me, Blaze?'

I hesitate, incredulous.

'You don't mind, do you, Marina?' Prince Haldyn asks, glancing at her.

Marina looks like she minds a great deal.

'Not at all,' she simpers, shooting me a parting glare before stalking off.

The dance taking place around us comes to an end. The reedy string music starts up again, and half dazed, I let the prince begin to lead the way around the floor, his hand cool and smooth in mine.

Grandmother taught Flint and me how to dance. She was dictatorial with her lessons, having us glide and spin around this very ballroom again and again until we were perfect. I make a mental note to thank her for it later.

'What were you doing?' The prince is looking down at me in amusement, his face mere inches from mine.

'When?' I ask. My voice sounds a little breathless, but I tell myself that's just from the dancing.

'Just now, when you crashed into us.'

'I was trying to catch my brother,' I explain. 'He likes to run off sometimes.'

Prince Haldyn frowns, bemused. 'Flint?'

I almost laugh. 'No, our younger brother, Renly. He's only six.'

'I see.' He spins me round then catches me again in time with the music, drawing me in close to his chest. He's a skilled dancer, graceful, well-practised and light on his feet. 'And where were you earlier when my father called you forward?'

I grimace.

The prince smiles suspiciously. 'What?'

I shake my head.

'Well now I'm definitely intrigued. I could order you to tell me, you know, then you wouldn't be able to refuse.'

I sigh, admitting defeat. 'Honestly?'

'Preferably.'

'I was hiding,' I tell him, holding on to my skirts as we spin around again.

His lips quirk. 'Hiding where?'

'Under the table.'

He laughs. 'You are . . . not what I expected.'

I raise an eyebrow. 'In what way?'

I'm surprised at my boldness, at how I'm conversing with him so easily. I might not be what he expected, but he's not what I expected either. He's not arrogant, in the way I might have imagined princes to be. Nor does he look at me as if I am dangerous or depraved, yet rather he holds me as though I were something rare and precious. His eyes are searching but his hands are steady, and I find myself leaning into his touch.

He considers my question. 'It's just, they call you the Storm Weaver.'

'Among other things.'

'People talk,' he says dismissively. 'It's what people do.'

I'm suddenly aware of the many faces turned in our direction.

'I suppose . . .' the prince continues, 'I suppose I expected someone who . . . *wanted* it. Enjoyed it. Being who you are, I mean. Knowing what you're capable of. Knowing that everyone else knows it too.'

I stare at him blankly. 'You thought I'd *enjoy* it? Enjoy the fact that I . . . that I . . .'

Nearly drowned an entire empire? An empire that will soon be yours?

Prince Haldyn scans my face as though trying to read my thoughts. When it becomes clear that I'm not going to finish my sentence, he speaks again, his voice slightly lowered.

'I apologize for being so direct. Only, in my experience, those with that kind of power, they . . . take pleasure in it. They like that it is known. They *want* it to be known.'

I swallow hard. I think I know who he might be referring to.

'*Blaze?*' Flint is dancing with a pretty Ventalla girl. His eyes are wide with astonishment, flicking between Prince Haldyn and me.

As the prince whirls me round again I catch sight of Grandmother, leaning on her stick. She's smiling at us. Beside her is Ember. She's not smiling.

I glance back up at Prince Haldyn. He's already looking down at me, one hand pressed to the base of my spine. He smells of summertime, like bottled sunshine and lemons.

'I'm sorry if I'm a disappointment to you.'

'Far from it, Blaze. I might try hiding under the table the next time my father summons me.'

I bite back a laugh. 'Please don't tell anyone about that.'

It's not long before the dance comes to an end, and Prince Haldyn offers me his arm, leading me off the dance floor towards Grandmother.

'I believe I have something of yours, Lady Harglade,' he says.

Grandmother's eyes glitter as she takes my hand. Ember curtsies, fluttering her eyelashes. The prince bows low, then excuses himself.

I watch him walk away into the crowd. The world around me suddenly seems brighter, as though everything were bathed in golden rays.

Moments later Flint appears at my side. 'Is that a ... *smile*?'

I elbow him in the ribs. 'Oh, shut up.'

4

It's late and I'm leaning against a wall, my tired eyes flicking between members of the Council and the colourful array of dancers. Aunt Yvainne dances with her wife, Seraphine. Aunt Hester dances with King Balen, his cloak of swirling fog cutting through the air as he moves gracefully around the dance floor. Prince Haldyn is dancing with his mother. Whether or not it was his intention, his dancing with me has made something of a statement. Ever since, I have been sought out by numerous guests and engaged in polite court chit-chat, during which I've exchanged anecdotes about my brother and steered conversations away from my mother.

Yet while this kind of attention is undoubtedly preferable to the substantially more hostile alternative, it has slowly started to drain me. So after a while I disentangle myself from my newfound friends and set off in search of Renly, eventually cornering him by the dessert table. Protesting is futile, and I sentence him to bed.

I catch sight of Grandmother standing a dozen or so yards to my right. The man she's speaking with has his back to me. Tall and broad-shouldered, with hair like fresh snow, he's dressed in a simple blue tunic and has what appears to be a

LAURYN HAMILTON MURRAY

small trident strapped to his belt. Grandmother notices me hovering by the wall and hurries over without so much as a word of farewell to her companion, rubbing exasperatedly at the chocolate smeared on my sleeve.

Suddenly the dancing stops and silence falls. I turn to see the emperor striding through the parting guests, flanked by his Court of Eyes.

'The time has almost come for us to take our leave,' he announces, his voice rebounding off the stone walls.

Relief floods through me.

'Almost,' he continues, 'but not quite. I am a patient man, but I have waited long enough. Bring me the Harglade twins. *Both* of them.'

The relief curdles like milk. The emperor has hardly travelled from the Golden Palace just to wish Flint many happy returns. Not when tonight is the Storm Weaver's first ever public appearance. My *debut*, as Grandmother called it. Some debutante I make.

Prince Haldyn's gaze meets mine from across the ballroom, and slowly every head begins to turn in my direction. I am pinned up by stares like a specimen on a wall.

Grandmother gives me a little push and my feet reluctantly begin to move. A path clears as we walk slowly through the crowd. Flint is already standing before the emperor, who says nothing as he takes me in, his head slightly tilted.

'Blaze,' he says eventually, the piece of irony that is my name uncertain in his mouth. 'We meet at last, Storm Weaver.'

His golden cloak looks heavy enough to flatten me. I sink into a deep curtsy, concentrating on keeping my voice, and knees, steady. 'Your Imperial Majesty.'

44

It's so quiet that I swear you could hear a raindrop.

The emperor turns to my brother. 'Flint, dear boy. What a fitting way to celebrate a young man such as yourself. A rare diamond if ever there was one. I have little doubt that when the next eclipse comes to pass, you will be branded an Heir to the Ignitia throne, continuing the legacy of the Harglade name. How proud your family must be of you.'

Flint bows. 'Thank you, sire. I strive to be worthy of their love and your words.'

The emperor smiles. Then King Balen is there beside him, appearing so suddenly it's as though he's materialized from thin air.

The Ventalla King's tone is conversational. 'Oh, I'm sure his thanks are not necessary, are they, brother? There are gifts far more valuable than gratitude.'

I can tell Flint is confused, but his smile never falters. 'Your Majesty?'

'Why don't you give us a gift, Flint Flameborn?' King Balen says smoothly. 'A trick you have been working on, perhaps. A display of your many talents. Surely the emperor must have something in return for the honour he has bestowed upon you this night?'

I glance at Flint, but he's already looking at Aunt Yvainne, who nods. Flint bows once more to the emperor, then raises his hands. I watch as every bud-like flame from every candle in the ballroom rises gently into the air until they are hovering above their wicks, burning freely. I clench my jaw to stop my mouth from hanging open in astonishment. My brother rarely uses his gift around me. I've always assumed it's because he feels sorry for me, since his power flows in abundance and mine is gone for good. No wonder he enjoys spending so much time at the Ignitia court, Fire Mountain, where he can revel in his abilities guilt-free.

With a small jerk of his wrist, the thousands of tiny flames begin to move, gliding over one another, filling the hall with flickering light. Next, he opens his arms wide, and the flames shoot towards him, skimming over the heads of the crowd and coming to rest in his outstretched hands. I watch, dumbstruck, as fire blazes in his palms.

Flint holds the fire there for a few moments, then, with a satisfied grin at Aunt Yvainne, he throws it up into the air. The flames cascade towards the ceiling in a roar of heat before drifting apart once more, floating lazily back to their wicks.

Grandmother is beaming, the guests are applauding and the emperor claps my brother on the shoulder, calling for a toast. Attendants dart among the crowd, laden with trays of glasses filled to the brim with wine. I accept one and hold on tightly to the stem.

'What better way to toast a Harglade than with the words of his House?' The emperor raises his glass high. 'Flicker, flare, flame.'

We echo him, then we drink. The wine tastes bitter.

'And yet,' says King Balen, his voice slicing through the air, 'there is one Harglade who has no affinity with the words of her ancestors. One who does not ignite the flame, but drowns the fire. If the brother is a rare diamond, then the sister is the rarest, the most exquisite, of pearls.' He smiles at me, his teeth sharp and white. 'Isn't that right, little dove?'

Once again, I feel like I might lose my footing.

The Ventalla King twists his golden signet ring round his finger. 'What do you say, brother, to receiving not one gift this night, but two? Two birds with one stone, so to speak.'

The emperor looks at him questioningly.

'Humour me,' King Balen continues. 'Young Flint here has delighted us with flame. Perhaps his sister could dazzle us with rain.'

The effect on the crowd is instantaneous. Some shriek, while others pale in horror. As for me, I've forgotten how to breathe.

'Come now,' King Balen soothes. 'Seventeen years ago a storm shook the world to its core, and for seventeen years we have lived in the shadow of the past. It is time, I think, to bathe in the light of the future.' I can barely hear his words over my heartbeat. 'Blaze, sweet girl. Tonight the emperor gives you the chance to prove to the people of our glorious empire that to them you mean no harm. That you are not a danger, but a gift.'

The crowd murmurs nervously.

'Lady Harglade,' says the emperor. 'Can you give us your word that there is indeed nothing to fear?'

Grandmother's eyes bore into me as she clears her throat. 'I assure you, sire, I assure you all, that my granddaughter is no longer a threat. If she were, she would not be standing among you. The days of storms are behind us.'

I look at the floor, my stomach curling in on itself.

Prince Haldyn said that those with devastating power take pleasure in it, that they want it to be known. Perhaps if I had any left, I would too.

But Grandmother is right. The days of storms are behind us. All that's left is me.

The emperor nods. 'Very well.'

A fresh wave of panic surges through me and I stare helplessly at my brother. Flint smiles encouragingly, but his eyes betray him.

King Balen takes a step towards me. 'Go ahead, little dove.'

I want to scream at him that I can't. That I can't do it. That I am empty. And that if he doesn't let this go, everyone here will know it too.

My hands begin to shake. Flint reaches out to take my glass.

'Come now,' King Balen's voice purrs in my ear. 'What would you show us? If Analiese were here, what would you show her?'

My chest aches at the sound of my mother's name. I have deflected it all night long, letting it bounce off me like a skimming stone. But here, now, at my most vulnerable, I don't want to hear another person say it. I don't want to hear it fall from the Ventalla King's lips. I want to take her name and keep it for myself, so that it is mine.

There is so little left of her, after all. She never cared much for jewels or trinkets, and her scent has long since faded from her clothes. My father has her wedding ring, Grandmother a lock of her hair. I have nothing. Nothing except my memories, each one carefully stowed away inside a box in my mind I seldom allow myself to open.

Only sometimes, she spills out. And sometimes, when I let myself think about her, it drizzles. Even when I'm indoors. Even when the sun shines.

Everyone is watching me, the silence brimming with expectation. I can't hide, so I close my eyes to escape the stares, and the moment I do, I see her.

And suddenly I'm nine years old again. I'm back in Nemeth, standing on the rocky beach below Bartell Manor. This is where my mother taught me to swim, smuggling me down to the cove whenever my father was away on a posting. It was our secret. My small taste of freedom, which only made me hunger for more.

One day, my girl, she would tell me, drawing a map in the sand. *One day, you'll sail across the Second Sea. You'll have a hundred adventures. And then, if I'm lucky, you'll come back and tell me all about them.*

Pain prickles behind closed eyelids. It crawls up my throat, threatening to choke me.

I watch as my mother walks out into the waves, beckoning for me to follow. All around her, the water sparkles.

Then I feel it – soft, hazy droplets falling from the stone ceiling. I open my eyes, my mother's face still glimmering faintly at the edge of my vision.

Grandmother is watching me intently. I can see her knuckles protruding from where she is gripping the hilt of her stick. Prince Haldyn gazes up at the cloud of mist, his expression slightly perplexed. Many of the guests nearest me begin to emerge from behind their arms, which were held over their heads as though to shield themselves from a torrent. Except this – this isn't a torrent. It isn't even rain. It's drizzle. Feeble, futile, insignificant drizzle.

Shame floods through me as whispers flit among the crowd. Some of the Etheri hold their hands out to catch the drizzle, or watch bemusedly as it falls into their glasses, mingling with the wine. What are they thinking? Have they figured out the truth?

Or . . . is it possible they think I did this on purpose? As a precaution, just to be safe? That the drizzle drifting down around them is a mere drop of the power I possess?

I mull this over. It seems plausible. Besides, why would they assume that I could no longer call the rain? It wouldn't make sense for them to come to this conclusion. Perhaps I should plaster on another smile, try to own it? Yes. Yes, that's what I'll do.

The corners of my mouth are just curving upward when somebody starts clapping. Slowly. Painfully, tauntingly slowly.

'Is *that* it?' Ember sneers, appearing at my side. 'Seriously?'

A few sniggers join the whispers. Grandmother checks Ember with a stern glance, and my cousin falls silent, smirking. I grit my teeth, hating her.

'Well,' says the emperor, exchanging a look with King Balen, 'it seems Lady Harglade was right. The Storm Weaver no longer poses a threat.'

Should I say something? Something to make it sound as though it was intentional?

It turns out I don't have to, for Grandmother must have been thinking the same thing.

'Blaze understands the devastation caused by her birth, Your Imperial Majesty, and she will do everything in her power to make sure we never see its like again,' she says, in a voice loud enough for all to hear. 'As you can see, her gift is now firmly under her control.'

King Balen gives a little cough. 'That is all very commendable, Lady Harglade, but I was under the impression that I asked for rain. Not this –' he gestures gracefully towards the ceiling – '*vapour*.'

Beside me, Ember snorts quietly into her wine glass. I flinch as she hisses in my ear, 'A family like ours was bound to have a rotten apple some day, cousin. And here you are, rotten to the core. You're not fooling anyone, least of all me.'

Her words are poison delivered in a voice like melted honey. My heart races, pounding against my ribcage, and something stirs inside of me. Something cold.

Flint steps forward then, smiling graciously at King Balen. 'I suspect Blaze was just being modest, sire.'

'Oh, I have no time for modesty,' responds the Ventalla King silkily. 'I wish to be entertained.'

'Come now, brother,' begins the emperor, but I don't hear what follows, because Ember leans in close once more.

'I'm just glad dear Aunt Analiese isn't around to see it. To see *you*.'

I feel myself go still, my whole body rigid, as though I am frozen in place. All at once, the drizzle stops.

'How burdensome you must have been to her, Blaze,' Ember continues softly. 'How . . . *disappointing*.'

I always thought fury would feel like fire, but I was wrong. Fury is ice. It burns cold, searing through my veins.

Ember opens her mouth to say more, but she doesn't get the chance. For in every wine glass in every hand, the dark liquid quivers, ripples, and then freezes solid. Seconds later the hall echoes with the sound of a thousand shattering glasses.

White noise fills my ears as the crowd staggers backwards away from me. I can't hear their screams, or Ember's shrieks as she holds up her hands, red trickling from a series of deep gashes on her palms.

My gaze falls on Prince Haldyn, his cheeks spattered with flecks of blood or wine or both. Next to him, Flint is looking at me as though he's never seen me before.

Then Grandmother seizes hold of me, debris crunching underfoot as she half drags me from the ballroom. But before the doors close behind us, I look back.

Among the sea of horrified faces, King Balen smiles on.

Still holding what remains of his broken glass, he looks into my eyes, and raises it.

5

I lie twisted in red-silk sheets, listening to the soft crackle of the fire. It had sprung to life in the hearth the moment Grandmother had marched me through the door to my rooms, and has remained burning long after she disappeared downstairs to clear up my mess.

Sleep.

That's all she said to me, as if I were no more than a cranky child in need of a nap. But I'm too shaken-up to do so much as close my eyes. I'm wide awake, skittish and deathly cold. The fire casts the room in a warm orange glow, yet I can't stop shivering.

Aside from the rain, which answers only to a Rain Singer, the Aquatori learn to harness three main kinds of water manipulation – simmer skimming, wave carving and ice making. After the storm, after my rain was replaced by drizzle, I long held out hope that my other water gifts would materialize one day, but they never did.

Until now.

The fury has all but drained out of me and I feel … I don't know what I feel. Horrified? That I gave the Etheri yet another reason to fear me? That I have served a seventeen-year sentence only to kiss any chance of exoneration goodbye?

I sit up, hugging my knees tightly.

I made my cousin bleed for what she did. And there was a part of me, a very small part, that had wanted to hurt her. Hurt her like she hurt me.

But hadn't she deserved it? Those things she said about my mother, they were unforgivable. She knew exactly what she was doing. Only, I didn't. It was unintentional, reflexive. Like a release. All that anger, all that fury, all of a sudden it was lifted. Redirected. Turned into something cold and sharp and vicious.

For the first time, I didn't feel powerless. I felt *powerful*. And I *liked* it.

So yes, I expect I am a little horrified by what I did. But what scares me more is not being able to do it again.

My head spins with unanswered questions.

I lie awake all night, then sit on the roof with Ren to watch the dawn. Word about my outburst must have made its way around Harglade Hall, because none of the sentries stationed outside my door seemed willing to object as I marched past, hand in hand with my little brother. They simply fell into step behind us as we made our way down to the kitchens, where Ren and I swiped a selection of fruit, pastries and a jug of mango juice before heading up the ladder and out the trapdoor on to the roof, the guards remaining below, lingering at the entrance to the attics.

The air smells of hot stone. Even at this early hour, Valburn is already bathed in hazy morning sun. Having thawed out during the night, I'm grateful for the flimsy material of my nightgown, though if Grandmother catches me wandering about wearing it I'm sure she'll lock me up for good, and this time melt down the key. But I can't find it in me to care. I have enough to think about already.

It all plays on a loop inside my head. The stirring in my chest. The bitter cold. The ice, the glass, the blood. My cousin's words echo softly in my ears.

How burdensome you must have been to her, Blaze. How . . . disappointing.

What would my mother have made of it, I wonder? Would she have screamed, stumbled backwards, looked at me with fear in her eyes like the other Etheri? Dragged me from the scene and hidden me away like Grandmother did? Maybe Ember was right. Maybe I was nothing but a disappointment to her.

To my dismay, I realize that a small cloud of drizzle has formed above my head.

'Not again,' I mutter, but Renly just laughs in delight, sticking out his tongue to catch the hazy droplets. I put an arm round his shoulders, pulling him close and breathing in the comforting scent of clean linen and chocolate. He smiles at me, his mouth full of pastry.

'You smile just like Mother did, do you know that?' I tell him.

'Do I?'

'You do.'

He smiles again, pleased, then says, 'You never talk about Mother.'

I swallow the lump in my throat. 'That's because it makes me sad.'

'That she's not here any more?'

I nod.

Ren nuzzles into me, his hair tickling my nose. 'You'll always be here, won't you, Blaze? You'll never leave me?'

Guilt slams into me so hard that I feel winded by it. Because there's something I haven't told him. Something I never could.

'How do you stand it?' Flint once asked me. 'Being shut up here while I can do whatever I like, go wherever I please?'

'I'm used to it,' I replied. 'I don't know any different.'

This was true enough, but not the whole truth. The whole truth is that I was able to stand it because I told myself that it wasn't forever. That one day, when I came of age, I would be free to sail across the Second Sea and start a new life far from Ostacre. It was my mother who first told me the tales of the rolling deserts of Veridia, the star-spangled skies of Obsidia, the endless grassy plains of Thresk – beautiful, dangerous isles saturated with ancient magic. Ever since, I've felt this strange, unmistakable pull towards the Otherlands, one that has only grown stronger in the years following her death.

I have it all figured out. In the depths of the old world, I could be someone new. I could reinvent myself entirely. I'd come back and visit, of course, yet I'd no longer be a burden to my family.

But leaving always means leaving something behind. Or in this case, someone.

Renly looks up at me, his dark eyes wide and questioning, but at that moment Flint appears through the trapdoor.

'There you are,' he calls.

'Here I am.'

He throws himself down next to us, snatching up a handful of berries. 'I knew I'd find you two up here.' He pauses, squinting at me. 'Gods. You look *awful*.'

'Charming,' I tell him, as the drizzle peters out. 'So are you here to lecture me or laugh at me? Because whichever it is, I'm really not interested.'

He brings a hand to his chest, wounded. 'Neither. I'm here to look after you. And, fine, maybe laugh a little. I'll leave the lecturing to Grandmother.'

I grimace.

'Oh, stop fretting. By all accounts, everybody had a smashing time.'

I let out a groan, burying my face in my hands.

'Blaze. *Blaze*. Come on, I'm kidding.' Flint prizes my fingers apart.

I relent, reaching out and taking a cautious sip of mango juice, half expecting it to freeze and the cup to shatter into pieces.

'What was *with* you last night?' Flint demands. 'Hiding from the emperor, speaking to Queen Hydra, dancing with the *Crown Prince* –'

My heart gives a sudden jolt at the memory of Prince Haldyn, of his raven eyes alight with curiosity, his cool hands pressed gently to the small of my back.

'And why didn't you tell me you could make ice?' Flint persists. 'Did you know?'

Renly sits up straight, interested. 'What?'

Flint pulls Ren's nightshirt over his head. I pull it back down again.

'No, I didn't know, and I don't know how I did it.

57

I just . . .' I think of Ember's cruel words, the cold fury that lanced through me. 'I couldn't control it.'

Flint huffs a laugh. 'I'll say.'

'What happened afterwards?' I ask.

'After Grandmother frog-marched you away, you mean? I won't lie, it was uncomfortable. No one seemed quite sure what to do.' He leans back on his elbows. 'I made the rounds for a bit, apologizing and things.'

I feel a dull ache of shame that my brother was forced to apologize for me. *About* me. The shame doubles when I notice that there's still some glass in his hair.

'Then Grandmother reappeared and had the attendants clear the ballroom,' Flint continues, as I pick out the shards one by one. 'King Balen made some joke about Harglade women and said how Grandmother's parties have always been eventful. You must have made quite the impression, by the way. He asked me to pass on his regards.'

A shiver runs through me. I hear the Ventalla King's voice in my head, as soft as silk.

Such a beautiful little thing. Tell me, how does one so pure sing a song of such destruction?

I swallow, my throat tight. Only then do I realize that Flint is still wearing his doublet. I nudge him in the chest with my foot. 'Have you even slept?'

He catches hold of my ankle. 'Who needs sleep? It wouldn't do for both honourees to abandon their guests, and besides, I live to entertain.'

'You mean there's still people here?' I say incredulously. 'But it's *morning*.'

'Trust me, this is nothing. At court, parties can last days, weeks even.' My brother laughs at the expression on my face. 'I know something that'll cheer you up,' he says, pulling a small, badly wrapped parcel out of his pocket. 'Here, catch.'

My Name Day present. I tear off the paper, and a tiny pearl-encrusted box falls into my lap. When I open it up, music begins to play, sweet and lilting. Smiling, I lean over and plant a kiss on Flint's cheek, which he pretends to wipe off in disgust.

Suddenly, without warning, the sky begins to darken. Shadows flood the city, swallowing the tinkling music. They climb up the sides of buildings, elongating themselves and merging together as they spread out across Valburn and beyond. Flint springs to his feet as though preparing for a fight. Bewildered, I follow his gaze upward, watching as the sun is obscured by the moon, partly at first, then completely, drenching us in gloom.

Silence sweeps over everything, ringing in my ears. My lungs feel compressed, smothered by the stillness.

An eclipse. It's an eclipse. And that means only one thing. I take a deep breath, steadying myself as the realization hits me.

When the Gods send an eclipse, it's a signal, a call for change, for the next emperor's reign to begin and a new Crowned Council to govern each of the four Crown Courts.

A new Council, a new era, a new Choosing Rite. The promise of power and the preservation of youth. Emperor Alvar, King Balen and the three queens are all nearing middle age, after all. It was always going to happen sooner or later, just as it has time and time before. But watching history unfold feels very different from reading about it.

I reach out through the darkness for Ren, needing something to hold on to.

That's when the world erupts.

The torches in the courtyard below spring to life. The wind begins to howl, whipping up our hair, our clothes. The earth trembles and quakes beneath us and I feel it in my bones. And I don't have to see it to know that the usually glass-still surface of the Creek is churning.

Renly clutches me tightly, burying his face in my neck as the elements unleash themselves upon the world.

I don't know how long it lasts. Minutes. Hours. I can't be sure.

But then, all at once, it stops.

Yet the darkness remains, thick and impenetrable. Except for . . .

'Flint,' I breathe into the silence.

Flint opens his eyes. I know this because I can see him. And I can see him because he is bathed in light.

When an eclipse occurs, the Gods select a number of worthy successors, and one by one, the Heirs' brandmarks are set aglow.

Only the most gifted Etheri are summoned to the Golden Palace for the Choosing, and only the most powerful Heirs are Chosen, for a throne, for a court, for a crown.

My stomach drops.

Heir. My brother is an Heir.

I stare at him, open-mouthed, but Flint isn't looking at his own hand. I follow his gaze and choke on a gasp, releasing my grip on Renly.

I stagger backwards, eyes wide as I take in the light emanating from the Aquatori waterdrop seared into my flesh.

It's glowing. My brandmark is glowing.

I stand there, clutching my wrist, lit up like the sun.

6

We don't utter a word as the unit of Harglade guards escorts us to Grandmother's parlour. She's standing by the window, watching the commotion unfold below. I can hear the Etheri shrieking, hooting, singing, their voices filling the torrid air with ... what? Uncertainty? Anticipation? Exhilaration? I can only wonder at how they feel, for I feel nothing at all.

'Sit.'

Perhaps if I wasn't completely numb, I'd be slightly more disgruntled at the way Grandmother has taken to addressing me of late. *Sleep. Sit.* What's next? *Fetch?*

Flint takes the armchair, Renly and I the small couch. No one speaks. Eventually, Grandmother turns and faces us.

'You do know what this means.'

She has this habit of turning questions into statements.

Renly starts nodding, then pauses, puzzled, the nodding turning to shaking. I just pull at the fraying edge of a red quilt.

'Yes, Grandmother,' Flint answers.

She eyes us beadily. I find that I can't quite meet her gaze, so focus instead on her earrings, studded with fat rubies and so long they stretch her earlobes.

'The Gods have spoken,' Grandmother says. 'There are to be new rulers. New blood.' She starts pacing the room, the sharp rapping of her stick a third footstep on the stone floor. 'I knew, right from the moment you were born, that you were both destined for lives beyond all imagining. Flint, a true son of House Harglade, you have been trained for this day since before you can remember. And Blaze, my darling one, the last Rain Singer, the girl who summoned the storm, now an Heir to the Aquatori throne.'

Heirs are meant to represent rebirth and rejuvenation. Life, not death. Yet my life caused death. They call me soulless, deadly, the beginning that brought the end.

The shock must be wearing off slightly, as the irony of the whole thing does not escape me. It's so ridiculous, so *impossible*, that it's all I can do to keep from laughing out loud. But any threat of laughter dies before it can reach my lips as Grandmother's gaze locks on to me, her expression charged with such intensity that it's almost ferocious.

'We must be ready,' she says, 'for they will come.'

I sink further into the cushions, squeezing my glowing brandmark between my knees.

'Flint, Blaze, you two are Heirs now. That means they will be watching you, more so than ever before. From the moment you set foot inside the Golden Palace, your every move will be scrutinized. Remember, the emperor's court aren't called the Eyes for nothing.'

A shiver travels uncomfortably up my spine.

'The Eyes live by a code of secrecy and deceit. Why do you think they only wear Imperial gold and not their gift colour? It's a disguise. And it is this act of concealing their powers that makes them dangerous. You must be wise about how you conduct yourselves. You must remain above reproach, in everything.'

I glance at Flint. His shock also seems to be wearing off, only unlike mine, it has been replaced by eagerness. While I feel drained by the news of our fate, my brother seems positively re-energized. There's a glint in his eye, a new poise to his usual easy confidence.

Flint leans forward in his chair. 'And the trials?'

'They will test you beyond your limits,' Grandmother says. 'They will coax out every last shred of power.'

My stomach churns. I hadn't even thought about the trials. I'm thinking about them now though, my mind reeling as I scrabble around for information, anything I might have retained – a line from a book, an old bedtime story of my mother's.

I hear her voice in my head.

Did I ever tell you about the time I walked through fire?

'Aunt Yvainne has told me of the last Choosing,' Flint says. 'Yet she also told me that mine would be different.'

Grandmother nods. 'Your aunt is right. No Choosing is the same. I should know, I've lived through two, one of them my own.' She pauses, as if lost in memory. 'But every trial, whatever form it may take, is designed to target weakness. To trick you. Break you. Victory is hard-fought. Play to win, by all means. But make no mistake, the real game begins when the winners take their thrones.'

I feel her words pull me further and further away from the shore. They strike me, one after the other, as though she delivers each with an accompanying jab of her stick.

'Your minds must be sharp, your judgements sure,' says Grandmother. 'For there is more than just the trials to contend with. Old magic still lurks within the Golden Palace.'

My eyes widen. I've heard stories about the ancient enchantments embedded deep within the golden bedrock of the Imperial Province.

'I don't ask that you win the Choosing, only that you uphold the honour of House Harglade, and keep yourselves safe. I will not always be there to protect you, and so you must help one another, lean on one another,' Grandmother continues. 'Today is the day your lives change forever. There is no going back, only forward. Do you understand?'

I open my mouth, and then close it again.

Forward.

I have always been looking forward, always thinking ahead. My life has been a countdown, sitting by the window, wishing the days away. I have dragged these seventeen years behind me, telling myself over and over that upon the eighteenth, I will be free. Free to leave this place. Free to invent a past and carve out a future.

Except now that future is receding before my eyes – because I am an Heir.

'Grandmother,' I whisper. 'I – I can't, I *won't* –'

'You can, Blaze, and you will.'

I shake my head. 'I'll withdraw. Someone else can take my place. I don't want it.'

Flint stares at me like I've gone mad.

'Heirs cannot refuse to attend the Choosing, Blaze,' Grandmother says with a sigh. 'You know this. To do so would be to turn one's back on the Gods.'

That might be so, though if anything, it feels awfully like the Gods have turned their backs on me. I look down at my glowing brandmark. What's their game here? Are they trying to humiliate me? It certainly feels that way. Why else would they brand me, the Storm Weaver, the most hated girl in all the realm, as an Heir?

There are four Heirs to vie for each of the four thrones. This means I will be pitted against three other Aquatori for Queen Hydra's crown of golden waves. Of course, I don't have the smallest chance of winning. Even after last night, even if I were somehow able to wield that ice again, my competitors will have years of training under their belts. How could I possibly hope to compete? By making it *drizzle* on them? What a joke that would be. And how the Etheri will delight in discovering the truth about my rain, or rather, my lack of it. Yes, I will be first out of the running, shaming my family even more than I already have.

But this isn't even the worst part.

The worst part is that whether they win or lose the crown, the Heirs are bound to it for life, granted high-ranking positions in their new sovereign's court.

Aunt Hester is Aunt Yvainne's seneschal, and before she died, my mother served as her adviser. Though she chose to raise Flint and me at our father's ancestral home in Nemeth, she was often summoned to Fire Mountain. As for my father, he is the Ignitia High General. Or at least, he used to be before he was enveloped by an impenetrable haze of grief that has kept him shut away inside Bartell Manor for six long years.

It hits me then, like a kick in the chest. Even after I inevitably lose the Choosing, there is still no way out. I will never travel to the Otherlands. I will never escape the land I almost destroyed and the people who wish me nothing but misery.

I will *never* be free.

Hope cracks like ice, splintering into nothing.

I have never felt smaller than I do in this moment.

When we are eventually dismissed, my brothers file wordlessly out of the door, but I remain behind, rubbing my scar hard enough to bruise the skin.

I don't look at Grandmother as she crosses the room and sits down beside me. When she speaks, her voice is gentle. 'Forgive me.'

I do look at her now. 'For what?'

'For ensuring Flint's training and neglecting yours,' she says. 'For wanting to protect you, from yourself as much as anything. For hoping that this day would never come.'

'Grandmother . . .' I begin, but I trail off, because I don't know what to say.

'Perhaps last night could have been avoided if only I'd acted sooner,' she continues. 'Perhaps you would not be feeling so helpless in the face of what lies ahead if only I'd made sure that you had been taught about your gifts and how to control them.'

'But how, Grandmother?' I say bitterly. 'Before last night, I couldn't freeze so much as an ice cube. And as for my rain, they may call me the Storm Weaver, but since that storm, the most I've ever been able to summon is drizzle. And even then, that's only when I'm thinking about –' I stop myself.

Grandmother stares at me, eyes blazing. 'Go on.'

I swallow, feeling somehow more exposed than I did yesterday at the dress fitting, standing in this very parlour in my underclothes. 'Mother,' I whisper eventually. 'It only drizzles when I'm thinking about Mother.'

The silence is abrasive. It rubs me raw.

Grandmother breaks it. 'All love has its price. The cost can be crippling. Yet if what you say is true, then you have found a way to turn pain into power.'

Her words are the spark of a match at the end of a tunnel, but I shake my head, stamping out the hope before it can spread. 'It's just drizzle.'

'There is no limit to what you can do or how you can feel, Blaze. Your gifts were never gone for good. They are a part of you.'

I run the tips of my fingers over my glowing brandmark. 'I thought I was empty.'

Grandmother smiles. 'You have never been, nor will you ever be.'

I bite the inside of my cheek. 'I'm afraid.'

'I know you are. But you must promise me something.'

I look up at her.

'You must embrace it,' she says. 'Fear, sorrow, anger, joy, you must embrace it all. Don't bury your emotions. You cannot hide from your heart. That is where your power lies; that is what will guide you.' Her expression softens. 'To feel is to be alive, Blaze. And I swear to you that no matter what, it is better to feel everything than to feel nothing.'

A familiar tightness lodges itself in my chest.

If to feel is to be alive, then to be alive is to hurt. And if I were to surrender myself to the pain I keep buried deep inside of me, I'm scared it would drown me. That is why I deny and deflect. That is why I have not shed a single tear since the day my mother died.

Grandmother claims I cannot hide from my heart, yet I have spent nearly seven years trying to.

But her gaze is unrelenting, and I yield beneath it.

'I promise.'

Grandmother takes my hands, my brandmark shining between us. 'Fate has many faces, my darling one,' she says. 'Make sure you look them all in the eye.'

7

I walk alone through a dark passageway upon a carpet of fallen leaves, their skeletons bone-dry and brittle. Something gold glimmers in the darkness beyond.

I hear a whisper. My name.

Blaze.

A sharp pain shoots through me. I look down to find that the leaves have become pieces of broken glass. With every step my feet are sliced and shredded. I watch, horrified, as hot blood pours on to shards of crimson ice.

I wake with a jolt, hitting my head against the side of the carriage. Judging by the grey half-light, it's almost dawn. Flint sleeps soundly on the opposite bench, his gentle snores drowned out by the rhythmic clopping of hooves. The Imperial Guard ride close by, visors gleaming in the light from the flickering torches.

They came for us a few days after the eclipse. I watched from the library window as the small legion of knights arrived at the gates, bearing an official summons from the Golden Palace.

Saying goodbye to Renly was painful. He had sobbed and wailed and clung to me so tightly that an attendant was forced to pry him off and carry him back inside Harglade Hall. Grandmother had cupped my face, brushing a kiss between my eyes. Then she was gone, disappearing from view as the carriage trundled down the hill.

As we passed through Valburn, people had poured out of inns and workshops and tall, slate-roofed townhouses, lining the streets excitedly to watch us go by.

'It's not every day you see an Heir,' said Flint, smiling genially out of the window while I ducked my head, shielding my face from view.

It was the same in the next province, and the next. Yet gradually, the bustling cities began to peter out, replaced by barren stone wasteland, and I felt as though I could finally breathe again. I leaned right out of the carriage, gazing around at the unfamiliar terrain, watching steam billowing upward in great plumes from the hot springs, which ranged from puddle-sized to craters so large that we were forced to take a detour. It was then that a small thrill went through me, and I realized that while I might still be stuck in Ostacre, I was no longer stuck inside Harglade Hall, and though this was a journey I'd never envisioned myself making, it was the closest to freedom I'd ever got. So I spent the long, hot days hanging out of the window, drinking in the world around me, and I spent my nights clutching a cup of water, trying – and failing – to freeze it.

I glare down at the now-abandoned cup, balanced on a pile of books, its contents still very much liquid, quivering with the motion of the carriage.

Combing my hair with my fingers, I lean over to peer out of the window, expecting to find us in the middle of yet another endless stone plain. Instead, I find that we are travelling through the deserted remains of a city.

Once a city, now a tomb.

My heart gives a nervous thud.

Six years ago – a few months after my mother died – Ostacre suffered untold devastation. It was a cataclysm unlike any other, one that claimed thousands upon thousands of lives. Only that time, I wasn't behind it.

This was not the work of the Storm Weaver, but of the Earth Cleaver.

He is considered to be the most dangerous Etheri in the world, which seems fitting, since he's the one who broke it in two.

I remember it so clearly, the deafening, agonized *ripping* as the realm was split apart. As *he* split the realm apart. I felt it in the innermost parts of myself. The hollows of my bones, the chambers of my heart. It was as if I were being cleaved in half, too.

Though I was lucky. What with its very foundations built into the dormant volcano it sits upon, Harglade Hall was left more or less intact. Yet the rest of Valburn suffered greatly, with much of the surrounding city collapsing and having to be built anew. However, this was nothing compared to the utter devastation that ploughed straight through the centre of Ostacre, from the northernmost tip to the southernmost lip of the empire, creating the gaping chasm known as the Rift. Bordering the Rift is what little remains of demolished towns and villages, all utterly ravaged by the force of the Cleaving, homes reduced to brick and dust, their inhabitants long entombed within them.

A City of Buried Souls – that is what they call places like this.

I gaze out at the sprawling unmarked grave, and shudder.

The slightly hunchbacked Riftkeeper eyes our procession as we approach the toll bridge, leaning heavily on a thick, gnarled staff. When he speaks, his voice is a rough scrape, like fingernails down bark. 'State your business here.'

A knight nudges his horse forward. 'Our business is that of the Crowned Council, Riftkeeper. We escort their guests.'

The Riftkeeper peers interestedly at the carriage. 'And what might be their names?'

'That is none of your concern,' growls the knight.

'Oh, but it is,' replies the Riftkeeper, reaching out a wrinkled hand to stroke the knight's horse. 'For none cross my bridge nameless.'

Flint yawns loudly beside me. 'Wasappening? Why've we stopped?'

The knight tosses a pouch towards the Riftkeeper, who makes no effort to catch it.

'You may keep your gold, sir, if you give me their names.'

'And you may keep your life, Riftkeeper, if you give us passage,' the knight snarls.

The Riftkeeper plants his feet, his mouth curving into a toothless grin. I gasp as the knight unsheathes his sword and swings it towards him in one smooth arc – a killing blow. But it never meets its mark. It's blocked by the Riftkeeper's staff.

I stare, incredulous. The knight lunges a second time, and a third. The staff does not bend or break, but blocks each strike as though it were steel rather than wood.

'Their names, if you would be so kind,' says the Riftkeeper pleasantly, as though the knight were not trying to decapitate him.

But now the other knights are advancing, swords in hand. The Riftkeeper's staff may be strong, but there are twenty knights of the Imperial Guard and only one of him. Before I realize what I'm doing I've kicked open the carriage door.

'Stop!'

The knights freeze, turning to look at me. The Riftkeeper smiles, delighted.

'Blaze,' I tell him. 'My name is Blaze.'

His smile grows even wider.

My brother pokes his head out over my shoulder. 'Well, I guess we're doing this. Her name is Blaze and my name is Flint. Can we go now?'

'My lady understands the value of a name,' says the Riftkeeper. He stands aside, moving slowly, as though his joints trouble him, as though he hadn't just fought an armed member of the Imperial Guard with a knobbly old stick. 'All may pass.'

The knights hesitate, then lower their swords. One of them ushers me back inside the carriage and I sit down opposite my brother, who is looking at me as if I've sprouted wings. There's a sharp *snap* of the whip and the carriage begins to move off.

'Wait!' I call suddenly, leaning out of the window. The carriage halts, and I turn to the Riftkeeper. 'You said I understand the value of a name. I gave you mine. Now give me yours.'

The Riftkeeper chuckles. 'A name is a gift. A name is a curse. A name is a riddle. My lady wishes to know the name I bear, and my lady shall have it. My name is Eldritch, Storm Weaver, and I am the Keeper of the Rift.'

I nod once in acceptance. The carriage rolls on, followed by the old man's eyes.

'Making friends already, I see,' my brother says wryly.

The pounding of hooves echoes through the emptiness of the Rift as we cross the bridge. After the Cleaving, a number of bridges were built in an attempt to connect the two halves of the empire. Yet the one we are crossing does not stretch all the way across the Rift, but rather stops midway, leading to the Imperial Province – the home of the emperor.

If the provinces are the bones, the courts the organs, and the Creek the veins, then Cor Caval is the beating heart at the centre of the realm. Golden to the eye and golden to the core, it sits upon an ancient goldmine belonging to the Gods – our principal source of wealth and trade. Though it was the site of the Cleaving, the city remains untouched. Entirely surrounded by the Rift, it is the only central province to have survived the desolation, having been built upon that which is uncleavable and protected by ancient enchantments. Lying on neither the left nor the right side of the Rift but in the very centre, Cor Caval is an island in the middle of an empire, a lighthouse in a dark, empty sea.

Even in the lower towns, the streets are paved with gold. I peer out at the markets, warehouses, apothecaries and forges, at the ramshackle, cramped little houses and lines of laundry that stream like banners overhead. Fidra, those with no magical ability, can be found in every province – they live scattered throughout the four kingdoms. But in Cor Caval, the vibrant hub of the empire situated in neither the Firelands nor the Waterlands, the Windlands nor the Wildlands, this is where many of them flock, all of them hoping to make a life for themselves in this breathtaking city of Gods and gold.

Unlike the Ignitia, Aquatori, Ventalla and Terrathian, the Fidra have no representative – they are governed solely by the Etheri. Yet although we live side by side, fraternizing is frowned upon, and intermarriage is entirely forbidden, for fear of diluting Etherian bloodlines. Still, the Choosing Rite is always cause for celebration among the commonfolk, many of whom revere our power. Some even sport ribbons and flags in various court colours.

The heat is unbearable. It clings close, like a second skin. I try to think of anything but the churning in my stomach.

'You've gone green again,' Flint says helpfully.

It's late afternoon by the time we reach the citadel. The dilapidated lower towns have melted away and been replaced by grand estates and sprawling villas. Over the tops of gold-pronged gates I catch glimpses of mansions, manors, exotic gardens and temples.

The golden streets are lined with Etheri. Flint leans out of the window, waving and smiling to the crowd. I shrink back against the bench. The sound of cheering unnerves me. And if the people knew who they were cheering for, it would unnerve them, too.

What will they say, I wonder, when they discover that the Storm Weaver is in Cor Caval? And what will they say when they find out why?

Murderer.

Changeling.

Freak.

Heir.

Suddenly Flint yanks me over to the window. 'Look, Blaze! We're here.'

My mouth falls open. My brother has told me of the splendour of the Golden Palace, but nothing could have prepared me for this. As high as a mountain, made entirely from gold as old as the beginning of time, it glitters, larger than life, like an earthbound sun. Turrets rise into the cerulean sky, tall enough to kiss the clouds.

It looks like a dream. A glorious, shimmering, terrifying dream.

Only this time, there's no waking up.

8

Ignoring a knight's proffered hand, I climb slowly out of the carriage. Flint jumps down beside me. The palace steps stretch out in front of us, steep and lined with sentinels, their golden uniforms emblazoned with the Castellion raven. I wonder how my mother felt, climbing these same steps all those years ago. I wonder if she was afraid.

I can still hear the faint rumble of the crowd in the streets below, yet they grow more and more distant with each step I take towards the towering golden doors. It's instantaneous the way the thick, heavy air becomes gloriously cool inside, the oppressive heat of the city gone in less than a blink. The entrance hall is vast. It is also empty.

My brother and I exchange an uncertain look.

Flint scratches his nose. 'Hmm. Is it embarrassing to admit that I was anticipating a *slightly* better turnout?'

Footsteps sound, accompanied by a shrill voice. '*Gods*, is that the time?'

The voice belongs to a girl who comes into view moments later, skipping daintily down one of the huge golden staircases. The first thing I notice about her are the tattoos on her face – golden whorls inked along both cheekbones.

She's small and impish with dark skin and jet-black hair that's been carefully styled into little gold-tipped knots all over her head.

Flint reaches an arm out to steady her as she skids to a halt in front of us. 'Careful!'

She takes a step back and cocks her head. 'You're very alike, aren't you? I can't decide which of the two of you is the better looking.'

This makes Flint laugh. 'And you are?'

The girl grins. 'My name is Spinner, Flint Flameborn.'

'Nice to meet you, Spinner,' my brother says. 'Quick question. Where is everyone?'

Spinner glances around at the empty entrance hall. 'Oh, they're in bed. The celebrations have been going on pretty much non-stop since the eclipse. All those festivities take their toll, you know. The palace is asleep. As was I until about five minutes ago.' She rubs her pond-green eyes for emphasis. 'So, as far as welcoming committees go, I'm afraid it's just me. And . . . ah. He was meant to be here by now.'

Spinner smiles at us, finally pausing for breath. Then she cups her hands round her mouth and screams, 'Sheen! Shee-een! SHEEN!'

'You called?' A boy seems to materialize behind us as if he has just stepped through thin air.

I jump with fright, moving closer to Flint.

The boy is tall and thin with pale, white-blonde hair. His eyes are a dark shade of violet, his smooth skin the colour of wet sand. Like Spinner, he is also dressed entirely in gold – an ornately embellished golden doublet and matching gloves.

Spinner points a finger at him. 'This is Sheen.'

'So we gathered,' says Flint.

Sheen's eerie violet eyes flit to my brother and rest there for a moment.

I decide it's probably time for me to say something. 'So . . . you two are . . . what?'

That came out slightly ruder than I meant it to, but Spinner only laughs.

'We're your chaperones, of course,' she says. 'Well, technically, I'm *your* chaperone, and Sheen is Flint's.'

I frown. 'Chaperone?'

'Yes. Every Heir is assigned a chaperone from the Imperial Court for the duration of their time at the Choosing. It's my job to escort you from place to place, plan your wardrobe, organize your schedule, things like that. Think of me as your guide, your stylist, your confidante, your shoulder to cry on. You don't have to worry about a thing.'

I listen out for any trace of hatred or fear, but find none.

'What about you?' Flint asks Sheen. 'Are you going to be *my* shoulder to cry on?'

Sheen purses his lips, unamused.

Flint chuckles. 'I guess not. So, what now?'

I'm suddenly aware of how dishevelled we must look after our journey.

'We're to take you to your chambers,' Sheen says, his voice a dry monotone.

'Unless you want the grand tour first?' suggests Spinner. She doesn't wait for an answer before skipping off up the stairs, leaving us with no other choice but to follow her.

The Golden Palace is dazzling. More than dazzling – it's magnificent.

As we make our way through long, gleaming corridors, I have to remind myself to close my mouth, which keeps falling open in shock each time we round the next corner. Flint is decidedly less awestruck, having already visited the palace on several occasions along with Aunt Yvainne and the Court of Flames. He seems far more preoccupied with grilling Spinner for information about the Choosing, questions which she either deflects or dodges entirely, prattling on excitedly about this parlour or that salon, pointing out ballrooms and galleries and banquet halls, rooms so grand and so *gold* that my eyes take time to adjust.

After what feels like an age, we find ourselves in a dome-like chamber that leads off in four different directions.

'This is where we leave you, I'm afraid, gentlemen,' Spinner announces.

'What?' I can't stop the panic from creeping into my voice.

'You mean we won't be together?' Flint asks.

Sheen scoffs. 'What did you expect, adjoining rooms?'

'Heirs are split by court,' Spinner explains, with a great deal more tact. 'Ignitia that way, Aquatori this way, and so on. But don't worry,' she continues, noting my expression. 'You're free to roam the palace as and when you like.'

Flint looks uneasy. 'I thought my sister might be placed closer to me. She's ... well ...'

The most hated girl in all the realm?

He clears his throat. 'I would just prefer it if she were nearby, that's all.'

'It's all right, Flint,' I tell him. The last thing I want is to appear weak.

His answering look translates as *Are you sure?*

Reluctantly, I nod.

'Sorted,' Spinner says happily. 'This way, Storm Girl.'

The Aquatori Wing is long and winding, adorned with blue tapestries. Spinner leads me to the very end of the corridor to a door with a knocker in the shape of an open eye.

'Here we are.'

The sheer opulence of my chambers takes my breath away. The walls are carved with leaping waves, the golden floor so painstakingly polished that I can see myself reflected in it, wide-eyed and bedraggled. The reception room is strewn with delicate ornaments and blue-velvet armchairs, and boxes of my belongings have already been piled up neatly in a corner.

'Is everything to your liking?' Spinner asks, pinching a fat grape from a bowl and popping it in her mouth.

'I . . . yes,' I say, still gazing around in astonishment.

'I'll leave you to settle in.' She skips back towards the door. 'Now, was there anything else? I think there was. Was there? Yes! Yes, your serf. The Crown Prince has gifted every Heir a personal serf as well as a personal chaperone, so you'll be well taken care of, to say the least. Between the two of us, I'm certain we can make you presentable.'

Coming from anyone else, I'm sure this would sound like an insult, but Spinner says it with such good-natured enthusiasm that I almost laugh. 'Right. Thank you.'

When she leaves, the silence is loud in my ears.

Through a golden archway lies my bedchamber. The glass doors to the balcony beyond are already open wide. I glimpse the Rift far off in the distance, yawning wide and empty. A shiver scuttles like a spider up my spine and I step back inside.

The golden taps in the bathing room are shaped like fish. I turn them on and bathe in rose-scented bubbles, gazing out at the city below.

When I return to my bedchamber, a girl is standing before the dressing table, draping my necklaces carefully over a jewellery stand. She starts as I enter, then bows her head so low that her curtain of butter-blonde hair swings in front of her face. I had forgotten that the Golden Palace would be full of serfs and not attendants. Attendants are paid for their service, whether that's with a few coppers or a roof over their heads. Serfs, on the other hand, are slaves. And all of Ostacre's serfs hail from the Otherlands.

The War of the Empires took place more than half a century ago, and yet this girl, and others like her, serve as a constant reminder of which side won. Their freedom is a price they're forced to pay for the crimes of their Magi ancestors. The people of the Otherlands are Magi no more, of course. They lost their magic when they lost the war.

How strange it must be, knowing there was a time when your homeland was prosperous and powerful. Knowing that you will never inherit that power, or any at all.

'Hello,' I say awkwardly.

Slowly, the girl looks up. I blink. She is beautiful, exquisitely so, as though she's been painted right in front of me. Tall and slender with fair skin, slightly flushed. And her eyes . . . her eyes are *autumn*. As warm and bright as amber stone, almost luminous in the last golden rays of the sun. I have never seen such eyes before.

'My lady,' she whispers.

As expected, I detect a slight telltale lilt to her voice.

'Blaze,' I tell her. 'Just Blaze.'

She dips her head again, busying herself with my jewellery. A thought strikes me. My plans to travel to the Otherlands may have been foiled by the Choosing, but here I have a part of the Otherlands standing right in front of me. Perhaps, if I tread carefully, she'll tell me about them. I'm sure I could learn far more from this girl than from any book or map.

'What's your name?'

The girl looks utterly taken aback, as though she'd never expect me to ask.

'Elva,' she says quietly, before peering behind me at the clock on the wall. 'The First Feast begins in an hour, my lady.'

'*Blaze*,' I correct, glancing towards the windows. The sky is pink, like a blush, and the sun is retreating. 'Then I suppose I'd better start getting ready.'

Right on cue, Spinner bursts through the door. 'Only me!' she calls, as if I somehow can't see her standing right in front of me. 'I have a surprise.'

A serf shuffles in behind her pushing a rack of the most extravagant clothes I have ever seen, the fabric all varying shades of blue.

Spinner grins. 'Storm Girl, you're going to be the best-dressed Heir in Ostacre.'

She selects a sky-blue dress bejewelled with diamonds the size of fingernails because *we really ought to keep it low-key on your first night, you know*, and Elva paints my eyelids blue and wrestles my curls into the usual two braids down my back.

Twilight has arrived, and the Golden Palace is now awake.

At that moment there's a knock on the door to my chambers. Elva hastens across the room to answer it, Spinner and I following along in her wake.

My breath catches as the door swings open.

'Blaze,' says Prince Haldyn. 'How glad I am that you're here.'

9

The prince wears a golden doublet with solid-gold epaulettes, and his dark hair has been neatly combed back from his face. He's just as handsome as I remember, if not more so. I'd almost forgotten about the way that light always seems to find him, glancing off his face, accentuating the curve of his cheekbones, the sharp angle of his jawline.

On his hand, his brandmark glows brightly, as though it really were a small sun. Beneath his right eye are two white scars that intersect like a cross. I stare at them in alarm, suddenly recalling the blood on his face at the ball.

Behind me, Spinner coughs pointedly.

'Your Imperial Highness,' I murmur, sinking into a curtsy.

Prince Haldyn smiles. 'Would you allow me to escort you to the feast?'

I gape at him. Is he serious? He *can't* be. But he must, for he hardly seems the type to play a cruel joke, and his gaze is steady and true, his eyes impossibly dark and yet somehow filled with warmth.

'Well?' he prompts, sounding amused. 'Don't leave me hanging.'

I take his arm, managing a shaky smile in return, and we emerge from the Aquatori Wing into hallways teeming with Etheri dressed in Imperial gold and the colours of the four Crown Courts. They goggle at us as we pass by.

That's her.

Are you sure?

Look at her brandmark.

Blaze.

Storm Weaver.

Murderer.

Changeling.

Freak.

I grit my teeth.

When we reach a quieter passageway, Prince Haldyn and I start speaking at the same time, then both trail off, smiling.

'Please,' he says. 'After you.'

I take a deep breath. 'I just wanted to say that I'm sorry. For what I did at Harglade Hall.'

'Don't apologize,' he says. 'You lost control. It happens.'

'How do you know?' I ask, surprised. 'That it wasn't intentional, I mean.'

'I didn't,' says Prince Haldyn. 'Not for sure, anyway. I imagine most of the other guests think you did it on purpose, but during our short acquaintance, Blaze, I've learned to expect the unexpected, especially when it comes to you.'

I glance away, not sure whether to feel embarrassed or pleased.

A flock of Eyes dressed from head to toe in gold silks gape at us as they pass by. I wait until they're out of sight before speaking again.

'I never meant to hurt anyone.' My gaze lingers on the criss-cross scar below his eye.

The prince reaches up, brushing it lightly with the tip of his finger. 'Put it this way,' he says, 'you certainly made your mark that night.'

A blush creeps slowly up my neck.

He makes me nervous, there's no use in denying it, but the sensation in my chest isn't sharp, or tense. It's unfamiliar but not unpleasant – warm and tingling and curious.

We round the corner into a large candlelit gallery where a gigantic tapestry adorns one wall. I stop in my tracks, stunned by the sheer size of it.

'*Gods*,' I mutter.

'Precisely,' says Prince Haldyn, adjusting the collar of his doublet.

As I peer more closely at the tapestry, I realize he's right. Five figures are depicted – three men, two women.

On the left, a beautiful man in nothing but a pine-green loincloth stands with his arms extended towards the under-growth, where an array of twisting plants and flowers bloom around his feet. This can only be Tellus of the Terrathian, God of the Earth.

Beside him is a woman wearing a long crimson gown. She cups a small fire in her hands, the flames reflected in her eyes, which are golden brown and eerily familiar. This is the Fire Goddess, Vesta. My own ancestor.

On the right, a man in billowing grey robes seems to be levitating a single feather. Avel, God of the Air.

And there, carving a perfect wave above her head, is a woman dressed in a flowing blue gown with hair as white as morning frost. The Water Goddess, Morwenna, Mother of the Aquatori.

Prince Haldyn watches me as I gaze up at the Gods, each of them as formidable and exquisite as I had imagined. 'I'm reminded of why I try to avoid this gallery,' he says mildly. 'Really feels like they're looking back at you, doesn't it?'

In the centre of the tapestry stands the fifth and final figure. He is the most imposing of all, and the most unnerving, for he is almost a mirror image of the prince at my side.

The Maker himself.

It was the Maker who created us. Etheri, I mean. He had the power to wield light – and life. My mother used to tell me the story. Thousands of years ago, at the dawn of the new age, the Maker moulded Tellus from the earth, forged Vesta in the fire, shaped Avel from the winds, and pulled Morwenna from the water.

The First Etheri – the four elements incarnate.

Gifts were spread among a chosen few, and passed down to offspring. The number of Etheri began to grow, the Noble Houses were born, and the Maker claimed this land for his people. He had Fidra build the Golden Palace and he had Magi fill it with enchantments. He formed his Crowned Council, quartering his empire and giving each of the First Etheri a kingdom to rule over in exchange for binding their power with his own. Then, once he was in possession of light, earth, fire, air and water, the Maker crowned himself Emperor of Ostacre.

It's little wonder he and Prince Haldyn look so alike, given that he sired the Castellion line. While the Maker decreed that every king and queen must win their thrones, he ordained that only the firstborn sons of his House would inherit the Imperial Crown, thereby ensuring that his legacy would live on, and that his face, or at least one chillingly similar, be worn by every Ostacrian Emperor, for all of time.

I wonder how the prince must feel, as a descendant of the Maker, knowing that soon, very soon, he will leave behind his life as the light-wielding Castellion Heir and take his rightful place as the most powerful Etheri in the world.

My eyes linger on Vesta, then Morwenna, the Goddess whose blood runs through my veins and the Goddess who never seemed to hear my prayers, my whispers in the dead of night, a single plea – for my own power to be returned to me.

I think of the storm, of my drizzle, of ice coating and cracking a thousand glasses, of the eclipse darkening the skies and the brandmark glowing softly on the back of my hand.

If the full impact of my situation has not yet entirely hit me, it does now, over and over, as vast and as intimidating as this tapestry.

I take a step backwards, away from the prince. 'Your Imperial Highness,' I begin.

'Hal,' he says.

'What?'

'Hal,' he repeats, glancing sideways at me. 'My friends call me Hal.'

How unimposing his name sounds, cut in half and devoid of titles.

'Hal, then,' I continue. 'I think there must be some kind of mistake. I don't think I should be here. I don't think I should be an Heir.'

The prince raises an eyebrow, jerking his head towards the tapestry. 'Did you just question the will of the Gods?'

My stomach sinks. 'I – no, I just –' That's when I notice he's smiling. I exhale in relief. 'Very funny.'

Hal's smile fades slightly as he fixes me with those Castellion eyes, which hold neither the calculating consideration of his father's nor the cold amusement of his uncle's. 'Like it or not, Blaze, you've been branded an Heir. And no matter what you feel, no matter what anybody says, I think you'd do well to start acting like one.'

I hold his gaze. 'Is that what you would do?'

'It's what I do all the time,' he says, his voice gentle. Then he grins. 'You can't hide under the table forever, you know.'

My blush deepens. 'I *really* wish I hadn't told you that.'

Hal moves forward, extending his arm once more. I take one last look at the Gods, then fall into step beside him.

As somebody unaccustomed to the company of others, I'm surprised by just how much I enjoy his, even if I can't account for why he would seek out mine. Much like during our dance at Harglade Hall, I find myself savouring his undivided attention, his closeness, the lingering scent of lemons on his skin.

We soon find ourselves in a crowded passage, winding our way through a throng of courtiers until we reach the teeming banquet hall. Without meaning to, I grip his arm tighter.

He glances down at me. 'You really hate all this, don't you?'

'I don't much like being looked at,' I admit as the stares burrow into me.

'Perhaps you'd blend in a little better if I made myself scarce?'

Whispers dance around us as Hal deftly unhooks my hand from the crook of his elbow and bends to kiss it. As his lips touch my glowing brandmark, that strange, warm feeling seems to grow. Then he's gone, disappeared into the crowd, and I feel suddenly cold.

The banquet hall is enormous. Five long tables are arranged at right angles to a golden dais. Five tables for five courts. Upon the dais is another table, smaller and made from solid gold. Behind it sit five golden thrones, the one in the middle the largest of all. Five thrones for five rulers. Below the dais, running parallel with it, is yet another table. I wonder who it's for.

Tucking my brandhand into the folds of my skirt, I begin to make my way around the perimeter of the room, searching for my brother.

Right on cue, Flint appears at my side, dressed in a lavishly embroidered red doublet. 'There you are.'

I manage a smile, relieved. 'Here I am.'

He gives me a reproachful look. 'I went to your rooms to find you and your serf told me you'd already left. Day one and you ditch me?'

'I didn't *ditch* you,' I tell him. 'What'd you want me to do, turn down the prince?'

His eyes widen. '*Hal* escorted you?'

'He did.'

'Let me get this straight,' my brother says, throwing an arm round my shoulders. 'So far, you've made two friends. A mad old Riftkeeper, and the Crown Prince of Ostacre.'

I lean into him. 'That's about the size of it.'

We walk together through the crowd. Everyone is dressed in their finery, expensive silks and brocades from Vost, glittering jewels from Thaven. The golden Court of Eyes are everywhere I look, and looking back at me.

'How's your chaperone?' I ask Flint.

'Sheen? Silent, morose and perfectly miserable. I'm sensing the start of a beautiful friendship. How's yours?'

'Very . . . *enthusiastic*.'

'Want to swap?'

'I'm afraid not. I doubt Sheen has such good taste in dresses.'

Flint lets out a sudden whoop of excitement and yanks me over to a couple of Ignitia courtiers. 'So it is true,' he says with a grin, gesturing towards their glowing brandmarks. 'It seems the Gods really are letting their standards slip. Cole, Elaith, I'd like you to meet my sister.'

The muscular, fair-haired boy, Cole, clasps my brother's hand and wrestles him into a one-armed hug. 'Wondered when you'd show up, Harglade.' He catches my eye and nods. 'Blaze. We've heard a lot about you.'

The girl, Elaith, rolls her eyes. '*Obviously*. We haven't been living under a rock.'

'Well,' says Flint, 'you live in Fire Mountain. So, technically, you kind of have.'

She laughs, punching his arm. Elaith is small, with blue eyes and flame-red hair that clashes frightfully with her dress. She holds out a hand. 'Nice to meet you, Blaze.'

I shake her hand, mirroring her smile. Flint accepts a glass from a passing serf and offers me a sip. I try not to wrinkle my nose at the tartness of the wine.

'It's not fair,' Elaith is grumbling. 'The emperor didn't come to *my* Name Day ball.'

'Which is probably a good thing, seeing as you threw up on your shoes,' notes Flint.

Elaith holds up a finger indignantly and points it at him. 'I blame you for that. I didn't exactly spin myself around the dance floor.'

'No,' Flint concedes. 'But you did drink enough champagne to fill the Lagoon.'

This time, Elaith holds up a different finger.

Flint chuckles. 'How long have you two been slumming it here, then?'

'Couple days,' says Cole. 'After your ball, Queen Yvainne sent us back to court. We'd barely been travelling an hour before the eclipse.'

A gaggle of Terrathian girls calls out Flint's name in greeting, and he waves to them over the sea of heads.

'We still have no idea what to expect for the first trial,' Cole continues. 'Elaith got Hal black-out drunk on wildfire wine last night and he wouldn't let anything slip.'

Elaith smirks. 'And that's saying something, as I can be *very* persuasive.'

I catch sight of Hal from across the room, laughing at something a pretty Aquatori girl is whispering in his ear.

'What about the Council?' asks Flint. 'How are they taking it?'

Elaith shrugs. 'They've mostly been shut up in the Council Chamber.'

'And our aunt?'

'Quiet,' Cole admits. 'Subdued.'

I can't pretend to have any strong feelings for Aunt Yvainne, but there's a part of me that pities her. To give a crown means to take a crown. This is only the beginning for the Heirs, yet it is also the end for the Council.

Elaith notices my expression. 'Listen,' she says gently, 'your aunt is beloved, by the court, by the realm. If I'm crowned queen –'

Cole pretends to cough. '*Unlikely.*'

Elaith narrows her eyes at him, then turns back to me. 'As I was saying, if I'm crowned queen, I hope that I could be half as good and gracious as her.'

Flint clinks their glasses together.

Cole lets out a whistle. 'Seriously, though. To spend all those years as ruler only to go back to being . . .' He trails off, taking a swig of wine. 'I can't imagine how that would feel.'

'Well, that's lucky,' Elaith tells him sweetly. 'Because you'll never have to.'

Cole just smiles to himself. A moment later the sleeve of Elaith's dress catches fire. I step back, alarmed, while Elaith shrieks and Flint roars with laughter.

'Bastard,' Elaith mutters, extinguishing the flames and dusting herself down.

'Easy, little girl,' Cole purrs, slinging an arm round her shoulders.

'Least you didn't drop your wine,' Flint tells her.

A group of Ventalla courtiers is watching us, not caring to lower their voices.

Is that the Storm Weaver?
Did you see her with the prince?

'Have you met the other Heirs?' Flint asks loudly, moving closer to me.

'Some,' Elaith replies. 'Most we know, or at least know of.'

Cole smirks. 'Training hasn't even started yet and the Eyes have already been placing bets. There's a couple of underdogs, so that should make things interesting. Nice trick, by the way, at your ball.'

Flint presses a hand to his heart in mock gratitude. 'Why, thank you.'

'Not *you*. I was talking to your sister. Smashing glasses is definitely one way to liven up a party, Blaze. You know you've had a good time when you're still picking ice out of your –'

'Shhh!' Elaith hisses, grabbing his arm. 'Look.'

All around us, voices are starting to fizzle out. The four of us turn just as the horns begin to sound.

As one, we sink to our knees.

10

The emperor strides through the centre of the kneeling crowd, his cloak of spun gold fastened across his chest with a thick golden chain. Behind him walk his Crowned Council. First comes Aunt Yvainne, wearing a garnet-red gown and a strained-looking smile. Queen Aspen wanders dreamily after her in a dress made from flower petals, her long coppery hair falling to her waist. My heart jolts as Queen Hydra comes into view, my gaze lingering on the Aquatori crown of curling waves perched atop her head. Last of all is King Balen, his raven eyes roaming the room, mouth curved in an amused smile, as though he alone were privy to some secret joke. I think of his soft voice, his cold lips pressed to my scar, the way he raised his glass to me among a sea of ice and blood.

The Council climb the steps to the dais and take their thrones.

'Rise,' booms the emperor.

Flint holds out a hand to help me to my feet as the crowd makes their way towards the banquet tables. The Eyes claim the one in the centre, with the four Crown Courts taking those opposite their sovereign. I swallow hard, pressing closer to my brother.

Elaith notices. 'It's all right, the Heirs sit together.' She points to the table below the dais, the one that had puzzled me earlier. The other Heirs are practically elbowing one another out of the way to secure a place near Hal, who is already seated at the head.

'*My lady.*' Cole offers his arm to Elaith, but before she can take it he darts off into the throng with a hoot of laughter. She scowls, stalking after him.

Almost every chair is occupied by the time we reach our table, which is piled high with honey-cured meats; strange, exotic-looking fish; melons and cranberries; tureens of stew; cheeses, olives, truffles; and oysters on ice.

Elaith decides to crawl underneath the table rather than walk round it, using Cole's knees to pull herself up and into the seat beside him. I don't hear what he says to her, but she swats at him with her napkin, smirking.

Many of the Heirs turn to stare as I sit down next to Flint, just as the Ventalla King's silken whisper slices through the din. '*Silence.*'

'I will *never* get used to that,' mutters Elaith.

I'm startled a second time when the emperor speaks, his voice a rumble of thunder that fills the hall. 'Tonight we celebrate the First Feast, which marks the beginning of the Choosing Rite, and the beginning of a new era.' His gaze falls on our table. 'My friends, it is my great honour to present the Heirs of Ostacre.'

Chairs begin to scrape back as those around me get to their feet. I count thirteen. No, fourteen, including myself.

There are supposed to be four Heirs from each of the four Crown Courts, which means that two of us are missing.

'Blaze,' Flint hisses, nudging my shoulder.

I make myself stand.

The banquet hall erupts with applause, and the Etheri crane their necks to get a good look at us. I remember what Cole said about the Eyes placing bets, and shiver.

The emperor raises his goblet, and suddenly the light in the room grows brighter. The candles burn more fiercely, the wine in our glasses ripples, and the ground begins to tremble, the sound of rattling cutlery joining that of the whistling streams of air.

'A toast,' he says. 'To the future.'

I wonder how it will feel, handing over all that power to his son. In our neighbouring kingdoms, Thaven and Vost, the transfer of power from sovereign to successor takes place only upon the sovereign's death. But in Ostacre, we have different customs. At the Binding Ceremony, the emperor will relinquish his throne, and at the coronation, he will be forced to bow alongside the rest of us as his son takes his place upon it.

Once the answering cheers eventually die down, excited chatter resumes, and we take this as our cue to sit. I catch a glimpse of Spinner at the Eyes' table. She gives me an encouraging thumbs up, her tattooed cheeks bulging with food.

My brother pushes a heaped plate towards me. Obediently I pick up my fork and begin to eat, listening to Flint, Cole and Elaith sizing up the other Heirs.

'So, who have the Eyes set their sights on, then?' Flint asks.

'Well, *you* for starters. No surprises there.'

My brother grins. 'Naturally. Who else?'

'Remember that Fish bitch?'

'Which one? There's a whole shoal of them.'

Apologetic looks are cast in my direction. Fish is the derogatory nickname for the Aquatori. I just smile blandly, concentrating on chewing.

'You know, the one who tripped Elaith up on Dawnday last year.'

'She's lucky I didn't incinerate her on the spot. I was *very* tempted.'

'Ah, that one. What about her?'

'Our carriage arrived at the same time as hers, and let me tell you she practically *ran* up the front steps.'

'Her family's supposed to be filthy rich. They own a bunch of ships. And her parents spend most of their time trailing round after Queen Hydra.'

'She's got her eye on the prince, I heard.'

'She'll be disappointed, then. I've never met anyone who guards their heart like Hal.'

I glance towards the head of the table. Sure enough, an Heir in a dazzling blue-and-silver gown is sitting on the prince's left. I almost let out a groan as I realize who she is. It's the courtier in the fish-scale dress who I crashed into while chasing Renly across the dance floor at Harglade Hall, the one who looked as though she had wanted to strangle me on the spot when Hal had asked me to dance. Marina, he'd called her.

'Seriously, that girl is so insufferable I'm beginning to pity the other Fish.'

'Oh, Blaze'll wipe the floor with her, I'm sure. Won't you, sister mine?'

I take a sip of something pink and sour as an excuse not to answer him.

'What about the Gusters?'

Gusters is the slightly less derogatory nickname for the Ventalla.

'Zeph,' answers Cole, jerking his thumb towards a boy in dark-grey robes.

Flint looks pleased.

'And of course, there's still one Heir yet to arrive,' says Elaith.

'Only one?' I glance over towards the two empty chairs at the end of the table.

'Oh, the last Pyro's here, all right,' Elaith tells me, making a face. 'She just considers the feast far less important than her training schedule.'

Flint leans on his elbows and begins to count. 'Full shoal of Fish. Full set of Pyros and Gusters. Which only leaves . . .'

The Terrathian.

'So, who's our last Green?' Flint asks, cracking open an oyster shell.

Elaith clicks her long red nails against the side of her wine glass. 'Well, that's the thing. Nobody knows. There are some rumours of course, but nothing particularly believable.' She nods in the direction of a girl wearing a gown of tightly woven grass. 'I tried asking Amaryllis, but they're all none the wiser. It's starting to cause quite the stir.'

My brother grins. 'How very mysterious.'

I look at him, and suddenly my heart clenches as I imagine him sitting upon the great stone throne in Fire Mountain. Flint, a king. Born of flame. Born to rule. And I imagine myself, trapped in the Lagoon, bound to the crown I wasn't powerful enough to win.

I think of the tapestry in the gallery, history stitched with needle and thread, and in my mind I weave a tapestry of my own, this one with Hal in the centre, a prince turned emperor, flanked by his Crowned Council – only I can't make out their faces.

I glance round at the Heirs, with their bright eyes and glowing brandmarks.

I think you'd do well to start acting like one, Hal had said.

Maybe he's right. There's no escaping this, which means I have a choice to make. I can choose to hide under the table, or play the game.

Even if I'm going to lose.

II

I walk along a winding path, feeling myself pulled, as if by an invisible tether, towards something gold up ahead, something that knows me, waits for me.

I hear a voice in my head, soft, like a whisper.

Blaze.

Just a little further.

Yet when I gaze up at the patches of sky between the canopy of leaves above, I find they are no longer blue, but as black as coal.

'*Blaze.* Wake up, you idiot.'

I open an eye, the dream disintegrating. Flint lounges at the end of my bed dressed in a plain red tunic, a spoon poised over a tray of half-eaten food.

'Finally,' he says, grinning. 'Rise and shine, sister mine. Today is a big day.'

I groan, burrowing down under the sheets and clutching at them with all my might as my brother attempts to yank them away. He wins the tug of war and I emerge, disgruntled.

'Is that my breakfast?' I ask, pointing at the tray.

He shrugs. 'If you're not fast, you're last.'

'Pig.'

Flint grins at me through a mouthful of porridge.

The sun streams through the open balcony doors, bathing the room in early-morning light. Birdsong mingles with the sounds of a city waking up.

'Here,' Flint says, pushing a bowl of berries towards me. 'Eat.'

I do as I'm told.

'Where's that chaperone of yours?' My brother glances around as though she were crouched under the dressing table. 'Isn't she meant to be, you know, *chaperoning* you?'

At that moment Spinner hurtles through the doors and screeches to a halt, nursing a stitch in her side. 'Oh, good,' she says, between pants. 'You're up.'

Flint throws a berry at her. 'No thanks to you. She'd have slept right through the first training session if it weren't for me.'

Spinner just blows him a kiss.

Elva appears behind her, amber eyes downcast. Draped over her arm is a tunic exactly like Flint's, only this one is blue. Spinner ushers me behind a screen to change. The tunic fits perfectly, as did the dress from last night. This strikes me as odd, given that I was never asked for my measurements. Perhaps Eyes have a knack for these things.

Flint and I follow a couple of Ventalla Heirs through long corridors and echoing galleries until we reach the entrance hall.

'Morning,' says Elaith. 'Sleep well?'

'Like a baby,' Flint tells her.

'What's with these, d'you reckon?' Cole pulls a face as he gestures to his tunic.

'Can't say I mind them,' says Flint, flexing his shoulders.

'I'm lucky, though. You can pull off just about anything when you're as pretty as me.'

Elaith snorts. 'Sure.'

She's customized her own tunic with a red leather belt, and gold bangles glitter round her bare forearms from where she's rolled up the sleeves.

'How convenient for you, Elaith,' my brother says. 'I didn't realize the training tunics came in children's sizes.'

Elaith elbows him in the chest. Moments later a man appears at the foot of the largest staircase. He smiles widely, displaying two rows of solid-gold teeth, and introduces himself as Alator, the court official overseeing the day-to-day running of the Choosing Rite.

'Training will take place at the Golden Keep,' Alator says, moving to stand over by the towering doors to the palace. 'Who can tell me something about the Keep?'

I can. I've read about it. The library at Harglade Hall has a whole shelf dedicated to the Imperial Province. The Keep was built by Rekar Castellion, the second emperor of Ostacre and firstborn son of the Maker. It's protected by ancient enchantments and was used as a site of refuge during the War of the Empires. Not that I plan on saying any of this out loud. I expect I wouldn't be doing myself any favours in being branded a know-it-all.

When no one responds, an Aquatori Heir clears his throat quietly. He's a good-looking boy, tall and lean and angular, his long dark hair tied back from his face with a scrap of blue cloth. 'The Keep was designed to protect those inside from invaders,' he says. 'Many sought shelter there when the citadel was under siege from the Magi.'

Alator looks pleased. 'Excellent, Kai. It appears someone knows their history.'

A Ventalla girl in a pearl-grey tunic steps forward. 'So what happens now? Will Hal be joining us?'

'His Imperial Highness, *Prince Haldyn*,' corrects Alator, 'has far more pressing matters to attend to at present. Your trainers will oversee every aspect of your tuition. The prince will watch each of the three trials, alongside the Crowned Council.' He claps his hands together briskly. 'Now, before we depart for the Keep, is there anybody missing?'

'Well, that depends,' says a voice from above. 'I'm not just anybody.'

My body turns rigid. I know that voice, honey-sweet and hateful. No. Not here. Please not here. Not *her*.

Slowly, I turn round.

Ember saunters towards us, skipping lightly down the last few steps and walking straight through the middle of the Heirs, who part for her with only muttered indignation. Her hair is threaded with golden beads, her lips painted the same shade of red as her tunic, and there, glimmering on the back of her hand, is the unmistakable glow of her brandmark.

Horrified, I turn to Flint, who's looking pretty sheepish.

Ember smirks. 'What's the matter, cousin? Didn't you miss me?'

An echo of the rage I felt at the ball thrums through me. Why must she torment me so? What have I ever done to her? If I didn't know any better, I'd think she was *jealous*. As if she fears she's being overshadowed. Which is perfectly ridiculous, of course. From where I'm standing, my infamy serves only to cast her in a brighter light. She is everything a daughter of House Harglade should be – poised and bold, fearless and flame-wielding, just like her mother, and mine, and our aunt, the Fire Queen.

Alator peers at us, his interest piqued. 'Three Harglades at the Choosing. How history does enjoy repeating itself.'

The sun beats down mercilessly as we make our way through the palace grounds towards the Golden Keep. I hang back, skulking at the rear of the group. Part of me is just angry that I didn't figure it out. My cousin may only be fifteen years old, but she's powerful, and she knows it. She's always taken considerable delight in her gift, ever since we were very young, when she would singe the hair off my dolls or burn the very last page of my book.

I think back to last night. What was it Elaith had said when I noticed that the fourth Ignitia Heir was missing?

Oh, the last Pyro's here, all right. She just considers the feast far less important than her training schedule.

So, Ember has already started training. Judging by her blatant absence, she's not making any secret of it either. If she were keeping her extra training sessions a secret, it would suggest that she needed them. But she's not. Which means she doesn't feel threatened. Which means she thinks she might actually be in with a shot. Dread courses through me as I consider what could happen if my cousin wins the Ignitia crown.

Ember. *Queen.*

I'm so absorbed in this nightmare that Elaith has to wave a hand in front of my face to get my attention. She and Flint have broken away from the group to wait for me.

Elaith cocks her thumb at my brother. 'He said you wouldn't take it well.'

'Oh, he did, did he?' I snap. 'How intuitive of him.'

Flint suddenly becomes very interested in the sleeve of his tunic.

Elaith shrugs. 'I don't blame you, Blaze. I swear that girl came out of the womb a raging bit–'

'*Elaith*,' Flint warns, trying his hardest not to smile.

I watch Elaith glance over to where Ember is whispering something in Cole's ear.

'If it's any consolation,' Elaith says tightly, 'I've never liked her either.'

The palace gardens spread out for miles, enclosed by a wall of solid gold. Paths spiral off in all directions from the one we follow, winding through the perfectly manicured lawns, the grass soft and vivid green despite the heat. All around I can see serfs pruning, weeding, watering flowers, planting seeds.

'Is that a maze?' I ask, pointing at a cluster of high hedges far in the distance.

Elaith nods. 'It's enchanted. Few have ever found the centre – it likes to move around. Piece of advice – don't play hide-and-seek in the maze after dark.'

'What she *means* is don't play hide-and-seek in the maze after dark after drinking your weight in wildfire wine,' Flint tells me.

Elaith is unperturbed. 'Seriously, it seemed to go on forever. I had to send up a flare.'

'And *I* had to find you and carry you out of there,' Flint mutters.

We pass a row of rosebushes. At first I thought it was a trick of the light, but no, the roses themselves are *gold*, their thorns glittering in the morning sun.

I flinch as Elaith loops her arm through mine, then instantly feel foolish.

'Come on,' she says. 'Let's catch up.'

The tower stands at the edge of the palace grounds. It stretches high into the sky, windowless, doorless and impenetrable.

'Welcome to the Keep,' says Alator.

Elaith frowns, puzzled. 'There isn't any door,' she points out.

Alator turns his smile on her. 'Quite right, Elaith.'

'But if there isn't a door, then how do we get in?' asks Cole in a voice one might use when speaking to someone incredibly dim.

Alator glances round at the group of Heirs. 'Someone's been skipping his Imperial History lessons. Would anyone care to tell Cole why the Keep has no door?'

Once again, the Aquatori boy, Kai, fills the silence. 'The door to the Keep only reveals itself to those it deems worthy of its protection.'

Alator beams at him. 'Precisely. This sacred tower sheltered many Etheri during their time of need, regardless of rank or title. You must present yourselves to it and prove your worth.' He laces his fingers together in front of him. 'Do I have a volunteer to go first?'

At once, the Heirs begin to raise their hands eagerly. Some even step forward. Elaith, who's at least a head shorter than everybody else, stands on her tiptoes. I remain where I am, arms planted firmly at my sides, eyes fixed on my feet.

'Blaze,' says Alator genially. 'What about you?'

My heart sinks. Slowly, I glance up. Everybody is looking at me. 'I . . . don't really . . .' My voice trails off limply.

'Come,' Alator presses, his gold teeth gleaming in the sunlight. 'There is nothing to fear, and I must say, there is a beautiful sort of symmetry to it.'

I frown, confusion swamping my embarrassment. 'What do you mean?'

Alator smiles. 'Only that the first Heir to enter the Keep at the last Choosing was your mother.'

I blink, glancing at Flint, who looks just as surprised as I am.

'Blaze?' Alator prompts.

I take a few small steps towards the Keep. 'What am I supposed to do?' I ask, privately thinking that if Alator is expecting me to introduce myself to a solid-gold wall in front of all the others then he has another thing coming, symmetry be damned.

'Extend your hand,' he tells me. 'Let it feel you're there. Let it know you.'

From his place among the crowd of Heirs, Flint gives me an encouraging smile. I turn back to the Keep. Feeling foolish, I press my palm to the golden wall, which is smooth and remarkably cool despite the glaring sun.

I'm here, I think. *I'm letting you know me.*

Nothing happens.

I'm letting you know me like you knew my mother.

Again, nothing happens. Behind me I can hear Ember's hateful, tinkling laugh.

I don't pretend to be worthy. I have killed people. Drowned people. Ruined lives. I don't know why it happened. I don't know what any of it means. The storm. The ice. My dreams. Perhaps I really am soulless like they say.

A lump forms in my throat and I swallow it down.

My mother believed I would do great things. She told me so herself, and she always told the truth. And I'm here, aren't I? I'm an Heir. That's got to be worth something. That's got to be worthy of something.

Please.

All at once, the wall beneath my hand begins to shift and change, tingling and pulsating with ancient enchantments. I open my eyes.

Before me, where there was previously solid wall, is a gleaming golden door.

12

Tentatively, as though it might vanish, I take hold of the handle. The door to the Keep is as light as breath and yields immediately to my touch. As it opens, I feel this strange phantom weight pressing down upon me, like I'm being watched by a thousand pairs of eyes.

'Thank you,' I whisper as I step inside.

There are no windows, yet the tower is lit from within, the sunlight permeating the walls as if they were made from glass rather than gold. A winding spiral staircase wraps itself round the perimeter, extending upward as far as I can see.

Unsurprisingly, Ember is next to appear. 'Come now, cousin,' she croons, skipping over to me. 'No need to look so nervous.'

'I'm not nervous,' I lie. 'But I appreciate your concern.'

'Glad to hear it.' She leans closer. 'Though just between you and me, you should be.'

I drop Ember's gaze, my hand moving instinctively to rub my scar.

'Ladies.' Flint smiles as the door melts away behind him. He strolls over to us, coming to a stop by my side. 'Playing nice, I hope, Ember?'

She smiles sweetly at him. 'Always.'

Soon enough, all fifteen Heirs are assembled inside the Keep. We climb the seemingly endless staircase until Alator signals for us to stop.

'Here we have the Keep's training facilities,' he says.

Elaith raises an eyebrow. 'Is he seriously expecting all of us to train together in *one* room?' she whispers. 'He must be mad. We'll practically be on top of each other.'

Cole grins. 'Well, I for one won't be complaining.'

She shoves past him with her sharp little elbows, pulling Flint and me with her just in time for Alator to open the door.

Elaith *should* be right. Judging from the proportions of the Keep, which is built tall rather than wide, this door should lead to a fairly small, narrow room. But this room is quite the opposite. In fact, it can hardly be described as a *room* at all. The space is impossibly vast, the ceiling so high that I wonder if there's even one there at all.

Flint lets out a low whistle. 'Holy –'

'*Gods*,' Elaith breathes.

I catch sight of four figures making their way across the stone floor towards us – three men, one woman, each wearing a different court colour.

'Allow me to introduce you to your trainers,' says Alator.

The only female trainer, a severe-looking woman in robes of steel grey, steps forward. 'Welcome.' She nods briskly at Alator. 'We'll take it from here.'

Alator smiles graciously, and the golden door shuts behind him with a clang that seems to reverberate through my entire body.

'One of their number is missing,' muses the trainer dressed in evergreen. 'I was promised four Children of the Earth, and yet I count no more than three.'

It's true. The fourth Terrathian Heir is still missing.

'Let me look at them,' murmurs the trainer in robes of deep crimson. He's ancient, with a beard so long he's tucked it into his belt. 'I see generations in their faces,' he says, more to himself than to anyone. 'In the hue of an eye, in the curl of a lip, I see fragments of those who came before.' He inhales sharply, tilting his head to the side. 'I smell ambition on their skin.'

Beside me, Elaith wrinkles her nose, as though she can smell it too.

The Ignitia trainer beckons. 'Come to me, my little flames.'

A wedge of something jagged and anxious lodges itself inside my chest as Flint, Elaith, Cole and Ember break away from the group and make their way over to him. They are followed by the Ventalla and Terrathian Heirs, who set off after their respective trainer.

This leaves the Aquatori trainer. His hair is a piercing white, brighter than snow, his skin fair and slightly wrinkled, his eyes a dark, depthless blue. He's dressed in a simple tunic and belt, attached to which is a leather sheath that holds a small silver trident. There's something familiar about him.

'We meet at last,' he says softly. 'My name is River.'

River leads us past the Ignitia Heirs, who stand in a large stone pit a few metres below floor level, while far above, the Ventalla Heirs are climbing a flight of rough-hewn steps cut into the walls of the chamber, which seem to stretch on endlessly up into the air.

Quite suddenly, the ground beneath my feet is replaced by soil and roots as we begin to make our way through a thicket of trees. I stare around at the large boulders and bushes with rows of sharp thorn-teeth gleaming in the dappled light from an absent sun, branches hanging low enough to stroke the tops of our heads like fingertips.

A forest inside a tower.

I take it all in, eyes wide.

We pass the three Terrathian Heirs and their trainer standing in a clearing, and soon emerge out of the other side of the trees. Over the heads of my companions I can make out something shimmering lying just up ahead. As we get closer I see that it's a pool of water. River asks us to spread out around it. Kai moves to stand on my left, the other boy, Fjord, on my right, and Marina, or 'Fish Bitch', as Cole had called her, directly opposite.

River clears his throat. 'Welcome to training,' he says. 'These sessions are designed to prepare you for the trials ahead. There are three in total, each set a month apart. After every trial, the weakest link will be eliminated from the Choosing, yet they will remain here, at the palace, to attend the Binding Ceremony and coronation.'

Marina glances round the pool, sizing up her competition. 'When is the first trial?'

'That is for the emperor to decide,' River tells her.

'Has anyone ever died during the trials?' Marina asks this question casually, as though she were enquiring about the weather.

There is an uncomfortable pause, then River says, 'Once or twice, over the years.'

I feel myself grow cold.

'While the death of an Heir is not unheard of, it is a rare tragedy, and one we strive to avoid at all costs,' River continues. 'And, though I cannot tell you what the nature of these trials will be, I will do everything in my power to ensure that you are ready to face whatever the Council intend to throw at you. All I ask for in return is your trust. Do I have it?'

I force my head to nod along with the others. River smiles. 'Good. We will begin, I think, with a small display of your talents. Fjord, shall we start with you?'

Fjord is a sickly-looking boy, pale and thin with eyes that are a murky colour, like puddles at the side of a road. I watch as he makes a small curving motion with his hand, as though painting a spiral on a canvas. The pool begins to churn, the water slapping the sides and sloshing over the edges. Fjord repeats this same movement until a large, perfect wave rears and breaks before him. The moment he drops his hand, the water calms.

'Good,' says River. 'Kai, you next.'

Kai raises both hands above the pool and closes his eyes. For a few moments, nothing happens. Then I hear a harsh, scraping sound. I watch as a thin layer of ice spreads across the water, coating the surface, crackling and hissing as it goes.

River nods approvingly. 'Excellent. Marina?'

Fish Bitch steps forward, shooting me a particularly dirty look as she holds out a hand, palm facing upward. Slowly, her fingers begin to curl into a fist. For a moment nothing happens. Then steam erupts from the frozen pool, bursting up in great plumes through the sheet of solid ice, filling the air with hot, heavy moisture.

I wipe my sleeve across my brow. Marina's eyes meet mine – a challenge.

Suddenly the water begins to froth violently. With a delicate flick of her wrist, Marina carves a perfect wave, which comes crashing down in front of me, spraying my legs with boiling water. I spring backwards with a yelp, causing Fjord to hoot with laughter. I stare at the floor, my cheeks burning hotter than my shins.

'That is quite enough, Marina,' says River sharply.

'Sorry,' she replies, not sounding sorry in the slightest.

River turns to me. 'Blaze. It's your turn.'

That wipes the smirk off Fjord's face. 'Are you sure that's a good idea?' he splutters. 'I mean, given who she is.'

River turns his head a fraction to look at him. 'I thank you for your guidance, Fjord.'

Pink blotches appear on Fjord's pale neck.

'I am going to say this once and once only,' River continues, his hand resting on the silver trident at his hip. 'To those among you who bear any animosity or prejudice towards *any* of your fellow Heirs, I would ask you to leave those feelings at the door. For those who do not heed this request will find themselves in very deep water.'

I stare at him in astonishment, but he's not finished.

'No student of mine will resent another for that which was outwith their control. No student of mine will pass judgement, hold grudges or flaunt their ignorance of matters about which they understand *very* little. Do I make myself clear?'

One by one, the others begin to nod. Solemnly, like Kai, and sourly, like Marina and Fjord. I look down at my feet. No one has ever defended me like that. Not even Grandmother, who trained me from childhood to be grateful and graceful, or Flint, who prefers to act as though the storm never happened at all.

When River speaks again, his voice is softer. 'Blaze. Please, go ahead.'

I swallow hard, tucking a few loose wisps of hair behind my ears.

It's said that when the Rain Singers called the rain, they heard a song of such indescribable beauty that it pierced the soul. I've often wondered whether I heard such a song all those years ago when I summoned that storm. Whether I will ever hear it again.

Taking a deep breath, I wait, or rather *hope*, for something to happen.

A painful minute trickles by, the silence broken up by a few muffled sniggers.

If my gifts are not gone for good, if they are a part of me like Grandmother said they were, then why is there no sign of the rain I was born with? Why doesn't the pool freeze and crack, just like those wine glasses did at Harglade Hall?

There's nothing else for it. Closing my eyes, I picture my mother. She's sitting in a rocking chair by the fire, telling me a story.

There was once a girl with eyes like rainclouds and sea mist, and a heart of purest gold, and when she came into the world, she sang to the rain, and the rain sang back.

I watch as tears begin to roll down my mother's cheeks.

Then I feel it.

Slowly, I open my eyes. My mother is gone but the drizzle remains, hazy droplets smattering soft ripples upon the surface of the pool.

Marina is smirking. Kai is staring at me, his expression slightly bewildered. Fjord has his eyes screwed shut, as though waiting to be blasted into oblivion. He opens one eye cautiously, followed by the other, then straightens up, clearing his throat.

At my Name Day ball, Grandmother claimed my drizzle was intentional, that I was merely demonstrating control, while Flint suggested that I was just being modest. Here, I have no such excuses. Nothing to hide behind. Now, they see me for what I am.

Or rather, for what I'm not.

'Thank you, Blaze,' River says quietly.

For the rest of the morning, I try my best to steer clear of Marina, who has taken to standing, watching and even commenting as I endeavour and ultimately fail to conjure anything more than a light shower, although she does so always when River is out of earshot.

I'm relieved when we break for lunch, joining the other Heirs at a large table that I'm almost positive was not there when we arrived.

I sit, self-conscious and irritable, taking a long time chewing and swallowing as an excuse not to speak to anyone. It doesn't surprise me in the slightest that Ember greets Marina like an old friend. They sit with their heads together, shooting smug glances in my direction. And they're not the only ones. News of my failure seems to have made its way around the table. Whispers dance from ear to ear, some barely whispers at all, and I sink further into my seat, wishing I could drop through the floor and disappear entirely.

It hurts, knowing that they look at me and expect *more*. They expect cloudbursts and flash floods and downpours and rainstorms.

But I am only drizzle.

13

B y the time I reach my chambers the sun has dipped low beyond the horizon line, painting the sky a deep gold.

Since collecting me from the Keep, Spinner appears to have given up asking me how training went and continues to chatter on about a multitude of things I can't find it in me to care about – who said what about someone I've never met and which Heirs have the most beautiful clothes or expensive jewels. I pretend to listen, nodding occasionally.

I'm relieved when she eventually leaves, though she does so with the promise to return later on and help ready me for the evening's festivities. Last night we celebrated the First Feast, and tonight there is a ball to celebrate the first day of training. It seems to me like the Choosing Rite is just one big excuse for the Imperial Court to throw a party. And having spent my life entirely isolated from society, I admit I'm finding it all rather exhausting. Before, I could spend entire days curled up in the library with only Renly for company, but now, I am on near-constant display, paraded under the watchful gaze of the Eyes and the four Crown Courts, who I suspect at this very minute are learning about my lamentable performance at the Keep.

I slump down on to one of the divans just as Elva arrives. It startles me how silently she can move.

'My lady,' she murmurs.

I dredge a smile from somewhere. '*Blaze.*'

She bows her head, then disappears to run me a bath.

I slide unceremoniously off the divan on to the floor, then slink through to my bedchamber and lie on my bed, staring listlessly up at the golden whorls and spirals engraved on the ceiling, tracing their outlines with my finger.

This afternoon had been no better than this morning. I am, as Marina had so kindly pointed out during one of River's strengthening exercises, useless. I can't simmer, nor can I carve waves, and in spite of what happened at Harglade Hall, I can't even make ice, which would come in handy right at this moment, since my skin still prickles with heat.

Scowling, I roll up my trouser leg to examine my stinging shins.

I'm about to fall back on to my pillows when something catches my eye. Curious, I step through the open glass doors on to the balcony. Sitting on the golden ledge is a small silver pot, and next to this pot lies a note – two words written in lazy, looping scrawl.

For you.

I glance around, which seems foolish given that I'm several hundred feet high in the air. Slowly, I take off the lid of the pot and peer inside. It's filled to the brim with what looks like thick green slime, the scent sweet-sharp and cloying – medicinal.

Could this be what I think it is?

I dip my fingers into the concoction and gingerly spread a little on to one of my burned shins. The pain recedes almost instantly, the medicine leaching the heat from my skin, leaving behind a glorious cooling sensation. I don't hesitate before applying the rest of the stuff all over my legs. Then I straighten up, confused.

I haven't told anyone about what Marina did – not Spinner, not even Flint. Only the Aquatori Heirs and River saw what happened, but neither Kai nor Fjord seem particularly keen to befriend me, and though I met my trainer only this morning he doesn't strike me as the type to leave secret gifts in any of his students' rooms. It couldn't have been Elva, either. Aside from the fact she didn't know about my burns, she arrived in my rooms after I did.

My thoughts turn to Prince Hal. He surprised me last night, offering to escort me to the feast. Because no matter what impression I might have made during our dance, I'm not exactly everyone's idea of a desirable companion.

My eyes linger on the pot of medicine. Would it be utter madness to believe he is paying me more attention than he perhaps should?

Madness on his part, maybe, if not on mine.

An hour later I stand with Spinner in a gigantic golden ballroom, trying to ignore the stares.

'Drink?' my chaperone asks, as a serf comes darting through the crowd carrying a tray of thin-stemmed glasses.

I shake my head, but Spinner takes two anyway, sipping from each in turn, her large triangular earrings clacking metallically as she tilts her head to the side, admiring her handiwork. Tonight's theme – pearls. They hang from my earlobes, are wound round my wrists, threaded through my hair. Even my pale-blue gown is studded with them, the skirts of which brush against my shins as I shift uncomfortably under Spinner's gaze, yet thanks to the ointment, the pain from my burns is almost entirely gone.

Though I'm grateful to whoever sent the medicine, I suspect that scalding wave is only the start of Marina's antagonism. It feels personal, somehow. More than that of a competitor, more than loyalty to my cousin. I thought it was about the prince at first, but now I'm not so sure.

I wonder what her next attack will involve. Freezing me to the floor? Pushing me into the pool?

It appears I don't have to wonder for long, however, as she and Ember suddenly emerge from the crowd, walking arm in arm, their faces twisting into gleeful smiles.

'Oh, *Bla-aze*,' my cousin sing-songs.

My heart plummets. Instinctively, I begin to edge behind Spinner, who, to my horror, pats my arm encouragingly and says, 'I'll leave you to your friends!'

I watch helplessly as the two of them advance. For a moment I consider darting away, only it seems I still maintain some dignity, for my feet refuse to move. I glance around desperately for Flint, but there's no sign of him.

Yet just as Ember and Marina reach me, just as I've lost all hope of being rescued, someone appears at my side. Someone dressed in a soft golden shirt, his raven hair combed elegantly back from his face. Relief cascades through me. I don't think I've ever been so pleased to see anyone in all my life.

'Blaze,' says Prince Hal warmly. 'Ember. Marina.'

The three of us curtsy in unison, and I experience a brief spark of satisfaction as Ember's eyes shutter in surprise.

'How was your first day of training?' Hal asks, adjusting his cufflinks.

'I was just about to ask my cousin the same question,' Ember simpers.

'Oh, yes,' Marina chimes in. 'I must congratulate you, Blaze. Your performance today was . . . *quite something*.'

I lower my gaze, my face flooding with heat.

Hal glances sidelong at me. 'Sounds intriguing.'

Marina smirks. 'Well, put it this way, it certainly gave us all something to talk about.'

I have nothing to say for myself, and so I stay silent, burning with shame.

Hal, seeming to sense my discomfort, changes the subject. 'It's a little gloomy in here, don't you think?' He glances around the ballroom, where the flickering candles cast long, undulating shadows across the walls. Then he holds out a hand, the Imperial sun and eye glowing softly on the back of it. 'Blaze,' he says, 'would you do me the honour?'

I blink. 'What?'

'I'll show you.'

Puzzled, I do as he asks. Hal clasps my hand in both his own, and closes his eyes. For a moment, nothing happens.

Then – *light*.

Pure light emanating from our hands, as though our brandmarks are fusing together, growing brighter and brighter until Hal lets go of me and throws the beams upward, banishing the shadows and bathing the room in a dazzling golden glow.

The crowd gasps and bursts into applause.

'Excuse us,' Hal says to a dumbstruck Ember and Marina before guiding me away.

Everyone is staring at us, and for once, I find I don't care. Hal nods courteously to the onlookers, but when he turns to me, he smiles, and I wonder what it must feel like to possess his gift. The Maker's gift. To be born of sunlight.

Prince of the Dawn.

'Impressive little trick, Your Imperial Highness.' A boy dressed in long grey robes is striding towards us. He bows low, then claps Hal on the shoulder.

Hal grins. 'Blaze Harglade, I'd like you to meet Zephyr Graven, who, in my extremely biased opinion, is the greatest Guster of his age. Zeph, this is Blaze, who of course needs no introduction.'

Zephyr is tall and handsome, with dark skin and deep-set eyes the colour of honey. I remember Cole singling him out as the Eyes' favourite to win the Ventalla crown. He reaches for my hand, his brandmark – a single feather – glowing softly on the back of his own.

'Nice to meet you, Blaze,' he says.

'How was training?' Hal asks him.

Zephyr shrugs. 'Can't say it was particularly challenging, though it was only the first session.' Behind him lingers a rather bored-looking Eye, who I take to be his chaperone. 'You can go now,' Zephyr tells him. 'No need to baby me.'

The boy straightens his golden doublet and nods, disappearing into the crowd.

Zephyr turns back to us. 'Gods, Hal, are the chaperones really necessary? I can tie my own shoelaces, you know.'

Hal just laughs. 'Tradition. And as for your training, Zeph, my uncle appointed the Ventalla trainer himself. Trust mc, she'll have you crying for your mother by the end of the week.'

Zephyr raises an eyebrow. 'Don't hold your breath. And speaking of mothers, yours doesn't look too happy.'

We turn to see Empress Goneril sweeping into the ballroom flanked by her ladies-in-waiting. Zephyr is right. She doesn't look happy. In fact, she looks downright enraged.

'Uh oh,' Hal says under his breath. 'I know what that means.'

I don't, but I get the feeling I'm about to find out.

Sure enough, moments later the horns are blown and we all sink to the floor, even Hal. The emperor appears in the doorframe looking magnificent in his golden cloak. But it's not him I'm looking at – it's the woman on his arm. With her creamy skin, bright-green eyes and auburn hair, she is as beautiful as a God. She wears a necklace of woven flower stems and a dazzling gown of gold-and-green leaves, and when the emperor looks at her, his expression entirely unguarded, I know there is only one person this woman can be.

Lady Kestrel Calloway, the emperor's mistress.

They make their way across the hall, sweeping past Goneril with not so much as a glance, her plainness rendered positively unsightly next to Kestrel's unearthly beauty. I am not prepared when they make a beeline straight for us.

'Father.' Hal straightens up before adding, 'My lady.'

But Kestrel is looking only at me. I get to my feet, bobbing a hasty curtsy, unnerved by her attention.

'How like your mother you are,' she says finally.

There is a long pause during which I think she might be about to say something more, but then decides against it. And the two of them walk on, just like that.

I can practically sense the tension wedged between Hal's shoulder blades, rippling in waves up his spine.

I can't imagine how it would feel to stand by and watch your father parade his lover before the courts, to see your mother humiliated, diminished. My own father has his faults, but his devotion to my mother could never be doubted. It was his lifeline, his redemption. It's what drove him into that unreachable void of grief.

My mother is gone, but she was loved. Hal's mother is here, but she is not loved. Nor does she appear to be hated. She is wholly disregarded, which seems even worse. No wonder she looks so sour all the time. It's said the emperor barely speaks to her. Her one duty, her one purpose, was fulfilled with the birth of their son – the prince at my side.

Yet while Goneril may have borne the emperor's only legitimate offspring, he has two bastards by Kestrel. Or rather, *had*. The little girl died young. Of the sweating sickness, I believe. They say she would have been as beautiful as her mother.

And as for the boy, if I am the beginning that brought the end, then he is destruction itself. That's why the courtiers treat Kestrel as though she were a queen, why they don't sneer as she walks by, but rather bow and scrape and smile. Because she may be the emperor's whore, yet she is also the mother of the Earth Cleaver.

She bore the boy who broke the world.

14

'We will spend today focusing on the art of water whispering.'

There is a collective sigh of disappointment among the Heirs sitting round the pool.

'You mean we won't be training?'

River just smiles. 'On the contrary, Marina. Water whispering is one of the most important lessons you will ever learn. Nobody can ever hope to draw fully from power which they do not understand, and which does not understand them in return. So, as I was saying, we will spend today focusing on the art of water whispering, and we will embrace it, with open minds and closed mouths.'

This shuts Marina up, and the lesson begins with no further objections.

Hours pass, and I hear nothing. We break for lunch and then resume our positions. Still nothing. I lie stretched out next to the pool, trailing my fingers through the water, straining my ears for the faintest, slightest whisper. But none comes.

At least I'm not alone. Fjord is concentrating so hard that beads of sweat have broken out on his forehead and upper lip. As for Marina, every so often she lets out a theatrical gasp and leans closer to the water, cupping her ear for emphasis. Judging by his expression, Kai's not falling for her little performance either.

It's been a week. A week at the Golden Palace, a week of training for the first trial, a week of being totally and utterly useless. Every morning I drag myself out of dreams, pull on my blue tunic and join the other Heirs at the Keep. Every evening I let Spinner and Elva dress me in one of my many new gowns, plaster a smile on my face, and submerge myself in the gold-tinted sea of simpering courtiers.

What little drizzle I had managed to summon on the first day of training has been reduced to a miserable mist-like substance that tends to linger above my head. And for all River's unwavering patience and my brother's gratingly optimistic encouragement, it appears that I am not getting better. If anything, I seem to be getting worse.

Already rumours are circling about the announcement of the first trial, and the thought fills me with dread. Which is unsurprising, really, since I could wind up dead. It's not unheard of for an Heir to die in the Choosing – River said it himself. But if, by some miracle, I manage to pull through, what then? Being first out of the running is one thing, but to be first out of the running because I don't even have the skills to compete is quite another. It seems I'm to be humiliated, made into a laughing stock. And won't my cousin just love that?

The day shuffles by on two large and uncoordinated feet. When River eventually announces that the four of us can return to the palace, Marina has to nudge Fjord awake before skipping off through the forest, presumably to track down Ember and delight in ridiculing me some more. Sighing, I sit up and stretch.

River moves round the pool to stand at my side. 'Hear anything today?'

I shake my head. 'Nothing.'

He smiles gently. 'I've been thinking about the trouble you've been having with your rain. I wondered if I might set you some homework.' In the dappled light reflecting off the water, his hair really does look like snow. 'I gather you like to read,' he says.

I frown a little. 'How'd you know that?'

'I know a great deal about a great many things. I tell you, I have visited many fine libraries in my time, Blaze, but the Golden Library is the finest of them all. It's also a rather comfortable place to spend an evening when one is seeking peace and quiet. I assume you are familiar with the legend of the Rain Singers?'

I nod. 'Of course.'

'They make for very interesting reading, don't you think?' muses River.

'Any book in particular?' I ask.

'Perhaps.'

'How do I find it?'

'Oh, it'll find you,' he says. 'Now, off you go.'

As soon as I walk through the doors to the Golden Library I understand why River called it the finest he'd ever visited. I'm standing in what appears to be an ocean of books. The towering golden shelves stretch all the way up to the ceiling, which must be at least sixty feet high, and attached to each is a sliding ladder. The air smells of old parchment and ink and leather. There are no candles, but the library is lit by hundreds of tiny orbs of light. One of them floats lazily over to me as I begin to weave in and out of the shelves.

It's very quiet, but I can just make out the faint scratching of quills and the rustle of pages. There's no sign of a librarian, and given the size of the place I'm sure the Choosing will be over by the time I manage to track down River's book.

I discover a cosy alcove and perch for a moment in the largest of the two armchairs, deciding where to begin my search. But when I glance to the side, there, on the table next to me, is a book. The title is emblazoned along the spine in faded silver lettering.

Rain Song.

My heart races as a wave of excitement surges through me. There are so few books about the Rain Singers. Very little is actually known about them, given that they lived in the treacherous gorges of Brava, the most dangerous province in the Waterlands, where very few Etheri have dared to tread. But part of me has always wondered whether this dearth of information about the Singers is also an attempt to erase them from history. They were powerful and they were dangerous, and severing ties with the Aquatori gave rise to centuries' worth of resentment. Bad blood stains, after all.

Though if the plan were to erase all memory of the Rain Singers, I certainly must have complicated things.

I slide the book on to my lap, and as I open it up a cloud of dust engulfs me. I swat the dust away impatiently, the sound of my coughing amplified by the silence of the library. Tucking my feet up beside me, I begin to read.

Situated in the rocky depths of the Waterlands, Brava was once home to a colony of Aquatori who possessed the power not only to manipulate water but to summon the rain. The Rain Singers dwelled in caves known as crevices, took to the skies on the backs of giant dragonflies, and were renowned for their ancient customs and rituals. Over the centuries, they adapted to their inhospitable environment, sustaining themselves on a diet consisting of rainwater, fish and mountainous plants.

I skim through the next few pages, all detailing their perilous habitat.

The Rain Singers believed themselves to be servants of a figure known as Om Shikara, whom they claimed to be the one true God. Consequently, they did not worship the Etherian Gods and thus did not recognize Etherian royalty.

My brandmark glimmers as I trace the lines with my finger.

When I flip over the next page, I stop short. For the paper is covered in handwritten notes, the margins filled with spidery lettering.

At the top, someone has scrawled: *All Rain Singers are born with the ability to Meld.*

I peer closer, holding the book up to the light.

Melding is the anchoring of a gift to a particular emotion.

I sit up straighter in my chair, vaguely aware that I'm gripping the book so tightly my knuckles are protruding.

Once discovered, anchors allow the wielder to call forth their gift.

I think of my drizzle, how it only ever falls when I'm thinking about *her*. My mother. When I allow myself to mourn, if only for a moment.

I think back to what Grandmother said on the morning of the eclipse.

You have found a way to turn pain into power.

It's just drizzle, I had replied, dismissing her words.

But I remember the fierce look in her eyes, the promise she had me make her.

Don't bury your emotions. You cannot hide from your heart. That is where your power lies; that is what will guide you.

I swallow hard.

I thought my rain gone for good. But what if it's not? What if it's connected – *anchored* – to an emotion that I do not allow myself to feel?

You never talk about Mother, Renly had said to me on the roof of Harglade Hall.

That's because it makes me sad, I told him.

If my power is Melded to the sadness I keep locked away inside a dark corner of my mind, then the only way to access it fully is to let myself feel it, to feel all of it. But there's a reason I've never allowed my eyes to spill over – I'm afraid they'd never stop.

I turn back to the words inked into the book.

Rain Singers teach themselves how to harness their power through emotion without letting that emotion overcome them.

My hands are trembling. I read the notes again and again, and then I close my eyes.

I think back to the day she died. I remember the pain. It felt like . . . *tearing*. And I remember my father screaming. No, not screaming. There's not a word that could ever truly describe the agonized sounds fighting their way out of his mouth that day. The baby was screaming, though. Baby Renly. Tiny and squawking, covered in blood.

Oh, the blood. There was so *much* of it. You'd think I'd have been used to the colour red, having grown up a daughter of two Ignitia Houses. But this was not the red of flames. This was the red of death, the blood thick and dark and unforgiving. I could smell it.

Midwives. Stained sheets. Sterile water. Sharp instruments laid out on the bed. The physician shaking his head. I saw it all. Flint was herded from the room but I wouldn't move. I was frozen to the spot. My father was bent over my mother as if shielding her with his body would somehow stop death from taking her. She was fading fast, her eyes hazy and unfocused. But just for a moment, which held inside it pain enough to last a lifetime, they fixed themselves on me. She smiled. And the fire in the hearth went out.

Drizzle kisses my cheeks. My throat is closing up and I gasp for air, my entire being folding in around the dull ache inside my chest.

You cannot hide from your heart.

Then, I do something I have not allowed myself to do for six long years.

I cry.

And when the tears begin to fall, so does the rain. Not drizzle – *rain*. The droplets come thick and fast, and I hold on to the sadness, letting myself feel it, gazing up in astonishment as it takes form above my head, streaming down my face, soaking the book in my lap.

After all these years of believing myself empty, it appears

my gift is not gone for good. My gift is anchored to my grief. To sadness. To *her*.

Power that arose out of pain.

And somehow, I find I'm smiling.

I turn back to the book. Already ink is running down the margins. I squint at the words scrawled there, attempting to blot the page dry with my sleeve.

Conceal, I read. *Conceal, contain, control.*

I take a few deep, shuddering breaths until the tears subside. Blinking hard, I push the memory of my mother away, watching it recede before my eyes. Then I concentrate on reeling my power in, as though it is something tangible, something alive.

Conceal, contain, control.

I watch as the rain slows before stopping entirely.

Drenched to the skin, heartsick but grinning, I grab the book, stuff it under my tunic and don't stop running until I reach my chambers.

15

'And why do you seem so cheerful all of a sudden, sister?' Flint asks as we make our way up the spiral staircase towards the training room.

I shrug innocently. 'Maybe I've just decided to be more positive about my situation.'

'How very intriguing,' he says. 'You see, you've always struck me as such a carefree, optimistic sort of person.'

I raise an eyebrow. 'Would you prefer it if I went back to being miserable?'

'By no means,' says Flint, tugging on one of my braids. 'But does this drastic change in mood have anything to do with a certain prince? Only, last night you were nowhere to be found and I noticed Hal slipping out of the banquet hall during the speeches, and I just wondered if maybe you ... you know, were together.' He clears his throat. 'And as your brother I feel it's my duty to make sure that you're being ... *sensible.*'

'Sensible?'

'Responsible, then.'

I stare at him with unconcealed horror. 'Are you trying to give me the *talk*?'

Flint shudders theatrically. 'I don't know. Do I have to? I mean, you're seventeen and it's not like you have much experience with the ways of the world, and what with all the attention he's been paying you recently, I'm just saying –'

'Well, don't,' I interrupt. 'I spent last night in bed.'

Flint looks aghast.

'*With a headache*,' I add, jabbing him in the ribs.

I'm not ready to tell Flint about my discovery. It still feels too raw, too personal, and I'd rather keep it to myself, for now at least.

Elva had been waiting in my chambers when I arrived back from the library, clutching the book to my chest. She left without a word when I dismissed her, and I spent the entire night in the bathing room practising, surrendering to my emotions without letting them swallow me, letting myself cry and calming myself down. Gradually I was able to tap into that sadness without letting it show, concealing as well as containing and controlling it, forcing my eyes to remain dry and my face to remain impassive, even when it felt like my heart was breaking. I did it again and again. I must have got through two dozen candles. I also must have nodded off at some point, because I awoke on the cold, wet tiles to Flint and Spinner hammering on the door, shouting at me that I was going to be late.

'What time do you call this?' Marina asks loudly as I approach the pool.

'Thank you, Marina,' says River. 'Blaze, please join us.'

He sets the Heirs a few exercises to do and makes his way over to me, a question in his eyes. I nod, biting back a smile. 'The book. You were right – it found me.'

'And was it helpful?'

I don't answer him. I don't need to. Someone – I think it's Fjord – audibly gasps as rain begins to fall from the ceiling above.

River is smiling. He gestures for me to walk with him, and we break away from the others, skirting along the edge of the forest. I glance around briefly to catch sight of Marina looking murderous, shaking the droplets from her hair.

I turn back to River. 'The notes in the margin. That was you, wasn't it?'

He inclines his head. 'All you needed was a little push in the right direction.'

'But how did you know?' I press. 'That my gift was Melded, I mean.'

'You're a Rain Singer, Blaze,' River says. 'It wasn't a question of your possessing power, but of unlocking it. The answer was always inside of you. You just had to find it.'

I let this sink in before I ask, 'Why do you know so much? All that stuff about Melding – it wasn't in the book.'

River pauses, then says, 'I was always fascinated by the Rain Singers. I knew there was much I could learn from them, and so, many years ago, when I was the same age as you are now, I travelled to Brava.'

I stare at him, wide-eyed. 'You *saw* them? The Rain Singers?'

'I did.'

'What were they like?' I breathe.

River closes his eyes for a moment. 'They were ... remarkable. Their gifts had no equal, not in strength nor in beauty.'

I swallow. 'All the stories say they were dangerous. Even savage.'

'You'll come to find, Blaze, that many stories are spun from lies,' says River softly. 'The truth can often get lost within the tapestry.'

I feel overcome with relief that not all the legends are true, that the Rain Singers were not wild or vicious, or a threat to their fellow Etheri.

We walk in silence for a time, listening to the soft patter of my rain. The shower intensifies twofold as I'm struck by a sudden desperate sadness that, unlike River, I will never get to meet them, the only people capable of truly understanding who I am.

And who am I, exactly?

The question tumbles out of my mouth. 'If you can explain all this, then how do you explain me? I come from a long line of pureblood Ignitia, and yet somehow, I was born a Rain Singer. It doesn't make sense. *I* don't make sense.'

A strange expression crosses River's face, fleeting and entirely indecipherable. When he speaks, his voice is gentle. 'I'm afraid I can't give you all the answers you seek, Blaze.'

Disappointment coats my tongue. I swallow it down.

'So, what now?' I ask, cutting off the shower.

'Well, now that you have claimed your rain,' River says, 'I would like you to try your hand at ice.'

'Oh,' I respond, a little disgruntled. Some time to revel in the fact that I'm not a complete failure might have been nice.

River simply smiles. 'Melding can help concentrate power, but it can also have consequences. These can consist of sporadic outbursts and flare-ups, especially in those as yet unfamiliar with their gifts. Though perhaps you know this already.'

I nod slowly, remembering the sound of a thousand shattering glasses.

'Being unaware of which emotion is the key to unleashing a particular gift can prove dangerous because it results in a loss of control,' he says. 'You've figured out which of your emotions is anchored to the rain, Blaze. Now you must discover the same for ice.'

And suddenly I'm not with River in the training room of the Golden Keep. I'm in a crowded ballroom at Harglade Hall while a sweet voice spouts cruel words in my ear. I feel something sharp and cold spreading inside of me. Anger. No, not anger. *More.*

I clear my throat, my gaze landing on the small silver trident strapped to River's belt. It's always seemed so familiar to me, and suddenly I realize why.

'You were there,' I say. 'On my Name Day. You were speaking with my grandmother.'

River runs his hand down the rain-slick bark of a sapling. 'I was. Queen Hydra was most insistent that the Court of Waves attend the occasion.'

I take a breath. 'I'm worried about ... about what happened last time. With the ice. I couldn't control it.'

'Discipline is an art,' says River. 'Be patient with yourself. Don't be afraid of what you can do, embrace it. And most importantly, learn from it.' He glances back towards the pool. 'Perhaps the others could be of some use to you.'

I make a face. 'I'm not sure the others want anything to do with me.' I watch Marina smirk as she carves a perfect wave. 'They're not Rain Singers, so their water gifts aren't Melded, are they?'

River shakes his head, drops of rain still clinging to his snow-white hair.

'But doesn't that make them stronger than me?' I say, frowning. 'I mean, I have to rely on channelling the right emotion to call the rain, but Marina can carve a wave simply because she *wants* to.'

River studies my face, as though reading something written there. 'Some see emotion as a hindrance rather than a strength,' he says quietly. 'But that is because they forget how powerful emotions can be. Never underestimate the way you can feel.'

I hear Grandmother's voice in my head.

To feel is to be alive, Blaze. And I swear to you that no matter what, it is better to feel everything than to feel nothing.

'As for your Melding,' River continues, 'I'd like you to keep it to yourself. It is a secret that has been protected for hundreds of years.'

'I will,' I promise him.

When I return to the pool, Kai offers me a half-smile. 'Congratulations.'

I'm slightly taken aback. The other Heirs rarely deign to speak to me. But I just shrug casually. 'Took me long enough.'

'You know, if you need any help, I'd be happy to show you how to make ice.'

'Really?' I ask, startled by his generosity.

Kai glances at Fjord, who looks away quickly, pretending not to be listening to our conversation. 'Sure,' he says. 'Why not?'

I hesitate. It's a kind offer, only it's not as straightforward as simply accepting, not after learning my water gifts are Melded. Kai's methods won't work on me. We would just be wasting each other's time. But I can't tell him this, and he's looking at me, waiting for an answer.

'Thank you,' I say tentatively. 'I'd like that.'

First Kai gets me to clear my mind, which is a lot easier said than done. We sit facing one another at the edge of the pool, my hands folded in my lap. I meant what I said to River, about being worried. I don't want to lose control. I don't want to hurt anyone.

In the darkness behind my eyelids, I see the criss-cross scar on Hal's cheek.

'I want you to think about nothing but ice,' Kai says. 'Think about the way it coats the ground, the sound it makes when it cracks. Think about frost, icicles, frozen dew. Lean into the coldness.'

After a while, I open my eyes, frustrated. 'It's no use. I can't do it.'

Kai appears to be contemplating something. 'New plan,' he announces. 'You realized you could freeze water after breaking a bunch of wine glasses, yes?'

A grimace is my only response.

'All right, then. Ask for a glass.'

I frown. 'Ask who?'

'The Keep.' Kai chuckles at my expression. 'My father told me that the Keep will give you anything you desire, so long as you ask it politely.'

I can't help but stare at him. I doubt I'll ever get used to the enchantments in this place.

'Go on,' he says. 'Try it.'

I glance around to make sure Marina isn't anywhere in earshot, then clear my throat.

'Give me a glass.'

Minutes pass, and I remain glassless.

I try again, a little louder this time. 'I need a glass.'

Kai raises a dark eyebrow. 'I said you have to ask it *politely*.'

'Since when did an old siege tower have a thing about manners?' I grumble.

'Oh, just do it, before we both grow old and die.'

'Fine,' I say with a sigh. 'I would like a glass. *Please*.'

In the time it takes for me to blink, a glass goblet appears out of thin air in the space between us, teetering to a standstill.

'See?' Kai dips the glass into the water then pushes it towards me. 'Now freeze it.'

'But I –'

'You did it before,' he says. 'You can do it again.'

I catch sight of River watching us from the far side of the pool. He nods.

I think I already know which of my emotions is anchored to ice, and as soon as I close my eyes, I see her, standing in that rust-orange dress, lips curved in a cruel smile.

Is that it?

I hear the sniggers from the crowd.

Murderer.

Changeling.

Freak.

I feel it again, that coldness.

A family like ours was bound to have a rotten apple some day, cousin. And here you are, rotten to the core. You're not fooling anyone, least of all me.

I watch Ember smirk as she readies herself for the killing blow.

I'm just glad dear Aunt Analiese isn't around to see it. To see you. How burdensome you must have been to her, Blaze. How . . . disappointing.

The coldness is spreading, blazing through me like fire, and I give myself over to it, letting it fill me to the brim. It's not anger. It's not even rage.

It's ice-cold fury.

So strong it engulfs me. So cold it burns.

Conceal, contain, control.

It takes everything I have to push back against the feeling, and eventually, with one last gasp of effort, I reel my power in.

Panting, I open my eyes, expecting to see the glass of water coated in a glistening layer of ice.

Instead I find the entire pool has frozen solid.

16

The carpet of pine needles beneath my feet gives way to an expanse of glittering snow. I walk across this frozen wasteland as an icy wind begins to blow, my gaze fixed on a glimmer of gold lying up ahead. With every step I feel its pull growing stronger.

Even over the howling gale, I hear my name.

Blaze.

I wake with a start. Wrapping a rug round my shoulders, I push open the glass doors and sit on the balcony to watch the sunrise.

The dreams started shortly after the eclipse. I'd be lying if I said they didn't unsettle me, but more than anything, I find them frustrating. Infuriating, even. Because whatever it is that waits for me in the distance, I can never reach it.

I wonder what it's supposed to symbolize. The Aquatori crown? The future I had planned for myself? My mother? I considered telling Flint, but I didn't want to bore him. They're just dreams, after all.

It's not long before my thoughts turn to my water gifts. All those years thinking I was empty. Hating myself for it. Now, I understand. The rain, the ice, they're both Melded, both *mine*. I have what I always wanted – power of my own. And I intend to make the most of it.

Elva appears, placing my breakfast tray down on the balcony. If the Etheri are scared of me, then the Fidra can barely meet my eye. Yet Elva's eyes, almost luminous in the early-morning light, do meet mine. She turns to go but I stop her with a question.

'Do you want to join me?'

She looks frightened, and a little bewildered.

'There's more than enough for two,' I say, gesturing to the tray, which is heaped with cinnamon bread, three different types of jam, melon, fried mushrooms, coffee and pomegranate juice. I'm not sure what they feed the serfs down in the kitchens, but I know it'll be nothing like this. I don't press her though, suddenly embarrassed that I asked.

She pauses for a long moment before sitting down beside me warily.

'Which isle of the Otherlands are you from?' I ask, pouring myself coffee and adding a generous helping of cream and sugar.

Elva doesn't answer, just picks up some bread and holds it to her nose, inhaling the scent before tearing off a tiny piece and chewing it very slowly.

'Do you have any family?'

She hesitates, then nods.

'And did they come here with you? To Ostacre?'

A shake.

'Do you miss them?'

A nod. Another bite of bread.

'I have a younger brother back home. His name's Renly. I miss him a lot. I've never been away from him before.'

Elva accepts a slice of melon.

I blow on my coffee, trying to think of something else to say. 'My hair looked beautiful last night.'

It really did. She'd threaded tiny moonstones through my braids, each one glinting as it caught the light.

'Where'd you learn how to do that?' I ask her.

She blinks. Pauses. Opens her mouth. Closes it. Then says quietly, 'Amma.'

I stare at her. Over the years, I have had a lot of time to read a lot of books, and in every language I have ever studied, there is one word that always sticks out to me. I know it in a number of dialects. This one in particular originates from Obsidia, an isle far across the Second Sea, known as the Land of Eternal Night.

Amma. Mother.

That's when I realize Elva has answered not one but two of my questions. Because she gave me her answer in her native tongue – Obsidian.

The sound of a door slamming shatters the stillness, and Elva gets to her feet quickly, backing away as Spinner hurtles into the room. I pull on my tunic and let my chaperone drag me down to the entrance hall. It's not my brother waiting for me there, but Kai.

'Ready for training?'

'Looking forward to it,' I tell him, and it's the truth. The other Heirs have had years to figure out the complexities of their gifts, and I have a lot to learn before I'm anywhere near ready for the first trial.

Shaking all thoughts of Elva from my head, I smooth my features into a smile as we walk together across the palace grounds towards the Keep.

That evening I stand in front of the mirror while Spinner fusses with the hem of my dress and Elva wrestles my hair into two thick braids. We haven't spoken since her revelation this morning. There's still so much I want to ask her, about Obsidia and the Otherlands, about how she came to be in Ostacre, about what happened to her family.

Spinner holds up two sets of earrings. 'Pearls or sapphires?'

I shrug. 'Either is fine.'

'Sapphires, then. No, maybe pearls. Or how about both?'

My chaperone is wearing what is without a doubt the shortest dress I have ever seen. She has me spin for her, then selects a pair of bright-blue slippers. As she bends down I get a good look at the tattoo on the nape of her neck. It's of an open eye.

'I always thought it was a myth that the Eyes have those,' I say.

'Nope, no myth.' She straightens up and smiles wickedly. 'It means we can watch you even when our backs are turned.'

I scoff, but her words still send sharp prickles up my spine.

At that moment there's a knock on the door. Spinner skips across the room to open it, revealing Hal. It's only been a few days since I last saw him, yet I'm struck again by just how beautiful he is. Raven hair, ivory skin, eyes gleaming black in the candlelight. The spitting image of his ancestor, the Maker. God of Gods, come to life.

To my embarrassment, I find myself momentarily tongue-tied, an affliction that, fortunately, my chaperone does not share.

'Your Imperial Handsomeness. To what do we owe this unexpected pleasure?'

I'm convinced that no one would ever risk curtsying in a dress as short as hers, but Spinner proves me wrong.

Hal smiles. 'I was just passing and wondered if Blaze might like an escort.'

A familiar blush creeps into my cheeks.

'How very thoughtful. Isn't he thoughtful, Blaze?' Spinner winks at me, and I find myself wishing I could fall through the floor. I just about manage a small curtsy before she gives me an indiscreet shove in the prince's direction.

Hal seems pleased to find me in better spirits, even more so to hear about the resurgence of my water gifts. Each time I glance up to look at him, I discover that he's already looking down at me, which makes me feel slightly giddy, as though my veins were filled with champagne bubbles rather than blood.

Tucking my hand into the crook of his arm, he guides me through the sea of stares and whispers, and for once I barely notice them.

'No ball this evening?' I ask as we reach the throne room.

'My father has requested that the courts gather here,' he says.

Unease pools in my stomach as Spinner ushers us over to where Flint is standing with Cole and Elaith. Sheen hovers moodily at the edge of their circle, neatly sidestepping my chaperone as she attempts to kiss him on the cheek.

'I'll take it if he doesn't want it,' Flint tells her.

Spinner grins, rising up on to her tiptoes and planting a kiss on his cheek instead.

'Where did you disappear off to after training, Blaze?' Elaith asks.

'I was in the library.'

'I didn't even know this place had a library,' she says. 'Whatever do you do in there?'

Flint rolls his eyes. 'What do you *think* one does in a library, Elaith?'

'Oh, I'm sorry,' she says, pressing a hand to her chest. 'I didn't realize you were such an expert, *Flint Flameborn*. In fact, I didn't even realize you could read.'

Flint wags a finger at her. 'Now, now. Though it is true that my sister employs her time far better than I do. She's the clever one, and I'm the –'

'Drunk one?' Elaith suggests.

'Amusing. I was actually going to say the –'

'Vain one?' Cole finishes, swilling wine round his glass.

Flint shakes his head. 'I see how it is. Cruel, the both of you. Heartless and cruel.'

Moments later the sound of the horns drowns out the din, and we sink to our knees, watching as they stride through the doors – the emperor and Lady Kestrel, followed by the Crowned Council. King Balen's raven eyes find me among the crowd, flitting amusedly to his nephew at my side. I'm anticipating it, but it still unnerves me when it comes, that soft, silken whisper, meant only for me. 'Making friends, little dove?'

I clench my jaw to keep from shivering.

The emperor mounts the golden steps leading up to the Imperial throne, and every last shred of newfound confidence turns to dust in my mouth as he announces that a date has been set for the first trial. And it is tomorrow.

Tomorrow. The word echoes through me, blunt and harsh.

I'm not remotely ready. Not yet. Maybe if I had more time . . . but then what's the point in speculating?

'I thought we'd have weeks yet,' Elaith hisses as the crowd erupts.

'Scared, little girl?' Cole smirks. 'That's music to my ears.'

Elaith stamps on his foot, a few of the candles nearby flickering out. 'You wish.'

Hal shoots me an apologetic look. He must have known the whole time. But before he can say anything, Flint puts an arm round me. 'All right, sister mine?'

No, Flint, I'm not all right. I feel as though the emperor just announced my execution.

'Fine,' I say. 'You?'

'Fighting fit.' There's not even the slightest glimmer of uncertainty in his eyes. 'I always have a few tricks up my sleeve.'

'Oh, good,' says Elaith, tugging at the sleeve of his red doublet. 'Give some to me.'

The Heirs are soon herded towards the centre of the throne room, which is filled to bursting with the sound of voices as the Etheri descend on us. It turns out what Cole said about the Eyes placing bets on who will triumph in the trials was no fabrication. I hear the odds being discussed loudly among the courtiers.

Four to one on the Harglade boy.

No deal, he's a shoo-in. His sister, on the other hand . . .

What's the latest? Can she call the rain or not?

I bet fifty gold pieces she'll summon another storm.

I bet fifty gold pieces she'll crash and burn.

Elaith brings her head close to mine, her hair tickling my ear as she whispers, 'Don't worry, it's all just a big game to them. Pay no attention.'

But that's about as impossible as the crowd is impenetrable. We're hemmed in so tightly that I can hardly move. I consider trying to crawl through them, but run the risk of being trampled. I'm also not sure this is what Hal had in mind when he told me to start acting like an Heir. And I doubt calling down a shower of rain would cast me in a particularly favourable light either. Though it might alter some bets.

When it gets to the point at which I think I might scream, a hand reaches through the throng and takes my arm, the grip strong but gentle.

'Thank you,' I say, as River guides me safely out of the throne room.

We walk together through the blissful silence of the hallways. After several minutes River glances at me.

'May I ask what you're thinking, Blaze?'

I stop walking. 'For the first time in my life, I felt as though I was managing to stay afloat,' I admit. 'And I suppose I've just been reminded that I will always be out of my depth.'

River doesn't respond, sensing that I have more to say.

'I won't deny that the thought of tomorrow terrifies me,' I say, leaning back against the wall, 'but it's *more* than the trial. You've seen how the others act around me, and

I don't blame them for it, truly. But when all this is over – that is, if I make it through – I am bound to serve the new Aquatori sovereign, in any capacity they might wish. And if that person is Fjord or Marina, I will be forever bound to somebody who despises me.'

I can see it clearly now, this bleak, lonely future that has haunted me from the moment the moon eclipsed the sun. Whiling away my days at the Court of Waves, never to leave, never to sail to the Otherlands, being reminded every moment that I am and will forever remain the most hated girl in all the realm.

Sheer misery clasps me tightly and won't let go. I don't even have to think about my mother. The drizzle begins to fall, clinging to my eyelashes.

River reaches out automatically, but seems to think better of it, his hand falling back to rest on the silver trident at his hip. 'You have already decided that you will not succeed, and I will not attempt to convince you otherwise,' he says softly. 'But strength, like weakness, is a choice. I trust you will make the right one.'

I look at the floor.

'As for the others,' he continues, 'you know, perhaps better than anyone, that hatred can sink its claws in deep. And if I were you, Blaze, I would start sharpening my own.'

17

I walk through a forest so close and dense that it blocks out any sunlight. Just up ahead lies something gold and gleaming, small enough to fit in the palm of my hand.

Blaze.

I can feel its power, crackling like lightning, radiating around me in great waves. I'm getting closer now, close enough to see it clearly.

It looks like . . . like . . .

That's when the ground begins to tremble beneath my feet, fault lines spreading out across the earth. Fear courses through me and I start to run. Only the forest floor is gone. I'm plunged into dark nothingness, falling through the world.

I wake to the sound of sharp, impatient rapping.

'Go away, Spinner,' I mumble into my pillow.

'Oh dear,' says a familiar voice. 'It seems we've left our manners at home.'

My eyes fly open. '*Grandmother?*'

And there she is, standing over my bed, hands clasped over the hilt of her ruby-encrusted stick, wearing a thick red gown and a worried frown. Her expression softens slightly as she takes me in, reaching out a hand to cup my cheek.

'What're you doing here?' I ask.

She props her stick against the nightstand and sits down beside me. 'Did you really think I'd miss your first trial?'

I must still have been falling, because I hit the ground hard enough to knock the wind out of me. Of course. My first trial. And undoubtedly my last. Today I will be humiliated before the Crowned Council and seal my fate as the next Aquatori sovereign's lackey.

The sun streams through the windows, illuminating the silvery streaks in Grandmother's dark hair.

'Nice day for it,' I say.

She gives me a look, then snaps her fingers. A moment later Elva appears carrying my breakfast. My stomach churns as she sets it down in front of me.

'Eat,' commands Grandmother.

'I'm surprised you came all this way just to see me fail so spectacularly,' I tell her, ignoring the food. 'I'd have thought you'd had your fill of watching me shame the family.'

Grandmother tuts. 'The only person you shame by talking in this way is yourself. You are no more a source of shame to me than your brother is.'

'Ah, yes. How is Flint Flameborn? He seemed pretty chipper last night. Have you been to see him already?'

She shakes her head. 'I go where I am needed. Now, eat.'

To appease her, I nibble on an apple slice. Then I ask, 'Did you visit Mother before her first trial?'

A flicker of pain passes across her face. 'I did.'

'Was she afraid?'

'Yes. But I told her that true courage is born from great fear.'

'And what about you?' I say. 'Were you afraid, Grandmother?'

She smiles slightly. 'Terrified.'

Suddenly there's a clattering in the reception room and Spinner comes racing through the doors. 'Sorry I'm la– Oh. Hello. I mean, good morning, Lady Harglade.'

Grandmother gives her a curt nod. 'Your services are not required today. I will ready my granddaughter for her trial.'

Spinner blinks, stooping into an awkward half-bow before shuffling out.

'Incompetent girl,' Grandmother mutters.

'Harsh,' I say. 'Spinner's nice. Not the best at timekeeping perhaps, but nice. Even you have to admire her taste.' I gesture towards the rack of dresses but Grandmother pays them no attention.

'*Nice* or not, Blaze, she's still an Eye. I warned you about the Eyes before you left Harglade Hall.'

I take a sip of water, remembering her words.

The Eyes live by a code of secrecy and deceit. Why do you think they only wear Imperial gold and not their gift colour? It's a disguise. And it is this act of concealing their powers that makes them dangerous.

Not for the first time, I find myself wondering which brandmark is concealed beneath Spinner's golden glove, which element she secretly wields.

Grandmother reaches for her stick and stands, whipping back the bedsheets. 'Up.'

Dread gnaws at me as I rise, wash and dress. There's no such thing as coaxing with Grandmother – she practically shovels a bowl of oats down my throat before sitting me in front of the dressing table and braiding my hair back from my face.

'Can't you just tell them I've got the flu or something?' I ask hopefully.

A hairpin jabbing into my scalp is the only response I get.

I gaze out at Cor Caval sprawling beneath me, glittering in the sunlight. Far beyond in the distance, the Rift gapes wide and empty, encircling it all.

'Did you give your name to the Riftkeeper?' I ask Grandmother.

She straightens the collar of my tunic. 'I didn't need to. He knows it well.'

Rather than taking me to the entrance hall, Grandmother leads me down into the very depths of the palace. I want to ask where we're going but my throat feels as though it's collapsed in on itself, my voice box reduced to rubble. Torches in brackets along the walls illuminate the winding passageways, each one burning more fiercely as Grandmother passes by.

Eventually I hear voices up ahead. Grandmother clasps my shoulder, turning me round to face her. She's surprisingly strong for somebody who requires a stick to walk.

'Listen to me,' she says. 'You can do this. You can.' She takes my hand, lifts my chin. 'Stand up straight, my darling one.'

Then she's gone, disappearing back the way we came.

Alator is waiting with the rest of the Heirs at the end of the passageway. I count them as I approach. Four Ignitia. Four Ventalla. And as of now, four Aquatori. Only three Terrathian. With or without the missing Heir, the Choosing is going ahead. Whoever they are, it appears they're too late.

When I reach the group, Alator explains that we're making our way to the Keep through the ancient evacuation tunnels used when the palace was under siege. I watch in astonishment as a concealed door swings open at the touch of his hand.

Several of the Heirs make attempts at conversation, but most remain silent. Elaith mutters quietly to herself as we walk, and even Cole seems uncertain, last night's bravado replaced by a clenched jaw. Flint meanwhile looks positively carefree, his arms swinging loosely at his sides. As for me, I'm just trying to hold on to the contents of my stomach.

Kai falls into step beside me. 'How're you feeling?'

Like I'm going to throw up on your shoes.

'Fine,' I tell him.

We emerge through a trapdoor on to the ground floor of the Keep. Instead of taking us to the training room, Alator comes to a stop outside a door which opens to reveal another set of four doors, each of them a different court colour. Flint barely has time to squeeze my hand before the Ignitia Heirs are herded through the red one.

Behind the blue door is a room strewn with chairs and a small table heaped with food. On the other side of the room is yet another door, this one gold. Fjord tries the handle, but it won't budge. The four of us sit in uncomfortable silence until Alator reappears, informing us that the Drawing is complete. The Drawing is an ancient ritual in which the Crowned Council each place their signet ring in a golden bowl, and the emperor's son – so in this case, Hal – picks them out one by one, thus determining the order of the trials.

'The Aquatori are up first,' announces Alator cheerfully.

The moment the blue door closes behind him, the golden door on the other side of the room creaks open.

'What are we waiting for?' says Fjord. 'Somebody go.'

'I don't see you rushing forward,' Kai points out.

Fjord rounds on him. 'Are you calling me a coward?'

'No,' says Kai calmly. 'I was just stating a fact.'

Fjord forces out a derisive laugh. 'Perhaps the Storm Weaver would like to go first? That'll certainly make the rest of us shine in comparison.'

'Leave her alone, Fjord.'

'Always jumping to her defence. Come on, Kai. Why don't you take her place?'

Marina tosses her hair over her shoulder. 'Oh, please. *I'll* go.' She flounces across to the golden door. 'Good luck measuring up to me,' she calls, smirking. 'You'll need it.'

The door shuts with a clang behind her.

I rub my scar, trying to focus only on the sound of Fjord's foot tapping against the floor. There's not a clock in the room, so I can't tell how much time passes before the door swings open once more and Fjord disappears through it without a backward glance.

When the door opens for a third time, I'm light-headed with nerves.

Kai looks at me. 'Ladies first.'

I shake my head. 'I can't.'

'You can,' he says.

'No, seriously, I can't.'

'All right.' Kai takes a deep breath and gets to his feet. 'See you on the other side?'

He walks through the golden door, leaving me alone.

I rest my chin on my knees, arms wrapped round my legs, until the door eventually opens for the fourth and final time.

At first I don't move. Everything has taken on a dreamlike quality. The blue walls seem bluer, the chairs seem to shrink, the ground seems to shift beneath my feet as I force myself to stand.

You can do this, Grandmother had said.

Can I? I'm not so sure. Running away and hiding somewhere nobody can find me sounds like a far more appealing alternative. But could I really do that to Grandmother? Could I really do that to myself, after everything?

I think of my mother. Not as I remember her, but as she was before, when she was my age, when she was an Heir. She was scared, too. Yet she still walked through that door.

I take a step, then another, and when I find myself in the passageway beyond, it's as though I can feel her beside me. So I keep walking. On and on until I see the mouth of the tunnel up ahead. My heart has climbed into my throat. I think I might choke on it.

I say a silent, futile prayer before stepping out into the light.

18

My eyes take a few seconds to adjust, then I begin to piece together my surroundings.

Rocky terrain, jagged and imposing. Miniature mountains with solid-gold summits, peaks glittering in the bright sunlight. Water. Tributaries running down the mountains, merging into little pools, and at the bottom, a lake, glistening blue and deep.

This place seems to be a gigantic arena. The tunnel opening has led me out of the side of the largest mountain, and I just stand there, looking around at this enormous spherical stage. It's so unnaturally silent that my foot dislodging a pebble sounds like an avalanche.

Where is the Council? And what is it, exactly, that I'm supposed to be doing? Do they want me to call the rain? Freeze a stream or two? And why the peculiar setting? I could do just as much by the pool in the training room.

I dig my nails into my palms and try to think. I have a pretty good view of my surroundings, but perhaps I should try to secure an even better vantage point. My gaze lands on the gold-tipped peak in the centre of the arena. It takes several minutes to climb it, my boots rasping against the stone. Soon I reach the top, breathing hard.

That's when I hear it – a soft, tinkling laugh. I whip round.
Ember is standing a few feet away from me.

'Hello, cousin.'

I back up automatically, staring at her in astonishment.
'What are you doing here?'

I notice she's wearing that same rust-orange gown she
wore at Harglade Hall.

'You know, Blaze,' says Ember, twirling a lock of dark
hair round her finger, 'it never ceases to amaze me just how
pathetic you are.'

I grit my teeth.

'How I laughed when I discovered you were an Heir.
Nobody can say the Gods don't have a sense of humour.'

'Ember,' I say, trying to keep my voice level.

'I've often wondered,' she continues, 'how does it feel to
be in a room full of people and know there is not a soul
among them who does not despise you?'

I look down at my feet, refusing to let her see the hurt on
my face.

'Do you ever think about how many of their loved
ones you killed with that storm? How many lost children,
brothers, sisters, fathers, mothers?' She pauses, a cruel smile
curling the corners of her mouth. 'Of course, you know all
about losing a mother, Blaze. Tell me, what was it like to
watch the life drain out of dear Aunt Analiese?'

Bile rises in my throat.

'Such a waste,' Ember says with a sigh. 'Especially since
the child responsible for her death appears to be even more
of a burden than you are.'

I ball my hands into fists. 'Leave Ren out of this.'

Ember steps closer, her dress rustling across the golden rock. 'Poor, sweet little Renly. Utterly powerless. Who ever heard of an Etheri without a gift? How breakable he is. How unwanted. Your father hasn't even laid eyes on him since he was born. I wonder what it must be like to know that everybody he loves wishes he had never existed at all. How, if given the choice, they would trade his life for his mother's in a heartbeat.'

Her words are poisonous. 'Shut your mouth.'

'No wonder you love him more than anyone, Blaze. He's just like you. *Empty*.'

I want to slap the smile off Ember's smug face. But I don't get the chance, because my cousin disappears. I blink in confusion.

That's when I hear another voice.

'Foolish girl. You really thought I loved you?'

I spin round.

Grandmother's stick raps loudly on the golden bedrock as she moves closer to me. 'How could anybody love *you*? You, who have brought such shame to our good name. To me. Who could ever love you after what you did? Who could ever love you for who you are?'

My eyes are wide with shock.

'You are nothing but a disappointment. You are *nothing*. You will always be nothing next to Flint Flameborn.'

'It's true, Blaze,' comes Flint's voice from behind me. 'You know it's true. Do you have any idea how much I hate you? My freak sister, a constant thorn in my side. Why do you think I spent so much time at court?'

Hot tears prick behind my eyes. 'Flint,' I begin, unable to keep the plea out my voice.

'*Blaze*,' he responds mockingly, mimicking my tone. 'You're a disease. A plague upon our House. Though, at least you give us all something to laugh about.'

And then Spinner and Elaith are there, stepping out from behind him, grinning maliciously. The three of them begin to laugh, their voices high and cruel, echoing around the arena. Nausea writhes in my stomach. *What is going on?*

My brother cocks his head to the side. 'Oh, I'm sorry. Did you think they were your friends? Don't you know? Can't you see? None of it was ever *real*.'

I stumble backwards away from them, scanning the mountainside for the best route down. But when I turn back round, Flint, Spinner and Elaith are gone.

It's Kai who steps forward, his face flooded with concern. 'Blaze. Gods, are you all right?'

I flinch as he touches my shoulder.

'It's me,' he soothes, his dark eyes kind and sincere. 'It's over now, I promise. Come on, let's get you out of here.'

Shaking and disorientated, I lean heavily on Kai's arm as we start making our way down the mountain, glad for something to hold on to.

He glances sidelong at me. 'It was so *easy* to convince you that I liked you.' Panicked, I jerk away from him, but he holds on tightly, his fingers digging into me. '*So pitifully easy.*'

I wrench my arm free from his grip and start to run, but someone blocks my way, appearing so suddenly, as if out of nowhere.

'Well, if it isn't the most hated girl in all the realm,' Marina hisses.

Where did she come from? Why is she here? Why are any of them here, in *my* trial?

That's when realization dawns on me, shining like a beacon through the haze of confusion and despair.

'You're not real,' I breathe. 'This is all just a trick.'

Marina's smirk doesn't falter.

My hands are trembling, but I stand my ground. 'Move.'

'Or what, Blaze? You'll go running to our trainer? Look around you. There's no River here to protect you now.' She moves towards me, coming close enough to whisper in my ear. 'I'm going to make you a promise, Storm Weaver. I vow that when I'm crowned queen, I will make your life a *misery*.'

With that, she shoves me hard in the chest and I tumble backwards down the mountain.

It's not like the free falling in my dream. I can feel every point of impact as my body slams repeatedly into the stone, the breath knocked clean out of my lungs as I flip over and over, limbs flailing as I try to grab hold of something, anything. It's only when I come to a stop, curled in a heap at the bottom of the rock, that the pain finally arrives. All different kinds of pain at once. I lie there gasping as it washes over me. I think I'm sobbing, but can't hear anything over the ringing in my ears.

Catching my breath feels like inhaling shards of glass. I try propping myself up into a sitting position, but something – I think it's my tailbone – protests, and I slump back down with a yelp. Head pounding, I try again.

Once I'm sitting up, I examine myself. My hair is untethered from my two braids, my tunic ripped and tattered, and already I feel bruises blooming across my skin. My face smarts with grazes, and I dread the thought of putting weight on my right ankle. And my left wrist . . . Searing pain. Bent at an odd angle.

My head continues to throb like a heartbeat behind my eyes, blurring my surroundings. Dazed, I cover my face with my hands, and when at last I emerge, it is to see a woman standing before me. A beautiful woman, tall and graceful with flowing dark hair.

'Mother,' I whisper.

How is this possible? Am I hallucinating? Am I *dead*?

I don't know. I don't care. The pain recedes. All that's left in the world is her and me.

My mother pulls me up into an embrace. 'Oh, Blaze,' she murmurs, stroking my hair.

My voice trembles. 'I – I never thought I'd see you again.' A tear leaks out of the corner of my eye and I hold on tightly to her, my heart bobbing up and down in the tide of emotion that threatens to sweep me away.

She's here. She's really here. I can feel her. I can smell her perfume. I'm nine years old again, and I'm safe.

My mother plants a kiss atop my head. 'My girl. My raincloud. My sweet little curse. If only the storm had taken you with it.'

A chill runs through me. No. *No*.

She continues stroking my hair. 'It would have been better that way, for everyone. An abomination like you should never have been allowed to live. But the people were frightened, you see. If your birth almost drowned an empire, one can only imagine what your death could do. And so, here you are.'

I'm shuddering uncontrollably, still wrapped in her arms. This is no hallucination. This is all part of my trial. A test designed to deceive. And this, the cruellest deception of all. I didn't just fall into the trap – I jumped. Blindly. Eagerly. Because I so wanted it to be real.

'You know, Blaze, in many ways dying was a gift. It meant I no longer had to live with the shame of knowing it was I who brought you into this world.'

Falling down a mountainside hurt less than this.

With everything I have left, I push my mother away from me, shooting pains licking up my wrist. Her golden-brown eyes are now narrowed with loathing, her soft smile a hateful, mocking sneer. I watch, horrified, as her face begins to contort, her features twisting, her skin stretching thin over her bones and then melting into nothing, replaced by hard, shiny scales. Her eyeballs fall out of their sockets, rolling across the rock and coming to rest by my feet. She rises taller and taller until she towers above me, and from her hands sprout sharp silver claws, as long and deadly as daggers.

My mouth is open in a silent scream. Every instinct is telling me to run, but it's as if my brain has disconnected from my body, because I can't move.

The beast looks down at me with eyes as red as blood, and when it speaks its voice drips out of its gaping mouth in a sibilant hiss. '*Storm Weaver.*'

My breath hitches.

'Come, little Singer. Let me slit you open. Let me suck the marrow from your bones. Let me see if you bleed red, or rain.'

I am rooted to the spot.

The beast moves closer. 'Let me slice your skin. Let me carve the shell of your skull. Let me wear your teeth round my neck like a talisman for all to see.'

I am utterly defenceless. No one is coming to help me. I am going to die here on this gilded stone stage. I am going to die broken and bloody and afraid.

When the beast speaks again, it is with a different voice, heavy with grief. 'I would rather a daughter dead than a daughter damned.'

I almost topple backwards. The voice is my father's.

Then it changes again, becoming cold and contemptuous.

'A waste of space,' Aunt Hester spits. 'That's what you are. Unworthy of the Harglade name.'

Next comes King Balen's voice, a silken purr. 'Hello, little dove.'

Suddenly the voices start coming all at once, oozing contempt like congealed blood from a deep wound. Some I don't recognize. Nameless enemies with endless names for me.

I try to run, stumbling over the terrain on my throbbing ankle, clutching my wrist to my chest. By the time I realize the stretch of rock leads to nothing but a thirty-foot drop, it's too late. There's nowhere left for me to go. I stand at the very end of the jutting ledge and watch my death approach. The beast advances, accompanied by a torrent of resentment. Loudest of all is my mother's voice, her words cutting me into pieces.

My drizzle begins to fall, the light rain clinging to the

beast's scales, dew drops glittering like jewels on the ends of its sharp claws. It's so close to me now that I can smell the blood on its breath as it bares its teeth.

Then, another voice. It's not coming from the beast but rather from inside my head, drifting through a fog of memory, soft and light like ocean spray. I remember the way Queen Hydra had leaned in close, as though she were telling me a secret.

Sometimes, we must lose our footing in order to find our balance.

For a moment I hear nothing but the drizzle pattering against the beast's scales before it lunges towards me with a deafening roar.

But I have already stepped backwards into the air.

I hit the surface of the lake with such force it sends shock waves through my body, jolting me awake. And I see it now. I understand. There's no one more suited to this trial than me. River had said it himself only last night.

You know, perhaps better than anyone, that hatred can sink its claws in deep. And if I were you, Blaze, I would start sharpening my own.

The claws that cut deep, the words that cut deeper. The dark, twisted creature that plagued me long before I set foot inside this arena.

The beast. It's *hate*. It is hatred itself.

I move faster in the water than I ever did on land, even without the use of one arm. I was always a strong swimmer, even as a child. My mother taught me well. For a moment I feel as though I'm back there, in the cove below Bartell Manor, racing her to the shore.

Only it's not my mother on my tail, but the beast – and it's gaining on me.

I keep swimming, urging myself on until the water becomes shallow and my feet can touch the bottom. Staggering up the rocky bank, I surrender to my anchors, letting sadness fill me up, letting fury seep into my bones.

As the beast slithers out of the lake, I unleash my rain. Moments later a thin layer of ice begins to form, coating its dripping scales. The beast snarls, shaking it off, but I persist.

Murderer.

Changeling.

Freak.

The ice is thicker now. I hear the sharp crackle as it finds purchase. As I turn hatred into something I can shatter.

The beast's eyes are wild, flicking frantically from side to side. The stream of voices slows, petering out as my ice spreads over its jaw, its teeth, its long forked tongue.

I'm gasping with the effort, but I don't stop until the beast looks as though it is encased inside a thick layer of glass.

Then I bring my hands together and a thousand splintered fragments explode outwards, obliterating the frozen statue in front of me.

I shield my face from the worst of the blast, and when I look up again I see that nothing remains of the beast but blood-soaked shards of ice, scattered chunks of scaled flesh, and a few deadly, dagger-like claws.

19

I come to in a brightly lit tiled room surrounded by physicians. They scuttle about like insects, murmuring softly to one another. Someone is holding my hand – the one not trapped in a sling. I turn my head to the side and then lurch back in fright.

'It's all right, it's all right, my darling one. You're safe. It's over. You did it.' Grandmother's voice is gentle and soothing, but still I narrow my eyes distrustfully.

'Are you the real one?' I demand, my own voice a little slurred.

'I am.'

A wave of pain washes over me and a low groan escapes my throat. Grandmother taps her stick impatiently and a physician bustles over, peering at me from under his spectacles.

'You were lucky,' he says earnestly. 'It could have been a lot worse.'

'I don't feel lucky,' I mutter.

Gingerly, I try to sit up, but Grandmother pushes me gently down again. 'Rest now. You've been through quite an ordeal.'

I gaze down at my battered body. 'What's the damage?'

Another physician glances over at me from where she's grinding something up into a powder and adding it to a vial. 'Your left wrist is broken, but thankfully it's a clean break. Bruised ribs, bruised tailbone, sprained ankle and a concussion.'

'The full works, then.' I squeeze my eyes shut as the pain laps over every nerve ending, radiating a dull, aching heat.

'Nothing we can't fix,' the physician responds, holding out the vial of liquid, which manages to make mud look more appetizing. 'Drink this.'

'What is it?' I ask as Grandmother takes it from her.

'Sedative,' she says. 'It should knock you out for a couple of hours.'

I have never felt more exhausted, but the last thing I want to do is sleep.

There's a knock at the door and Spinner enters, shooting Grandmother a nervous glance before coming over to stand at my bedside. 'How're you feeling?'

'You know, I think that might be the first time you've ever knocked,' I observe.

Spinner proceeds to tell us that Hal has drawn Aunt Yvainne's ring, meaning that it's the Ignitia Heirs up next.

'I can stay with her, Lady Harglade, if you want to go and watch Flint and Ember,' she says to Grandmother, nodding at me.

Flint and Ember. I try not to shudder as I remember their sneering faces, their cruel, mocking voices. There is no love lost between my cousin and me. Truthfully, I owe the discovery of one of my anchors to Ember, meaning that in a twisted, roundabout way she actually helped me defeat the beast in that arena. But hearing Flint's words, watching *him* laugh at me, taunt me, was unbearable. My heart clenches at the memory.

It wasn't real, I tell myself. *It wasn't real and it wasn't him.*

Grandmother glances at me, still brandishing the vial of sedative.

'I'm not taking that. I want to watch Flint, too.'

Spinner shakes her head. 'Heirs aren't allowed to watch the trial, Blaze.'

I ignore her, turning to the physician. 'Can't you give me something to keep me going?'

'You do realize it's not just you who's in the infirmary, right?' says Spinner. 'Some of the Gusters are in a pretty bad way.'

I learn that the Ventalla arena was nothing short of an abyss, just empty space interspersed with a few stone ledges hovering over the void. One of the Heirs misjudged his ability to levitate, and another lost her balance as she attempted to freeze her beast in place with a dense current of air, which caused her to topple from the ledge she was standing on.

'They practically had to scrape them up off the floor.'

My eyes widen in horror.

'I'm just kidding. King Balen slowed their fall. Still, they'll be out of action for the foreseeable. Nobody's died yet, though,' Spinner adds, as if to make me feel better.

Grandmother kisses me lightly on the forehead and leaves to take her place in one of the private viewing rooms overlooking the arena, which are reserved for family of the Heirs, trainers, and Etheri of high status.

She's followed by a couple of physicians.

Spinner grimaces. 'There'll be a lot of burns to tend to after this next trial.'

I refuse the sedative again, but accept more painkiller, opening my mouth obediently to take the strong-smelling vial of purple liquid the physician tips down my throat. It's instantaneous the way the pain dulls, and I become absolutely, intensely fascinated by the sight of my brandmark.

'Look, Spinner,' I breathe. 'Look at the way it glows. It's like a little star. I like stars.' I look up at the physician. 'Do you like stars?'

Spinner's shoulders shake in an effort not to laugh. I start laughing myself because everything suddenly seems so much more vivid and interesting and amusing. But the laughter soon sputters out when a wheelchair appears by the bed.

'We'll take you back to the palace now,' says one of the physicians.

'No.' My voice increases slightly in pitch. 'No. I'm not going in that. I'll walk.'

'You're not walking anywhere for a few days,' another physician informs me. 'There is to be no weight placed on that ankle. Do you understand?'

I turn to Spinner. 'Why do people always say that? *Do you understand?* Of course I understand, I'm not *stupid*.'

Spinner snorts loudly, pressing her lips together.

I try to sound authoritative but my voice comes out all drunk and dreamy. 'Listen to me. I'm not being *wheeled* anywhere. I am an Heir, and you will all do exactly as I say.'

'I certainly wouldn't cross her if I were you,' says a voice from the door.

I don't register Spinner's sharp intake of breath, or the looks on the faces of the physicians. I barely even notice as a glass vial shatters on the floor. My eyes are fixed on the boy leaning against the doorframe, smiling at me. I scarcely have time to blink before he's at my bedside, lifting me gently into his arms, a finger pressed to his lips as he whisks me from the room. I'm so woozy with painkiller that I can only form one clear thought.

'You're very handsome.'

And he is, with his sun-kissed golden skin, untidy waves of dark hair and piercing leaf-green eyes. He's tall, a good head taller than me, with high cheekbones and a little gold hoop dangling from one ear. His shoulders are broad, his jawline angular, and I can feel the corded muscles of his forearms as he holds me against his chest.

His is the kind of beauty one might call devastating. The kind that almost hurts to look at.

The boy chuckles softly, his face just inches from mine. I find myself gazing at his eyelashes, which are jet black and long enough to be enviable. He doesn't so much as hesitate as he navigates his way through the depths of the Keep.

It takes me a while to notice that I'm wearing nothing but a thin nightgown.

'Don't let Grandmother see me,' I tell the boy in a loud whisper. Then I take in what he himself is wearing. 'Oh, are you a serf?' I ask, fingering the collar of his white tunic.

'Only when it suits me,' he replies, his voice deep and velvety. 'And you don't have to worry about being seen, not where I'm taking you.'

I frown, unable to untangle what it is about this boy

that doesn't quite sit right through the heady haze of drugs, but I'm soon distracted by the sight of my toenails, which Spinner insisted on painting bright blue.

After a time we come to a door which leads into a small circular room, empty but for a chair sat in front of a porthole cut into the far wall. On the other side of the glass lies an arena. Fear takes over and I turn rigid.

The boy shifts my weight so that he's holding me with one arm, using the other to brush a strand of hair from my face with a gloved hand. I relax a little at his touch, breathing in the scent of fresh mint leaves and something earthy and sweet, like pine.

He lowers me carefully into the chair, then kneels down beside me. 'If anyone comes looking for you, it'd be best not to mention this,' he says. 'I don't want anybody knowing I'm here yet, you see.'

I nod slowly. 'All right. Your secret's safe with me.'

The boy smiles. 'Oh, that I never doubted.'

Then he's gone.

I sit gazing out at the arena. This time there's no miniature mountains or pools or lakes. Nor does it resemble the void Spinner had described. This arena is made entirely from stone, with a curved floor and high walls lined with flaming torches. The Crowned Council are seated on golden thrones atop a platform just metres above it. So there *is* an audience. Only they're invisible to the Heirs, just as this porthole must be too. Hal is with them, perched stiffly next to his father. On the emperor's other side is King Balen, his expression bored, his fingers drumming a silent tune on the arm of his throne.

Suddenly a small figure emerges from the tunnel below. Flame-red hair, knee-high red leather boots. Elaith swivels her head from side to side, staring straight through the Council, who she can't see peering down at her. She takes a step forward, just as Flint and Cole appear behind her.

Elaith whips round, her face flooding with confusion. 'What do you two not understand about waiting your turn?'

I want to pound on the glass, to scream at her that it's not them, that it's not real. But it's no use. She can't hear me. So I just sit and watch as her best friends tear her to shreds with their cruel words, pushing and shoving her until she is weeping on the ground.

Then Flint is gone and it's just Cole, kneeling down beside her, stroking her hair, murmuring kind, comforting words. Elaith raises her head, and the way she's looking at him confirms what I've long suspected.

Suddenly, Cole begins to transform, morphing into a creature so terrifying that I almost fall out of my chair.

Where mine was dark and reptilian, Elaith's beast is pale and disturbingly human. It resembles what I imagine a long-dead body to look like, blanched and bloodless. Her scream echoes around the arena. Then she's up, she's running.

But that's just it – there's nowhere to run to.

The beast moves after her with disjointed, staggering steps.

Fire, Elaith, I think desperately. *Use your fire.*

It's like she hears me. As she runs she raises a hand and a torch extinguishes, the ball of flame shooting into her palm. She splits the fire in two and throws it with all her might at the creature pursuing her. It shrieks as the flames make contact, licking up its sallow, almost translucent skin, melting part of it away to reveal the bone underneath.

The beast begins spewing out different voices. A male voice, her father's perhaps, telling her what a disappointment she is to him. Flint again, taunting her. And Cole. Her face twists with pain and humiliation as he tells her that he doesn't love her, that he never will, that she is a fool for ever imagining that he would.

I'm beginning to wish I had just taken the sedative.

Elaith is sobbing as the voices descend like a flock of birds, pecking and clawing at her as she tries desperately to concentrate.

Eventually, just when I think she's about to give up, she blasts the beast with enough fire that any remaining skin hanging off its frame melts away, leaving nothing but a grotesque, charred skeleton, the bones clattering to the ground.

Two physicians dart into the arena and begin examining Elaith's hands. She must have been so focused on burning the beast that she ended up burning herself in the process. They lead her back into the tunnel and out of sight.

It's not long before the next trial begins. I watch as Cole is encircled by a host of fair-haired, hazel-eyed Etheri that I take to be his family pressing in on him from all sides, spitting on him, spouting hateful words. Then his beast is there, a monstrous wolf-like creature with a long, flicking purple tongue. But try as he might, Cole can't seem to best it, and when the horns to signal the end of the trial are eventually blown he stalks out of the arena, roughly shaking off the physicians who run in to tend to his angry-looking burns.

I'm not prepared for when Flint emerges from the tunnel, even less so as I watch myself appear beside him, my voice cold and hateful and laced with derision as I tell Flint that our mother loved me best and he knew it, that he was a coward for not remaining at her side while she died.

I am followed by his friends, Grandmother, Father, Aunt Yvainne, Spinner, even Sheen. Then comes his beast, a gigantic snake with glistening golden fangs, large enough to crush a carriage. It's only when I take in its red scales and beady, brown-gold eyes that I realize. It's not just a snake – it's a cobra. A Harglade cobra, the emblem of our House.

Flint starts to run, bolting along at a slight angle from where the walls slant upward like a giant bowl. One by one, every flaming torch in the arena is extinguished, reduced to wisps of smoke as Flint passes by. Sure enough, in his outstretched hands he holds a ball of fire, which grows steadily larger with each flame he gathers.

The beast slithers after him, voices dripping like venom from its mouth.

Suddenly, Flint stops. He turns, panting, brandishing the fireball. His curls are stuck to his forehead with sweat. The snake is near enough now to run him through with one of those deadly fangs. I'm frozen with fear, unable to tear my eyes away from my brother.

Flint holds on to his flames until the voices reach a crescendo, until the beast opens its mouth wide enough to swallow him whole – and hurls the fireball down its throat.

There's a sickening screeching sound, and I watch as the snake burns to death from the inside out, writhing and twisting until it flops to the ground, dead.

My brother waves the physicians away good-naturedly and disappears through the tunnel.

I let out a huff of laughter, light with relief, then wince. The pain is returning. If only that handsome boy would come back, I could send him for more painkiller. I'm just considering whether to ask the Keep for some medicine when my cousin struts into the arena.

Grudgingly, I'm forced to admit that Ember handles the first part of the trial well. Perhaps she's just too arrogant to believe any of the cruel words thrown in her direction.

Failing to faze her as either Aunt Hester or Aunt Yvainne, Ember's beast sheds its disguise and claims its true form – that of a towering dragon.

The Firelands were once home to a great number of dragons, but during the war, many of them fled Ostacre, never to return. The closest I've ever come to seeing one is in Renly's picture books. It's incredibly, horrifyingly beautiful.

My cousin runs straight at the dragon while expertly dodging billowing bursts of fire. She directs her own flames up towards its eyes, and in the time it takes for the dragon to jerk its head away, she's climbing up its leg and swinging herself on to its back. The creature roars and arches, but Ember clings on tight, crawling up its neck until she's gripping the dragon's head between her hands. It's not until the smoke begins to rise that I understand.

Ember is sizzling its brain.

The dragon barely has time to spew out a few tendrils of flame before it collapses to the ground. Ember slides delicately off its ridged back and skips away from the smouldering body as though she'd just made a pot of tea rather than fry a fully grown beast.

I slump back in my chair, sickened.

Moments later I'm looking at an entirely different arena, a large meadow dotted with trees. I watch dazedly as the Terrathian Heirs complete their trials. One girl, Amaryllis, manages to ensnare her beast, a monstrous spider, in its own sticky web.

By the time the third Heir has been carried out on a stretcher, the pain from my injuries is unbearable. The completion of the trials must have put an end to whatever enchantment has been concealing the Crowned Council. I can hear them talking to one another as I drift in and out of consciousness.

Then something tugs at my attention, and I find myself gazing down into the arena just as the fourth Terrathian Heir emerges into the light.

I sit up, ignoring my aching limbs. The *fourth* Heir? But there are only three, there have only been three since the very start of the Choosing. Everyone has long given up hope of the fourth Heir making an appearance.

Yet there he is, grinning lazily up at the Council.

'Sorry I'm late,' is all he says.

My brows shoot up in surprise. Because I know him. Only he's no longer wearing a drab serf's uniform, or his pair of thin leather gloves. He's dressed just like the other Terrathian Heirs – in a green tunic that matches his eyes. I catch sight of his tree-shaped brandmark glowing brightly on the back of his right hand, which he rakes through his untidy dark hair.

The faces of the Crowned Council paint a picture of undiluted shock. Aunt Yvainne is shaking her head while Queen Aspen has both hands clapped over her mouth.

My surroundings seem to tilt as the boy turns his gaze on me, and slowly I begin to piece it all together. For there is only one person who could warrant such a reaction, only one person who is even more infamous, more feared, than I am myself.

The emperor's illegitimate son. The bastard prince.

His name is Fox Calloway Castellion, but they call him the Earth Cleaver.

20

I was eleven years old when the earth was ripped in two.

I can still see it all so vividly, sitting by the window in Harglade Hall as the ground began to tremble and quake. Everybody was ordered to take refuge in the crypt. I detest it down there, surrounded by urns and towering stone statues of our ancestors. Still, it felt fitting to wait the whole thing out in a tomb, especially since the attendants were helpfully wailing that we were all going to die. And many did. Thousands upon thousands of them. More were swallowed by the Rift than were drowned by my storm.

Aside from Cor Caval, which is built upon a bedrock of enchanted gold, every central province was destroyed. Many obliterated. For some, no trace of them remains or, like the Cities of Buried Souls, their remains serve as a reminder of all that was lost. Ancient Houses. Entire bloodlines. Countless lives. Etheri and Fidra alike, all dead, all gone, never to return.

And the boy responsible for their deaths, the boy responsible for breaking the world, is looking right at me as though I am the only person in it.

Only when Fox's gaze eventually drops do I find I can breathe again. His arrival has shattered through the haze, leaving me aching, reeling and painfully alert.

The Earth Cleaver. The Earth Cleaver is *here*. And not only is he here, he's an Heir to the Terrathian throne. Beast-Ember was right. The Gods must really have a sense of humour. Or some deeply questionable intentions.

Fox returns his attention to the Crowned Council, who are all whispering frantically to one another, and dips into a sweeping bow. 'Father. Uncle. Your Majesties.' Then he turns to Hal, and smirks. 'Brother.'

The prince grips the arms of his throne. 'Fox. It's been a while.'

This doesn't surprise me, given Fox's vocation. I imagine it must be pretty time-consuming being a slaver, what with all those trips across the Second Sea on expeditions to the Otherlands. They say he hunts magical creatures too, in his spare time. With all those delightful hobbies, it's a wonder the Earth Cleaver comes back to court at all. But return he does, every year on the anniversary of the Cleaving. Perhaps he enjoys commemorating it. Maybe he raises a toast, congratulating himself on perpetrating the greatest massacre in Etherian history at only thirteen years old and walking away unscathed.

A memory surfaces.

In my experience, those with that kind of power, they ... take pleasure in it. They like that it is known. They want it to be known.

Even then, I'd guessed who Hal might have been referring

to, and here, now, looking down at the Earth Cleaver, I think I guessed right.

Fox cracks his neck. 'Let's get this over with, shall we? I've been travelling for weeks and could really use a hot meal or three.'

The emperor still appears stunned, but the small smile he shoots Fox is one I've never seen him give to Hal. 'Very well, my son. Let the final trial begin.'

Fox paces up and down the arena with hands behind his back as numerous people spit out terrible things. It's almost amusing how unfazed he is by it all.

Only once does his smirk falter. It happens when a child appears in front of him, a little girl with flowing hair the colour of autumn leaves. But after a moment Fox just turns his back on the girl and uproots the ground she is standing on without even bothering to watch as she morphs into his beast – a tentacled creature with bulbous milky eyes.

He makes short work of it. With a few casual flicks of his wrist, tree vines begin to curl round the beast's tentacles until the thing is completely ensnared. Fox sidles over to where it waits, strung up and almost pitiful. Then he holds out a hand, and a large branch soars into his palm as if pulled by a magnetic force. The Earth Cleaver snaps the branch across his knee and doesn't hesitate before driving the splintered end into the beast's heart.

He wipes the sleeve of his tunic across his blood-spattered face and grins up at the Council. 'Well, that was diverting. Now, if you'll excuse me.' He gives a low bow. 'Oh, and brother?' he says, turning once more to Hal. 'It's good to see you, too.'

With that, he disappears through the tunnel.

Rigid with shock, I watch as the pool of blood Fox left behind begins to spread, staining the green meadow crimson. I realize my mouth is hanging open and snap it shut, swallowing a whimper as the pain in my limbs becomes unendurable.

The last thing I remember before the darkness drags me under is the sound of a door opening, the back of a hand pressed gently to my burning forehead, and a low voice murmuring softly in my ear.

When I open my eyes several hours later I'm lying in my bed in the Golden Palace. My cuts and grazes have been cleaned and bandaged, and a small pillow has been propped under where my broken wrist sits in a sling, alleviating some of the weight round my neck. I turn my head to the side and find a vial of medicine waiting for me on my nightstand. There's a sound, too, soft and tinkling – Flint's music box, propped open beside it. The pain is still there, but it's kept at bay by whatever new painkiller is surging through my veins.

I screw up my face as I come to, unable to recall how I got here. Perhaps Grandmother managed to track me down and sent for a physician?

At that moment, a few orbs of light float gently into my bedchamber, banishing the shadows from the walls. They are followed by Hal, holding an enormous bunch of golden roses. My heart leaps at the sight of him, then sinks slightly as I imagine the sight of me. I must look a mess – exhausted, battered and bruised, my hair still wild and loose around my shoulders. Yet Hal doesn't seem to mind. His gaze is nothing but warm.

He lays the flowers on a chair before sitting down gently on the side of my bed. 'How are you feeling?'

I shrug, then wish I hadn't as heat sears through my joints.

'You were incredible out there,' he tells me. 'You had more to face than anyone else and I'm sorry for that.'

'You mean you're sorry so many people hate me?' I ask wryly.

Hal half smiles. 'If it's any consolation, Blaze, I don't hate you.'

'Thank you, Your Imperial Highness. I'll try to remember that while I'm polishing Marina's boots.'

This makes him laugh. 'Don't count yourself out just yet,' he says. 'Look.'

Hal gestures to my left hand, and my jaw drops.

When an Heir is axed from the Choosing, their brandmark ceases to glow. Yet the Aquatori waterdrop seared into my flesh continues to glimmer faintly beneath the bandages.

'The trial was designed to test how the Heirs react to hostility and respond to fear,' says Hal. 'It seems Fjord was ill-equipped to deal with either.'

Fjord. Smug, stuck-up Fjord is first out of the running. Which leaves Marina, Kai . . . and *me*. Conflicting emotions jostle one another for space, but for a moment all I can think about are the orbs of light reflected in Hal's raven eyes, and the scent of lemons on his skin.

'Your brother performed well, too,' he says. 'Very well, in fact.'

I'm about to tell him that I know, that I was there, but I stop myself. Because I wasn't supposed to see Flint's trial, or anyone else's. Especially not –

Just then Flint comes bounding into the room, followed by Spinner and Elaith, whose hands are thickly bandaged. Hal stands up so quickly he practically gives me vertigo.

My brother raises an eyebrow before throwing himself on the end of my bed, causing me to wince. He whoops gleefully, pointing at my brandmark. 'I *knew* it!'

I take in his own brandmark, and Elaith's, both of them glowing. I imagine Ember's must be too, if her trial was anything to go by. That means Cole has been cut from the pool of Ignitia Heirs. Elaith seems a little subdued, which only confirms my assumption.

To my disappointment, Hal crosses to the door. 'I should return to the party. Congratulations, all of you.'

'Hal?'

He turns back round to face me.

'Thank you for the flowers.'

The prince smiles, then leaves, the orbs of light floating along in his wake.

Flint flutters his eyelashes at me. '*Thank you for the flowers.*'

I make a gesture I would never dare make in front of Grandmother.

'We heard about what happened during your trial,' says Elaith, pulling at the fraying edge of her bandage. 'You were really brave.'

'I've certainly had better days,' I concede. 'Though things could be worse. I could have broken both wrists.'

Flint pats my foot affectionately, sending a jolt of pain up my leg. 'That's the spirit, sister mine. Speaking of breaking things, you'll *never* guess who the fourth Terrathian Heir turned out to be.'

My chest constricts as I recall being cradled in a pair of strong arms, peering dazedly up into the face of the most beautiful boy I have ever seen.

Spinner busies herself fetching a vase for Hal's roses and doesn't meet my eyes.

Elaith leans forward, lowering her voice theatrically. 'He's here. In the palace.'

'Who?' I make myself ask.

'The *Earth Cleaver*,' says Flint. He seems to interpret my silence as my being paralysed with terror, because he then adds, 'It's all right, Blaze. You don't have to speak to him. You don't even have to go near him. I'll make sure of that.'

A little too late, brother, I think.

21

After seven full days of bedrest, I am exceedingly restless. Etheri tend to heal more quickly than Fidra. Because of our power, our bodies are more durable, drawing from magic to mend. My cuts have long since scabbed over, the steady influx of drugs has turned my broken wrist from a painful inconvenience to just an inconvenience, and I can even walk with the help of a ridiculously ornate golden crutch. When Spinner first presented it to me, Flint had pretended to mistake me for Grandmother and then rolled about laughing. His laughter soon turned to spluttering after I'd brandished the crutch and jabbed him in the ribs.

I reach for it now as I carefully manoeuvre myself out of bed. Grandmother had wished to stay longer to nurse me, but I insisted she return to Renly as soon as possible.

It's late evening, and I can hear the muffled sounds of a revel several floors below, meaning that the rest of the palace is pretty much deserted. I meet only a couple of drunken courtiers and a handful of serfs before the towering doors of the library come into view.

I limp between the groaning shelves and tiny orbs of light until I find the comfortable alcove. As before, as soon as I take my seat a book appears on the golden table beside me – another of River's recommendations. I pick it up, expecting to find a title detailing the lives of the Rain Singers or an advanced guide to ice making, but instead I find a small, slightly battered volume entitled *The Dance of the Waves*.

Wave carving. River must think it time I discovered my third water gift. A shiver of excitement runs through me as I prop the book open in my lap.

The first section revolves around the art of water whispering. I swallow a groan, remembering the day River had us sit by the pool, straining our ears to catch the faintest sound carried on the still – and stubbornly silent – surface.

I pore over the pages until my eyelids begin to droop.

I'm just snapping the book shut when a voice startlingly close to me croaks, 'So, you're her, are you?'

I look up to find an old man I've never seen before sitting in the armchair opposite. Everything about him is pale, from his sagging skin to his wispy beard to his crumpled golden robes. Everything apart from his eyes, which are so dark they seem to be all pupils.

'I'm . . . what?' I stammer, taken aback.

The old man smiles crookedly. 'The girl they call the Storm Weaver.'

'Oh, right. *Her*. Yes. I mean, yes, I am.'

He studies me thoughtfully for a moment and then says, 'I thought you'd be taller.' The lines on his face look as though they've been engraved there. I watch his gaze drop to the book in my lap. 'You won't find the answers in that, girl.'

I frown, defensive. 'Why not?'

'Books are for those who have lived,' he tells me. 'You? You have not lived. Not yet. You have your own pages to fill. You want to know how to carve a wave, Storm Weaver?'

I nod.

'Don't read about it,' he says. 'Do it.'

'It's hardly that simple,' I mutter peevishly.

The old man merely chuckles. 'You think that book is going to tell you which of your emotions is anchored to the waves?'

I stare at him. 'How do you –'

'There was a time my advice was worth its weight in gold,' he says, ignoring me. 'And now here I am, merely giving it away. Close the book. Open your mind. Carve the wave.' He lifts a gloved hand and points a long, gnarled finger at me. 'Now, be off with you, girl. You're in my seat.'

Disgruntled, I reach for my crutch, leaving the book on the table. Before turning the corner, I glance back to find the old man settling himself comfortably in my armchair.

I limp back to my chambers, irritable and confused.

What business is it of his how I learn to carve? Who is he, anyway? And more importantly, how does he know that my gifts are Melded? There is nothing about Melding in any of the history books. The Rain Singers kept it secret so that the rest of the world would never find out the source of their power.

As Elva helps me prepare for bed, I realize sleep is the last thing on my mind. The old man's words have got under my skin, so much so that I fill my wash bowl, place it on the floor and sit in front of it, unsure where to begin.

Rain is sadness. Ice is fury. But as for waves … I don't know. It could be anything. Anything at all. Which isn't exactly much to go on. In fact, it's nothing to go on.

I think about the years of drizzle, about the glasses shattering at Harglade Hall. How they just sort of … happened. I was never trying to discover those anchors. They found me.

Feeling foolish, I stare into the water, waiting for inspiration to strike.

I end up falling asleep in front of the wash bowl, then groggily heave myself into bed a few hours later, just as grey dawn light is beginning to leak through the windows.

Hal comes to visit me that evening.

Ever since the first trial he's taken to bringing me bunches of gleaming golden roses. My rooms are overflowing with them, their sweet scent perfuming the air.

Naturally, I'm flattered. Delighted, even. Yet still I find myself mystified by his attentiveness, and what's more, I'm afraid of misinterpreting it. Because what if he's just being kind? What if I'm simply reading too much into things?

Though if I am, then I'm not the only one.

'Everyone's talking about the two of you,' Spinner told me yesterday, wiggling her eyebrows as she handed me another vial of medicine.

'What? Who?'

'You and the prince, of course. There's been quite a bit of gossip surrounding all his visits to your chambers.' I must have looked stricken, because she continued quickly, 'Don't worry, I've assured them it's nothing untoward. Hal's a perfect gentleman, after all.'

I couldn't argue with that.

'You really shouldn't have,' I tell him as I admire the roses. 'This room is practically a rose garden already.'

He just smiles, then hands the flowers to Elva, who heads off in search of a vase. She returns a few moments later, setting a jug and two glasses down on one of the low tables. Hal pours the pale-green liquid into one of the glasses and offers it to me, but I decline. After my encounter with the Earth Cleaver, I've taken to avoiding consuming anything that will make me even slightly uninhibited. Spinner has reluctantly given up asking me about it, since I did a pretty convincing job of feigning amnesia.

I wonder what Hal would say, if he knew. Nothing good, I suspect, if their brief exchange in the arena was anything to go by. He hasn't once mentioned his half-brother's arrival during any of our conversations, seemingly keen to avoid the subject completely.

The prince takes a sip of wine. 'I imagine you're looking forward to getting back to training. Last I heard, River seemed most impressed with your progress.' He lets out a sudden bark of laughter. 'And River's not the only one,' he says, holding up his glass and running his forefinger over the fine layer of frost on the rim.

'You might want to pour another one of those,' I reply. 'I've not figured out how to melt ice yet.'

'Why don't you ask Marina to help you?'

I arch an eyebrow. 'Pass.'

'Oh, come on. She's excellent at simmer skimming, and

she's all right when you get to know her. The Kalparas are one of the last pureblood Aquatori families in Ostacre, and very proud of it. Marina's an only child, and her parents have always put an awful lot of pressure on her to be . . .'

'A tyrant?' I suggest.

Hal chuckles. 'I was going to say perfect. Sure, she can be a little prickly. But you never know, you might come to like her.'

I don't bother telling him that I find this highly unlikely, or that I would rather throw myself down the Rift than ask Marina for help.

Hal places his glass down. 'I know these past few weeks haven't been easy,' he says. 'I imagine it's all incredibly overwhelming, especially for someone like you.'

'Someone like me?' I mean it to sound teasing, but it comes out slightly defensive.

'I just meant with you having not really left home before,' Hal explains.

'Try ever,' I say, perching on the edge of an armchair. 'That is, unless you count the carriage ride from Nemeth to Valburn when I was ten.'

'And what was the reason for that?'

I pause, suddenly self-conscious. My first instinct is to deflect. I don't talk about my parents, not to anyone.

But there's just something about Hal. Lots of somethings. I was drawn to him the moment I met him, and not only because of the way he looks but also because of the way he looks at me. He makes me feel special and beautiful and admired – as though I am some kind of rare jewel, shining all the brighter under his gaze. And he makes me feel like I can trust him, even with the most breakable parts of myself.

'When my mother died,' I begin, 'my father, he . . . well, he sort of . . . withdrew. He wouldn't come out of his rooms, wouldn't eat, wouldn't speak to anyone.' The words leave a bitter taste in my mouth. 'He couldn't take care of us any more, my brothers and I. So our grandmother decided that it would be best if we went to live with her – at Harglade Hall.'

Hal sits down opposite me. 'And was it?'

I consider this for a moment. 'Yes,' I say finally. 'At least, I think so. Flint thrived in Valburn. He loves to be in the thick of things. And Renly, he never knew any different. As for me, I suppose it was just . . .'

'Trading one prison for another?' Hal finishes.

I blink in surprise.

'I've often wondered,' he continues, 'what did you do? To fill your days, I mean.' When I don't answer right away, he glances up, catches sight of my expression and backtracks. 'Forgive me, I don't mean to pry.'

'No,' I say, shaking my head. 'It's just, nobody's ever asked me that before.'

Hal inclines his head. 'Well, I'm glad to be the first.'

I settle myself more comfortably in my chair. 'Books, mostly. I could spend entire days reading. It made me feel less removed, somehow. It probably sounds stupid.'

'It doesn't sound stupid at all.'

'I wanted to learn everything I could,' I say. 'I studied history and poetry and cartography. I even learned six languages, just to pass the time.'

Hal's eyes widen in disbelief. '*Six?*'

'Well, six and a half. My Thavenian still isn't up to scratch.'

He exhales in a low whistle, and says, 'You're remarkable.' Which makes me blush. And forget how to speak. But before I can summon the means to string a sentence together, Hal's smile suddenly wavers, then slides right off his face. 'I don't pretend to know anything of the pain you must have endured,' he continues. 'My mother is alive and well, and I accepted a long time ago that my father is first and foremost father to the realm.' He clears his throat. 'But I do know something about growing up in a gilded cage.'

I try to picture him as a boy of four or five, scampering through echoing hallways filled with golden-clad courtiers. 'I can't imagine being a child in this place,' I say. 'Being surrounded by so many people, all the time.'

'And yet what I remember most about my childhood is feeling lonely,' says Hal. 'You know, when I was younger, my friends were actually selected for me. Seriously, they were hand-picked by my parents. Young Eyes in training, reporting back on my every move. There was very little that wasn't chosen for me, and look what's changed.' He glances down at his brandmark. 'It's strange. To have everything you could ever want, and yet not the freedom to decide your own future.'

I think of the future I had planned for myself, all that time spent daydreaming about salt air, the steady slap of waves, the strange, mythical beauty of the Otherlands. I can't seem to let it go, because it's all I had to hold on to.

'I thought I could decide, once,' I admit. 'When I turned

of age. Before the eclipse. But then again, I'm not the Crown Prince of Ostacre.'

'No,' says Hal wryly. 'You're the Storm Weaver.'

'Glad we've straightened that out.'

He grins, then shakes his head. 'Ironic, isn't it? They call it the Choosing Rite, only we have no choice in the matter.'

'Don't you want it? All that power?' The words are out before I fully understand the weight of them. They sit heavily in the air between us. Hal's expression darkens, and I curse myself. 'I'm sorry. I spoke out of turn.'

'Not at all,' he says, pretending to adjust his cufflinks, which are engraved with the Imperial sun and eye, matching his brandmark. 'I prefer it when you speak your mind. So few people do.'

I rub my scar self-consciously. Stupid. I was stupid to ask such a thing. Even now, sitting straight-backed and elegant, hands resting lightly on the armrests of a blue armchair that may as well be a throne, Hal is every bit the future emperor.

'It's . . . my birthright,' he says eventually. 'My one true purpose.'

I say nothing, sensing there's more. I may regret the question, but I find I still want the answer.

'But it can also be a burden,' Hal continues. 'My position is more fragile than you might think.' He takes a deep breath. 'I suppose I've always felt . . . I don't know, like a performer. Like I'm forever on stage, playing the same role over and over. Only if I were to drop the act, even for a moment, I'd jeopardize everything.'

I'm reminded of standing with him in front of that tapestry depicting the Gods, when he told me to start acting the part.

Is that what you would do? I'd asked him.

To which he'd replied, *It's what I do all the time.*

I meet his gaze and hold it. There it is again, that shadow of vulnerability amid the brightness of his disposition. I've seen it pass across his face on more than one occasion. His father escorting Lady Kestrel into the ballroom. Fox appearing in that arena. And every time, it takes me by surprise. Because Hal is so warm, so steady, so full of light. When I'm with him, I feel lit up by it. And I'm not the only one. Everybody always wants to be near him. I suppose he's a bit like the sun in that way. People tend to bask in his presence.

Hal gets to his feet and crosses to the window. Outside, the night sky is speckled with stars. They're especially bright tonight, shining silver and infinite against the inky blackness.

'Do you ever wish you were someone else?' I whisper.

I'm not sure what makes me say it. I'm not sure I'd have had the courage to, had the question been directed at Hal's face and not to his back.

There's a long pause.

'Sometimes,' he says, without turning round. 'Do you?'

'Sometimes.'

I rise from my chair and join him by the window. Silence descends, but it's not uncomfortable. It feels sacred, somehow. Like some unspoken oath.

Then Hal says, 'Though if that were the case, then we wouldn't have our gifts. Which reminds me . . .' He slips a hand into his pocket. 'I have something for you.'

In his palm sits what appears to be a small glass box.

Heart pounding, I reach out and pick it up. 'What is it?'

Hal's fingers wrap round mine as he raises the box gently to my lips. 'It's a nightlight. Enchanted to respond to your voice alone. Go on, say something.'

'Like what?' I ask, then gasp in surprise as the box lights up, illuminating our faces.

'Think of it as your very own sunbeam,' he says softly. 'As though I'm giving you a little piece of my gift.'

My stomach flips over. His gift, inherited from the Maker himself. Light. Pure and golden and full of hope. A reminder that darkness is temporary, and the dawn will always arrive to chase away the shadows.

'Thank you,' I say, slightly breathlessly. 'It's beautiful.'

'It's nothing.'

'No, it's not nothing. I love it, really.'

He's still holding my hand, raven eyes boring into mine, questioning, conflicted. My heart beats loud in my ears. I don't move. I hardly dare breathe.

Then, just when I think he's about to bridge the small gap between us, he breaks it.

Later, as I drift into sleep, I leave the nightlight glowing gently on my nightstand, guarding me from dreams.

22

My week-long reprieve from stares and whispers soon comes to an end.

Elva helps me into a light, sleeveless blue dress while my brother lies on my bed, eating a plum and complaining about Sheen, his sullen chaperone.

'He's just so . . .' Flint gestures with his hands as though looking to snatch the right word straight out of the air. 'So . . . *sour.*'

'Maybe you're too sweet?' I suggest.

'True enough,' he says. 'But I've just never met anyone who doesn't –'

'Like you?'

'I was going to say *adore* me, but I suppose like will do.'

I roll my eyes.

Spinner appears just as Elva finishes braiding my hair. 'Here,' she says, holding out my crutch.

I shake my head. 'No way. I'm not using that. Not in front of everyone.'

'Ah, see, I thought you might say that.' Flint gets to his feet and extends his arm towards me. 'Worry not, sister mine. I'll be your crutch. Lean on me.'

I smile gratefully, and with that, the three of us slowly make our way towards the banquet hall. Spinner winks at Flint before she skips away towards the Eyes' table.

'What are we talking about?' Flint asks, ruffling Elaith's hair out of place as he sits down next to her.

'What d'you think?' says Zeph, handing him a glass of purple wine. 'What's all anyone's been talking about? Or rather, *who*.'

'I see. So, what do you make of the Imperial Bastard, then? I notice he's not graced us with his presence tonight.'

'Well, it's not hard to see why he's caused such a stir. The Earth Cleaver, Heir to the Terrathian throne? It's unprecedented. I mean, after everything he's done ...' Zephyr trails off, shooting an uneasy glance in my direction before quickly looking away.

I know what he's thinking, and I don't blame him. The Earth Cleaver, Heir to the Terrathian throne, the Storm Weaver, Heir to the Aquatori. He's right. It is unprecedented. Inconceivable, even. It's little wonder the eclipse caught me completely off guard, why any rumours concerning the missing Green were dismissed as ludicrous. Heirs are selected for their power, yes, but that power is supposed to symbolize rejuvenation, not destruction.

'Fox is mythic,' says Elaith dreamily, swirling her wine inside her goblet. 'Not to mention *gorgeous*.'

Kai raises an eyebrow.

'What? He is. Objectively, I mean. You have to admit it.'

Flint nods wisely. 'She's got a point.'

'He's the perfect conundrum,' continues Elaith. 'I find him fascinating.'

'What d'you mean?' I ask, without looking up.

'Well, he's the most dangerous Etheri in the realm. That goes without saying. Not to mention sadistic – and cruel. But he's also confusingly . . . charming. *Terrifying*, but charming. Like you're not sure whether he's planning to kill you or kiss you. It's exhilarating.'

'It's easy to see why the Eyes fawn over him,' says Zephyr. 'The other courts are warier, of course. Most are afraid of him, many despise him, but they wouldn't dare show it. He's already treated as though he were a king.'

I frown at my empty plate. I am reviled for summoning that storm, meanwhile, despite literally breaking the empire apart, Fox has somehow amassed a legion of admirers? Charm or no charm, that hardly seems fair. Nor does it seem fair that he is permitted to travel the world as he pleases, and I was locked away for seventeen years. I suppose being an emperor's son comes with its benefits.

'They say his father favours him,' says Elaith. 'Right, Zeph?'

Just then, Hal appears, a gaggle of courtiers in his wake. He manages to shake them off and slides into the seat next to mine, shooting me a small smile just as serfs begin to swarm into the hall carrying platters of food – crab cakes served with seaweed and lime; honey-drizzled pork; tomatoes the size of my fist sliced and scattered with basil leaves; potatoes swimming in butter; apricots, pies, pastries. Flint takes my plate and starts filling it for me, while Zeph takes Hal's arrival as his cue to change the subject.

'How's Cole doing? I haven't seen him since the first trial.'

I watch as Elaith stabs a potato a bit too forcefully with her fork.

'He'll be fine,' says Flint. 'He's just blowing off some steam. That reminds me, how are your water gifts coming along, sister? Mastered simmering yet?'

I shake my head. 'I'm trying my hand at wave carving, but I can't say it's going well.'

'You'll get there,' Kai assures me. 'The girl I met on that first day at the Keep could barely manage drizzle, and now look at you.'

'I second that,' says Hal, raising his glass.

The others follow suit, and as they clink their glasses together I become aware of a warm feeling taking root inside my chest.

After the feast I slowly make my way to the library, where I limp through the maze of bookshelves towards my usual alcove. But once again, I find my armchair occupied. Only this time, not by the old man.

'Hello, Storm Weaver,' says Fox Calloway Castellion.

I start in surprise, and then, for some inexplicable reason, dart behind a nearby bookcase. 'Are you *following* me?' I try and fail to keep the embarrassment out of my voice.

He chuckles. 'Well, I was here first, so I suppose I could ask you the same thing.'

'You're right,' I snap. 'I'll go.'

'Oh, I wouldn't hear of it,' Fox says pleasantly. 'There's plenty of room for two. And what a perfect opportunity to get to know one another, don't you think? Now, why don't you come out from behind that bookcase and let me introduce myself.'

'I *know* who you are. We've already met.'

'Then I do hope I made a good impression.'

Spurred by irritation, I step out into view. Fox is lounging in the armchair. He wears a loose green shirt that gapes open to a frankly indecent degree, dark breeches and a pair of slightly scuffed riding boots. His hair is just as untidy as it was before, a few strands falling into eyes the colour of spring leaves, which fix themselves on me, rooting me to the spot. A traitorous blush stains my cheeks as I remember what I said to him at the Keep.

You're very handsome.

Fox smirks, as if he's remembering too. Round his neck is a simple golden chain. He runs the crook of his forefinger along it as he nods to the chair opposite. 'Be my guest.'

I stay put. 'Why did you come to the infirmary?'

'Because I wanted to see you.'

My heart races uncomfortably. 'Why?'

'To put a face to the name. And what a beautiful face it is, too.'

My breathing turns shallow, but this time I refuse to blush. 'Why did you trick me into thinking you were a serf?'

'I didn't trick you,' he says innocently, taking a sprig of mint from his pocket and popping it into his mouth. 'You made an assumption. I simply chose not to correct it.'

I narrow my eyes. 'I'm guessing you watched my trial?'

He nods, chewing thoughtfully. 'I confess I did. It was . . . interesting.'

'Interesting,' I repeat. 'In what way?'

'Watching you make a decision like that.'

'Like *what*?'

'You had all but decided to give up,' he says. 'But then you didn't. You decided to *win*. The others, they fought against their beasts, but *you*, you fought it by turning it against itself. All that anger, all that pain it inflicted, you used it as a weapon.'

I stare at him, unsettled by the shrewdness of his observation. Fox smiles, twisting a gold signet ring round his finger. He has two, I notice. One engraved with the Castellion raven, the other with the Calloway falcon. Traditionally, Etheri adopt the surname of the more powerful House. Fox's father is the emperor, the Castellions are the Imperial family, and yet he chose to take his mother's name as well. He makes no attempt to deflect from his unconventional parentage, nor from his illegitimacy, but rather he flaunts it. He *owns* it.

Fox leans back in his chair. 'Any more questions?'

'Why were you so late to the Choosing?' I ask. 'Or was the dramatic entrance all part of the plan?'

He grins. 'I'm not the only one with a flair for the theatrics, it seems. Been smashing many glasses lately, Storm Weaver?'

I scowl. 'That was an accident.'

He waves my words away. 'Sometimes we must claim our accidents. Intention can define you. And better to appear wilful than witless, wouldn't you say?'

He stretches, cracking his neck, the sound of it so loud in the silent library that it makes me jump, which makes him smile.

'When the eclipse happened, I was in the middle of the Serolian rainforest,' he says. 'The timing was really most inconvenient.'

Serolia. That's one of the Otherlands, an isle consisting mostly of jungle, once home to Magi with the ability to shape-shift, sprout wings, and even communicate with animals. Part of me longs to ask him what it was like. The other part is telling me to run.

I clear my throat, hoping the harshness in my tone disguises the fear. 'So now that you're here, what is it that you intend to do?'

He considers this for a moment. 'I'm looking for something.'

I swallow. 'And what's that?'

Fox tilts his head to the side, sizing me up. 'Oh, Storm Weaver,' he says. 'Are you sure you want to know?'

Everything about him – his soft voice, his piercing gaze, even the way he's positioned, casually, lazily, but really lying in wait, poised to strike – all speaks of a distrustful and dangerous threat. A predator. And if he's the predator . . .

Suddenly I want to put as much distance between myself and the Earth Cleaver as possible. I take an unsteady step backwards.

Fox rises from his chair. 'Going so soon?'

'As delightful as it's been, yes.'

He smirks. 'Scared, Storm Weaver?'

Yes.

'No,' I say tersely, turning away from him, wincing as my bad ankle protests.

'Need any help storming out?'

I grit my teeth as I walk away, and I just know he's grinning.

23

I weave through a field of wildflowers. The air is sweet, the sky a brilliant blue. Rays of sunlight reflect off something gold up ahead.

Blaze.

I hear my name, whispered like a caress.

Then the flowers begin to wilt and wither. There's a splintering sound, followed by a thunderous, deafening *crack*.

When I open my eyes Elva is standing over me holding a breakfast tray, concern creasing her face. That's when the pain hits me, in my wrist, my ribs, my tailbone, and I realize that I'm all tangled up in bedsheets. I must have been thrashing around in my sleep.

I become aware of a lingering sense of irritation that is undoubtedly linked to Fox, to our conversation last night, to his answering my questions with statements that were somehow both direct and evasive. Elaith was right. He was confusingly charming. Vexatiously pleasant. Maddeningly beautiful. I find him infuriating.

Elva helps me into a sitting position. We haven't really spoken since that conversation on the balcony. I remember how tentative she was about accepting the food I offered her, the way she held the bread up to her nose and inhaled it, as if hardly daring to believe it was real. It's the memory of this that prompts me to invite her to join me for breakfast again.

She perches nervously on the end of my bed as though it might burst into flames. I spoon some oats into my mouth with my good arm then push the tray towards her.

'How old were you when you were . . . when you came here?' I can't bring myself to say *taken* or any other word that implies what we both know to be true.

When she speaks, her voice is little more than a whisper. 'Ten.'

Ten. My heart clenches at the thought.

It's been more than half a century since the War of the Empires, since Ostacre triumphed over the Otherlands and defeated the Magi. Grandmother doesn't like to talk about it. She says some things are best left in the past. Only it's not in the past, not really. For Elva, and those like her, it's ongoing. Endless. I wonder just how many children have been enslaved over the years, made prisoners of a war they never started.

It was a brutal war, the kind that leaves a stain on the pages of a history book.

When the Maker and the First Etheri claimed Ostacre for their own, they lived in peace with the Magi, who were once nomadic and could be found scattered across the world. Yet over time, tensions began to grow, with the Magi's powers being deemed unnatural, even wicked, and so the Magi, tired of not having a land of their own, retreated to a distant group of islands, which were henceforth known as the Otherlands.

Centuries later, the rulers of the Otherlands came together, and seven isles united to reclaim Ostacre from the Etheri. They sent their battleships across the Second Sea, and the War of the Empires began. It lasted a year and a day, but ultimately Ostacre triumphed, with the four High Generals leading their armies to victory.

Then the unexplainable happened. When the Magi lost the war, they lost their magic.

Some say their Gods abandoned them, that it was punishment for their defeat. Others believe that fighting the Etheri over such a long stretch of time weakened them until their powers were entirely depleted.

It's a mystery. A question that has gone unanswered for over fifty years.

I've read about the Magi more times than I can count. About those who could get you to spill your darkest thoughts using their voice alone. Those who could plant visions in your head that ate away at your subconscious until you went mad. Those with the power to manipulate the body and the senses, who could blind and maim and curdle blood. Those who shared a deep, telepathic connection with animals, or could take the form of anyone or anything they chose. Even those with the power to communicate with the dead.

But without their magic, the Magi were defenceless and the Otherlands fell. Their people, once deadly and dangerous, are now nothing but Fidra, forced to pay for the crimes of their forebears. Though not with jewels or oil or spices. No, the Otherlands provide something far more valuable. Slaves. Or as we call them – serfs.

Being from Obsidia, the Land of Eternal Night, Elva's ancestors were once Shadow Magi. They wielded darkness, ruled over the dusk.

She's sipping tea, not looking at me.

I clear my throat. 'What was it like?' I ask quietly. 'Obsidia?'

Elva goes still, then carefully places her cup back down on the tray. I'm convinced I've thrown away what little of her trust I've managed to earn, but then she finally whispers, '*Beautiful*.' Then she shuts her amber eyes tight.

I fall silent, thinking about Elva being ripped away from her family, a child shackled and put on board a ship bound for the land that conquered her own, sailing towards a future without freedom, emptier than the Rift, darker than the midnight skies of her homeland.

Tonight the emperor is throwing a ball in his brother's honour, so in true Ventalla fashion, the ballroom is filled with feathers. They're everywhere – adorning dresses and doublets, handed out as favours, floating around the ceiling, and fluttering around the dance floor, swept up on the breeze created by the twirling ring of dancers. I myself sport a large peacock feather in my hair. Spinner gave Flint one too, but he's mostly just been using it to tickle her. Sheen stands a little off to the side, watching them with a distinctly unamused expression.

Most of the Crowned Council are dancing. The emperor dances with Aunt Yvainne, though he can't seem to take his eyes off Kestrel Calloway, who looks radiant in a feathered gown complete with a pair of falcon wings. I spot Ember too, wearing her usual shade of burnt orange, spinning smugly around the floor with Hal. I experience a brief stab of jealousy just as a sudden hush falls over the room.

I turn my head to see the Earth Cleaver striding through the doors. He removes a hand from his pocket and holds it out expectantly, and a serf rushes over to him with a tray. Fox takes a single sip of wine, then tosses the glass over his shoulder. I flinch as it shatters, shards skittering across the golden floor. The courtiers nearest to him have backed away, some of them even bowing their heads as he passes by. His green eyes come to rest on me, glittering with amusement, and I hear an echo of his words from the night before.

Been smashing many glasses lately, Storm Weaver?

Heat prickles up my neck. Why is he taunting me? And why must he call me that, as though it were a badge of honour?

He himself has many names. Maybe even more than me. But ever since my conversation with Elva this morning, there's one I can't seem to ignore.

Prince of Slavers.

As if he wasn't already utterly irredeemable.

'Gods, he's gorgeous,' says Elaith with a sigh.

'Seriously, Elaith, I think you've got a problem,' Kai tells her.

Elaith is unfazed. 'Oh, I love this one!' she exclaims as the musicians begin playing the fast-paced music of the Firelands. Handing me her glass of champagne, she tosses her hair over her shoulder and yanks Flint through the crowd and on to the dance floor.

With them gone, and Kai now deep in conversation with Spinner, I am left standing alone as Fjord sidles over to me, a cruel smile splitting apart his face.

'So,' he says, his nose just inches from mine, 'I believe congratulations are in order.'

I say nothing, desperately hoping for someone to come to my aid.

'Tell me, Blaze, because I'm curious – how did you do it?'

I stare at him. 'What do you mean?'

'Oh, I don't know. Maybe how you managed to blag your way through the first trial. Or how you managed to trick the Council into believing that *you*, of all people, are worthier of the Aquatori throne than I am.'

I take a step back, swallowing my indignation.

'Or *maybe*,' Fjord continues, taking a step forward, 'it wasn't the Council you tricked. Maybe it was someone else, someone with the power to influence such decisions. Someone you've made it your mission to become close to ever since you arrived here.'

I frown. But before I can ask who he means, Hal's eyes find mine from across the dance floor. He smiles, almost shyly, ignoring my cousin as she prattles into his ear.

Fjord watches this exchange. 'Touching,' he says. 'Though I must admit, I underestimated you, Blaze. It shows real resourcefulness on your part, selling yourself like this, using what meagre advantages you have to win the prince's favour. After all,' he continues, gesturing to my glowing brandmark, 'it seems to be working.'

A familiar coldness begins to spread through my chest at his insinuation.

'I had you down as many things,' says Fjord, not bothering to lower his voice. 'A murderer, a changeling, a Gods' damned little freak.' He pauses, his eyes travelling slowly down the length of my body and back up again. 'But I never had you down as a *whore*.'

It happens so fast.

A blur of colour, a terrified scream, and Fjord is lifted clean off the ground. He hangs there, suspended high above the heads of the crowd, held in place by what seems to be thick green rope. As I look closer I realize it's not rope – it's *vines*, coiling themselves round Fjord's wrists like snakes, slithering along his arms and up his back.

All around the room voices are petering out, instruments falling silent. Dragging my gaze away from Fjord, who is dangling trussed-up and helpless in mid-air, I see that a small clearing has formed below him, and feel someone brush past me as they walk straight into the middle of it.

'It seems a pity to spoil such an occasion,' says the Earth Cleaver. 'Only it appears someone has forgotten their manners.'

My chest rises and falls rapidly, my breaths coming fast and shallow.

'What is the meaning of this?' Emperor Alvar demands, parting the crowd. I notice that he looks rather weary. Haggard, even. He makes to speak again, but Kestrel Calloway places a hand on his arm, silencing him.

Fox doesn't spare his father even a glance.

'Let me down,' hisses Fjord, his pale face pink with humiliation and terror.

'Would you like to repeat what you said?' Fox's voice is unwaveringly pleasant.

Fjord swallows hard, the vines undulating as they wrap themselves tighter and tighter round him. 'I didn't say anything.'

Fox shakes his head fondly. 'Oh, but that's simply not true, is it?' he says in a tone one might use to admonish a small child. 'You see, I overheard you. And I would like to see if you're brave enough to say it again, for all to hear.'

I am rooted to the spot as if bound by vines myself. Fjord struggles against his restraints, but they hold fast. His eyes flit between the Earth Cleaver and me, confusion furrowing his brow, which is already damp with sweat.

When he speaks, his voice is stretched taut. 'I. Didn't. Say. *Anything.*'

Fox smiles up at him. 'That's the wrong answer, I'm afraid.' He glances around at the stunned crowd. 'What do you think, shall we teach him a lesson?'

The Etheri gaze back at him, horrified, exhilarated.

'Let's see,' Fox continues, his brandmark glowing brightly on the back of his hand as he raises it. 'Why don't we start by washing your filthy mouth out?'

I gasp as a vine disentangles itself from the others and shoots into Fjord's open mouth. His eyes bulge and he begins to choke, turning his head this way and that, staring wildly at the crowd of onlookers. No one moves to help him. No one dares. They just watch, utterly transfixed.

There's a kind of sickening intoxication to the fear Fox inspires. I can't seem to look away, no matter how hard I try.

He waits until Fjord is seconds away from asphyxiation before deeming himself satisfied. The vine halfway down

Fjord's throat grows limp, and he coughs and splutters, his entire body heaving. Then he vomits all down himself.

Fox snaps his fingers and the rest of the vines release Fjord, who falls ten feet to the ground, landing in the contents of his own stomach. He tries to stand, but loses his balance and goes crashing down once more, letting out a low groan of pain.

The crowd are whispering. Some are sniggering. A couple of Aquatori courtiers move forward, pulling Fjord up and supporting him between them.

Fox isn't paying attention. His eyes are fixed only on me, and it burns, the intensity of his gaze. It burns and keeps burning, long after he turns away.

'You might want to clean that up,' he says to no one in particular, gesturing to the pool of vomit. 'We wouldn't want anyone to slip.'

24

My heart beats loudly in my ears as I hasten from the room, pushing my way through a golden sea of whispers. I don't stop, not even when I've put three floors between myself and the Earth Cleaver, walking without direction, trying desperately to come up with an answer to the question that pummels at me relentlessly.

Why?

Why would he do that? What possible reason did he have to come to my defence? We're not friends. We're not anything.

'Blaze!'

I turn to find Hal striding towards me. At the sight of him, the tension in my chest eases, just a fraction.

'I saw you leave,' he says, as he draws level. 'Are you all right?'

'I'm fine,' I lie, willing my hands to stop trembling.

'Fjord's been taken to the medical wing,' he tells me. 'Though I think it's his pride that's hurting more than anything. You were speaking to him, right before all the commotion. Do you know what it is he said that got Fox so riled?'

My heart jolts furiously at the memory of Fjord's words,

at his accusation that I have been offering myself to the prince in exchange for my place in the Choosing.

'No.' I shake my head. 'I don't.'

Hal nods, torchlight glancing off his face. There isn't much of a resemblance between him and Fox. Hal is a Castellion through and through, a mirror image of the Maker – his frame lean, his skin porcelain, his eyes a deep raven black. Fox, on the other hand, has his mother's eyes, and his skin is golden, his build more athletic. And while they both have the same dark hair, Hal's is forever sleek and neat, and Fox's is longer and permanently untidy.

I wonder when the dislike between them began, or whether it's always been there, growing worse with every passing day, like a festering wound.

Hal sighs. 'Knowing Fox, he was probably just looking for a fight. He likes to make a spectacle out of it. A show of his strength. It's utterly deplorable, but hardly out of character. You'd do well to steer clear of him entirely.'

'Yes,' I agree, trying not to think about the way Fox had smiled as that vine slithered down Fjord's throat.

Tension ripples across Hal's clenched jaw, and I get the feeling it's not just his half-brother who's plaguing him.

'Was there anything else?' I ask tentatively.

There's a long pause, during which Hal seems to deflate. He glances around, as if making sure we're alone, then, taking my hand, he pulls me through a nearby door and into complete darkness. I tense up reflexively, bewildered. Moments later an orb of light materializes in the prince's palm and floats gently upward, illuminating our surroundings. We're standing in what appears to be a broom cupboard. It smells strongly of polish, and is so cramped that Hal's head almost brushes against the ceiling.

'I didn't want to be overheard,' he says.

A spark of unease. My gaze snags on the dark circles beneath his eyes, the way he keeps flexing his hands, as if he's not aware he's doing it.

'All right,' I say, shifting slightly as something digs into my back. 'I'm all ears.'

'I've spoken with my father. That is, if you could call our exchange a conversation,' he says, grimacing. 'It is his view and the view of the Imperial advisers that . . .' He trails off, clearing his throat. 'After I'm crowned emperor, it has been decided that I must marry.'

My stomach curls in on itself. Of all the things I expected him to say, it wasn't this.

'An Imperial marriage is first and foremost a political alliance,' Hal continues, his voice strained. 'It is a widely observed tradition that a bride be selected from a neighbouring kingdom, whether to open up trade routes or simply to ensure peace between the two lands.'

I think of the emperor, about how he could never have married Kestrel Calloway, a Terrathian commoner with a hastily assigned title, how he was forced instead to marry Goneril, a Vosti princess, and, in doing so, sealed our alliance with Vost, the kingdom with which we trade gold for expensive fabric and materials.

The already tiny broom cupboard seems to shrink around me.

'I was delusional to think for even one second that I might be allowed to choose my own bride,' Hal says bitterly.

He looks as though he's trying to hold himself together. I fear that if I reach out and touch him, he might fall to pieces.

'And does your father . . . does he have someone in mind?'

Hal takes a long, deep breath. 'I am to marry Princess Mirade of Thaven.'

Thaven. The land of jewels and precious metals.

'An emissary is being sent to draw up a marriage treaty. Upon its completion, our betrothal will be announced before the courts.'

I taste blood and realize that I've been biting the inside of my cheek.

It's stupid, really. I'm not a fool. I always knew, deep down, that nothing could ever happen between us. Nothing serious, nothing binding. He's the prince, after all. Soon to be the emperor. And I am the most hated girl in all the realm.

'Have you ever met her?' I ask quietly. 'The princess?'

For some reason my lips don't want to form her name.

'Once or twice. Our fathers are old friends. She's nice enough. But she's not . . .' He swallows. 'She's not my *choice*. I . . . I don't have a choice, Blaze.'

My fingers trace the scar on the back of my hand.

'Do you know what my father said to me?' Hal's tone is infused with a venom that does not suit him. 'He said that as soon as I get an heir out of her, I can do as I want. As if I would ever do what he did to my mother, discarding her like she was nothing and letting that *woman* parade around court as if she were his wife.'

I think about the way the emperor looks at Kestrel – like she is the only person in the room, like she is the only beautiful thing left in this world.

'And it's . . . it's decided?' The words are thick and clumsy in my mouth.

'I keep trying to come up with ways to get out of it, but there's nothing,' says Hal. 'Not unless I want to jeopardize an extremely powerful alliance and put the entire empire at risk before I even take the throne.'

'I understand,' I tell him. I don't, not really, but it's just something people say.

'The only thing left for me to do is accept my fate. But I just *can't*. I can't accept it.' He steps closer to me, dark eyes pinning me to the spot. 'It kills me, Blaze,' he says. 'Knowing I can't have the one that I want. It kills me more and more every day.'

My breathing is uneven. Elaith's words echo in my head. *I've never met anyone who guards their heart like Hal.*

But what is any of this, if not letting his guard down? What is he doing at this moment, if not speaking from the heart?

And what of my heart? It feels bruised, and maybe a little foolish, though it still leaps when Hal pulls me closer, his cool hands wrapping themselves round my waist.

The orb of light above us seems to grow brighter, like a miniature sun. There is safety in sunlight. Warmth and certainty. And beauty so bright it blinds.

I look at Hal, at the scar below his eye, the shadows lingering in the planes of his cheekbones. He looks back at me, his gaze darkening with despair and something deeper, almost devouring.

He hesitates, as though wrestling against it.

And then he kisses me.

Having spent the last seventeen years locked away, it will come as no surprise that I have never been kissed before. The sensation is entirely new to me. I didn't think I'd know what to do, but my lips move instinctively, parting for his.

The kiss is slow, and achingly gentle. One of his hands glides up my back and into my hair, while the other bunches in the silk of my dress, just above my hip. My eyes have fluttered shut, my body moulding itself to his, my stomach flipping over with every touch, every press and slide of his mouth. My arms wind round his neck, reeling him closer.

The whole world seems to go quiet.

For a moment, nothing else matters. No one else exists.

But then Hal draws back sharply, startling me. I open my eyes to find his expression guilty.

'I shouldn't have done that,' is all he says.

I stand there in the darkness long after he leaves, leaning heavily against the door. Slowly, I trace a finger across my lips, while something warm stirs inside my chest, mingled with a sweet kind of pain I never knew existed.

25

For the next week, the news of Hal's secret betrothal looms over me.

That, and the kiss. I relive it over and over. The soft pressure of his lips, the scent of lemons on his skin.

I don't know what to make of it. I don't know where we stand now. He's spent most of this week shut away inside the Council Chambers with an army of Imperial advisers, yet despite this, and the fresh bunches of golden roses waiting for me in my rooms each day after I return from training, I can't quite shake the feeling that he's avoiding me. The thought fills me with dread. Because I want him to seek me out, just as he always has, time and time before. I want him to want me the same way I think I'm starting to want him.

Was this his way of breaking things off? A goodbye of sorts? A first kiss, and a last. Only, the thing is, it didn't feel like an ending.

Tonight, as Elva helps me dress, I rub my thumb over the cool glass surface of the nightlight, pretending to listen to Spinner's evaluation of the twelve remaining Heirs. It's only when she waves a hand in front of my face that I realize she's waiting on a response.

I blink at her. 'What?'

'Wake *up*, Blaze. *Flint*. Did he mention me at all today?' She examines her gold-silk gloves as though she isn't waiting for my answer with bated breath.

'I haven't seen him much,' I admit. 'Oh, but yesterday he said something about you saying something about . . .' I narrow my eyes, trying to remember.

Spinner hands me a set of pearl earrings, shaking her head in disbelief. 'You really are *awful* at this sort of stuff. You know that, right?'

'Harsh,' I tell her. 'I haven't exactly had a lot of practice. Besides, *you're* the Eye. If my brother is of that much interest to you, I'd have thought you'd have at least one of your three trained on him at all times.'

Spinner just tuts, and twirls her finger for me to spin.

Prince Hal doesn't eat with the Heirs this evening. Instead he sits on a golden throne set on the dais above, poker-straight and silent next to the emperor, who appears even more haggard than before. Both he and Hal have the same dark circles under their eyes, which are only accentuated by the paleness of their skin. I wonder if the pressure of what's to come is making them ill. For Hal, the burden of taking on the role of emperor. For his father, the idea of leaving it behind.

The prince's gaze is trained on our table, only not on me. It rests on the boy sitting at its head, who seems to have no end of adoring sycophants desperate for his attention. Perhaps Hal dining with the Council is a way of sending the Earth Cleaver a message, reminding him, reminding everyone, that while they may share blood, *he* is the prince, a trueborn Castellion.

Whether or not Fox has noticed his brother's attempt to pull rank, he doesn't seem to care. He's leaning back in his chair, sipping wine and smirking at something one of the Ventalla Heirs is whispering in his ear.

The image of Fjord tangled in a web of vines slips unbidden into my consciousness, and I look quickly down at my hands. I run my fingers over my glowing brandmark, reminded of the orb of light Hal had conjured in the broom cupboard, so similar to those that float gently around the Golden Library, where I've taken to spending most evenings. I was apprehensive about returning after my late-night run-in with the Earth Cleaver, and yet my armchair has remained steadfastly empty, with no sign of either Fox or that strange old man. I want to find the old man, to find out how he knows about my gifts being Melded, and to discover whatever he thinks he knows about the art of wave carving, especially since I haven't been able to carve so much as a ripple. And mastering this skill would not only please River and wipe the smirk off Marina's face but might also prove useful in the second trial, which, terrifyingly, is just two weeks away. Though, of course, to do that I first have to determine what my anchor is, which so far is not proving to be an easy task.

The sight of Hal makes my chest ache, and I find I don't have much of an appetite. I'm just about to slink off to bed when I notice Flint's eyes widening in surprise at something behind me. Before I can turn round, somebody covers my own eyes with their hands. Their very small hands. Small and slightly sticky with . . . chocolate.

'Renly!' I exclaim, as my little brother throws his arms round my neck.

Even over the din, I can hear the rap of her stick.

'Maker almighty, Blaze, I tell you I did not know a moment's peace until I agreed to bring him here to see you.' Grandmother pats Renly's tangle of curls. 'You have your sister's stubbornness and your brother's powers of persuasion, don't you, little one?'

Renly giggles while the rest of the Heirs bow their heads respectfully, even Fox. Grandmother kisses Flint and me before departing for the Ignitia table.

Renly clambers up beside me, touching my cheek. 'I missed you.'

I feel it again, that warmth inside my chest, a ball of light, a seed that begins to spread and grow, radiating outwards.

What happens next is unexpected and instantaneous.

Up and down the table the contents of every glass leap into the air, sloshing over half-eaten plates of food, splashing dresses and doublets with water and wine. Some of the Heirs shriek in surprise, jumping up from their seats. Ember is screeching, and a couple of panic-stricken serfs dart over to try in vain to mop up the crimson stain on her gown. Elaith rounds on Kai and Marina, clearly unable to decide which of them is responsible. Zeph is blinking champagne out of his eyes, and Flint, who was midway through taking a swig of wine, is now loudly attempting to eject a large quantity of the stuff from his nose.

'Again!' cries Renly.

I take my napkin and wipe his face clean, wondering if anyone can hear how loudly my heart is pounding.

Flint is now holding on to the back of Elaith's dress in an effort to stop her from marching over to Marina, who she's clearly singled out to be the culprit. But it wasn't her. Nor was it Kai. It was me. I know it was.

Ever since my mother died, I'd forgotten what it was to be truly happy. I wasn't miserable all the time, of course. Some days were better than others. But here, at the Golden Palace, I was reminded what it felt like – when I was with my friends, when I was with Hal. And just now, being reunited with my little brother after spending so long apart, a wave of happiness rose up and enveloped me whole.

So that's my anchor to waves.

Happiness.

I feel giddy, as if I might laugh out loud, but this seems like a bad idea given the circumstances, so I attempt to mirror the expressions on the faces of the other Heirs. Shock, annoyance, amusement, an amalgamation of all three. But it's of little consequence as everybody seems too busy squabbling to pay any attention to me.

Well, not everybody.

The Earth Cleaver is staring right at me, smiling. I try to look as innocent as I can, but either it doesn't work or those green eyes of his have somehow managed to pierce through my own and into my head, where he can read my every thought.

His dark hair gleams wet with wine, blood-red droplets forming at the ends of each strand. One falls and rolls down his cheek like a tear towards his lips. His gaze never leaving mine, I watch as he slowly opens his mouth and catches it on his tongue.

26

I wake with a start, my dream receding, but the tension soon drains out of me as I catch sight of Renly sleeping peacefully at my side. Quietly, so as not to wake him, I slide out of bed and fill my wash bowl, then take it out on to the balcony. I hold a hand over the still water and reach inwards for that happiness that glows warm inside my chest. A small, perfectly formed wave rears up, curves over and then curls in on itself. Closing my eyes, I switch my focus, grasping hold of a different emotion. Soon enough, the silent morning is filled with the crackling hiss of water freezing. And just for good measure, just because I can, I call the rain, letting it come splashing down around me, soaking my hair and nightgown, melting the ice.

'Blaze?' Renly's eyes are wide with surprise.

'Hello, you,' I say, cutting off the shower.

He sits down beside me, not seeming to care that the balcony is all wet. 'Grandmother said that you'd found your gifts. That you know how to use them now.'

I nod.

Renly traces his finger through a puddle of water. 'Do you . . . do you think that I'll ever find mine?'

My heart sputters. Of course Renly knows that he has no gift, at least not yet, but I've always tried to shield him from the fact that this is in any way unusual.

'Of course you will,' I say firmly.

Ren smiles. 'Then I hope my gift will be like yours.' He lowers his voice to a whisper. 'I don't like fire much.'

That makes me laugh. 'Me neither.'

As soon as I'm dressed in my training tunic, Spinner arrives to collect Renly.

'Only me,' she sing-songs as she comes skipping into the room. 'Chaperone and babysitter, at your service.'

Renly is fascinated by the swirling golden tattoos on her face and squeals with delight when she shows him the eye on the back of her neck.

'I think I'll take him for a walk first,' she says to me. 'Get some fresh air. Then I'll feed him. Then maybe a nap? Or perhaps I should give him a bath?'

'He's not a dog, Spinner,' I call over my shoulder before heading out of the door.

That evening, after playing several rounds of cards with Flint and Elaith, in which we all let Renly win every time, I leave my little brother fast asleep in my rooms with Elva watching over him, and walk the familiar route to the Golden Library in search of a book about the Thavenian royal family, thinking that maybe I can find out more about this Princess Mirade. Only when I get there, I discover that my armchair is now, once again, occupied.

'Good evening, girl,' says the old man, not even bothering to look up from his book. 'How's the wave carving coming along?'

I swallow my stubbornness. 'Fine.'

'Figured out your anchor, then?'

'Apparently. About that – how do you know about Melding?'

The old man turns a page. 'I know everything.'

'Right,' I say flatly, sensing a dead end. 'Well, great chatting with you again, but I'd best be going now.'

'The Storm Weaver seeks a book.'

I raise an eyebrow. 'You can hardly put that down to your all-knowingness. I mean, we are in a library.'

He chuckles, closing the volume in his lap, which is entitled *Ancient Curses and How to Break Them*, and places it carefully on the table beside him. Only then does he glance in my direction. 'I have a story for you, girl. Would you like to hear it?'

'Not particularly.'

The old man smiles crookedly at me. 'The girl is a strange little creature. Cold. Closed. The girl needs to open her mind.'

'Does she?' I say. 'Well, maybe the old man needs to learn how to mind his own business.'

A wheezy laugh. 'The girl has spirit. I can certainly see why the emperor's son has taken a liking to her.'

'I'm going now,' I snap.

'*Sit down.*'

I almost topple over at the *authority* in the old man's voice. Not a request – an order. One I find myself obeying.

'There now,' he says, resuming his former tone. 'That's better.'

I try not to scowl.

The old man clears his throat with a dull rasp, and begins.

'There once lived three sisters who were some of the most powerful Magi ever to walk the earth. Round her neck each sister wore a talisman. It was from these talismans that the sisters drew their power.'

I tuck my feet up and settle back into the cushions. This could be a long night.

'Sifa, the first sister, had the power to see the past. She could scour the secrets of history, discover that which was once lost in time, ease the pain of mourners with memories of their loved ones. She saw all that once was, all that had come before.

'Seera, the second sister, had the power to see the future. She alone knew the outcome of every harvest, the winner of every battle, the path each soul would tread on their journey towards fate. She saw what lay ahead, fragments of what was to come.

'And then there was Syla, the third sister, the most powerful of them all. For her power *was* power. She had the power to take power. To return it. Wield it. Protect it. Possess it. Power belonged to her. It ran through her veins.'

The old man closes his eyes for a moment, as though lost in recollection.

'For many years Etheri and Magi maintained a tentative peace, until one day that peace was broken, never to be repaired. You know, of course, the events of which I speak?'

'The War of the Empires,' I say.

'Precisely. Yet with her gift of sight, Seera was able to see glimpses of this future before it came to pass, thus buying herself and her sisters time to flee.'

'And did they escape?' The question slips out, betraying my curiosity. I've spent years studying the Magi, and yet this is a story I've never heard before.

The old man shakes his head.

'So what happened? Were they killed?'

'Sifa and Seera met their ends, yes. But not before they cast one last enchantment. You remember the sisters' talismans?'

I nod.

'Well, these talismans were no ordinary Magi relics. They were crafted by a Magi Goddess, each one a small golden pendant shaped like an eye.'

A strange shiver runs through me. 'An eye?' I repeat.

'Yes,' he says. 'The Eye of the Past, the Eye of the Future, and the Eye of the Soul, which was the key to power itself. Terrified of what would happen if these precious talismans fell into the wrong hands, Sifa and Seera decided to hide them. Together they scattered the Eye of the Past and the Eye of the Future where they believed they would never be found.'

'And the third sister? What happened to her?'

'Syla was captured by the Etheri,' says the old man. 'She was taken to Ostacre and brought before Emperor Caius.'

Caius Castellion, Hal's – and, I suppose, Fox's – grandfather, is rarely seen at court. They say he's crippled with age, muddled and confused, unable even to tell his two sons apart.

'Did he execute her?' I ask.

Thousands of Magi were executed after the war. As for those permitted to live, they returned home to the Otherlands, powerless and impoverished, forced to await the slave ships that arrived every few years to take their children.

I think of Elva, and my chest tightens.

'No, Syla was not executed.'

I try to sound indifferent. 'Then what became of her?'

'She lived out her days as a servant of the Etheri.'

I frown. 'I don't understand. You said she was the most powerful of them all. Surely she could have just killed the emperor. Killed everybody. Escaped.'

The old man angles his head. 'Is that what you would do, girl?'

I shrug, suddenly self-conscious.

A ghost of a smile tugs at his pale lips. 'Yet what if I told you that your life cost the life of someone you loved. Someone . . . breakable. Tell me, what would you do then?'

'But Sifa and Seera were killed,' I say slowly.

'This is a tale of the three sisters, yet what if I told you there happened to be a fourth,' says the old man. 'And in some ways she proved to be the most important of all. Senna was young, only a child, sweet and pure and defenceless. A little girl whom Syla loved more than anyone in this world. A sister whom she would do *anything* to protect.'

I shake my head. 'That's sickening.'

'Life is sickening, Storm Weaver. But it is always preferable to death.'

I swallow. 'So they took her? The fourth sister? They kept her as a bargaining chip, as *bait*, so that Syla would be their puppet?'

He claps his hands gleefully. 'Oh, very good.'

My heart thuds painfully. 'And did they hurt her? The little girl?'

'As long as Syla did the emperor's bidding, Senna was unharmed. She was given a room, here in the palace. Naturally, her identity was kept under wraps, but she had a nursemaid and was treated with kindness. She was even allowed to visit her sister.'

'Visit her where?'

'Where do you think, girl? Syla was kept where all criminals are kept. The dungeons. Though of course, not many prisoners of war can boast a cell made from purest crystal.'

A memory stirs – something I'd read before. 'Crystal weakens Magi, doesn't it?'

'That is correct.'

'So what did they do to her? To Syla?'

The old man's gaze shackles me to the spot. 'They used her. After all, what greater weapon could there be than power itself?'

There's a long, drawn-out silence in which I wait for my heart rate to return to normal. It was foolish, humouring him like this. The old man is clearly senile. That, or he's playing a game with me. Either way, I've grown tired of his company.

I get to my feet. 'That was quite the story.'

'It was indeed, and all the best stories are true.'

I roll my eyes. The tale is undoubtedly a fabrication. Does he really expect me to believe that such talismans existed, or that the former emperor had – what? A *pet Mage*? It's perfectly ridiculous. For starters, how could such things possibly be kept secret, and not just then, but for all these years since? It doesn't make any sense.

I nod once at the old man, brisk and dismissive. 'Goodnight.'

But as I turn on my heel and walk away, I hear Grandmother's words in my head, the warning she gave us on the morning of the eclipse.

Old magic still lurks within the Golden Palace.

The old man chuckles to himself.

'Sweet dreams,' he calls as I round the corner.

PART II

The Eyes

27

I walk across a desert plain, the hot sand undulating beneath my feet. Something gold glimmers up ahead. I can feel it, a second heartbeat thrumming with untold power. It urges me onwards, reeling me in until I'm standing right in front of it. I see it clearly now. And it sees me. For lying at my feet is a beautiful golden eye.

Blaze.

If I dared, I could reach out and touch it.

I sit bolt upright, heart thundering. I'm disorientated at first, then last night comes flooding back to me. The old man, the story, the sisters, the Eyes.

The Eyes.

I push back the sheets and draw my knees up to my chest. Beside me, Renly gives a little grunt of protest.

That glimmer of gold in my dream – was it an Eye all along? Or have the old man's words just got into my head? I screw up my face, trying to make sense of it.

As my breathing slows, logic returns. This is stupid. It was only a dream. They don't mean anything. And why should I take the word of a senile old man? No doubt he would have rattled off that very same tale to anyone who would listen.

I imagine he has nothing better to do. Besides, I have more important things to worry about – like the second trial, which is in only thirteen days' time.

Just as before, the Heirs have been given no idea of what to expect. But now, with more training and three water gifts under my belt, at least if I lose, it'll be with some dignity. And the Heirs are expected to attend the Binding Ceremony, meaning I can stay here, at the palace, close to Flint, to my friends, to Hal.

'Blaze?' Renly gives a yawn.

I look down at him, soothed by his presence. 'Yes?'

'I'm hungry.'

'You're always hungry,' I say, tickling him.

An hour later, as I walk across the palace grounds towards the Keep, I realize something. Tomorrow is Renly's Name Day. I've been so preoccupied lately that I almost forgot.

In our family, Name Days are not always cause for celebration. Just as mine marks the anniversary of the storm, the day Renly came into the world was also the day our mother left it. Being Ignitia, my mother was cremated, which meant that her soul could be returned to the Fire Goddess, Vesta. Her ashes are enclosed within a golden urn that stands before a tombstone in the gloomy crypt beneath Harglade Hall, and that is where Grandmother usually spends this day, sitting by candlelight, lost in a haze of grief. Flint is often away at court, and I imagine our father is even more unreachable than usual. Renly doesn't even remember him. Grandmother came for us when he was but a few months old, after our father had shown no sign of emerging from his seemingly endless state of suffering, and we have lived with her at Harglade Hall ever since. Because Ren never knew him like Flint and I did, I think he's come to accept our father's absence. His abandonment.

But I haven't.

It wasn't Renly's fault that our mother lost too much blood giving birth to him. It wasn't his fault that she died, ripping an irreparable hole in our lives forever. He was only a baby, after all. Just like I was when I summoned that storm.

Because it is a day of such sadness, I try to make it a happy one for Renly, and I always make sure to get him a present. Or rather, I send an attendant out to the markets for one, what with being forbidden to go myself. But with a full day of training ahead of me, that leaves only this evening to find the perfect gift for him.

I spend the day carving wave after wave upon the surface of the pool, and experimenting with different intensities of rain, from drizzles to downpours. After lunch I partner with Kai to work on our ice making. River watches us a while, advising us here, instructing us there, until by the end of the training session I can freeze a dew-soaked leaf from twenty yards. I even manage to catch a faint whispering sound dancing across the surface of the pool.

Satisfied, I walk back to the palace with Flint, who promises to leave tonight's festivities early to help me find a present for Renly.

Back in my rooms, I take a long bath, catching sight of myself in the mirror before pulling on a robe. My body is still decorated with yellowing bruises, but my ankle, ribs, wrist and tailbone are now almost entirely healed. I'll be *as*

good as new in no time, as the chirpy physician keeps telling me. I'm glad. I'm sick of feeling like an invalid.

Renly soon arrives back with a haggard-looking Spinner. We eat dinner on the floor like a picnic, and Renly soon falls asleep with his head in my lap. I coax him into bed, then settle myself in a chair with a book to wait for Flint.

Only Flint doesn't appear.

One, two, three hours pass, and still he doesn't come.

He can't have forgotten, I think, turning Hal's nightlight over and over in my hands. He promised.

The clocks are just about to strike midnight when there's a knock at my door and Elaith appears, Zephyr and Sheen behind her, supporting a very drunk Flint between them.

Flint squints at me, then grins vacantly. 'There you are!'

'Here I am,' I say grimly, taking in the rips in his doublet and the bruise blooming on his jaw. 'What happened?'

'He drank the palace wine cellars dry and then proceeded to fall down four flights of stairs,' Elaith informs me.

'It's not easy being this graceful,' Flint slurs as Zeph and Sheen deposit him, sprawling, into a chair.

'And what happened to finding a present for Renly?' I demand.

'What?' Flint asks the vase of roses on the table next to him.

I pour a glass of water and hold it up to his mouth. 'Drink,' I order him. 'Now.'

As he slurps the water, I turn to Zeph and Elaith. 'Thank you.'

'Don't thank us,' says Zeph, massaging his neck. 'It was Sheen who found him.'

I turn to look at Sheen lingering by the door and nod my thanks, but his violet eyes are fixed unblinkingly on my brother.

'Look, Blaze!' Flint calls merrily. 'The room, it's spinning!' He laughs and then stops abruptly, a hand on his stomach. 'Oh no,' he says thickly.

As quick as a flash, Sheen is beside him, handing me a bunch of dripping golden roses, holding the vase underneath Flint's chin, and wearing a vaguely disgusted expression as my brother proceeds to vomit loudly into it. Zeph wrinkles his nose.

'This is the way he usually gets through it,' Elaith says quietly. 'I should have stopped him before it had gone too far. I'd forgotten what tomorrow is. I'm sorry.'

Tomorrow. The anniversary of our mother's death.

I look at Flint, who's now lolling sideways in his chair, eyes half closed. So this is what he does each year to numb the pain – drinks himself into oblivion.

My brother is not someone I associate with hurt. He's too warm, too cheerful, too bright to be blue. But clearly, I misjudged him. Flint does hurt, I realize. It's just that people wear their hurt differently. Nobody hurts the same.

'Come on,' I say to him, my voice gentle. 'Time for bed.'

I urge the others to return to the party, but Sheen refuses to go with them. I'm grateful because Flint seems unable to stand without falling over. Together we manage to get him into the bathing room, where we wash his face and strip him down to his underclothes. Then we tuck him into bed next to Renly.

I shut the door to my bedchamber and thank Sheen for his help.

'I'm his chaperone.' That's all he says. Then he leaves.

For a moment I find myself wondering if maybe he's not quite as sour as Flint believes. The gentleness with which Sheen sponged my brother's face clean didn't seem like the behaviour of someone who disliked him. In fact, it seemed like quite the opposite.

Suddenly bone-tired, I sink down into the chair Flint was sitting in, right next to the vaseful of vomit. I take a deep breath then force myself to stand.

My first thought for a gift is a book, one with lots of pictures. Renly likes it when I read to him. But that's no good, since I've decided to avoid the library. I'm in no mood for another of the old man's peculiar stories.

I rack my brain.

Finally, I decide to try the kitchens, thinking that maybe I could swipe a cake, chocolate preferably, and decorate it.

The palace is filled with the muffled sound of music rising up from a few floors below, and I meet no one as I make my way along the empty hallways. There's just one problem – I have no idea where the kitchens are. And I dismissed Elva hours ago, so she's not around to ask. I'm busy contemplating whether to track down another serf when I round the next corner – and crash straight into the Earth Cleaver.

I yelp in pain and surprise, and he holds out an arm to steady me.

'Easy. You don't need any more injuries.'

'Sorry,' I snap.

'You sound it,' he tells me.

I scowl, which makes him smile. He's dressed in a pale-green shirt several shades lighter than his eyes, and which is only half tucked into a pair of leather breeches slung indecently low on his hips. I've noticed that Fox often appears distinctly unkempt, as though he's just ridden for miles or been in some kind of fight.

I clear my throat. 'Why aren't you at the party?'

He leans against the wall. 'Perhaps my mind was elsewhere. Perhaps I'm not so easily entertained. And you, Storm Weaver? Why aren't *you* at the party?'

'I have things to do,' I say tersely, pushing past him.

He blocks my path. 'Anything I can help with?'

I sidestep round him. 'I doubt it.'

He cuts me off once again. 'Try me.'

I stare at him in bewilderment, heart thumping. What is his game here? I can no more understand his motive now than when he came to my aid with Fjord. But he seems unwilling to take no for an answer, and I'm hardly going to turn and run.

'Fine. If you must know, I'm looking for a Name Day present. So unless you somehow have the perfect gift for my seven-year-old brother, no, you can't help me.'

His lazy smile widens. 'What if I told you I did?'

I raise an eyebrow. 'Is that so? How convenient. And what, exactly, is this gift you have in mind?'

He grins, straightens up and starts sauntering off down the corridor. I stare after him, half irritated, half intrigued.

'Well, aren't you coming?' he calls.

I hesitate. Why should I believe a single word he says? This is the Earth Cleaver, after all. The boy they call destruction itself. He can't be trusted. Not by me, not by anyone. I'd be a fool to follow him. I don't have to follow him. I don't *want* to follow him.

Fox only smirks. 'Scared, Storm Weaver?'

Yes.

'No,' I mutter, and follow him.

28

We walk in silence through golden hallways. The silence soon becomes decidedly competitive – amused on his end, stubborn on mine. He seems to want me to be the one to break it, but I stand my ground, refusing to give him the satisfaction.

I find myself stealing glances at him, my gaze grazing over his mud-stained boots, the rings on his fingers, the little gold hoop in his ear, the wicked-looking dagger at his hip. His hair appears even more tousled than usual tonight, as though someone had just been running their fingers through it. To my annoyance, the thought makes me blush.

Eventually he says, 'I enjoyed your little display the other night.'

I experience a brief moment of victory at him being the one to speak first. Then I narrow my eyes. 'What do you mean?'

He glances sideways at me. 'What is it with you and wine glasses?'

I bristle, remembering the way he'd watched me in the banquet hall, the crimson tear on his tongue, the smile that said *You can't fool me, but points for trying.*

'I don't know what you're talking about,' I say stiffly, which only makes him laugh.

'This way,' he says, leading me through an archway at the bottom of a long staircase.

Night air caresses my face, silken and cool. 'Where are we going?'

'To the stables,' Fox replies.

I frown. 'Why?'

'You'll see.'

'This gift you have in mind, it'd better not be a horse. It's not a horse, is it?'

'You ask a lot of questions, Storm Weaver.'

'What else am I supposed to do when you're so cryptic all the time?'

He smirks. 'Another question.'

'Seriously?'

'There you go again.'

I glower, clamping my mouth shut, ready to resume our game of silence, determined to hate whatever it is he's about to show me.

The palace stables are extensive and, like everything in this place, hewn from solid gold. Fox leads me past countless horses, golden thoroughbreds, charcoal-black ponies, even a number of silvery Threskan stallions belonging to King Balen. We soon come to a stall containing a velvety brown horse with a fine dark mane.

'This is Cedar,' he says.

I reach out a hand to stroke Cedar's muscular flank, feeling his strength ripple beneath my fingers. 'He's beautiful.'

'He is,' Fox agrees, as the horse nuzzles into him, nickering sleepily. 'But he's not why I brought you here. Why don't you have a look in that basket over there?'

So I do, and all my resolve to hate whatever I find inside crumbles on to the hay-strewn floor. For in the basket, sleeping close to their mother, are half a dozen kittens. I let out a sharp gasp of delight and the cat, a plump, smoky creature, opens one beady orange eye and fixes it on me suspiciously.

'Sorry,' I whisper.

The musty air in the stables is suddenly replaced by the scent of pine and fresh mint as Fox settles himself beside me.

'Pick one,' he says, nodding towards the kittens.

I blink at him. 'What?'

'Pick one,' he repeats. 'For your brother. I said I had the perfect gift for him, didn't I? Take any one you want. Take them all, if you'd like.'

I choke out a laugh. 'Really?'

'Really,' he says.

I swallow, my mind suddenly filled with the image of Fjord, strung up with vines, his face a picture of humiliation and terror.

'That night, at your uncle's ball . . .' I begin.

He leans back on his elbows. 'I remember.'

'Why . . . why did you . . .' *Defend me?* '. . . hurt Fjord like that?'

Fox considers this. 'That snivelling excuse for an Heir chose to ally himself with slander rather than concede his failure. He sought to tarnish you with his own shame.'

'That still doesn't explain why you intervened,' I say quietly.

He smiles, one side of his mouth tweaking upward before the other. 'If there's one thing I abhor, Storm Weaver, it's injustice.'

I furrow my brow, perplexed. How can he possibly mean that, given who he is? I wouldn't have thought a slaver could feel so strongly about injustice.

Fox watches me, unblinking.

I'm forced to break away from his gaze, charged as it is with an intensity that I don't understand, one that seems to burn right through my skin, brushing bone.

I turn back to the basket of kittens, some of which have started up a chorus of mewling as they scramble over one another. Gently, I disentangle a little grey one from the pile and scoop it up into my arms.

'Nice choice,' says Fox, who is now sitting with a pearly white kitten perched on his shoulder. 'What's her name?'

I shrug. 'Isn't that up to Renly?'

'Oh no,' he says. 'That one's yours. She's the same colour as your eyes.'

I don't know what to say to that. I don't know if I can accept this gift from the Earth Cleaver. It's too peculiar, too intimate. And besides, I didn't come here for myself. If this kitten should belong to anyone, it should belong to Ren.

Just then, as if it had heard me, the tiny white kitten climbs down Fox's arm and clambers up my leg.

'Hello,' I murmur as she curls up in my lap next to the other. Renly will *adore* her. I look up at Fox uncertainly. 'Thank you.'

He gives a small nod and reaches out to stroke the cat, which purrs at his touch.

'Is she yours?' I ask.

'Yes, but she wasn't always mine.'

'Oh?'

Fox runs his finger along the length of his golden chain, the pendant concealed beneath his shirt. 'She belonged to my sister,' he says eventually, in a voice like a door shutting. I can almost hear the bolt being slid across in the silence that follows.

His sister? A memory tugs at me. My mind was still clouded from painkiller at the time, but I remember her – the little girl with hair like autumn leaves who appeared in the Terrathian arena. That must have been his sister. But her name escapes me. I'm about to ask him what it was, but I'm stopped in my tracks by the expression on his face. It's one I recognize all too well, one I myself have worn for years.

Grief.

Fox stands abruptly, holding out a hand to help me to my feet. 'It's getting late.'

'It was already late,' I point out, handing him Renly's kitten.

We make our way back to the palace. Streams of courtiers are flowing merrily along the corridors. Many are too inebriated to notice us, but several Eyes watch us steadily until Fox grabs the back of my tunic and yanks me roughly through a concealed door in the wall.

'What are you doing?' I hiss. 'Where are we?'

'Serf tunnels,' he says, wrenching a flaming torch from a bracket. 'Best we remain out of sight. I don't want my brother thinking I'm after his girl.'

Heat floods my cheeks. 'I'm not – We aren't –'

But Fox is already striding ahead. Sometime later he comes to a stop. Light leaks into the tunnel as he shoulders open another door that, to my surprise, leads out into the Aquatori Wing. He hands me back Ren's kitten, which nestles into my arms beside its sister.

'How did you know?' I say, curiosity getting the better of me. 'At the feast, I mean. The waves, the wine. How did you know it was me? Nobody else did.'

Fox's eyes glitter green in the flickering light from the torch. 'I might be an Heir to the Terrathian throne, but I think you're forgetting I was raised an Eye,' he says. 'Where others look, I see. And I see you, Storm Weaver. I see all of you.'

His words prickle like thorns down the notches of my spine. I hate that I'm scared of him. I hate that he knows it.

'Wait,' I say quickly, as he turns to leave. 'Why?'

'Why what, O Queen of Questions?'

'Why did you help me?' I force myself to meet his gaze.

Fox is silent for a moment, as though weighing his response on a set of golden scales. One tips the balance. He smiles. 'Goodnight, Storm Weaver.'

I watch him disappear back down the tunnel before I slip quietly into my chambers, settling the kittens on a cushion and crawling into bed between my brothers. Flint is sleeping soundly on his side, mouth slightly open, his face peaceful.

Renly lies spreadeagled, his curls strewn over the pillow, his little fists clenching and unclenching in his sleep.

I think of Fox's sister, that poor dead girl, and shudder, not able to fathom the depths of such a pain.

That night, my dreams are filled with eyes. Some golden, some green.

29

I wake to squealing. Renly is hurtling about the room, a kitten in each hand, the expression on his face brighter than the sun.

Beside me, Flint groans loudly. 'What time is it?' he mutters, pulling the sheets up over his head.

Renly pulls them down again. 'Look, Flint! Look, Blaze! *Look!*'

Flint blinks groggily at the kittens as Renly plonks them on his chest.

'Happy Name Day, Ren,' I say, leaning over to hug him. 'See the little white one? She's yours.' I scoop up the grey kitten. 'And this one's mine.'

'What?' says Flint, bleary-eyed and outraged. 'Where's *my* cat?'

I fix him with a stern look. 'Darling brother, if the events of last night are anything to go by, you can barely look after yourself.'

I don't think the words have much of an impact, however, as Flint has already started snoring again. Still, I brush a stray curl from his forehead, all too aware that today is not just the day Renly was born, but also the day our mother died. They tend to overlap, beginnings and endings. Whether peaceful or painful, they always leave their mark.

'What are you going to name her?' I ask as Ren studies his kitten, holding her up close to his face.

'Milk,' he says decidedly.

I burst out laughing, because his answer is just too perfect, what with the frothy white moustache he currently has smeared above his upper lip. 'Milk,' I repeat, wiping his mouth with the sleeve of my nightgown. 'I love it. Milk it is.'

'What about yours?' Renly asks.

'I don't know what her name is yet. But I'm sure it'll come to me.'

Ren babbles happily away to Elva while she helps ready me for the day. She's just finishing braiding my hair when there's a knock at the door.

Prince Hal straightens up as I emerge from my bedchamber, Elva a silent shadow behind me. He looks effortlessly handsome in a fine burnt-gold doublet, a simple crown glinting atop his dark hair, which appears to be still damp from bathing.

A soft blush blooms across my cheeks, and I feel suddenly shy. I look at him, and all I can think about is that kiss. About whether he thinks about it.

Adopting a false air of normalcy, I force the memory of his lips on mine to the very back of my mind and sink into a curtsy. 'Hal.'

'Blaze.' He clears his throat. 'And this must be Renly,' he says as my little brother joins us, Milk snuffling quietly in his arms. 'I've heard a lot about you.'

Ren ducks his head and moves closer to me.

Hal points at the kitten. 'And what do we have here? A gift from your sister?'

I tense up, swallowing nervously, but Hal doesn't seem to notice.

Renly nods.

'Well, I'm not sure I can top that,' he admits. 'But what d'you say to another gift?' I watch in astonishment as he takes the crown off his own head and places it carefully on Ren's. 'There. Tell me, Renly, how does being prince for the day sound to you?'

My little brother's face floods with delight.

'That is, of course, if your sister has no objection?' Hal adds.

Renly turns to me, eyes shining. The crown is slightly too big for him, and slides further down one side of his forehead than the other. My heart swells.

'None,' I say, smiling.

'I take it this means I'm off the hook?' Spinner asks hopefully from the armchair.

I give her a look.

Hal winks at Renly before dipping into a graceful bow. 'Your Imperial Highness.'

My brother giggles, handing Milk to Elva before taking Hal's outstretched hand and following him from the room. Hal shoots me a grin over his shoulder before the two of them disappear out of the door.

It's very sweet of him. And incredibly thoughtful, which also happens to be entirely in character. Unlike some people, his generosity doesn't take me by surprise.

What would Hal say, I wonder, if he knew about my midnight trip to the stables?

I don't want my brother thinking I'm after his girl.

Am I Hal's girl? I'm not sure. I think I might want to be, but being and wanting are different things. What does it mean when someone pulls you into a broom cupboard, tells you they're betrothed to somebody else, then kisses you? And what does it mean when that someone's half-brother, who also happens to be the most dangerous boy in all the realm, asphyxiates your adversary in front of the entire palace, and then gives you a kitten?

If only there were a book about these sorts of things. Then perhaps I'd find some answers.

By the time I manage to coax Flint out of bed, we're very late for training. Spinner has him drink a foul-smelling concoction she claims eases the after-effects of alcohol. He grimaces but chokes it down dutifully, even pausing to kiss her on one of her tattooed cheeks before the two of us make our way down to the entrance hall.

'So, about the cats . . .' he begins.

'Kittens,' I correct.

'Whatever. I take it they're yet another offering from your *very* good friend the future emperor?'

I avoid his gaze, pretending to examine my brandmark.

Flint elbows me in the side. 'You and your secrets, sister.'

Because it's his Name Day, Grandmother lets Renly come to the feast tonight. He sits at the head of the Heirs' table, Hal's crown still perched lopsidedly atop his curls. Afterwards, Flint carries him back to my chambers and I tuck him into bed, the kittens stretched out beside him on the pillow. He falls asleep mid-sentence.

'Right,' says Flint, throwing a dress at me, a deep-blue silk number studded with tiny iridescent pearls. 'Put this on and let's go.'

'Where?' I ask apprehensively.

He grins at me. 'A very exclusive event.'

I raise an eyebrow. 'A party?'

'Not a party, sister. Think of it as a small, intimate gathering among friends.'

I shake my head. 'No.'

'Yes.'

'But I'm tired.'

'Tough.'

'And I wanted to read my book.'

Flint looks at me as though I'd just announced my plan to assassinate the emperor. 'Sometimes, I wonder how we ever shared a womb.'

I roll my eyes. 'Flint, what would you say if I told you that for some people, attending parties every single night can seem a *little* excessive?'

'I would say that those are exactly the kind of people who could use one. Now get dressed and quit complaining.'

Reluctantly, I do as he asks.

'Ah, there's that sweet smile,' he says as I emerge, scowling, from behind the screen. 'Now, come on.'

I sigh loudly. 'Just let me blow out the candles first.'

But Flint only snaps his fingers, and every candle in the room sputters out. He loops his arm through mine. 'Shall we?'

My brother steers me out of my chambers and along the Aquatori Wing, coming to a stop outside the very next door.

'You've got to be joking,' I say.

'I know, she doesn't seem the throwing-a-party type,' he says, rapping the golden knocker. 'She's exceedingly uptight for a Fish.'

The door swings open. Marina's eyes are lined with silver, her hair pinned back with those fish-shaped clips. She's forced to raise her voice to be heard over the noise coming from inside her rooms. 'Flint. And you brought your sister with you, too. How *delightful*.'

She shoots me a particularly nasty smile as she stands back to let us pass.

Marina's rooms are identical to mine in every way but one – they are filled with people. I tuck myself into a corner by the window while a group of chaperones in glittering gold robes all swivel round to stare at me. I linger there for nearly an hour, watching from the sidelines, counting down the minutes until I can slip off to bed.

A shriek of laughter rises above the din, and I glance up to see Zeph swinging Elaith on to his shoulders. She's brandishing a bottle of champagne, giggling as she pours some into Flint's open mouth. My brother wipes the back of his hand across his chin before turning back to the handsome Ventalla boy he'd been in the middle of kissing.

Kai appears at my side, grinning. 'Are they always like this, d'you think?'

'Definitely,' I say, as Elaith proceeds to down the contents of the bottle and Flint turns his attentions to a golden-haired Terrathian girl.

'Blaze!'

I look round to find Spinner sitting a short distance away, playing a game of cards with a handful of Eyes.

She beams as I approach the table. 'Want me to deal you in?'

Before I can respond, a silence sweeps through the room, voices dwindling as the Etheri turn their heads towards the door.

My breath hitches.

Fox stands framed in the doorway. His loose green shirt gapes open at the neck, exposing several inches of smooth golden skin, his thin gold chain glimmering as it catches the light. He smiles, slipping his hands into his pockets, dark leather quenching the glow of his tree-shaped brandmark. Almost immediately he's swarmed by his usual gaggle of sycophants. I watch, disgusted at the way they fawn over him, at the way he lets them. But rather than stop, he keeps walking, the Etheri parting down the middle as he makes his way directly towards the spot where I am standing. I freeze. Yet when he speaks, it is not to me.

'Move.'

Spinner's companions get up hurriedly, but she remains seated, her mouth hanging open with shock and indignation.

Fox angles his head. 'Did you hear me, Eye? Or are you too busy catching flies?'

Several of the Etheri laugh. Spinner blinks, then gets to her feet, teetering slightly in her heels as she stalks away.

Fox settles himself comfortably in her chair. One hand rests behind his head, and the other, to my horror, pats his knee. 'Care to join me, Storm Weaver?'

Whispers dart among the crowd.

I stand there, resenting the heat flaring up in my face, resenting *him*, with every thunderous beat of my heart.

The boy sitting in front of me bears little resemblance to the boy I was with last night in the stables. Perhaps he never existed at all.

'What's going on?'

I almost sag with relief as Hal appears at my side. His voice is carefully neutral, yet his raven eyes, trained unblinkingly on his brother, flash with barely concealed rage.

'Your Imperial Highness.' Fox's own voice is thick with feigned deference. 'How changed you are since last I was home. I confess I once found you to be somewhat lacking in taste, but now it seems you've set your sights on quite the prize.'

Hal takes a step towards Fox, his hands clenched into fists.

Fox's smile widens. 'I'm flattered, brother, yet my offer did not extend to you.'

Hal's skin is flushed. They stare at each other, the Prince of the Dawn and the Earth Cleaver, for a long, breathless moment.

My stomach lurches violently, my gaze flitting between them.

Then, without breaking eye contact, Hal slips an arm round my waist. I hesitate, just for a second, before letting him pull me close.

I feel Fox's gaze burn into the back of my skull as we walk away.

Hal waits until the room is once again filled with chatter before releasing his grip. 'I'm sorry,' he says quietly, his mouth twisted in anguish. 'I can't stand that he's here. I can't stand that he's an *Heir*. Each time he returns I'm reminded of how much I wish he wouldn't. He doesn't belong here. He never has.'

I glance over his shoulder to where Marina is now perched smugly on the arm of Fox's chair. She giggles loudly at something he murmurs in her ear, fists bunching in his shirt as he leans into her.

'He has no honour,' Hal continues. 'No respect. No sense of decency, or loyalty.'

I can't seem to tear my gaze away from where Fox and Marina sit, obscenely intertwined, his hand snaking slowly up her throat.

'I want you to stay away from him, Blaze. He only means to scare you.'

A voice fills my head, amused, taunting.

Scared, Storm Weaver?

'I'm not scared,' I say, a little too forcefully.

Hal looks at me curiously, but doesn't press me further. Brushing his fingers lightly against mine, he mutters something about a Council meeting, and leaves.

'Blaze?' Flint appears at my side, along with Elaith, Spinner and Kai. 'What's happened? Are you all right?'

Fox appears to have lost interest in his choice of diversion. I watch as he pushes Marina roughly off him and turns away, picking up the abandoned deck of cards, shuffling them, and dealing them out to a group of his gleeful companions.

'Nothing. I'm fine.'

Flint grimaces. 'Well, the Earth Cleaver's certainly put a damper on the evening.'

'Arrogant bastard,' mutters Spinner.

'Not to make matters any worse,' says Kai, 'but it seems we have company.'

We turn to find Cole walking towards us. I say walking, but perhaps *staggering* would be more accurate, for he is clearly incredibly drunk. He sways to a stop, a cruel smile spreading across his face as he sinks unsteadily into a low, mocking bow.

'The Heirs,' he says, his voice slurred. 'What an honour it is to stand in your presence.'

Elaith's shoulders curve inwards, and I move to stand beside her.

'Cole.' Flint nods coolly. 'Been a while.'

'Flint Flameborn,' says Cole slowly. 'The pride of his House. Nephew to the Fire Queen. How very . . . *convenient* for you.'

'What's that supposed to mean?' Spinner's eyeing Cole as though he were something unpleasant she'd scraped off the bottom of her sparkly gold heels.

'Let's just go, all right?' Elaith says quietly.

Cole turns to her, reaching out and tilting her chin up so that she has no choice but to look at him. 'What's the matter, Elaith? I must say, I've missed you. I've missed you following me around like a dog looking for scraps.'

Elaith's face crumples.

The words are out before I can yank them back. 'Leave her alone.'

'There she is,' Cole says, letting go of Elaith and turning to me. 'Ostacre's favourite little freak.'

'That's enough,' snaps Flint. 'Get lost, Cole.'

But Cole pays him no heed, stepping closer still until I can smell the soured spirits on his breath. 'I've often wondered, Blaze,' he says, 'how does it feel to always be the most *loathsome* person in the room?'

I look at Cole, and I can hear Ember in his voice. I find Fjord in the curl of his lip. I see a pair of blood-red eyes lurking just beneath the surface of his own, waiting for a sign of weakness. His words land with all the force he intended, but this time, I don't flinch.

'You tell me,' I say. 'It seems I may have been bumped to second place on this occasion. So congratulations, Cole. You've finally managed to win at something.'

Spinner snorts. Even Elaith bites her lip.

'You have no idea who you're dealing with,' Cole hisses.

I raise an eyebrow. 'Don't I? Well, why don't you enlighten me?'

Cole opens his mouth to respond, but no words are forthcoming, only gargled, choking sounds. He clutches at his neck, bleary eyes widening in shock as he realizes what I've done. As he realizes that his tongue is now frozen to the roof of his mouth.

He tries to speak, to scream. But he can't.

Many of the Etheri have turned to watch, sniggering as Cole claws at his tongue, attempting to pull it free.

I thought it would be appalling, hurting someone like this. It ought to be. But if anything, it feels *powerful*. Almost intoxicating. There's a sense of justice to it – tormenting the tormentor. Watching him suffer the consequences.

With one last murderous look at me, Cole turns and stumbles from the room. Through the sea of drunken revellers, a pair of eyes finds mine.

The Earth Cleaver is grinning. There is no surprise written across his features, only amusement. Amusement and satisfaction and something else, something like ... *pride*.

All triumph drains out of me.

In my head I see Fjord, humiliated, strung up by vines. I see Fox standing below him, smiling as a crowd watches on, horrified, transfixed.

I can hear his voice, clinging to the corners of my mind.

Where others look, I see. And I see you, Storm Weaver. I see all of you.

I kept wondering what it was he saw when he looked at me.

Now I think I have my answer.

And I turn away, because he has no right to look at me this way. Like he knows me. Like I know him. Like I could shake the world to its core and he would just laugh, and watch.

30

'What do you think?' Elaith asks, twirling around in front of the mirror.

I glance up from my book. 'Very nice.'

'You said that about the last eight dresses.'

'Eight*een*,' I mutter.

'I heard that. Now be honest, which one do you prefer?'

'The red one,' I say, turning a page.

'They're *all* red, Blaze!' cries Elaith, throwing up her hands in frustration. 'Oh, Spinner, thank Gods you're here. Blaze is being about as helpful as that cat she insists on carting around everywhere.'

My kitten fixes its pale-blue eyes on Elaith, affronted.

'Don't listen to her,' I murmur, stroking her ears. She lies back down and goes to sleep on Elaith's pillow.

Spinner folds her arms, looking Elaith up and down. 'No,' she says at last. 'No, this simply won't do. You must look your best tonight.'

Tonight the emperor is throwing a banquet, but unlike any other banquet, the list of attendees is far smaller than usual, consisting only of the remaining Heirs, their trainers and the Crowned Council. It's now exactly a week until the second trial. Time keeps on slipping away, and every day I try my best to ignore the nerves gnawing incessantly at my insides.

After sifting through the pile of discarded dresses, Spinner pulls out a red chiffon gown fringed with teardrop garnets. She helps Elaith into it, cocking her head to the left, then the right. 'I think we can make this work.'

And she does. Tearing off a bit here, pinning up a bit there, altering the neckline, adjusting the hem. By the time she's finished, it could be an entirely different dress. The bodice is now shapely and sleeveless, the skirts, simple and unappealing before, are now shorter and ruched, flaring out impressively just above the knee.

'I love it!' Elaith squeals, sweeping around the room as though dancing with an invisible partner. 'Spinner, you're a genius.'

My chaperone bobs a curtsy. 'I thank you. But my work here is not yet done. You,' she calls, pointing at me. 'Up.'

Grumbling, I get to my feet just as the door opens and Elva appears clutching a long dress made from indigo satin.

Elaith smiles when I emerge from behind the screen. 'Gorgeous,' she says.

Spinner nods approvingly. 'I really am good.'

Elva seems distracted as she weaves pearls through my braids, as if something is troubling her. Perhaps our conversation about her past dug up painful memories.

'Are you all right?' I whisper as Spinner and Elaith gossip loudly about someone I've never heard of.

She doesn't meet my gaze.

'Is His Imperial Handsomeness coming to escort you tonight, Blaze?' Spinner calls.

'I don't know,' I say, holding still while Elva dusts my cheekbones with shimmering silver powder. 'I haven't seen him for a while.'

It's true. Hal has been absent from the evening festivities during the past few days. More Council meetings. More roses. There's no use in denying that I miss him. And I miss the way I feel when I'm with him. The way *he* makes me feel.

Elva bows her head and slips silently from the room. My kitten sidles over to me, and I reach down and pick her up.

'Have you still not come up with a name for it?' Elaith asks, handing me a glass of champagne.

'*Her*,' I correct. 'And no. I told Renly I would write to him as soon as I do.'

He and Grandmother had returned to Harglade Hall a couple of days previously. Saying goodbye hurt just as much the second time as it did the first.

Suddenly Elaith lets out a blood-curdling shriek, causing Spinner to spit out a mouthful of champagne. 'What is it?' she splutters.

Elaith is standing on her bed, stabbing her finger at the floor. 'Mouse! Mouse!'

I catch sight of it darting around frantically for cover. '*Really*, Elaith?'

'Get it!' she wails, hopping from one foot to the other. 'Set the cat on it! Quick!'

I look down at my lap where my kitten is cowering, mewling pitifully as she tries to hide herself among the fabric of my skirts.

'*Blaze!*'

'Do you know,' I say, 'I think I've found the perfect name for her.'

'What?' Spinner asks from where she is perched on the dressing table.

The kitten peers up at me, trembling. I smile, stroking her soft grey fur. 'Mouse.'

Spinner snorts, hopping from chair to chair until she lands beside Elaith, who clings so tightly to her that she loses her balance and the two of them fall backwards on to the mountain of pillows.

'Well, well, well. What do we have here?'

I look up to see my brother standing in the doorway dressed in a striking scarlet doublet, Kai at his side.

Flint grins at me before throwing himself on to the bed. 'Ladies. Mind if I join you?'

'Not at all,' Spinner replies, fluttering her lashes.

I make a face.

'Come on, Blaze,' Flint calls. 'What're you waiting for?'

Kai holds out a hand. I hesitate, just for a moment, taking in the scene, taking in my *friends*. Then I scoop Mouse up into my arms and let Kai pull me into the centre of them. We lie there, a tangle of limbs, a blur of red and gold and blue, and I feel sure that in this moment I could carve a wave the size of a kingdom.

Spinner walks us to the banquet hall, and Kai and Elaith head inside. She hugs me lightly before turning to my brother. 'Have fun tonight.'

'Don't have to tell me twice,' says Flint, then kisses her full on the mouth. Spinner winds her arms round his neck, running her hands through his curls.

I just stand there, slightly amused, vaguely horrified, not sure where to look. When neither of them surfaces, I bob my head awkwardly. 'Right, well, I'll just . . .'

I practically hurl myself through the doors.

The long golden tables have been removed, the banquet hall empty but for a large circular table in the centre. I scan the handful of guests for the one face I don't wish to see. I've not encountered the Earth Cleaver since that night in Marina's chambers. Perhaps he's grown bored of whatever game he decided we were playing together. I can't work out whether that means he won, or I did. Maybe both. Maybe neither. Not that it matters.

Drawing myself up to full height, I head over to where Kai and Elaith stand talking with Zeph and the rather eccentric old Ignitia trainer.

Elaith peers behind me. 'Where's Flint?'

'Don't ask,' I mutter.

Flint appears several minutes later, looking very pleased with himself. 'The Council running late?' he says, wiping a smear of gold lipstick on to the back of his hand.

'The Council are never late, young Harglade,' murmurs his trainer absently.

Elaith rolls her eyes.

I spot River standing by the table and start making my way towards him, just as Ember sticks a delicately pointed foot out in front of me. I don't react quickly enough before it's hooked itself round my ankle and I trip, lose my balance, go crashing to the floor –

And am caught. Just in time.

Fox sets me back on my feet, rakes a hand through his dark hair, looks at me for a little longer than a heartbeat, and walks away without saying anything at all.

I don't have time to process what just happened, because at that moment the Council sweep into the banquet hall, as magnificent and as imposing as ever.

Reeling, I take my place at the table, waiting to see who will claim the empty seat beside me. My answer wears a doublet of purest gold, his brandmark, the Imperial sun and eye, glowing gently as he tucks my chair in. With the news of Hal's betrothal to Princess Mirade of Thaven still a secret, his attentiveness causes many eyes to flit towards us and linger, including Ember's, who looks as though she'd like to flay me alive.

The emperor welcomes us all, and I notice again just how ill he looks. It's worse than before, the dark circles under his eyes even more pronounced. He also appears to have lost weight – that resplendent golden cloak of his now positively swamps him.

As he makes a few introductory remarks, I watch the Ignitia trainer's beard dip in and out of his goblet each time he nods his head.

It's not long before the feast begins, and the emperor sits down heavily, two fingers pressed to his temple. It can't be easy, being father to the realm. It's aged him. But then I suppose that's the whole point of the Choosing – replacing those past their prime with the next generation.

Various conversations ensue. Several of the Heirs seem to be trying desperately to impress the Council. Some sit silently, seemingly overwhelmed. Then there's those like my brother, who's not paying attention to anything other than his food, and Fox, who seems to be bored senseless by the whole thing as he leans back in his chair, one foot propped on the other knee, swirling wine inside his glass.

I can still feel his hands – one on my back, the other on my waist, breaking my fall.

Elaith called him the perfect conundrum, and she's right. I can't work him out, no matter how hard I try. Does he pay me attention because he knows it'll score him a point against Hal? But then why does he see to it that our meetings always take place away from prying eyes? If it were really about provoking his brother, then surely Fox would have taken every opportunity for him and me to be spotted together.

He's disconcerting. Unpredictable. I never know which side of him I'm going to get, and I don't know what it is he wants from me. Because if he thinks we're the same, he's mistaken. I regret what I did to Cole. He deserved it, but I regret it. I am not the Earth Cleaver. I do not take pleasure in other people's pain, and I never will.

Hal touches my arm, startling me. 'I'm sorry for my absence this past while.'

'You're the prince,' I say, as if he's somehow forgotten. 'You have far more important matters to attend to than visiting me.'

Hal smiles. 'More pressing, perhaps, but not more important. I assure you, Blaze, visiting your chambers is my most favourite part of the day.'

My heart leaps feverishly. Does he really mean it? I lower

my gaze to the small criss-cross scar on his cheek – the scar I gave him. 'I don't believe that.'

'Try,' he says. 'For I'm not a good liar. Never have been.'

'What gives you away?'

'I'm told it's my eyes. I can never seem to look the person I'm lying to in the eye.'

Raven eyes that can't lie.

A tinkling sound fills the air, and I glance up to see King Balen holding his glass in one hand, his knife in the other. 'A toast,' he says, his voice wrapping round me like silk.

More serfs appear, placing a fresh glass of wine down in front of every Heir. Twelve brandmarks glimmer like stars as we raise them high.

'To you, my young friends,' says King Balen. 'May you continue to shine as brightly in your second trials as you each did in your first.'

We toast. We drink.

Flint downs the contents of his glass in one gigantic gulp. Fox wears an odd expression on his face, as though it were soured milk and not wine on his tongue. His brows are furrowed, fists clenched. He does not swallow. Puzzled, I turn to Hal.

Who does not meet my eyes.

All at once, my surroundings start moving. Gently at first, as if I'm on a rocking boat, and then faster, spinning like a top. I lose my grip on my glass and it falls to the floor. One by one, the Heirs slump down on to the table.

The last thing I hear before the darkness descends is a soft, silken chuckle.

31

When I wake, the banquet hall is deserted.

My head throbs dully as I raise it from the table. I glance around at the empty chairs, unfinished food, sharp slivers of glass strewn underfoot. Slowly, I get to my feet, swaying slightly. The silence amplifies my footsteps as I cross to the double doors at the end of the room. I try one handle, then the other. Both are locked.

Panic pools in my mouth. It tastes a bit like metal. I spit it out.

I call for help, but no one comes. I run back to the table, pick up a knife and wedge it between the doors, but nothing happens. I kick the doors hard and then clutch my foot, wincing. The pain gives me some clarity and I return to my chair.

The wine – it was drugged. It must have been. But why? What possible reason would the Council have for *drugging* us? And where is everyone?

I screw up my eyes. The fog clouding my mind reminds me of the painkiller I was given after the first trial.

Just then, a soft whisper slinks through the haze.

To you, my young friends. May you continue to shine

as brightly in your second trials as you each did in your first.

No. Not now. Not like this. There's still a week to go. A whole week. This *can't* be my second trial. Can it?

As if in answer, the room starts filling with water.

Cursing, I climb on to a chair. The Aquatori might be nicknamed Fish, but that doesn't mean we have gills. We can still drown, just like anybody else. Perhaps they plan to unleash another beast for me to fight, some kind of sea creature this time? My insides twist like snakes. If there's any of that wine left in my system, I think I'm about to throw it up.

Think, Blaze, I order myself. *Concentrate.*

Water laps at the hem of my dress. It's rising fast. Too fast. I have to stop it, and the only way is to freeze it.

Closing my eyes, I reach inwards for that cold shard of fury lodged deep inside my chest. I think of Ember tripping me up in front of everyone. I think of the Council tricking us into drinking wine laced with sleeping potion, inviting us here under false pretences. I think of Cole, his casual cruelty towards Elaith, the way she had folded in on herself, crumpled . . .

There's a crackling sound as the surface of the rapidly rising water begins to solidify, a layer of ice spreading around my feet. I step up on to the table.

The water is freezing. It's working. *It's working.*

It's not working.

The flow is increasing, fresh water breaking through the sheet of ice. I gather up my skirts and try to think. Rain won't help, clearly. As for waves, I don't see what use they would be, either. Surely they would just make things worse. Unless . . . My eyes tilt upward. Hanging above my head is a gigantic chandelier.

I must be mad, I think, as I prepare to jump off the table.

I am mad, I think, as I jump off the table.

I plummet, crash, sink, then drag myself upward until I break the surface. The water is neither hot nor cold – it's like it's the same temperature as the room. No, not the room. It seems to be the same temperature as my *skin*. Shuddering, I flip on to my back and float for a moment, weighed down by my dress.

Happiness. I try to find it.

I think about Renly surprising me in this very banquet hall after weeks apart. About Hal kissing me under the soft glow of a miniature sun. About how, after years of drizzle and emptiness, I know what it is to feel, to have courage, to have *friends*.

Small waves begin to curl and break. I twist round and tread water, still concentrating on that warm glow inside my chest, letting it wash over me. All around, the water is writhing, the waves growing stronger, rising higher. I duck beneath the surface as a gigantic wave looms over me, bracing myself as it comes crashing down. I swim up and try again. Another monstrous wave swells, but it's not close enough for me to catch it.

The candles are starting to flicker out, the room growing steadily dimmer.

I try once more, and this time it works. The wave envelops me, the sheer force of it knocking the remaining breath from my lungs as it sweeps me upward in a great, churning arc.

I ride the wave to its apex and, with a strangled scream, launch myself at the chandelier.

There is a moment in which everything hangs in the balance.

A breath, a heartbeat, and then my hand closes round solid gold.

I hold on tight, gasping at the wrenching in my shoulder joint as my arm takes the full force of my weight. The chandelier is huge, suspended from the ceiling by a thick golden chain.

I start moving in jerking motions, like a fish out of water, kicking my legs back and forth until I manage to hook one foot over the lowest tier. I dangle for a moment, panting, gathering enough strength to heave myself up.

Sitting astride the chandelier, I stare down at the rising water. Chairs and debris from the banquet table float atop its surface, lit up by the few remaining candles.

Now what? I think, pushing a dripping strand of hair off my face. I've bought myself time, but to what end?

That's when I hear it.

It's faint. So faint, and eerie, like ... hissing. No, not hissing.

Whispering.

Is somebody here? Or some*thing*? I whip my head around, searching for the source of the sound. It grows louder, filling the room. I can't distinguish the words. They blend into one another, a sweeping wave of indistinct voices. My instincts tell me that I am alone, but if that's true, then who, or *what*, is making that sound?

Then it hits me. It's coming from the water.

I think back to those long hours I spent sitting by the pool in the Keep, straining my ears to catch the slightest whisper. I understand now why River was so adamant that we learn the art of water whispering – because he knew we would need it. Before, I'd barely heard anything, but now I'm listening like my life depends on it, which maybe it does.

All of a sudden, the last candle sputters out. The room is lit only by my brandmark, glowing softly amid the gloom. I close my eyes, concentrating hard. But the surface is still several metres below. Perhaps I'm too high up to hear.

Steeling myself, I drop down into the water.

I hit the surface and allow myself to sink, drifting through the whispers. The words caress my skin, breathing themselves into my ears.

> *I am something that is given, but can't be taken.*
> *I am often borrowed, at times forsaken.*
> *I am easily remembered, I am easily forgot.*
> *Perhaps you may know me, perhaps you may not.*
> *Some say I'm a gift, some say I'm a curse.*
> *Sometimes I'm for better, sometimes for worse.*
> *My sound can bring joy, or heartbreak, or dread.*
> *I live on your lips, I live in your head.*
> *Tell me, Storm Weaver, what am I?*

It's a riddle. I listen again and again, then swim up for air, my mind racing at a million miles a minute.

I am something that is given, but can't be taken.
I am often borrowed, at times forsaken.

My thoughts wander to the Golden Library. Perhaps . . . perhaps a book? Books can be given. They can be borrowed, too. No. No, that's not it. A book can be taken away. Grandmother's confiscated plenty of mine over the years. I wouldn't call them a curse, either.

I am easily remembered, I am easily forgot.

A dream? Dreams can stick in your mind, or slip away, unbidden. Dreams live in your head. Or at least they do in mine. But it doesn't all fit.

The water is rising steadily.

Perhaps you may know me, perhaps you may not.

I think of the Keep, about how I pressed my hand to the door and let it know me, surrendering myself to the enchantments within. My heart clenches. *Enchantments.* An enchantment can be remembered, forgotten, forsaken . . . but not borrowed.

The last line tugs at me.

I live on your lips.

A kiss? A kiss can be given. It can be for better, or for worse . . .

My sound can bring joy, or heartbreak, or dread.

No. Surely the *sound* of a kiss is not what incites such emotions.

Something collides with the back of my head and I let out a shriek. But it's just a chair, bobbing beside me in the water. I push it away. The darkened room is filling up fast. Soon it will be entirely submerged.

I think back to what Spinner said about the Ventalla Heirs toppling from their stone pedestals in the first trial, how King Balen had intervened and manipulated the density of the air to slow their fall. So maybe I should just give up? Float on my back until Queen Hydra stops the water, until I'm whisked out of here, no longer an Heir, disqualified but alive.

But then I think of Grandmother and the way she looked at me the morning of the eclipse. I think of River – his kindness, his patience, his willingness to help me in spite of who I am. And I think of my mother. Would she have just cried off? Admitted defeat? Gone down without a fight? I already know the answer.

The water persists in rising. Time is running out.

I remember what the Earth Cleaver said to me that night in the library.

You had all but decided to give up. But then you didn't. You decided to win.

All that sadness, pain and fury – it didn't break me. I didn't let it. Using it – that was how I fought back. That was how I *won*.

Memories surge. Rain-soaked scales. Ice-frosted flesh. And the names, spat out like broken teeth.

Murderer.

Changeling.

Freak.

They will always be with me. They always have, since the day I was born. Names are curious creatures, so much more than words. I have so many already. Those that hurt me, humiliate me. Those that make my skin crawl. Names have lived with me these past seventeen years. I know them well. I can't imagine anyone knowing them better.

Or maybe I can.

I picture him in my head. Crooked teeth, his voice a rough scrape on the eardrum, a wooden staff that cannot be broken, not by strength or steel.

The Riftkeeper.

Gold will not grant you safe passage over the toll bridge. He requires something far more valuable than that. I wonder how many names he has collected over the years. I wonder if mine is his greatest prize.

My head knocks against the ceiling. I take one last desperate gulp of air before the water claims me completely.

The whispering grows louder. Lungs burning, I squeeze my eyes shut and wait. To be rescued, to drown – whichever comes first.

And then I hear something, something other than the water. The image of the Riftkeeper still swims across my vision, and this time I catch his words.

A name is a gift. A name is a curse. A name is a . . .

My eyes shoot open.

A name is a riddle.

Realization buoys me up, sending the answer skyrocketing to the surface of my mind.

Tell me, Storm Weaver, what am I?

'A name,' I say, my voice distorted by the water, hundreds of silver bubbles streaming from my mouth and rising up into the darkness above. 'The answer is a name.'

For a moment, nothing happens.

Then the water begins to drain away, as if someone has pulled a gigantic plug out of the floor below. I kick my legs hard, swimming upward and breaking the surface, sucking in great, ragged lungsful of air. The room is suddenly lit with orbs of bright light, and I almost sob with relief when my feet finally touch the floor.

When the last of the water has drained into nothingness, I find myself lying on the ground, sodden and trembling as the adrenaline subsides.

River says nothing as he kneels down and gathers me up into his arms. He takes me back to my chambers, where Elva is waiting. I let her dry me off, wrap my wet hair and cover me with layers of blankets. I can still hear the riddle whispered over and over, punctuated only by the chattering of my teeth. I clamp my mouth shut. Clamp my eyes shut too.

I spend my dreams drowning, and I wake to find my brandmark still glowing.

32

The final two Heirs from every court were announced last night.

Zephyr made it through, along with a boy called Eriq from the Court of Wind. Elaith couldn't figure out her riddle and was forced to concede, which left Flint, to my delight, and Ember, to my horror. Fox and Amaryllis are the Terrathian Heirs. They say the Earth Cleaver leaped like some kind of animal from tree to tree, that he felt a tremor in their roots before the ground gave way. And as for the Aquatori, Kai swallowed several mouthfuls of water early on and almost drowned, leaving Marina and me to vie for Queen Hydra's crown.

I have a month to prepare to fight her.

One final battle stands between me and the throne. I can't seem to wrap my head around it. I never expected to make it this far. And now I don't know how to feel.

Victorious – that I managed to succeed, against all odds?

Or terrified – that whatever its outcome, the third trial will shape my entire future?

Just like the first trial was designed to test our courage, it seems the second trial was designed to test our minds.

Time was a factor in each, with the Ventalla facing rapidly thinning air, the Ignitia an encroaching wall of flame, the Terrathian unsteady ground and the Aquatori rising water. Each trial was difficult. Each was dangerous. The Council really knows how to play the game. But then it's easy to play the game when you make the rules.

'Blaze, it's almost time.' Spinner appears by my side, tongue between her teeth as she assesses every last detail of her handiwork. 'I must say, I really have outdone myself.' She shoots me an impish grin, nudging me towards the mirror.

My reflection is of a stranger. For tonight I am not Blaze the Aquatori Heir, or Blaze the Rain Singer, or even Blaze the Storm Weaver.

I am Blaze the Eye.

My eyelids, lips and cheekbones have been dusted with glittering golden powder. Elva has threaded gold beads through my curls, some of which frame my face, while the rest are piled up on top of my head in a popular Imperial style. A pair of dark-gold gloves conceals the telltale gleam of my brandmark, and as for the dress . . . I run a hand wonderingly over the fabric. Light as air, it ripples and flutters with every slight movement. And that's not all. The dress *glows*. It's as though I am wearing a thousand flakes of gently glimmering sunlight, each one woven together like golden scales.

Tonight is the masquerade ball. The entire palace will be in attendance. But here's the catch: for one night, everyone – every king, queen, Heir and courtier – will be dressed in gold. It's tradition, a display of loyalty to the future emperor, a means of showing him, showing *Hal*, that no matter which court we belong to, the Etheri stand united under one rule and bend the knee to one leader, above all else. Yet what with their inexhaustible penchant for parties, the Imperial Court have found a way to make this show of allegiance into a pageant of their own. Namely, a ball. One that requires a disguise. Tonight, you can shed your colour and step out of yourself.

Tonight, I can be anyone I choose.

'And now for the finishing touch,' announces Spinner, producing an ornate golden mask and slipping it over my eyes.

It's shaped like a dragonfly, the slender body stretching from just above my hairline to the tip of my nose. I peer at myself through small holes cut into its wings, which span the width of my head and more, each one speckled with tiny pearls, sapphires and amethysts.

It's beautiful. More than beautiful – it's a work of art.

'I found it on your dressing table,' says Spinner. 'Along with this.' She reaches down the front of her dress and pulls out a slightly crumpled note. It's almost identical to the one that accompanied the burn ointment. Two words, the penmanship lazy and looping.

For you.

My heart leaps into my throat. Could it be from Hal? But then, why the secrecy? And why does he continue to send me gifts when he's promised to another?

I feel a knot in the pit of my stomach every time I'm reminded of it.

'He must like you very much, you know.' Spinner winks at me before breezing past towards the door. 'I'm off to find your brother. Flint seems in need of a good *chaperoning*.'

I pretend to gag. Then I slip the note underneath my pillow and follow her.

The palace is awash with noise and excitement, and I let myself be swept along by a sea of Eyes, their faces concealed by masks: some big, some modest, some ridiculously flamboyant. One girl is wearing a golden headdress that creates the impression of a lion's mane. Nobody gives me a second glance and I relish it, this feeling of anonymity. It's a taste of the future I'd always planned for myself. Nameless. Free. I only wish it could last.

Spinner and I squeeze into the largest ballroom, skirting the perimeter until I catch sight of a shock of flame-red hair. Elaith looks dazzling in a skin-tight golden jumpsuit. Even in perilously high heels, she still looks tiny standing next to two others I realize upon closer inspection are Flint and Sheen, who appear to be engaged in some kind of disagreement. Kai must still be recovering from the second trial.

'You took your time,' says Elaith, leaning in to embrace me.

'I'm sorry,' I murmur into her hair. She knows I'm not referring to my lateness.

'Don't be,' she whispers back. 'It's their loss, of course. But I'm fine, really.'

When I pull back, I can see in her eyes that she means it.

She grins. 'Let's just hope Ember catches some awful illness before the third trial. The very *thought* of being lorded over by that arrogant, insufferable –'

'*Elaith*,' warns Flint.

'Fine – that obnoxious, intolerable –'

Sheen stoppers her mouth with a champagne bottle.

Spinner leans against Flint's shoulder. 'I overheard some of the Eyes talking about heading down to the palace grounds. There's a competition taking place, apparently.'

Elaith takes a swig of champagne. 'Well, I'm up for a challenge. Flint?'

My brother wraps an arm round Spinner. 'Count me in.'

Sheen frowns. 'I'm not sure this is a good idea.'

Flint just rolls his eyes. 'That's because you're allergic to fun. And parties. And seemingly, me. So why don't you take the night off, Sheen? I've already got one chaperone here who appears more than willing to keep a *very* close eye on me.'

He nuzzles Spinner's neck and she giggles, swatting at him. Sheen shoots him a withering look, but makes no further protest.

Elaith hands me the bottle. 'What about you, Blaze?'

I hesitate. Tonight is the one night I can be anybody. So, with this in mind, I think about what I would most likely do in this scenario, and then do the opposite. Tipping my head back, I drain the rest of the champagne. 'Let's go.'

Spinner whoops. A few people turn to stare at us and I beam brightly back at them.

The five of us weave through the crowded ballroom and down the first of many flights of stairs. Elaith teeters and totters so much that eventually Flint just sighs, bends down and tosses her over his shoulder. She props herself up on her elbows and I follow along behind so as to continue our conversation.

'A *name*? Gods, I'd never have got that in a million years. Mine was something about . . . Oh, what was it? Something broken, something fixed . . . something about a gap . . . or was it a map? I can't remember. Anyway, I guessed teeth.'

'*Teeth?*'

'All right, genius. How was I supposed to know? Not all

of us are sharp enough to outsmart the Council.' Still slung across my brother's back, Elaith reaches out and plucks a glass off a passing tray. 'Boys are a bit like riddles, don't you think, Blaze?'

Voices mingle with the faint chimes of music drifting from the palace as handfuls of golden courtiers make their way across the moon-bleached lawns towards the maze looming tall and dark in the distance. The effects of the champagne are starting to kick in. I feel slightly disorientated, as though a thin layer of fog is clouding my brain.

Alator is waiting at the entrance to the maze. He grins at us, showing off his rows of solid-gold teeth. 'Ready to play?'

'Definitely,' someone responds. I think it might have been me.

'Rules are simple,' he says. 'You enter alone, and no revealing your gifts. Remember, everybody is an Eye tonight. Whoever makes it to the centre of the maze wins.'

'But nobody *ever* makes it to the centre!' cries Elaith. 'It likes to change.'

'Please don't go getting yourself lost again,' Flint tells her, grimacing. 'I don't want to have to carry you out a second time.'

Elaith blows him a kiss.

Alator claps his gloved hands. 'Who's first?'

Spinner nudges me forward. I'm about to mutter an excuse, to turn back. But I don't. Taking a deep breath, I walk straight into the maze.

The air around me is gloomy and eerily still, the silence swallowing my footsteps. My dress lights the way, its gentle glow illuminating the path ahead, which forks into three.

I choose the one veering off to the right. At the next set of paths, I choose the one on the left.

Soon I begin to lose track, my feet aching in the pointed slippers Spinner picked out for me. I slip them off and toss them behind me, the soil now soft and cool beneath my feet.

Then, voices. Muffled but growing gradually closer. I recognize neither.

'They say the Fire Queen favours him.'

'That might be so, but I wouldn't underestimate the cousin, if I were you. She's a ruthless little thing. You heard about the way she fried that dragon's skull.'

I freeze.

'True enough. But the boy's just as gifted, and better-liked.'

'Being well-liked has nothing to do with it. Smiles don't win you a crown.'

The voices are so close now. Their owners must be standing right on the other side of the hedge. I remain completely still, listening.

'And what of his sister?'

There's a guffaw, then an unpleasant sound – the sound of a man spitting on the ground. 'It's a Gods' damned miracle they've let her get this far.'

'I have to say, she's surprised me.'

'Surprising or not, there's not a soul alive who would accept her as a ruler. Mark my words, the Veridian desert will turn to ice before the Storm Weaver is crowned Queen of the Fish.'

Their voices fade out of earshot, but their words remain, lingering on the air, turning it sour. I stumble blindly down a pathway, then another.

I thought tonight I could be anybody, but I was wrong. The past is not a skin I can shed. I carry it with me every day of my life. And it doesn't matter how grateful or graceful I am. It doesn't matter how hard I try. Because it will never be enough. *I* will never be enough for these people, who would sooner see me dead than sitting on a throne.

It hurts, accepting something that you've known all along.

I break into a run, darting between the high hedges, utterly directionless, until suddenly I hurtle round a sharp corner and collide with something tall and solid. Wincing, I pull down my mask and cradle my forehead in my hand. My nose is instantly filled with the acrid scent of liquor. When I look up, squinting into the face of the person standing before me, I feel my heart sink into the pit of my stomach.

'You know, I wasn't sure I believed them when they said the Storm Weaver made it through the second trial. But here you are, alive and well. Or at least, alive. I must say, you've looked better.' Cole smirks as he reaches out and plucks a twig from my hair then lets it fall to the ground between us. In his other hand he holds a half-empty bottle. 'What a perfect spot for a catch-up, don't you think? I so enjoyed our last get-together.'

I remember the way his eyes had bulged while he choked, trying desperately to prise his frozen tongue from the roof of his mouth. Warily, I take a step back.

'What's the matter, Blaze? Have somewhere you need to be?'

'Actually, yes.'

'And where's that?'

'Anywhere,' I say. 'Anywhere away from you.'

Cole smiles. The next moment we are encircled by a ring of fire.

'I think it's time you were taught some respect,' he murmurs softly.

My voice sounds strangled. 'You wouldn't *dare*.'

'Oh, wouldn't I?' Cole brandishes the liquor bottle and sloshes the contents over my dress. 'You underestimate me, Blaze. And you're not the only one, it seems.'

My gown is dripping in spirits. One flick of his wrist and I will be engulfed by flames.

'See, the only reason you're still breathing is because most people are scared of what your death might bring. Another storm, a plague, a curse, perhaps? Meaning that your miserable little life is untouchable, for the foreseeable at least. But, aside from killing you, there really are no limits to the ways in which I can make you suffer.'

I grit my teeth so hard I wonder if they might crumble into dust. 'Even you wouldn't be this stupid.'

Cole shrugs. 'There's no stupidity in justice.'

Justice. I think about the guard who tried to poison me all those years ago. He thought he was carrying out justice, too.

'I'm not scared, you know,' Cole continues. 'Of retaliation from the Gods. Why would I be, when I'd simply be righting a wrong? Destroying something that should never have existed at all. They'd call me a hero.'

The flames leap higher. I try to summon the rain, to conjure ice. But fear, raw, genuine fear, has taken over, clouding my thoughts.

'You're no hero,' I breathe. 'You're nothing but a coward.'

Cole steps closer. 'What did you say to me?'

'You're a coward,' I repeat. 'Just as you were in the first trial, just as you are now, just as I suspect you've always been. And I feel *sorry* for you.'

He grips the back of my neck. 'I'll burn you,' he hisses. 'Just watch me. I will *burn you* until you are nothing but ashes in my hands.'

'We'll see about that,' says a voice from behind him.

Cole whips round. There's the sound of a fist hitting flesh, the sickening crunch of bone, and suddenly Cole is on the ground, crying out in pain. The fire surrounding me vanishes, receding into the earth, leaving nothing but smoke in its place. But the newcomer isn't finished. He reaches down and yanks Cole to his feet. Cole barely has time to try to stumble backwards before he's sent flying by the force of another blow. He shudders, spitting out mouthfuls of dirt and blood, one arm raised in surrender.

I blink up at my rescuer, eyes straining through the smoke-filled gloom. Tall, dark hair, golden doublet, a mask shaped like a raven's wings obscuring half his face.

Hal.

He takes my hand and pulls me away round corner after corner until we reach a large clearing shaped like an eye – the centre of the maze.

Hal is panting. I am shaking. He opens his mouth to speak, but I don't get to hear whatever it is he's about to say, because before the little voice of reason inside my head can begin to talk me out of it, I close the distance between us and press my lips to his.

It seems to take him by surprise. He tenses up as my arms snake round his neck. For a long moment, he's completely still, as though deciding whether or not to reciprocate.

Then, it's as if he melts. He kisses me back. Hesitantly at first, then hungrily.

The kiss.

It's better than before. Better than I could have imagined.

Every nerve ending in my body is alive with it. Stars are born and burn and light up the sky with it.

It's feverish, all-consuming, charged with a delicious sense of daring. It feels like a secret whispered in the dead of night. It feels like diving down deep into the ocean on a single breath. It feels like falling. But then his arms slide round me, catching me, holding me close. His gloved hands graze my back, my waist, the nape of my neck, his fingers tangling themselves in my hair. Thoughts are drowned by sensation as I allow my own hands to roam, tracing the sculpted lines of his chest, all grooves and ridges and hardened muscle.

He brushes a thumb along my jawline, angling my face the way he wants it, tilting my head back for better access to my mouth before slowly slipping his tongue inside. My stomach tumbles as it begins to explore, sweeping gently over mine. He tastes like wine and green apples and something herbal, cool and fresh, a little sweet.

Emboldened, I press closer, then closer still, my own tongue sliding experimentally against his. He groans softly into my mouth and I shiver.

Then he's effortlessly lifting me up into his arms, pressing me backwards into the thick hedge surrounding us. But I can barely feel it – all I feel is him. Every point of contact. My arms round his neck. My legs round his waist.

He grips me tighter, trailing soft kisses down my throat and along my collarbone. I cling to him, arching my back as his eyelashes brush against my jaw.

I've never felt anything like this before – the headrush, the heat. He saved me from Cole's fire, and yet my whole body is burning, every inch of my skin electrified by his touch.

He draws back slightly, as though about to say something, but I just reel him closer. I don't want to stop. I don't want this to end. I want to freeze time, immortalize this moment, and relive it over and over.

I gasp as he tugs my lower lip between his teeth, drawing a spark of pain, and I feel him smiling against my mouth as I respond by digging my nails into his back.

He kisses me until my lips are swollen and my heart is pounding and my body is molten and boneless and trembling.

When at last we break apart, we're both breathing heavily. Reluctantly, he relaxes his grip, letting me slide slowly down to the ground.

With my hands still curled into fists upon his chest, I look up into his eyes.

His green eyes.

Green as leaves in springtime.

His mask falls to the ground and I realize then that the wings are not those of the Castellion raven, but of the Calloway falcon. I jerk backwards, horrified.

Fox rakes a hand through his hair, a small smile playing at the corners of his mouth. 'Well,' he says. 'That's certainly one way to thank me.'

33

'Concentrate, Blaze,' River says patiently.

'I am,' I lie.

But I'm too distracted to concentrate. I'm as inept as I was when I first arrived here, my rain mere drizzle, my ice a scattering of frost, my waves little more than ripples on the surface of the water. I can't focus on my anchors because my emotions are all over the place.

Dread plagues me, regret fills me up and the *guilt* – it chews me into pieces, all because of *him*. The Earth Cleaver. I *kissed* the Earth Cleaver.

I'm tortured by the memory of his lips on mine, soft and devouring, the way he'd –

I swallow hard, wiping the back of my hand across my mouth as though some trace of the kiss still lingers there, telling tales on me.

He tried to reach for me, after. But I shook him off, shook my head, backing away until I had summoned enough strength to turn and run. He made no attempt to follow me. Yet a single vine came slithering in my wake, guiding me safely out of the maze.

My skin prickles with heat and I squeeze my eyes shut.

What have I done?

Just then, someone barges past roughly, almost knocking me headfirst into the pool.

'Oh, how clumsy of me. Sorry, Blaze. Didn't see you there.'

I glower, reminded of just how much I miss Kai. He turned training from something that must be endured into something I actually looked forward to. But now he's no longer an Heir, and I'm stuck with Marina. She's wearing her usual contemptuous smirk, yet there's now an edge of uncertainty to her resentment. Because for all her jibes, here I am. And if I weren't in the midst of a moral crisis, I'm sure I would take considerable pleasure in being the one to knock Marina Kalpara's unfaltering sense of superiority.

I spend the rest of the session sitting by the pool, listening to the whispers dancing across the surface. At the end of the day, River takes me aside.

'Tomorrow, you will have your first lesson with your queen.'

I stare at him in alarm. 'What?'

'It is custom for the reigning monarch to offer one-to-one lessons with the remaining Heirs before the third trial. You still have much to learn, and Her Majesty is an excellent teacher. I can say this with authority and a hint of self-indulgence, since Queen Hydra was once, too, a student of mine.' River smiles gently. 'Off you go now.'

And off I go, rubbing my thumb over the mottled skin of my scar as I make my way across the palace grounds, trying and failing to banish the Earth Cleaver from my mind.

Back in my rooms, Spinner is sprawled over a silk chaise, gazing into space.

'And what are you daydreaming about?' I ask, sitting down on the window seat.

She sighs theatrically. '*Your brother.*'

I roll my eyes. 'Naturally.'

Elva hovers in the doorway holding a new bunch of golden roses from Hal. The sight of them sends a fresh pang of guilt coursing through me.

'I'll fetch a vase, my lady,' she says quietly before slipping out of the room.

Spinner yawns loudly. 'She's a timid little thing, isn't she?'

'Hard not to be, really, after all she's been through.' As soon as the words leave my mouth I want to snatch them out of the air and cram them back in.

Spinner is looking at me strangely. 'Whatever do you mean?'

'Nothing,' I say, too quickly.

'Has she said something to you, Blaze?'

'No.' Again, too quickly. I grit my teeth. 'I mean, she's a serf, isn't she? She's not exactly living a life of luxury, waiting on me all day.'

Spinner relaxes. 'Oh. Well, if you're sure.'

I nod, inwardly cursing my own carelessness. What Elva did, telling me about her past, is forbidden. If it was ever discovered, she would be punished. Spinner can never know what I know about Elva. She is my friend, yes, but she is also an Eye of the Imperial Court. It's easy to forget sometimes that Spinner has loyalties that extend far beyond me.

The setting sun paints the sky peach, and I wander through to my bedchamber to watch it from the balcony. The moment I swing open the glass doors I see something wrapped in fine blue silk waiting for me on the golden ledge. Beside it lies a note.

For you.

Another gift.

I glance over my shoulder before unwrapping it. It's a dagger, the handle silver and shining, the blade curved like a scythe, like a . . .

I flinch and the dagger clatters to the floor. Because I have seen this blade before, only it wasn't a blade then. It was one of many vicious, razor-sharp claws attached to the body of a creature with hideous black scales and blood-red eyes – the beast from my first trial.

Slowly, I pick it up.

Why would Hal give me a dagger? And not just any dagger, but one made from that *thing's* claw, as if I wanted some twisted memento of my time in that arena. It doesn't strike me as something he would do. It's not his style. Besides, he makes no secret of the roses. As for the nightlight, he put it straight into my hands. There was no note, no doubt.

I nibble the inside of my cheek.

First the burn medicine, then the dragonfly mask, and now this.

What if the gifts were never from Hal at all? What if they were from someone else?

Footsteps sound. I quickly hide the dagger behind my back and crumple the note in my other hand.

It's Elaith.

'Which one?' She holds up what appear to be two identical red dresses. 'I just can't decide. They're both so different.'

298

The following day I arrive at Queen Hydra's quarters, apprehensive and exhausted. I had lain awake for hours, thinking about Hal, trying not to think about Fox, and when I had eventually drifted off to sleep, the golden eye was waiting for me, only this time at the centre of a maze.

A serf leads me through a number of interconnecting chambers until we reach a large room overlooking the city. The Aquatori Queen is seated at a long golden table, facing away from me. She wears a modest gown in a light shade of azure, her flowing silvery-white hair a curtain of snow around her shoulders. She turns as I approach.

'Blaze Harglade. What an honour it is to meet with you again.'

I curtsy deeply. 'Your Majesty.'

'Sit with me.'

The chair makes an awful scraping sound as I pull it out and perch nervously on the edge.

'I must say, your performance in the first two trials was unforgettable,' remarks Queen Hydra as she boils the water in the teapot with a small flick of her wrist. 'Most unforgettable indeed.' She leaves it to brew for a moment, then proceeds to pour the tea into a little silver cup. 'Honey? Lemon? Milk? Sugar?'

'Honey. Thank you, Your Majesty.'

She stirs in a generous spoonful of the stuff and hands me the cup. I take a scalding sip and place it back down on the table.

'I'm told that you have now mastered the gift you were born with?'

I manage a small smile. 'Yes, Your Majesty.'

'Remarkable,' she murmurs. 'To have the power to summon the rain. To bend the weather to your will. And you, the last of your kind.'

I glance down at the table, finding that her words weigh heavily.

The last of my kind.

I thought I was something of an expert on solitude, but I've realized that being isolated is in fact entirely separate from feeling alone.

Queen Hydra, seeming to sense a shift in my countenance, pushes a plate of iced biscuits towards me, all of them shaped like snowflakes. 'Tell me about your training,' she says. 'I believe you have been progressing well with your other water gifts.'

I clear my throat. 'I've been working on my ice making and my wave carving, but I'm yet to learn how to simmer. Is that what you're going to be teaching me, Your Majesty?' I ask, glancing at the still-steaming teapot.

Queen Hydra shakes her head. 'I'm afraid that won't be possible. You are a Rain Singer. Your gifts are Melded, anchored to your emotions, and so in order to learn how to simmer, you must seek out the anchor yourself, just as you did for the others.'

'You know?' I say, startled. 'About Melding?'

She nods. 'I am one of the few who know the secret of the Singers.'

Yes, I think. *You, me, River and the old man in the library.*

The queen leans back in her chair, her slender fingers interlocking on the table in front of her. 'Are you happy here, child?'

I blink, taken aback.

'Forgive me,' she says. 'I only ask because I myself have never felt at home in the Imperial Province.'

'I've never really felt at home anywhere,' I say without thinking, then blush furiously. 'I'm sorry, Your Majesty. I only meant that –'

'I know exactly what you meant, child, and you are perfectly justified in feeling as you do. I confess I have thought of you often over the years, and when the invitation arrived from your grandmother, I knew I had to sail to the Firelands to meet you.'

Self-conscious, I look down at my teacup. 'I remember thinking you wouldn't come. I'd heard that you prefer to remain at the Court of Waves.'

Queen Hydra dips a biscuit delicately into her tea. 'That is true.'

'What's it like?' I ask, unable to help myself. 'The Lagoon.'

The queen smiles. 'Paradise,' she says softly. 'It will always be my haven, even when this crown is no longer mine to wear.' She reaches up and touches the circlet of golden waves sitting neatly atop her head, then rises from her chair. 'Come.'

I follow her to the large window and together we gaze out at Cor Caval, encircled by the yawning darkness of the Rift.

'I think perhaps the reason I feel so ill at ease in this city is because I am cut off from that which connects me to my home,' says Queen Hydra.

I frown. 'What do you mean, Your Majesty?'

'I refer to the Creek, child. You are aware, of course, that it flows through each and every province?'

I nod.

'Well, here, because of the boy they call the Earth Cleaver, that is no longer the case.'

I tense up at the mention of Fox. I'd never really considered before that since he turned the Imperial Province into what is effectively a land-locked island, the glistening blue vein which connects every region across Ostacre is now severed.

Queen Hydra places a gentle hand on my arm. 'Know, child, that when you leave this place, no matter what path you might tread, so long as you follow the Creek, you will always find what you are looking for.'

I find this strangely comforting, and am startled when the queen abruptly turns and walks away into the centre of the room.

'Now,' she says. 'Shall we begin?'

I don't have time to respond before a gigantic wave rears up in front of me, large enough to knock me flat. I brace for impact. Only none comes. I peer out from behind my arms and gasp. For the wave is suspended above me, completely immobilized.

I stare up at the motionless water, my hand passing straight through it as I reach out to touch the surface.

'This is incredible,' I whisper.

At that moment the wave comes to life once more. I stumble backwards, but it doesn't break over me. Instead it changes direction, receding towards Queen Hydra, who, with a slight crook of her finger, reduces it to foaming surf that laps at my ankles. I watch it darken the soft leather of my boots. But when I try to move, I find I can't.

I glance up at the queen, then back down at my feet, where a thick layer of ice now shimmers beneath them, freezing me to the floor.

Queen Hydra smiles gently. 'First lesson. Never take your eyes off your opponent.'

34

When the doors to the Aquatori Queen's chambers shut behind me several hours later, I lean against them and exhale right down to the very bottom of my lungs.

Rubbing my scar, I seek comfort in the sliver of darkness behind my eyelids.

Eyes.

They are everywhere. Some watch you behind golden fans, whisper about you behind golden gloves, are etched with needle and ink on to the napes of necks wreathed in golden chains. Some look like home. Some gleam like amber stone. Some you could drown in, as blue as deep water. Others are black like ravens' wings. Greener than spring leaves. Grey as storm clouds and sea mist. And some are steeped in enchantments, carved from solid gold.

Suddenly there is a sharp gust of wind, followed by a voice. 'Hello, little dove.'

Thoughts scatter and spill out over the top of my head.

King Balen stands barely more than a foot away from me, his own eyes dark pits cut into the centre of his skull. They bore into me, unblinking.

My words emerge flimsy and weak. 'Your Majesty. You startled me.'

The Ventalla King tosses one side of his cloak over his shoulder and extends his arm towards me. Hesitantly, I take it. A cool breeze accompanies us as we walk.

'It seems like yesterday I was travelling to Valburn for your first public appearance, and now here you are, one victory away from the Aquatori throne. Remind me, sweet one,' he says, 'how does it feel to stand on the brink of destiny?'

King Balen's crown glimmers in the light from the flickering torches, a wreath of golden feathers atop his straight black hair.

'I suppose . . . a little daunting?' My tone is disjointed, my tongue feels too big for my mouth. Everything about this man makes me nervous.

'I confess I, too, was daunted by the prospect,' says King Balen silkily. 'But one should not fear the future, one must seize it. Those were the very words my father spoke to me before I won my throne. Perhaps they may be of some comfort to you as you cross the bridge into the unknown.'

I plaster on the most gracious smile I can muster, stretching the muscles in my cheeks so taut I worry they might snap. 'Thank you, Your Majesty.'

We come to a stop outside a large antechamber. A serf rounds the corner ahead of us, starts, turns on his heel and scurries back the way he came.

'I will leave you now,' King Balen says, to my relief. 'Although I do hope to see you at the ball this evening.'

'*Another* ball?' I'm almost starting to miss my days of confinement. Then I clear my throat, embarrassed. 'I mean, I think I might retire early tonight, Your Majesty. I haven't been sleeping so well of late.'

It's true. Every night when I close my eyes, the dreams are waiting.

Amusement languishes in the creases next to King Balen's mouth. 'A pity, for my nephew seems *very* taken with you. Would you really deprive him of your company?'

I flush. 'I'm sure Prince Haldyn never wants for a dance partner, Your Majesty.'

King Balen chuckles lightly, leaning down to press a cold kiss to the scar on the back of my hand, just like he did at Harglade Hall. 'Forgive me, little dove. Only I said *my nephew*. I never said which one.'

A heartbeat – that's all I get before I manage to smooth my features into a politely perplexed expression, but not before the king catches the flicker of unfiltered shock that passes across my face.

His soft laughter continues to echo long after he disappears down the passageway.

'There you are,' says Flint as I join him by the edge of the dance floor an hour later.

I summon a smile. 'Here I am.'

My brother wears a thick magenta doublet and slim-fitting trousers. The golden flecks in his deep-brown eyes are brought out by a thin slick of gold lining his eyelids. Sheen stands sour-faced and silent beside him, and I find myself wondering if he picks out Flint's clothes just as Spinner does mine. Tonight she's selected a pale-blue number that shimmers like ice on water whenever it catches the light.

'How was it with Queen Hydra?' Flint asks.

'Fine. Good. How was Aunt Yvainne?'

'Ember had her lesson today, so I got stuck with our trainer.'

'And how'd that go?'

'Oh, just excellent. He fell asleep midway through telling me this story about the time he won a three-headed lizard in a duel.'

'A three-headed lizard,' I repeat. 'And what, exactly, did your trainer do with this three-headed lizard?'

'That's the thing,' says Flint, 'I never found out. He didn't even make it to that part. I practised some flame flinging, stared vacantly out the window for a bit. Eventually he woke himself up with a particularly loud snore and told me I could go.'

'Do you *ever* stop talking?' Sheen mutters.

'I'll stop talking when you crack a smile,' Flint tells him cheerfully. 'Though something tells me that day will never come, which is lucky for me, as I do love the sound of my own voice.'

I can't help laughing, and I feel the tight knot in my chest begin to unravel. We're soon joined by Elaith, Spinner and Zeph, who are deep in discussion.

'If Amaryllis had any sense, she'd cry off.'

'She can't just refuse to fight him, Elaith. That's not how it works.'

'Do you think he even wants to be king?'

'Of course he wants to be king. Why wouldn't he?'

'It just seems a pretty big adjustment is all. To go from travelling the world for six years to sitting on a throne in the Grove, deciding taxes and entertaining ambassadors.'

'Well, why don't you go ask him how he feels about it?'

'Shut up.'

I try my best to ignore their conversation. I don't want to think about the Earth Cleaver. Because if I do, I'll think about that kiss.

Just then, Spinner nudges me in the side. I follow her gaze to where a dark-haired figure is striding through the parting crowd. Ripples of silence spread unevenly around the room as he makes his way across it, straight towards me. I tense up as he approaches, guilt and longing battling one another, wrapping themselves tightly round my heart.

Hal holds out his brandhand. 'May I have this dance?'

I look at the prince. Raven eyes, fair skin. So unlike his brother. But it was dark in the maze, I remind myself, and Fox had been wearing a mask shaped like the wings of a bird, and everybody had been dressed in gold, and Cole had just tried to burn me alive, and I wasn't thinking clearly, and everything had happened so fast and . . . and . . .

Elaith prods me hard in the small of my back.

I sink into a curtsy. 'I would be honoured, Your Imperial Highness.'

I let Hal guide me out into the very middle of the dance floor. At once, courtiers begin following suit, couples streaming along in our wake. Music starts up, slow and dreamlike. My feet find the rhythm as Hal's other hand moves to cup my waist.

'Thank you,' I say softly. 'For asking me to dance.'

'I wasn't sure whether you'd want me to.'

Panic jolts through me. What if he's heard something? What if Fox and I were seen together in the maze? 'Why not?'

But Hal just smiles. 'I know you dislike attention.'

I feel myself relax. 'Is that why you come to my rooms to see me?'

'Why else?' Hal glances down almost shyly at our joined hands as we change direction. 'You value privacy. As do I. And I prefer it, speaking to you away from all the chaos, no Eyes hanging on our every word.'

I glance around. Everywhere, people are watching us. Even the other dancers crane their necks to get a good view. I catch sight of Ember in the crowd, wearing an expression that seems to say *Oh, cousin, if only you'd break both your legs.*

'You disappeared the other night,' Hal says. 'I searched everywhere, which I assure you was like looking for a needle in a very large, very gold haystack.'

The panic returns and I rack my brain for a response.

'A few of us headed down to the maze.'

This is true.

'But I'd had a little too much champagne.'

Also true.

'So I decided to return to my chambers.'

Lie. Lie. *Lie.*

I don't know why I feel so desperately guilty. Kissing Fox was an accident. Besides, Hal is as good as betrothed. It might still be a secret for now, but when it is announced, when he is forced to marry Princess Mirade of Thaven, what then? He will be lost to me forever. Not that he was ever mine to begin with.

The music becomes louder and I welcome it. It fills me up until there's no room for anything else. Stares bounce off me, whispers dissolve before they reach my ears. I'm spun from Hal, to Flint, to Zeph, and back to Hal again, until suddenly I find myself in the arms of someone new, someone tall and strong and impossibly, *irritatingly* beautiful.

The Earth Cleaver grins down at me. 'Aren't you a sight for sore eyes?'

I freeze mid-step as it all comes flooding back – the memory of his hands, his mouth, of running my fingers through his hair. Heat spills into my cheeks. 'Let me go.'

'Really?' His voice is amused. 'Because I will, you know. If you ask it of me. But I warn you, it'll make quite the scene. *What did he say to her?* someone might ask. *What did she say to him?* another may wonder. What could have possibly happened between them to make the Storm Weaver flee the dance floor in front of the entire palace?'

I open my mouth and then close it again, furious. He's right, of course. Meaning that there is no escape. Meaning that I will have to dance with the reason my heart feels as though it's about to burst out of my eardrums and make a break for it without me.

'Fine,' I say. 'But no talking.'

'As you wish. Although I must say, you look particularly lovely this evening.'

'I mean it.'

'As do I,' he says, dropping his gaze to my lips. 'Positively bewitching.'

I glare at him. Fox is wearing a loose-fitting forest-green shirt, his golden chain tucked beneath the collar. His hand is warm in mine, his grip firm. I can feel the calluses beneath my palm, from years of doing . . . what? Slaving? Trekking through jungles? His other hand rests on the small of my back, pressing me gently into his chest.

'So, Storm Weaver. What were you speaking to my brother about? Only you seemed a little . . . tense.'

I bristle. 'None of your business.'

'Just think, depending on the outcome of the third trial, the three of us might soon be spending an awful lot of time together.'

I grimace, wondering whether Marina winning the third trial wouldn't be such a bad thing after all. Then I remember what Elaith was saying moments before Hal asked me to dance.

'Do you even want to be king?' I ask bluntly.

Fox seems to consider this. He twirls me twice, then says, 'I like winning.'

I don't know how to respond to that.

'And you, Storm Weaver? Do you want to be queen?'

The question pins me to the spot. I've spent so long convinced I was going to lose, that I never really considered what it would be like if I didn't. Anyway, what is the point in speculating? Marina is formidable, ambitious, almost regal in her arrogance, and her ability to simmer gives her an advantage. And even if I could beat her, those men I overheard in the maze were right – the people would not accept me as ruler. I'm a Rain Singer. An outcast. And I summoned a storm that almost drowned an empire.

But what if I were to strip that all away?

Do you want to be queen?

I'm not much interested in glory, or status. But I'd be lying if I said I wasn't interested in power. Because I know what it is to feel powerful, and I know what it is to feel powerless, and I know which I'd choose, every time.

'I . . .' My mouth is dry. I wet my lips. 'I don't know.'

'You might want to figure that out,' says Fox wryly, pulling me closer as we change direction. 'Let me know when you do.'

I let out a squeak of surprise and protest as he lifts me up effortlessly by the waist.

Fox does not dance like a courtier. His movements are not poised or practised. He dances roughly, wildly, his body cutting through the space like a blade and taking mine with him.

Faster.

Colours blur and bleed into one another.

Faster.

The air around me fills with the scent of pine and fresh mint.

Faster.

I twirl. The world spins. A pair of green eyes is all that tethers me to the earth.

When the dance eventually comes to an end, clarity hits me like a cold, hard slap across the face. I stumble, my feet suddenly clumsy and graceless, my gaze snagging on stare after stare.

Beside me, Fox bows sharply from the waist before striding from the dance floor without a backward glance.

35

The golden eye rests at my feet, watching me.

I sense its power, raw and devastating. It reels me in and I am overcome with the desire to let it consume me.

Blaze.

So close.

My fingers have yet to brush the surface when the ground begins to quiver, then shake. I lunge for the eye, but I'm too late. The abyss swallows me whole and I fall down, down, down, landing in a pool of shimmering gold.

I jolt awake, gasping for air. Propping myself up, I knit my hands together to stop them from trembling.

The eye continues to gleam in the corners of my mind. It remains with me all day. Nothing can distract me from it. Not my training session with River, not Fox, not Hal, not even the thought of the third trial, which is now less than a fortnight away.

It was easier to dismiss the dreams at first. But the old man's story has got under my skin. I don't believe it, of course. At least, I don't think I do. But either way, it's getting harder and harder to pretend that it doesn't unsettle me, and I want some answers.

Spinner pounces on me the moment I return to my chambers that evening, steering me towards the pile of expensive fabrics fresh off the ship from Vost. She starts jabbering on about silks and satins and sapphire-blue velvets, but I brush her off gently.

'Where are you going?' she calls as I scoop a sleeping Mouse up into my arms and slip out of the doors.

When I reach the library, the old man is waiting for me.

'The girl is back. And she's brought a cat.'

He gestures for me to take the armchair opposite but I remain standing. 'I came to hear the end of the story.'

'What more is there to tell?'

'You said that Syla spent her life as a puppet of the Etheri. You didn't say what happened when her life came to an end.'

'Your point being?'

'When she died, what became of her Eye?'

The old man grins. I notice some of his teeth are missing. 'The girl is learning.'

'Well? What happened to it – the Eye of the Soul? If it exists, where's your proof?'

There is a pause, during which a flash of anguish ignites his ink-blot eyes, so fleeting that I can't be sure if it happened at all. 'Lost.'

'Lost?' I repeat. 'What do you mean *lost*?'

'When Syla died, her Eye vanished. One last enchantment, it seemed. And one that, as yet, remains unbroken.'

Unease twists my insides. Mouse mewls dolefully in my arms, and I realize I've been squeezing her tightly. I take a deep breath. 'Why did you tell me that story?'

The old man strokes his beard. 'Why do you think I told you that story, girl?'

'No, don't do that. Answer the question.'

'It plagues you.'

'*No.*'

He raises an eyebrow. 'You expect my truth in exchange for your lies? I think not.'

I scowl. 'Fine.' Then I pause, swallow. 'I've been having these . . . *dreams.*'

'How illuminating.'

I glare at him. 'Dreams about . . . about . . .'

'Speak, girl.'

'About an eye,' I say, the words tumbling out. 'A golden eye.'

A slow, crooked smile spreads across the old man's face. 'The girl came to me seeking an ending,' he mutters thoughtfully. 'But the girl forgets that one cannot have an ending without a beginning. As one thing ends, another begins. She knows this well, I think. She who has seen both. She who *is* both.'

The beginning that brought the end.

That is what the Fidra call me. Death born from life. Life born from death.

Nausea churns in my stomach. 'I don't understand. What do you want from me?'

A raspy chuckle. 'You must forgive an old man his ramblings. I fear you have indulged me too long. Now, leave me to my book. I require solitude.'

For a moment I just stand there, Mouse clutched to my chest. Is he out of his mind? Or am I, for letting him get in my head?

I draw myself up to full height, resolved not to dwell on

the story any longer. After all, whether she existed or not, Syla is gone, and so is her Eye.

The old man looks at me, head slightly tilted. 'You remind me of her,' he murmurs.

And for all my resolve, his parting words chill me to the bone.

That night, I walk through a winding, windowless passageway lined with flaming torches. There's something familiar about it, like I've been here before. Then it comes to me – I'm in the evacuation tunnels beneath the palace grounds, the ones that lead to the Keep. My feet are bare and the ground is cold. I wait for it to tremble, shake, break in two.

But it doesn't.

As I near the Keep, I become aware of the voices. The sound of my name envelops itself over and over.

Blaze.

I follow the whispering up the spiral staircase.

Blaze.

I push open the door to the training room, pass the fire pit, walk through the forest.

Blaze.

I reach the pool.

Blaze. Blaze. Blaze.

I crouch down beside it, listening. The water. It called me here. But why?

Slowly, I reach out my fingers, gently caressing the surface, and in that moment the glassy stillness shatters. The pool becomes a frothing frenzy and I jerk my hand back in shock. And that's not all. The water is glowing. Glowing gold.

Blaze.

'I'm here,' I whisper back.

It's like it hears me, and grows still once more. I peer down into this pool of liquid sunlight. There's something at the bottom. I can see it. I can *feel* it.

Blaze.

My mind is swimming inside my head. It floats on golden water.

I don't even take a breath before I jump.

Cold – the water is deathly cold. And deep, as deep as the ocean. Screwing my eyes shut, I wait to hit the bottom or wake up, whichever comes first. But I don't. Instead I fall right through the pool . . . and out the other side.

Wincing, I get to my feet. Strange light dances across the floor, and I look up to find a watery ceiling suspended above me. What is this place?

The chamber is spherical. No doors, no windows. Empty but for a single object lying in the centre.

Round her neck each sister wore a talisman.

I walk towards it, water dripping from my nightdress. Whispering fills my ears. My name, repeated like a pledge.

When Syla died, her Eye vanished. One last enchantment, it seemed.

I stare at the golden eye in front of me.

The key to power itself.

My arm shakes as I tentatively reach out my hand, and finally, *finally*, touch it.

Agony.

Euphoria.

Currents of something that exists beyond the realm of

words travel through me, surging through my veins, singing through my blood. Every fibre of my being is set ablaze, and I wonder through screams if this is what swallowing lightning feels like.

I am life. I am death. I see stars. They skim my skin. I am a star.

I am nothing at all.

When I wake the sun is streaming through the windows.

The dream clings to me. I shake my head to clear it and realize that my hair is damp, as if I've just bathed.

Did I make it rain in my sleep?

I sit up, and that's when I become aware of something else.

My hand. My brandhand.

The bones are so stiff that my joints seem locked in place, curled tightly into a fist. Trembling, I unfurl my fingers.

There, sitting on my palm, is the golden Eye.

36

Without thinking, without breathing, I fling the Eye across the room, the metallic clattering a second heartbeat bouncing off the floor.

I choke on disbelief, my head spinning as I try desperately to rationalize, to come up with some sort of explanation. Is this real? Or am I still dreaming?

Yes, that must be it.

I blink hard several times. I even pinch myself on the arm. But when I look back, the Eye is still there.

Cautiously, I slide out of bed and crawl towards it. There's nothing particularly special about it. I doubt I'd give it a second glance if it was worn as a piece of jewellery.

I reach out my hand instinctively, then draw it back as I remember what happened when I touched it – the way it had felt, the way *I* had felt. A shudder scuttles down my spine.

Steeling myself, I grit my teeth and pick it up.

Nothing.

The Eye is cold and lifeless.

Had I dreamed that part? The part where my skin was set aglow, my blood thrumming with something strange and ancient and *alive* . . .

At that moment Spinner bursts through the door. 'Rise and shine!'

Quickly, I drop the Eye into an open jewellery box, where it nestles inconspicuously among an array of golden brooches, and turn to face her.

'Oh, good,' she says. 'You're up. Queen Hydra is expecting you.'

I stare at her uncomprehendingly. 'What?'

'*Hello?*' Spinner pretends to knock on the side of my head. 'For your lesson.'

My heart plummets. How am I supposed to focus on anything after what's just happened? Come to think of it, what *has* just happened?

Spinner tosses me my tunic and pushes me behind the screen. 'Chop, chop. You don't want to be late.'

I dress quickly then trip out of the door in a daze. But I don't plan on going straight to the Aquatori Queen's chambers. There's someone else I have to see first.

The words are out of my mouth before I even turn the corner into the familiar little alcove in the library, but they fade on my tongue. Both armchairs are empty. An open book lies on the table between them, a tiny orb of light hovering above it.

'I know you're here,' I say impatiently. 'I need to speak with you.'

The old man does not appear.

'*Please.*'

Nothing. Not even a rustle. I wait as long as I dare, then mutter a word that would earn me a slap from Grandmother and stalk out of the library.

'Again.' Queen Hydra melts the wall of ice in front of me. 'And faster this time, child.'

I nod, trying to concentrate. We stand several yards apart, the blue marble floor submerged under a few inches of water. My muscles tense as I wait for her to strike.

I've spent the better part of the morning flat on my back. My thoughts are elsewhere, tucked away inside my jewellery box.

An enormous wave rears up and charges towards me. I stand my ground, raising my hands above my head. The ice numbs my fingertips as it shoots into the air, forming a shield around me. A split second later, Queen Hydra's wave slams down on to the frozen barrier with such force that it causes the ice to hiss and crack – but it doesn't break. I watch the water fall to the floor, frothing around my legs.

'Good.'

The ice shield melts and I'm left standing face-to-face with the queen. She waves a hand and at once the water in the room drains away to nothing.

'Take a seat, child.' Queen Hydra pours a cup of steaming tea from the silver pot on the table, stirs in a heaped spoonful of honey and pushes it towards me. 'You seem distracted. Something on your mind?'

Yes, I've lost it.

'No, Your Majesty.'

'Very well.' The queen looks unconvinced. 'Now, there is something else I wish to show you. Something that few Aquatori have ever learned, and even fewer have mastered.'

I sit up a little straighter in my chair, intrigued. 'Tell me.'

'Why don't you drink your tea, and then I will do more than tell you. I will show you.'

I do as she says, scalding my tongue in the process. When I'm finished, Queen Hydra glances down at the table between us. Moments later it's covered by a thin layer of water. She takes a finger and runs it over the surface, drawing a perfect circle no bigger than my head. If I'd blinked, I'd have missed it. For no sooner is the ring drawn, does the section of table it encircles melt away, leaving a small bottomless pool in its place.

I stare at it, then up at the queen. 'What does it do?'

She makes no reply, but rather reaches out and picks up my teacup. Then she rises from her chair and walks to the end of the table, where she proceeds to draw another circle. I dip my hand in the one in front of me and discover that it seems to extend on and on. I watch, bemused, as the queen holds the teacup out over the second pool, closes her eyes and drops it. The water ripples slightly before smoothing over once more.

'How –' I begin, but my words are cut off by the cup's reappearance. Only not in the pool in which it disappeared, but in the one in front of me. I see it – a flash of silver beneath the surface. Glancing uncertainly at Queen Hydra for confirmation, I lower my hand into the water, grasp the handle of the cup and pull it out of the pool.

'Water portals,' she says quietly. With a twitch of her hand the pool recedes into the centre of the circle until only the golden surface of the table remains.

'*Portals?*' I repeat, as she returns to her chair.

She nods. 'Think of them as gateways, as *waterways* – a means of travelling that involves no horses or carriages.

The Ventalla, too, have a similar method, a practice known as flitting, which allows them to travel through the air at great speed, disappearing in one location and reappearing somewhere else entirely. King Balen is an accomplished flitter.'

I think about possessing the power to go anywhere in mere seconds. *Anywhere.*

'Teach me,' I say quickly. Then add, 'Please, Your Majesty.'

Queen Hydra smiles. 'Mastering a skill such as this can take time. But I believe you have what it takes to learn.'

'You do?'

'I do. But I warn you, child, water portals carry their own risks. Very real, very dangerous risks. Therefore I ask that you treat them with caution.'

The queen offers me a plate of little cakes and I take one. 'What are the risks?'

'Well, to start with, one must know exactly where it is one wishes to go before stepping into the portal. If for some reason there is any confusion surrounding the destination, the subject may not reach it.'

'What – so they get *stuck*?' I say, horrified.

'The portal may transport them to a different destination, or yes, it is entirely likely that they could end up stuck – in limbo, so to speak.'

'And what happens then? How do they get out?'

Queen Hydra leans forward, her signet ring gleaming in the afternoon sunlight, engraved with her emblem – the swordfish. 'Either they somehow find a way back to the source portal, or they manage to remain calm enough to refocus their destination.'

'And if they can't?' I ask, already knowing the answer.

'They drown,' she says simply. 'Their body is lost forever between waterways.'

The ghost of a shiver runs through me.

'You understand now just how important it is to possess the right training, discipline and concentration required to use water portals?'

I nod, realizing that I'm still holding the silver teacup. 'And what of this, Your Majesty? Teacups can't drown.'

'No, indeed they cannot, which makes portals an excellent means of transporting inanimate objects from place to place. Or, alternatively, excellent places to store such objects, if you wished to preserve or perhaps conceal them.' The queen holds my gaze, her eyes two more portals, deep blue and boundless. 'There is much I wish to teach you, child,' she says. 'But time trickles on, ceaseless as a stream.'

When I arrive back at my rooms several hours later, I have almost managed to convince myself that I'd imagined the Eye. But as I peer warily into my bedchamber, there it is, sitting in my jewellery box, glinting gold in the early-evening sun.

I pace aimlessly for a while, trying to think. Eventually, I decide that until I get some answers, the Eye is safer being carried on my person. I thread it carefully on to a thin golden chain and fasten it round my neck. Despite the contact with my skin, the Eye remains permanently cool, sitting small and cold next to my heart.

It called to me. It haunted my dreams and it led me straight to it.

But *why*?

Elva draws me a bath, and I sink down beneath the water, letting the old man's words wash over me once more.

Sifa, the first sister, had the power to see the past.

I imagine being able to go backwards, to watch events play out just as they had minutes, or days, or even centuries before.

Seera, the second sister, had the power to see the future.

That would be something. To watch what is yet to come to pass.

And then there was Syla, the third sister, the most powerful of them all. For her power was power. She had the power to take power. To return it. Wield it. Protect it. Possess it. Power belonged to her. It ran through her veins.

Syla, the girl who played with power. I reach up and touch the Eye round my neck.

Three sisters. Three Eyes. I think of Sifa and Seera, hunted, captured and executed, but not before they had hidden their talismans where they could never be found. I think of Syla, hunted, captured and enslaved, bound for the rest of her life to serve her sisters' killers, imprisoned like a criminal and then taken out and exploited like a puppet. A cell made from purest crystal – that's where the old man had said Syla was kept.

An idea begins to form – a reckless, foolish idea.

I dress quickly, braiding my wet hair back from my face and tucking the Eye beneath the collar of my shirt. As I slip Hal's nightlight into my pocket, my gaze lands on the dagger. I hesitate, then stuff it inside my boot.

Elva looks startled as I sweep through the reception room.

'I'm going for a walk,' I lie. 'If anyone comes looking for me tell them . . . tell them I'm indisposed.'

It's common knowledge that the dungeons are located in the very depths of the palace, so I walk down winding corridors, down countless flights of stairs, down and down until the air grows cold and my stomach swoops nervously with every step.

Most of the Etheri are at the feast, though the handful I did encounter who were sober enough to register who I was hurried past without comment, eager to be out of my immediate vicinity. What I'm worried about are the palace guards. Somehow I don't think claiming to be lost is going to cut it.

Voices drift into earshot further down the gloomy passageway and I duck behind an ugly golden gargoyle. Taking my dagger, I cut off a piece of my shirt and wrap the fabric round my left hand to conceal the glow of my brandmark.

Suddenly my plan doesn't seem like such a good idea. What would Grandmother say if she found out I'd been snooping around the palace? What if I'm brought before the emperor?

It's some time before I muster enough courage to step out from behind the gargoyle.

At the end of the passageway lies a great gaping hole. This has to be the entrance to the dungeons. Sure enough, on either side are several armed guards. Yet to my surprise, every one of them appears to be fast asleep. A few scattered playing cards and an empty bottle of wildfire wine lie next to where the men sit slumped against the wall, snoring.

I frown, puzzling over the lax security. Perhaps there's not a prisoner valuable enough to place under strict watch, or perhaps it's a given that once someone is thrown into the dungeons, there is no getting out.

I take a deep breath. It's now or never, I suppose.

Darting out of the shadows, I edge quietly past the sleeping guards. Then I swallow my fear whole and slip into the darkness beyond.

37

I'm not sure what I expected exactly, but it wasn't this.

The dungeons are unfathomably large, larger even than the training room in the Keep, but just as gold. I peer over a railing and discover that they extend for what seems like miles, cut deep into the bowels of the earth. No, not the earth – the *mine*. Of course. Cor Caval was built upon an ancient goldmine. That's why it was the only central province unaffected by the Cleaving. The Earth Cleaver could not destroy the Imperial Province because its foundation is nothing less than the purest, most sacred solid gold.

I appear to be standing on the top level, and stretching down into the shadows are many more floors, each with countless doors set into golden walls. In the centre – nothing but empty space. I take the nightlight from my pocket and bring it close to my lips. It lights up immediately at the sound of my voice and I hold it out in front of me as I descend the staircase to the level below, peering into rooms containing sinister-looking instruments.

I don't stop, not until the top level disappears from view, shrouded in the gloom that seems to hang in the air like smoke.

After what feels like hours the staircase seems to come to an end, and I pause a moment to catch my breath. That's when the smell hits me – thick, acrid and unmistakable. Unwashed bodies, vomit, waste, blood. It is the scent of suffering and it threatens to suffocate me. I clap a hand over my nose and mouth, and force my feet to move.

I shine the nightlight through the small slot in the first door I come to and almost let out a shriek, for what must be two dozen pairs of eyes are looking right back at me. Old and young, thin and very thin, the prisoners are hunched against the walls of the cell or grouped together, attempting to share whatever body heat still lingers in their bones. Some look simply malnourished, whereas others are injured, cradling black eyes or trying to staunch bleeding wounds with dirty scraps of fabric. In one corner sits what looks like a horse trough, the contents of which send bile creeping up my throat. There is no food or water in sight, no blankets, no nothing. Just misery. The sort of misery that turns death from being something one tries to avoid into something desirable. It sickens me.

The old man's words elbow their way intrusively into my consciousness.

Life is sickening, Storm Weaver. But it is always preferable to death.

Yet looking into this cell, I find myself in disagreement.

What could anyone possibly do to deserve such treatment? Are they awaiting execution? Or have they just been left down here to rot?

My gaze lands on an empty pail. It's not difficult to summon the rain. There are gasps among the prisoners. I watch them fall upon the water, and I think about just how little I've seen of the world, its beauty and its brutality.

Then I turn and walk away down the passageway before I can do anything stupid.

At the next cell, a similar scene awaits me. And the next. Some of the prisoners bear features that are not native to Ostacre – oddly coloured eyes; swirling tattoos of strange symbols inked along their scalps, round their necks or down their arms. One woman, whose tattered clothes are stained with dried blood, nurses a newborn baby.

I've never experienced it before – this kind of pity. It's physical. I feel it in my chest.

Eventually I reach the last cell. It has only one occupant. A boy, not much older than I am by the look of him. Coppery hair falls into his strange yellowish eyes, and his skin is sallow and pale, almost grey. His wrists are bound with manacles that look like they're made from glass, from . . . My eyes widen.

There is only one reason this boy would be wearing crystal shackles.

He's a Mage.

But he *can't* be. The Magi lost their magic when they lost the War of the Empires. The people of the Otherlands are now nothing but Fidra, with each new generation being born powerless. Could it be that this boy somehow *retained* his power? But then, how is he still so young? The war took place over fifty years ago.

I waver a moment, caught somewhere between terror and pity.

The boy doesn't glance at the shower of rain falling into the empty pail beside him. He looks only at me. There is a long, still silence in which I have to remind myself to breathe. And when he speaks, it is in the native language of Nepta, an isle in the heart of the Otherlands that was once home to Magi with the ability to communicate with the dead.

'*S'ai nova sempara, Voya Ishraki.*'

My whole body goes rigid. Because what I said to Hal was true – I can speak six languages. And this is one of them.

S'ai nova sempara, Voya Ishraki.

I will remember this, Storm Weaver.

My skin turns deathly cold. I back away from the door. This was a mistake. I should never have come here. I don't know what I was thinking.

Extinguishing the nightlight and slipping it into my pocket, I lean heavily against the wall . . . and fall flat on my back as part of it swings open to reveal a hidden chamber made entirely from crystal.

The old man was telling the truth.

I scramble to my feet, heart pounding. This cell is larger than the others, more like a cave than a room. It glistens, and I see myself, a blurred mirror image reflected a hundred times around the walls, which curve round at odd angles. Large chunks of crystal taller than me are wedged into the ground, creating a maze of sorts.

I shiver as I walk slowly around the cell, waiting for the Eye to do something – grow heavy or light, pulsate or glow, send shock waves through my chest.

But nothing happens.

I imagine Syla here, shackled and weakened, bound to Emperor Caius's will. And I think about Senna, the fourth sister Syla gave up everything to protect. When I heard that part of the story I remember thinking she was selfish, abandoning her people, sacrificing thousands of lives in exchange for only one.

Then I thought of Flint and Renly.

And it's a terrible thing to admit, but I understood. Because it's frightening, looking at someone and knowing that there is nothing – *nothing* – you wouldn't do to keep them safe.

I'm startled by a sudden noise. Not something indeliberate like a scuffle, but something intentional like a scrape, as though someone were running a fingernail down the length of a wall. I move behind a tall block of crystal, reaching down to grasp the hilt of the dagger, unsheathing it slowly from my boot.

'Who's there?' I whisper.

There is no response. My body is frozen, my breaths coming in sharp, painful gasps.

Out of the corner of my eye I see something move.

I dart behind another wedge of crystal, then another, moving back into the centre of the cell. Silence has resumed, heavy and uncertain.

Then I sense the figure standing right behind me. With a surge of terror-fuelled adrenaline, I whirl round, instinctively lunging at them and slamming them backwards, brandishing the tip of my dagger at their throat.

'You know, if you'd wanted me up against a wall, you need only have asked.'

'What are you doing here?' I spit.

'There you go again with the questions, and it seems I could ask you the very same thing,' drawls Fox. 'What are *you* doing here, Storm Weaver? Good little Heirs don't go sneaking around the palace dungeons at night.'

I scowl. 'Don't they? How illuminating. Then I ask again, because I asked first, *what* are *you* doing here?'

Green eyes flash with amusement. 'Well, I am an Heir, like you, but I wouldn't say I was good, necessarily. Or particularly little, for that matter.' He smirks.

I adjust my grip on the dagger. It feels strange in my hand, like a living thing.

'Beautiful,' says Fox, glancing down at it. 'Delicate. Surprisingly lethal.'

'It was a gift.'

'I wasn't talking about the dagger.'

I blush in spite of myself, pressing the blade harder against the collar of his moss-green shirt. A thought hits me then, square in the chest.

'It was you,' I say slowly. 'The guards. They weren't sleeping, were they? You drugged them.'

Fox smiles in answer.

I glare at him. 'Would you be kind enough to explain why you just happen to be here, in the exact same place, at the exact same time, as me?'

He lounges back against the wall. 'I already told you.'

'*When?*' I ask, exasperated.

'In the library after the first trial. You asked me what I intended to do now that I was here, and I told you.'

I remember. I remember his response, too.

I'm looking for something.

'Perhaps you and I are more similar than you might think, Storm Weaver.'

I swallow, recalling the way he'd looked at me in Marina's chambers after I'd frozen Cole's tongue. He thinks we're the same, but we're not. He broke the realm apart and wears his notoriety like a crown. He takes pleasure in pain, revels in destruction.

And yet, there are these ... moments. Soft and quiet, or hungry and unguarded, in which I can almost glimpse another side to him.

Almost.

But then I remind myself who he truly is. *What* he is. A slaver. A monster. Vicious, volatile and cruel. And no amount of kittens or kisses will ever convince me otherwise.

'We are *nothing* alike, *Earth Cleaver*.'

Fox shrugs infuriatingly. 'If you say so. Although it seems you may have already found what I've been looking for.'

Fear strikes a chord in my chest. It skitters along the keys of an out-of-tune piano. It grows louder in my ears, building to a crescendo.

'Really?' I fight to keep my voice level. 'And what's that?'

It happens so fast. With one lightning-quick motion Fox has twisted the dagger out of my hand. With another he pulls me roughly against him and flips us round. My back slams into crystal and I gasp at the impact. I am pinned to the wall by his body, my own weapon gleaming at my throat.

The Earth Cleaver smiles down at me. A strand of dark hair falls into one of his eyes but he makes no effort to brush it away. I can feel the muscles in his legs, pressed up against mine, the solid planes of his chest as it rises and falls. I can feel his heart beating in time with my own. My whole body burns, and not just with hatred.

'How long were you waiting to do that?' I ask bitterly.

'Around about the moment you drew this pretty little blade on me.'

A stab of anger. 'Then what took you so long?'

Fox grins. 'Oh, Storm Weaver. There's just something about you holding a knife at my throat that makes my blood run hot.'

I seethe. There I was thinking I had him cornered, when all the while he was merely letting me. When all the while he was *enjoying* it.

I try to jerk one arm free, but he only presses me harder into the glistening wall. I struggle frantically underneath his weight, so much so that the blade nicks the soft skin on the underside of my throat. The brief spark of pain takes me by surprise. I stop fighting, slumping back against the wall as a single bead of blood slides slowly down my neck. Fox watches it for a moment. Then he leans in close, too close. And licks it away.

I'm so shocked that all I can do is blink. My voice seems to have got stuck on the way out. It takes me longer than I'd care to admit to find it again.

'Get. Off. Me.' Each word requires its own breath.

I'm afraid, and I'm angry. And I'm angry that I'm afraid.

Fox leans back until we are no longer touching. He cocks his head to one side, considering me. Then he takes the dagger and runs its tip gently down my neck, into the hollow between my collarbones.

I inhale sharply. I can't move. I can't form a single thought. My entire existence folds in on itself, reduced to nothing but the point at which the blade touches my skin, snaking lazily down my chest. A flick of his wrist and the top button of my shirt is severed. Even the echoes seem to echo as it falls to the ground and ricochets across the floor.

'You want to know what I've been looking for, Storm Weaver?' Fox cuts the second button. And the third. 'Well, I'll let you in on a little secret.' He lowers his voice to a whisper, leaning forward so that his lips almost brush against mine. 'You're wearing it.'

It's as though the very world explodes around me, with everything splintering into sharp shards of crystal, cutting me to shreds.

Fox lifts the talisman from my chest with the tip of the dagger, drinking it in with eyes like cool green pools. 'I knew it,' he breathes.

I wait for the chain to snap, for him to yank it from my neck and slit my throat for good measure. Maybe a minute, maybe an hour passes like this, standing face-to-face with the Eye gleaming gold between us.

'You can't have it,' I whisper. 'It's mine. I found it. It *wanted* me to find it.'

There is a shift in the air as Fox's eyes refocus on my face. He could take it right now, take it and leave me here to die, if he wanted to.

But he doesn't.

'I knew it,' he says again. 'I knew it was always meant to be you.'

My heartbeat patters like raindrops in my ears. There is a part of me, a strange, foolish part, that wants to trust him. I stamp down on it hard, crushing it with the heel of my boot.

'Let me go.'

Fox blinks in surprise. 'But I would never make you stay.'

I want to scream at him. I want to shatter this cell and myself with it.

'Good. Then give me my dagger and step aside. Then I can go back to avoiding you and we can both pretend that none of this ever happened.'

There is a pause.

'All right.' He holds up his hands in surrender. 'It's just, it seems only fair.'

'*What's* only fair?'

'Well,' he says, brushing a stray curl behind my ear, 'since you showed me yours, I figured it's only right that I show you mine.'

My stomach twists. 'What are you talking about?'

Fox smiles at me, and it's such a tender smile that it threatens to knock me off balance. 'I told you that you and I are more alike than you think,' he murmurs.

I'm about to protest when his hand moves to the chain round his neck. It's the one he's always worn since the very first day I met him. He reels the chain upward, winding it round and round his finger, revealing a pendant dangling from the end of it.

A small golden pendant, shaped like an eye.

38

I watch the morning sun glinting off my dagger and try not to come undone. I count the seconds, the inhalations, the heartbeats, the taunting *tick*, *tick*, *tick* of the clock on the wall and attempt to tackle time to the ground before it can run away like sand through my fingers.

Slowly, I begin to sift through the events of last night.

Fox. Fox knows about the three enchanted Eyes. He knows that I wear Syla's Eye round my neck. He has an Eye, too. But he didn't tell me to which sister it belonged, or why he let me go, or what he's planning to do. With the Eyes. With me.

He took me back to my chambers last night. Up the endless steps, past the sleeping guards and into the serf tunnels to avoid detection. When we reached the Aquatori Wing, he leaned across to open my door, but before I could slip past him he caught hold of me and murmured, 'I trust you to keep this between us, Storm Weaver. Because when someone breaks my trust, I break them.'

And when he said this I remember thinking about bones. The blunt snap of my wrist in the first trial. The sickening crunch of Cole's jaw in the maze. But something told me that Fox wasn't referring to mere bones when he spoke of breaking something. Someone.

I spend the rest of the night lying awake, wondering if I should throw the Eye right back into the pool in the Keep.

Maybe if I concentrate very hard on the patch of blue sky outside the window I could just melt into it. Leave my body behind and go live in the clouds.

But that might have to wait, because at that moment Flint bursts into my bedchamber. Mouse, who was asleep on the pillow beside me, starts awake and hisses at him furiously. For some reason my brother is holding a hand over his eyes.

'Just to be clear, I couldn't care less who you are,' he snarls. 'Unless your intentions are nothing short of *marriage*, I have no choice but to challenge you to a duel.'

I prop myself up on my elbows. 'Er ... who are you talking to?'

Flint is breathing heavily, as though he's marched all the way here, which I'm guessing he has. Splaying his fingers slightly, he peers cautiously through the gap. I give him a bemused little wave. He frowns, scanning the room before he yanks back my bedsheets and tosses them to the floor. I yelp, half indignant, half bewildered. But Flint isn't finished. He strides over to the armoire and begins pulling out dress after dress. Then, struck by a sudden idea, he crouches down on the floor and starts looking underneath my bed.

'What on earth do you think you're doing?'

He turns to me, eyes burning with rage. 'Where is he?'

'*Who?*'

Then I freeze. He doesn't mean Fox, does he? He can't know that I was with him last night, can he?

I decide to play the fool. 'Flint, I really don't know what you're talking about.'

My brother ignores me. I can almost see the steam coming out of his ears as he raises his voice, addressing the room at large. 'I know you're here, and I don't care who your father is, I don't care who you are, and I don't care who you're going to be. If you think I'm going to sit by while you *defile* my sister's honour, then you are mistaken.'

My stomach drops. Did Flint somehow find out about the kiss in the maze? But – but it was just a kiss. Just a mindless, misguided kiss. It didn't mean anything.

Trying to keep my voice as calm and measured as possible, I pat the bed beside me. 'Why don't you sit down? I think there's been some kind of mistake.'

Yes, a mistake. A cruel, sadistic, green-eyed mistake.

Flint doesn't sit down. His fists are clenched, knuckles protruding. 'There's no use denying it, Blaze,' he says. 'Spinner saw. She saw him.'

Heat creeps into my cheeks. 'I don't know what you're talking about.'

My brother sighs. 'How could you be so stupid?'

Embarrassment turns swiftly to anger. I stand up and face him head-on. 'Stupid?' I repeat. 'So I'm stupid now, am I? And how, exactly, am I stupid?'

'Nobody can find out about this,' says Flint. 'Nobody.'

I stare at him. If Spinner saw me with Fox in the maze, why hadn't she mentioned it before now? And if she'd seen us emerging from the serf tunnels together, the most she can do is accuse us of being in the same place at the same time. In any case, if she saw us last night she'd also have seen that

Fox left me at my door. So why is my brother ransacking my room? And why is he shouting about marriage and *defiling my honour* and –

'It's not your fault, Blaze,' Flint says quietly. 'It's mine. I should have . . .' He stops, takes a breath. That's when all the anger seems to drain out of him and he moves across the room, slumping down on to the window seat. 'I should have put a stop to it. I should have handled it differently. But I never expected him to take it this far.' An anguished look spreads across his face. 'You've lived a sheltered life. You're young –'

'You do realize you're only ten minutes older than me, right?'

Flint glares at me. I shut up.

'You're young,' he continues, 'and you're naive, and he's taken advantage of that and he's going to pay for it, prince or not.'

My chest constricts. 'Wait,' I say slowly. 'Who are we talking about?'

Flint looks at me incredulously. '*Hal*, of course. Who else? Or is this your way of telling me that you've been taking multiple boys into your bed?'

There it is, my jaw, lying cracked and broken on the floor at my feet.

Hal? My brother thinks that Hal spent the night here, in my bedchamber, in my *bed*?

Flint folds his arms. 'Well?'

Laughter bubbles uncontrollably up my throat. Relieved by the misunderstanding, I sit back down opposite my brother. 'Care to explain?'

'Spinner came by your rooms to check on you because you decided not to show up to the feast – *again*, I might add – and she saw Hal knock on the door, she saw it open, and she saw him go inside. Inside your chambers, late at night, when you were alone and unchaperoned.'

I frown, pinpricks of confusion stabbing into me as I try to make sense of his words. To reveal I know nothing about this is to reveal that I wasn't in my rooms last night, which will only lead to questions. But Flint is looking at me as though I'm this sad, foolish, ignorant little girl and it's making me so angry that I have to say something in my defence without incriminating myself in an entirely different way.

'I wasn't at the feast,' I begin. 'But I wasn't here either. I was . . . in the library.'

Yes, good. No one is ever in the library, so no one can dispute whether I was there or not. Apart from the old man, but he's apparently decided to disappear off the face of the earth.

'Oh, really?' says Flint, in a voice that tells me he doesn't believe a word.

'Really. I was reading up on . . . on the history of the Rain Singers. River lent me another book he thought I might be interested in. I'm sure Hal was just dropping off some roses from the palace gardens.'

'I see.' My brother nods once, twice. 'Then could you explain why Spinner also informed me that Hal did not return to the feast? If, as you say, you weren't in fact here, then whyever should the prince have cause to stay away such a great length of time?'

I stare at him, mystified and irritated, feeling somewhat as

342

though I were on trial for a crime I didn't commit. 'Maybe . . . maybe he waited for me to return. Or maybe he just didn't feel like going back to the feast straight after. Maybe he took a *walk*. Last I checked, he can do what he wants, being the prince and all. But whatever he did, I don't know, because I wasn't here. I was in the library, like I said, and I lost track of time. Happy?'

Flint picks at a loose thread on the hem of his doublet. 'Not particularly, no.'

I throw a pillow in his direction to get him to look at me. 'Flint, I'm your sister. Please believe me when I say that the Crown Prince of Ostacre *did not* spend the night in my bed. And nor did anyone else, for that matter, unless you count Mouse. All right?'

My brother squints at me, reading my face. Then he gets up from the window seat and sits down next to me. 'All right,' he says in a defeated sort of way. 'I believe you.'

'If you had found him in here, would you really have challenged him to a *duel*?' I ask.

Flint shrugs. 'If he'd added you to the list of girls used and discarded by powerful men, then yes, I would have challenged him to a duel, Blaze. And I would have bested him in front of his entire court.'

I roll my eyes. 'I had no idea you felt so strongly about these kinds of things.'

'Well, sister, I do. It's my job to look after you. Besides, depending on the outcome of the third trial, you could be *queen*. Remember what Grandmother said. She said you must be wise about how you conduct yourself here. That you must remain *above reproach*.'

I elbow him. 'She said that to you, too.'

'So . . . you and Hal, you really didn't – I mean, he didn't . . .'

'No, I didn't, he didn't, we didn't. But just so you know, even if I had, that would be my choice and none of your concern. And for the record, calling me stupid and naive and accusing me of hiding the Imperial Heir in my underwear drawer makes me angry, and as you know, when I get angry, things tend to get a little . . . *icy* between us.'

Flint cries out in surprise as a layer of frost coats his forearm. He wipes it off, wincing at the cold, then grins at me. 'Noted. But seriously, whatever is going on between the two of you – and please, *please* spare me the details – you've got to be more careful. Think what Grandmother would do if she heard you were sleeping with the prince.'

'Think what Grandmother would do if she heard you were sleeping with an Eye,' I shoot back. 'I can't imagine that going down particularly well.'

Flint points a finger at me. 'Now you,' he says, 'you are good.'

I bow my head. 'Thank you very much.'

'Care to be my escort to the party tonight?' he asks.

'I could be persuaded.'

'Great. Excellent.'

'That makes a nice change from stupid and naive.'

Flint exchanges an exasperated look with Mouse, but my kitten ignores him, nuzzling into my lap and purring softly.

'I still can't believe Hal got you a *cat*.'

'Oh, good,' I say, glancing up so quickly I almost get a crick in my neck. 'Breakfast.'

Elva moves silently across the room, amber eyes trained on the floor as she sets the tray down on the bed and leaves without a word. At the sight of the food, I recall the starving prisoners locked in the dungeons, pitiful and helpless. And I think of that boy, that *Mage*. For all I know, he could be the lone survivor of the Magi. The last of his kind, just like me.

'Isn't it strange?' Flint says through a mouthful of pastry. 'That in just a few weeks, you and I could be sitting here wearing crowns.'

I tense up. Since finding the Eye, I've barely given the third trial a moment's thought. And in answer to Flint's question, *strange* is certainly one word for it. I used to think it inconceivable. For me, that is. Not for him. My brother was born to be king. He has to be. Because if the idea of Marina winning is bad enough, the idea of Flint losing invokes an entirely different kind of dread altogether.

I haven't seen Ember for days. Word is she's spending almost every waking hour training. Flint, on the other hand, seems far more interested in drinking champagne until the small hours and going to bed whenever – and with whomever – he wants. Hypocrite.

Sighing, I reach towards the tray, finding nothing but a few crumbs and smears of jam. I glare at my brother, who's leaning back against the bedpost with a hand over his stomach.

'It was all that blind rage,' he says. 'It made me hungry.'

'I've never seen you like that before,' I tell him.

Flint raises an eyebrow. 'Well, if my darling sister's reputation is at stake, I'm afraid I'm going to have to turn off the famous charm, just temporarily. I'm not having

anyone say anything worse about you than they already –'
He clamps his mouth shut.

'Than they already do,' I finish for him.

I've often wondered whether Flint was somehow oblivious
to all the cruel things said about me, or whether he just tried
to shield me from them as best he could. I realize now that
the latter must be true. And I love him for it, for wanting to
protect me. But at the same time, I find that the word *protect*
leaves a bitter taste in my mouth.

All my life I have been protected.

To protect you, my parents said as they locked the gates
and doubled the guard and built the walls thirty feet high.

It's for your own protection, Grandmother told me when
I begged her to let me go with Flint and his friends to watch
a play at the theatre or swim in the hot springs.

After seventeen years, I've come to realize that *protect* is
actually just a pretty word for hide.

Hide her away. Lock her up. Maybe the world will forget,
if she's kept out of sight. Maybe she'll not look to leave, if
we give her no other choice but to stay. Maybe if we conceal
her well enough, she'll disappear entirely.

Heat prickles behind my eyes and I blink hard, sitting
up tall.

That was then. This is now. And I *refuse* to disappear.

'Are you all right?' Flint is watching me warily.

I force my features into a smile. 'Never better.'

39

I sometimes think of the Imperial Province as a web – finely spun, gleaming gold. Clinging to each silken strand are people from all walks of life, young and old, rich and poor, Etheri and Fidra, all of them bound up together. It is here they flock, weaving their lives among the gossamer threads all stretching towards the spider sitting in the very centre.

If the emperor appeared gaunt before, he is positively ghostlike now. I'd previously considered whether it was the idea of relinquishing his crown that was making him ill, but now I'm not so sure. I've never had the sense that Emperor Alvar feels particularly strongly about anything. He's difficult to read in that way. There was curiosity perhaps, with regard to me. Seemingly a fondness for his Council. Presumably an affection for his sons, although Fox is rarely at court, and as for Hal, I would describe their interactions as stiff at best.

The only time I have ever seen real emotion flit across his careful mask is when he looks at Kestrel Calloway.

I think of Empress Goneril, Hal's mother, the sour-faced Vosti princess who fulfilled her duty two decades ago and is now regarded as nothing more than an inconvenience. How they must resent one another, the unwanted wife and the beloved mistress.

I twirl the stem of a golden rose between my fingers. Hal was waiting for me when I returned from my lesson yesterday evening, a fresh bunch in hand.

When he marries, there will be no more roses. There will be no more visiting my chambers, or singling me out to dance, or secret kisses in broom cupboards. Because I know that Hal, of all people, who has watched his own mother dismissed by his father and disregarded by the court, could never inflict the same fate upon the Thavenian princess who will one day be his wife.

Bitterness claws at my throat. What am I *doing*? Why am I allowing myself to fall for a boy who I know will never be mine?

Maybe Flint's right. Maybe I am stupid and naive.

A sharp stinging sensation has me sucking in a breath through clenched teeth. I look down to find I've been squeezing the rose stem so tightly that a thorn has lodged itself deep in the soft flesh of my palm. Elva appears at my side, her beautiful face creased with concern as she dislodges the thorn with quick, careful fingers. I gaze bemusedly at the blood pooling in my hand. There's blood on Elva's hands too. It looks so red against her porcelain skin.

She bathes the cut in water, and I watch in surprise as she rips a strip of fabric from her white tunic and wraps it tightly round my hand, securing it in place with a small practised knot. I thank her, and she gives her head a little shake, as though her actions were not worthy of my gratitude.

'Blaze!' Spinner calls. 'Come on, we're going to be late.'

Since the night I danced with the Earth Cleaver, I have avoided all balls, banquets and parties. I say it's to conserve my energy for my training sessions with Queen Hydra, but really it's because the thought of seeing him again, especially after what I learned in the dungeons, makes me feel as though I'm about to turn to liquid, or fall through the floor.

I hate that he catches me off guard. I hate that I can't work him out, no matter how hard I try. I hate that he finds a way to burrow and bulb and bloom inside my brain, more than he should, more than I should admit. And I hate that I'm thinking about him now, even if it's only to list everything about him that I hate.

River's words come back to me.

Hate can sink its claws in deep.

My thoughts wander to the dagger wrapped carefully in my shirt, a silver claw cut from the body of a creature with no soul. I remember the way it felt pressed against my neck, that single bead of blood like a drop of dark wine on Fox's tongue.

Shaking my head to banish the memory, I offer Elva a small smile before Spinner tows me off towards the evening's festivities.

The palace gardens are strewn with tiny orbs of light, all of them floating a few feet off the ground. I tense up as I catch sight of the maze in the distance, but Spinner pulls me on towards a brightly lit patch of lawn where a crowd seems to be gathering. Music swells, lilting and melodic, mingling with the sweet-scented night air.

'Why does everything always smell of lilies in this place?' I wonder aloud.

'Lilies are Lady Calloway's favourite flower,' Spinner tells me.

'Oh.' I'm silent for a moment, then another thought strikes me. 'Spinner, you know how Lady Calloway and the emperor had a second child – the little girl who died?'

Spinner glances sidelong at me. 'Mm-hm.'

'What was her name? I can't remember it.'

There's a pause, then Spinner says, 'Her name was Freya.'

Freya. Fox and Freya. Born of love, torn apart by death.

'She died of the sweating sickness, didn't she?'

Spinner stops walking and turns to face me. 'What's brought this on?'

'What d'you mean?' I ask, self-conscious.

'All these questions about Freya. You've never asked about her before. Has someone said something?'

'No.' I swallow. 'No, I was just . . . curious. That's all.'

I sense her again, that other Spinner, watchful and suspicious, coiled just beneath the surface.

'I'll tell you something I'm curious about,' she says, seeming to let it slide and reaching out to touch the chain round my neck. 'Of all the beautiful jewellery from Thaven I spent *weeks* sourcing and selecting for you, why oh *why* do you insist on wearing this old thing?' With one quick tug she pulls the talisman out from underneath the front of my dress and examines it. 'I mean, no offence,' she continues, 'but it's not even that pretty.'

I brace myself, waiting for the Eye to come alive, for Spinner to scream in agony as the full force of its power surges through her the way it did me. But nothing happens.

Exhaling in relief, I shrug in what I hope is a casual, non-committal sort of way. 'You're right,' I tell her. 'It's just, well, it belonged to my mother.'

The lie immediately smooths over the sharp scepticism on Spinner's face. She lets go of the Eye and I tuck it back beneath my dress.

'And this,' Spinner says, nodding to my hand, where the bloodstained scrap of fabric is still wrapped round my palm. 'Would you care to explain this? It's not exactly complementing my masterpiece.' She gestures to all of me, from the silky sky-blue gown to the pearls woven among my hair.

I examine my hand, thinking about how hard I must have been squeezing that rose to lodge the thorn so deeply into my flesh. 'Sorry. Clumsy.'

Spinner rolls her eyes at me, the golden tattoos on her cheeks merging into different patterns as she smiles. 'Come on, then, Clumsy. I'm dying for a canapé.'

We soon reach a part of the palace gardens I've never been to before, where what appear to be gold-painted people are standing on small podiums dotted around the lawn. On closer inspection I realize that they are in fact statues, dozens of them, and no matter which way I turn, I am watched from every angle by blank, pupilless golden eyes.

Spinner spots Flint, Elaith and Zephyr in the crowd and bounds over to them, dragging me with her. But a familiar voice makes me stop short.

'Blaze?'

'Kai!' I exclaim. 'You're here! I mean, you're better. Are you better? You look – how – how are you?'

Kai wears a deep-blue doublet that suits his complexion, his dark hair tied back from his face with a strip of cloth. There's nothing – no scab or scar or bruising – that suggests he's been bedridden, but of course there wouldn't be. Coming seconds away from drowning doesn't leave a mark. Water doesn't cut – it chokes.

'I am better,' he says, smiling. 'Much better. And I wanted to congratulate you, Blaze. I always knew you had it in you.'

I return his smile, reaching to embrace him. He wraps his arms round me. As I draw back I become aware of someone watching us.

The Earth Cleaver leans against one of the golden statues, one ankle crossed over the other. He wears a loosely buttoned shirt in such a dark shade of evergreen it looks almost black, fitted leather trousers and scuffed, mud-flecked riding boots. His golden chain glimmers in the light from the orbs floating above our heads.

My breath catches. All week I've managed to avoid him. Now he's found me.

Fox pushes off the statue and strides towards us, his gaze only leaving my face to flit briefly over Kai.

'Storm Weaver. Friend of Storm Weaver. How are we this evening?' His voice is smooth and charming, laced with just a hint of sarcasm.

When I don't respond, Kai clears his throat. 'Well enough. Yourself?'

Fox doesn't answer him. I watch as he slides his hands into his pockets, stepping ever so slightly closer. He really is infuriatingly beautiful.

'What do you want?' I ask rudely.

'A word,' he says. 'Alone.'

'*Now?*'

'Now.'

Kai looks caught somewhere between fear of Fox and concern for me. He hovers for a moment, unsure of what to do, his eyes darting between us.

'It's all right, Kai,' I tell him. 'I'll find you later.'

'Yes, do run along,' says Fox without even glancing at him.

Kai hesitates a second longer, then walks hurriedly away into the crowd.

Fox holds out an arm. 'Walk with me.'

It's not a question, but I ignore his arm and brush roughly past him. I can hear the smile in his voice as he falls into step beside me.

'You know, you could do a whole lot better than a half-drowned Fish with a ponytail.'

I glare at him out of the corner of my eye and say nothing. We walk until we reach the outskirts of the crowd. It's quieter here, the floating lights fewer. Only a handful of stragglers gawk at us as we pass by, and one look from Fox sends them on their way.

'Can we keep this brief?' I say. 'I'd really rather we didn't discuss things so publicly.'

Fox's smile grows wider. 'I knew you liked being alone with me.'

I want to claw off my own skin as my cheeks begin to heat. 'That is *not* what I meant.'

'Don't worry, Storm Weaver. My dear brother is nowhere to be seen. And with regard to discussing things publicly, it may have escaped your notice that we are now right on the very edge of this tedious gathering and therefore attracting little attention.'

I pull a leaf off a low-hanging branch and rip it up into pieces.

Fox watches me amusedly. 'These statues,' he says. 'Do you know what they are?'

I let the mangled spine of the leaf fall to my feet. 'Should I know what they are?'

'That's an interesting way of saying no.'

I scowl.

Fox runs his hand down the nearest statue – a tall, bearded man gazing off thoughtfully into the distance. 'Each of these statues is a former emperor,' he says. 'This one is Rekar Castellion.'

'The second emperor,' I say. 'Son of the Maker. He built the Golden Keep.'

Fox nods. 'You know your history.' He leads me over to another statue, standing just a few yards away. This emperor is smaller, his mouth curved into a crooked smile. 'This is my father's father, Caius Castellion.'

A shiver runs through me as I stare into the face of the emperor who conquered the Otherlands and defeated the Magi. Who murdered Sifa and Seera while keeping Syla for himself, bound to serve him until she died.

Fox is looking at me. He is always looking at me.

'So,' I say briskly. 'Let's hear it.'

He arches a brow.

'You said you wanted a word. I want to keep it brief. So, get on with it.'

Fox's eyes glint with undisguised amusement. 'Nobody has *ever* spoken to me the way you do.'

I hold his gaze, irritation conquering fear.

'Very well,' he says. 'I wanted to ask what you have done to your hand.'

'My hand?' I glance down at the strip of white fabric. 'Oh, my hand. I – I cut it. On a thorn.' I frown. 'Why?'

Fox has a strange expression on his face. 'You cut it?'

'Like I said.'

'How deep was the cut?'

I stare at him. 'What has this got to do with anything?'

Fox ignores me. He reaches out, encircling my wrist and lifting my hand to his face, his fingers warm and rough against my skin. 'This fabric – it's from a serf's tunic.'

'So?'

'So, how did you acquire it?'

'How did *you* acquire the serf tunic you wore to the first trial?' I shoot back.

Fox smiles, but I can sense rather than hear the urgency in his voice. 'Was there someone with you? When you cut your hand?'

'I . . . Yes, my serf. She cleaned me up. Tore off a piece of her tunic and used it as a makeshift bandage. Again, *why*?'

'Your serf,' he repeats.

'Yes. Can I go now?'

There's an odd, strung-out pause during which Fox drops my wrist. 'I believe you have some questions you wish to ask me, Storm Weaver.'

I cross my arms over my chest. 'I might have some,' I say grudgingly.

Fox crooks his finger slightly and I watch as the scattered pieces of the leaf I ripped up float into the air and knit themselves back together. 'You may begin,' he tells me.

I take a deep breath. 'How do you know about the Eyes?'

'One hears many stories on one's travels.'

Well, that's irritatingly vague. I try again. 'Why were you in the dungeons that night?'

'The party lacked atmosphere.'

'*Seriously?*'

Fox examines his signet rings.

'Fine,' I say through gritted teeth. 'Then can you at least tell me whether your Eye belonged to Sifa or Seera?'

'Perhaps. In time.'

I stare at him, furious.

Fox smiles pleasantly back at me. 'I said I believed you had some questions for me, Storm Weaver. I didn't say anything about answering them.'

'You are unbelievable,' I hiss. 'You can't just spring something like this on me and expect me to figure it all out myself. I need answers. I feel like I'm going *insane*.'

A hush falls over the distant crowd as the Thavenian emissary is announced. My heart seizes up and sinks low as the emperor makes an announcement of his own, one that I have been dreading since the night Hal kissed me.

'It is my pleasure to inform you all that my son, His Imperial Highness, Prince Haldyn Castellion, is betrothed to Princess Mirade of Thaven.'

I feel it, then. I feel something snap.

'I can't do this,' I say, pulling the Eye out from under my dress. 'I don't know what's happening. I don't know what any of it means – the Eyes, the story, the sisters, and you know what? I'm beginning to think I don't want to.'

I curse as drizzle begins to fall above our heads. My hands shake as ice fills my veins.

Fox takes a step forward. 'Storm Weaver.'

'I mean it. I want no part in it.'

'What are you saying?'

'I'm saying . . . I'm saying I'm out. You want it?' I pull the chain over my head and dangle it in front of him. 'Then take it.'

I hurl the Eye at his feet. It bounces twice on the grass, coming to rest by the tip of his boot.

'Storm Weaver –'

'And stop calling me that,' I snap. 'It's *not* my name.'

'You're not thinking clearly. Calm down and we'll talk.'

'No.' I didn't realize how good that word felt to say. I say it again. '*No*. I don't want to talk. I'm done talking. Just leave me *alone*.'

I turn away and storm back towards the party.

Everything I said was true. I don't want the Eye. I never asked for it. But now that I am without it, I don't feel lighter. If anything, I feel weighed down by its absence. For days I have kept it close to me, this strange, ancient talisman. I have puzzled over the story, searched the library for the old man, risked being caught and brought before the emperor, all for nothing. The Eye is lifeless. Dead, just like Syla. I can't even be sure that the surge of power I felt in my dream wasn't just that – a dream. Besides, I have enough to think about. My lessons with Queen Hydra. The third trial. Hal.

I skirt the perimeter of the crowd, sifting through the mass of colours until I catch sight of Elaith. I plunge through the throng and grab her shoulder.

'Elaith. Have you seen the prince?'

'Blaze! We all wondered where you were. Nice dress. And no, I've not seen him. He doesn't seem to be here at all, which is slightly odd given they just announced his *betrothal*. Are you all right? Did you know?'

But I just turn and race away through the grounds and into the palace. By the time I reach my chambers, I'm ready to slump on my bed and sleep for a week.

Darkness.

That's what greets me when I open the door. Thick, impenetrable darkness, swarming around me, coating me in shadows. Even my brandmark can't make a dent in it.

Then, a voice, a familiar voice, stretched tight and stricken. 'Shut the door.'

An orb of light appears and floats up towards the ceiling, illuminating the scene before me. The floor is strewn with golden roses. Elva is lying on her back, eyes closed, seemingly unconscious. And clutching her protectively to his chest, burying his face in her hair as he pleads with her, as he *begs* her to wake up, is Hal.

40

I have never heard anything louder than the silence that fills my head.

It burrows into my ears, pours into my mouth. I drown in it. Because there is no mistaking the way Hal is looking at Elva. The desperation with which he clings to her. The terror in his voice as he tries and fails to rouse her.

Words dart through my mind, echoes of a conversation.

I know you dislike attention.

Is that why you come to my rooms to see me?

I remember Hal had looked down at our joined hands then, looked down and not at me, because he couldn't meet my eyes.

Why else?

I think I know why else. She's lying unconscious on the floor at my feet.

Elva.

Hal . . . and *Elva*.

Suddenly the pieces start falling into place. Last week. Spinner saw Hal slipping into my chambers when I wasn't there. I wasn't there, but *she* was. She is here all the time, moving silently from room to room, a kind, quiet presence

I have come to regard as being something close to a friend. And Hal. His seeming distracted. The roses delivered by hand. It was never about me, it was about her. It was always about *her*. All this time.

Truth is a ragged shard of glass to the jugular. It cuts me open and watches me bleed. It offers no consolation. Only cold, sharp clarity.

'Blaze,' Hal croaks. 'Please, please get help. I can't – I can't leave her.'

I assure you, Blaze, visiting your chambers is my most favourite part of the day.

I am frozen in place. I am a golden statue in a garden.

It kills me, Blaze. Knowing I can't have the one that I want. It kills me more and more every day.

Humiliation paints itself on to my skin. I want to curl up and die.

'Blaze. *Please.*'

I shake my head, swallowing hard. 'All right. All right, stay here.'

I stumble backwards through the darkness, my arm feeling disconnected from my body as I swing open the door.

'What's wrong?' One of Fox's hands is already outstretched, curled into a fist as though just about to knock. In his other he holds my Eye. 'What is it? What's happened?'

My voice quivers. 'I need a physician.'

His eyes search my face. 'I ask again, what has happened?'

'It's my – my serf, she –'

But Fox is already moving past me into my rooms. For a moment he takes in the scene. Then he reaches out and yanks me inside before shutting the door behind us.

Hal is still bent over Elva, shaking her gently, one hand stroking her face. He looks up, his expression twisting from fear to anger. 'What is *he* doing here?'

'And a pleasant evening to you too, dear brother.' Fox crouches down beside him, glancing first at Elva, then back at me. 'So, it seems your pretty little secret has been uncovered by your pretty little lie. How inconvenient for you.'

I clench my fists tightly, feeling the cut on my palm bubble up and bleed anew. 'Can't you see she needs help?'

A corner of Fox's mouth quirks upward. 'How very perceptive of you, Storm Weaver. Now be an angel and fetch a blanket, would you? We have to keep her warm.'

I just stare at him. '*You're* deciding to help?'

'Looks like it,' he says, pressing two fingers to a spot on Elva's neck.

'And what if I don't want your help?' Hal snaps. He's shaking.

Fox presses the same two fingers to the inside of Elva's wrist. 'You are perfectly within your rights to refuse, of course. But I feel I should inform you that the court physicians, most of whom are currently attending your betrothal party, would not consider the well-being of a serf to be particularly high on their priority lists. And if you did find one who was willing to help, your personal concern for the aforementioned serf would undoubtedly lead to a host of questions that I believe you would prefer to avoid.'

I watch as the cracks begin to form in Hal's resolve.

Fox's voice is quieter now. Not kind, exactly, but steady and sure. 'In any case, brother, you know as well as I do that I am worth ten of those physicians, and I offer my help without asking for anything in return.'

My eyes are wide with surprise and confusion. Hal looks from Fox, to me, to Elva in his arms, and then back to Fox again.

The Earth Cleaver shrugs. 'Your decision. But I would remind you that time is of the essence. The sooner I can take a look at her, the sooner I can prescribe a remedy.'

Suddenly Elva lets out a sharp gasp. Her eyes fly open for little more than a second and I stagger back against the wall, a small shriek fighting to escape from my mouth. Because in that moment, unmistakable in the thick gloom surrounding us, Elva's eyes gleamed the brightest amber. In that moment, her eyes had glowed in the dark.

'What *was* that?' I whisper.

Hal is breathing heavily, staring down at her. 'What – what just happened?'

Fox looks neither shocked nor scared. He places a light hand on his brother's arm. 'Haldyn,' he says evenly. 'Let me help her.'

Something seems to spark to life inside of Hal. 'Let's go,' he says.

Fox gets to his feet. 'We'll take the serf tunnels. Can you carry her?'

Hal nods, scooping Elva up and cradling her to his chest.

'That blanket, Storm Weaver, if you'd be so kind,' says Fox mildly, striding forward to open the door.

He leads the way through the serf tunnels, brandishing a flaming torch he plucked from a bracket on the wall. Hal follows him, holding Elva tightly, as though she might fall apart in his arms.

I can't think about Hal right now. I can't think about the fact that he has been using me. And I can't think about the fact that I fell for it. For *him*.

Up ahead, Fox comes to a stop. I watch in the flickering light as he reaches out and twists something on what seems to be a solid wall, which immediately swings open to reveal a room. The space is large, with a remarkably high ceiling, sloping walls and a strange, spongy floor. My nose is filled with the scent of pine and fresh mint.

Fox leads us inside. 'Some light perhaps, brother?'

Hal squeezes his eyes shut and a moment later the room is lit by a warm glow.

I can't help but gasp, for we are standing in what appears to be a garden. No, not quite – it's not as orderly as a garden. It's wilder, untamed.

Vines snake along the walls, long and thick like rope, sharing the space with a multitude of climbing plants. There's ivy, lots of it, and honeysuckle, its pale petals slowly unfurling in the light. The floor is a carpet of soft grass and wildflowers, hundreds of them, the colours vivid and beautiful, too many to count. In the centre of the room, stretching all the way up to the ceiling, is a gigantic tree. The branches are long and sweeping, the leaves as green as the eyes of the boy who places a gentle hand on the small of my back while he closes the door behind me. Something else about the tree catches my attention. I look closer. What appears to be a bed is positioned around halfway up the trunk, a large mattress tucked into the space where several branches have been entwined to resemble what looks like two cupped hands. There is no bedframe, only a mass of pillows and sheets.

Through one door at the far side of the room is a bathing room, its floor made from gleaming emerald. There is another door too, slightly closer to where we're standing, but it's closed, seemingly locked.

'Where *are* we?' I breathe.

'My rooms,' Fox says simply.

I take a moment to acknowledge how perfectly insane this is, that I am here, in the Earth Cleaver's strange jungle of a bedchamber. Oh, and we're joined by none other than the Crown Prince of Ostacre and my unconscious serf, who just so happens to have been conducting some secret relationship for months right under my nose.

Fox pulls a small silver key out of his pocket and unlocks the nearby door, and I step inside, mouth falling open as I take in the room beyond. In the centre sits a high wooden table littered with dried plants, powders, potions, potted herbs and strange curling stems. As for the walls, I can't even see them for the shelves, each one crammed with an assortment of glass vials of all different shapes and sizes, tinted green and neatly labelled.

Fox is looking at me, studying my reaction as he clears the countertop and gestures for Hal to lay Elva down.

'So ... so you're a *physician*?' My tone is light with disbelief.

He shakes his head. 'I don't like to think of myself as a physician. Physicians are cautious creatures, always relying on tried and tested methods and medicines. Their services are bought by coin. They are selective about who they treat. No, I'm no physician.'

'Then what is all this?' I ask. 'What are you?'

A faint smile flits across Fox's face. 'I'm a Healer,' he says. Cleaver. Slaver. Hunter. *Healer*.

I'm stunned into silence just as Hal finds his voice. 'You have to help her, Fox. You have to do something –'

'You found her like this?' Fox interjects, rolling up the sleeves of his shirt, exposing strong forearms, their golden skin weather-beaten and flecked with a series of small scars.

'Yes, I knocked and I waited but she didn't answer, so I went inside and that's when I found her lying on the ground, and I thought – I thought –' Hal takes a long, shuddering breath, leaning heavily on the table.

'Here.' Fox hands him a small green vial. 'Take this. It'll help with the shock.'

I press my lips closed.

'Don't worry, Storm Weaver,' says Fox, as though he could hear the comment I swallowed. 'I'll have a bucket of the stuff sent over to your rooms tomorrow.'

Hal takes a swig from the vial and I'm surprised by his willingness to trust his brother when mere minutes ago he was inclined, by some deep-rooted sense of pride, to refuse his offer of help, even with Elva's life hanging in the balance. And precarious as it may be, this new semblance of trust between them strikes me as not being *new* at all. It seems an old sort of trust, once binding and now fraying like a thread, yet still unbroken.

'Ten, nine, eight . . .' Fox begins counting down, glancing at neither Hal nor me, his eyes fixed firmly on his patient.

'What are you doing?' I ask.

'Seven, six, five – be an angel and pull up a chair for His Imperial Highness, would you, Storm Weaver? Four, three . . .'

I frown, but Hal is starting to look a little woozy and so I do as I'm asked. The moment I slide the chair behind him, he begins swaying on his feet.

'Two, one, and sweet dreams, dear brother.'

Hal collapses into the chair, eyes closed.

I gasp, fear stabbing at me, white-hot and fierce. Did I just witness the assassination of the Crown Prince? And am I next? Is this where I am to die, in this peculiar apothecary, surrounded by shelves and tinctures and medicines and –

'Oh, don't look like that. He's not dead. He's just sleeping.' Fox selects a couple of sprigs of something green and strong-smelling from the rack above the countertop.

My voice is barely more than a squeak. 'What did you *do* to him?'

'Knocked him out with some ragroot. I can't have him all hysterical while I'm trying to work. Hysteria is not good for my concentration. Besides, I reckoned his voice is one you most definitely don't want to hear right now, given the circumstances.'

I look at Hal spreadeagled in the chair. It's hard to be angry at someone when they're sleeping, but I'll do my best.

I turn my attention to Elva. 'What's wrong with her?'

'She appears to have fainted.'

'But it's more than that, isn't it?' I ask, as Fox reaches behind me for something.

Fox glances at me. 'Yes, Storm Weaver, and I will explain everything to you once I have brought your friend back to the land of the living.'

My eyes widen. 'You mean she's –'

'She's alive,' Fox assures me. 'But her pulse is slower than I would like.'

'What can I do?' I twist my hands together. 'I can't just stand here.'

Fox half smiles. 'Very well. Fetch me that green vial over there.'

I stare at him. 'Could you maybe be more specific? There's about ten thousand of them.'

'Don't exaggerate, Storm Weaver – there's only nine thousand four hundred and eighty-two.' He points. 'Third shelf, second from the left. The label should read *Bitterbloom*.'

I step over Hal's legs and retrieve the vial. Fox takes it from me, pulls out the stopper with his teeth and pours two drops into a mortar along with the pungent herbs, then begins to grind them up into a paste.

'What's that?'

'Lift her head up for me, would you?'

I move around the table. Elva's hair spills off the end, her skin deathly pale, lips slightly parted. The almost imperceptible rise and fall of her chest is the only sign she's still breathing. Gently, I slip my hands behind her head and prop it up. 'Like this?'

'Just like that. Now, I'm going to waft this under her nose, which will result in a shock to her system, meaning she's going to open her eyes for a moment or two.'

I shiver. 'Her eyes, they – they were *glowing*, they –'

'They were, and I need to get a better look at them to test my theory.'

'You have a theory?'

'I always have a theory,' says Fox. 'Now, whatever you do, don't let go of her head.'

I nod, deciding that now is not the time to question why I'm choosing to trust him.

Slowly, he lifts the small bowl up to Elva's face and her eyes shoot open, once fragments of amber stone and now slivers of molten sunset, luminous among the shadows.

Fox leans in close, examining them.

'Can she – can she see us?' I ask.

He shakes his head. 'She's still unconscious.'

Elva's eyes flutter closed once more.

Fox places the bowl down on the table and lets out a long, low whistle. 'Can you describe to me exactly what you saw upon entering your rooms?'

I swallow. 'Well, I opened the door and she was just lying there on the ground and Hal was bent over her and –'

'You misunderstand me,' he says. 'I want you to describe what you saw, the first thing you saw, when you opened that door.'

I frown, gently lowering Elva's head back down on to the countertop. 'I already told you, I saw her –'

'Not her, not my brother. Think about your surroundings. What did you *see*?'

'I saw . . .' Then I remember. 'I saw *nothing*. I couldn't see anything – it was all dark.'

'It was all dark,' Fox repeats quietly. 'Seems strange,

doesn't it? The candles are always lit well before dusk, the curtains were not closed, the moon was bright tonight, and yet you walked into a room that was in complete and utter darkness.'

I'm not following, but I can feel my muscles tightening, as though bracing themselves for something.

'You care for this girl, don't you, Storm Weaver? You respect her. Talk to her. Have you ever talked about where it is she comes from?'

I decide lying is futile. 'Yes, we have.'

'And can you recall the name of this place?'

'Obsidia.' I fold my arms. 'But what does that have to do with anything?'

Fox rests his head over a spot on Elva's chest, listening to her heart. 'Incredible,' he breathes. 'That she can withstand so much, that it hasn't killed her.'

'That *what* hasn't killed her?'

Fox straightens up. 'Tell me, how did Ostacre defeat the Otherlands during the War of the Empires?'

I raise an eyebrow. 'You're – you're seriously giving me a history test right now?'

'Answer the question.'

I answer the question. 'Well, because the Etheri were stronger, of course. Isn't that how people usually win wars? They overpower their enemy.'

'Overpower,' Fox repeats softly. 'Yes, you could say that. The Magi were left powerless, rendered no more than Fidra. Many were enslaved, just like your friend here.'

'So, Elva's ancestors lost their magic and now she's a serf. This I already know.' I fight to keep the impatience out of my voice. 'Tell me what's happening to her. Tell me what's going on. Please.' The last word slips out unbidden.

'You said the Magi lost their magic,' says Fox. 'Lost it how?'

I exhale, exasperated. 'Because it was depleted. Because their Gods decided to punish them. That's what everybody says. How else would you explain it?'

Fox rakes his brandhand through his hair. He hesitates then says, 'What if I told you there was a secret weapon? One that held unimaginable power.'

I shake my head. 'I don't understand.'

'The Etheri, they used it to strip the Magi of their magic. Their powers weren't depleted. Or taken by their Gods. They were *stolen* from them. Sealed, for more than fifty years, inside the weapon used to win the war.'

Reeling, I take a step backwards. 'What are you talking about? What *weapon*? And what has this got to do with Elva?'

Fox coaxes a spoonful of liquid into Elva's mouth. 'Before the war, Obsidia, the isle known as the Land of Eternal Night, was home to Shadow Magi – those with the gift of darkness.' He pauses. 'It seems . . . Well, it seems that Elva's powers, the powers stolen from her people, have been returned to her.'

My heart trips over itself, beating too hard, too fast. 'You can't be serious.'

Fox's steady expression remains the same.

'There has to be some other explanation,' I insist. 'There has to be something else, something –' I place both hands on the table between us. '*How?*'

'How,' says Fox, 'is always inextricably linked to who. You ask how her powers have been returned to her, but really what you should be asking is *who* returned her powers? How follows after.'

I choke back the nausea creeping up my throat. 'Fine. Who? Who could have possibly returned magic that was stolen from her ancestors before she was even born?'

Fox pulls something from his pocket and holds it out to me. I barely have time to catch my breath before his next words knock me off the side of the world.

'You did, Storm Weaver.'

Held in his hand, watching me, is the golden Eye.

41

Fox tells me that the War of the Empires wasn't started by the seven Magi rulers, but by his grandfather, Caius Castellion. That he invited their ambassadors to Ostacre under the pretence of forging an alliance and then slaughtered every last one of them, leading the Magi to declare war. Only when they sent their battleships across the Second Sea to invade and supposedly reclaim Ostacre from the Etheri, Emperor Caius sent his Imperial Guard to the Otherlands with orders to track down the three sisters.

When the emperor enslaved Syla, he had her seal the gifts of the Magi inside her Eye – the secret weapon, and the key to power itself. And I, unwittingly, have returned one such gift to its rightful owner.

Fox is still treating Elva, selecting green vials from the shelves and grinding up herbs into a powder.

'So . . . so when Elva touched me, when I touched her, the Eye gave her back her magic?' I say weakly. 'It made her a *Mage*?'

Fox nods, stepping back and wiping his hands on a scrap of cloth.

'Will she be all right?'

'I'm fairly confident that if she survived the bolt to the heart that would have been the decades' worth of raw power entering her system, then she'll pull through.'

'So she's out of danger?' I ask.

'She's out of danger,' Fox confirms. 'Let her sleep.'

I glance at Hal, who's still as unconscious as Elva. *That's another reason for knocking him out*, Fox had said. Aside from the fact that I would as soon punch him than look at him, it's best that we keep him in the dark about the Eyes, for now at least.

I take a deep breath. 'I still don't understand how all this could possibly have been kept a secret.'

'When so few people know the secret in question, it's not difficult to keep it,' Fox says. 'Especially since most of that number quite literally took it to their graves. There were some old Magi legends, of course, folktales about the sisters and their Eyes, but there was nothing to connect them to the war. And as for my grandfather, he was the one who made sure the truth never got out in the first place. It was easy enough. All he had to do was spin a few tales, speculation about wrathful Gods and the superior strength of the Etheri, and there you have it, the Eyes were erased from history.' He grimaces. 'Well, not quite.'

'What do you mean *not quite*?'

'Take the Imperial Court,' says Fox. 'Formerly the Golden Court, now the Court of Eyes. People think it a nickname picked up during the war, when so many of the courtiers turned spies for the emperor.'

Realization burns a hole through my chest. That's when

my gaze wanders to the prince's right hand. 'It was Caius Castellion who added the eye to the Imperial brandmark, wasn't it?'

'Before my grandfather's reign, it was just a sun.'

'Why?' I ask, appalled. '*Why* would he do that?'

'I imagine it amused him,' says Fox simply. 'Claiming the Eye as his own symbol, hiding the truth in plain sight, with everybody none the wiser.'

I shake my head in disgust. 'And what of your Eye?'

Fox leans against the table. 'You'll have to be more specific. Currently, I have five.'

'*Five?*'

He points once, twice, to his real eyes, then holds out both chains.

'And the fifth?'

He swivels round and lifts up his hair. There, seared into the nape of his neck, is an open eye, the trademark tattoo of the Imperial Court. If I found it unnerving before, it positively horrifies me now.

Fox turns back and holds up the second of the golden pendants. 'I presume you mean the talisman I spent several months scouring the Otherlands for?'

'How did you find it?' I ask incredulously, as he tugs it over his head and drops it into my palm.

He shrugs a shoulder. 'Intuition. A bit of luck. Excellent navigational skills.'

I turn it over in my hands. It's identical to Syla's in every way. 'Which one is it?'

Fox considers me for a moment. 'The Eye you're holding belonged to Sifa.'

I exhale slowly. 'You mean . . . this Eye can show you the past? That you can see the past, whenever you want?'

'Yes and no,' he says. 'For some time now I've been trying to figure out exactly how it works, but the Eye's visions are . . . subjective.'

'Meaning?'

'*Meaning* it's not as simple as asking to revisit a specific time or place. Sometimes it shows me glimpses of what I want to see, and sometimes it shows me a stream of recollections that flow from that particular moment or memory. Then there are times it'll give me a vision I was never looking for, almost as if it were trying to tell me something.'

'So *that's* how you know so much,' I say.

Fox pops a couple of mint leaves into his mouth and grins at me while he chews. I run my thumb across the Eye of the Past, imagining what it must be like for him, to have history at his fingertips. With this talisman, I could study the Rain Singers. I could unravel the mystery of the Mage boy down in the dungeons, whoever he is. And perhaps I could even discover the truth about myself. About my power. About the storm.

But what of Fox? Where does he fit into all of this?

'Why were you even searching for it?' I ask him.

I watch his expression flicker. He pauses, choosing his next words carefully. 'There were . . . some questions I wanted the answers to.'

'What questions?'

Fox twists his Calloway signet ring round his forefinger. 'You can't have all my secrets, Storm Weaver,' he says softly. 'There wouldn't be any left for me.'

I swallow my disappointment. Why must he be so infuriatingly cryptic?

'And what of the Eye of the Future? Where do you suppose it is?'

Fox sighs. 'Your guess is as good as mine.'

'So it really is lost forever? Safe and hidden, just like Seera wanted?'

'Oh, I doubt that,' he says. 'You see, the Eyes are much like their original owners. They're sisters. They like to be together. And if put together, all three of them . . .' He trails off. 'Do you understand that to be in possession of the past, the future and power itself would render the bearer *invincible*?'

The weight of Sifa's Eye in my palm seems to drag me down into the very recesses of the earth.

'Is that why you wanted to find them?' I ask quietly.

A smirk. 'Do you really have such a low opinion of me, Storm Weaver?'

'Do you really want me to answer that?' I shoot back. 'You ripped the realm in two.'

'And you summoned a storm that nearly drowned it. Same difference.'

'That's where you're wrong,' I snap. 'Because I regret what I did, but I don't think you do. In fact, you actually seem quite proud of it.'

Fox's eyes are fixed on me, unblinking and unreadable.

'Besides, I was a baby,' I continue. 'You have no such excuse.' My gaze falls on Elva. 'Then there's the fact that you're a *slaver* –'

'I'm not a slaver,' says Fox abruptly.

I stare at him. 'What do you mean? They call you the *Prince of Slavers*.'

Fox huffs a laugh. 'Oh, Storm Weaver. You of all people should know there's a difference between who you are and who people say you are.' He smiles slightly, though it doesn't reach his eyes. 'We all have our roles to play.'

Silence stretches between us, punctuated by my heartbeat. I can't work out if he's telling the truth. But then what reason would he have to lie?

'Believe what you will,' he says, holding out a hand for Sifa's talisman. 'We have more important things to discuss.'

I return it to him, watching as he pulls the chain over his head. 'How did you even find out about them? The Eyes.'

'I told you already. I heard stories on my travels.'

'And the emperor? Does he know?'

Fox shakes his head, dismissive. 'My father barely knows what day it is at present.'

I think of Emperor Alvar's haggard appearance, the dark circles beneath his eyes. He had seemed larger than life on my Name Day. How could he have changed so much in just a few months?

'Your father,' I say tentatively. 'Is he ... unwell? Only I couldn't help noticing that lately he's looked ...'

'Like death warmed up?' Fox suggests.

'I was going to say under the weather, but yes.'

Fox turns away and begins clearing the table, reaching across Elva for various pots and tinctures. 'He suffers from a hereditary ailment. Nothing to concern yourself with. Hand me that vial.'

I do as he asks, not wishing to pry. 'So, what are we supposed to do now?'

Fox smiles lazily at me. 'I love it when you say we.'

I shoot him a look.

'All in good time, Storm Weaver.' He dangles Syla's Eye in front of me. 'First I need to know – are you in or are you out?'

'But why would you give it back?' I ask, sensing a trick.

'Because it didn't choose me,' he says, matter-of-factly. 'It chose you.'

I force myself to hold his gaze, which is almost intimate in its intensity. He has always looked at me this way, like he knows me better than I know myself.

I wet my lips, self-conscious. 'That night in the dungeons, you said, *I knew it was always meant to be you.* What did you mean?'

Fox mulls this over for a moment, then says, 'Just a feeling. My instincts served me well. But don't you owe it to yourself to find out why? Don't you think it's fate?'

Grandmother's words come back to me.

Fate has many faces, my darling one. Make sure you look them all in the eye.

I hardly dare breathe as I let Fox slip the golden chain back over my head.

The darkness inside my chambers has long since dissipated, leaving no trace of Elva's newfound abilities behind. Golden roses still lie strewn across the floor. Slowly, I crouch down and pick one up. The petals are soft like velvet, the thorns glittering in the early-morning light. It's beautiful. Perfect, really. I hate it.

A strange sort of calm descends over me. I tug on a blue cord by the door, then gather up every rose scattered around my feet. Next I move over to the countless overflowing vases, pulling out stem after stem until my arms are full of them.

No more. No more will I think of Haldyn Castellion as anything other than the Crown Prince or the future emperor. An acquaintance, an ally, perhaps, but that's all.

There's a knock at the door. The serf gawps at me, his terrified expression tinged with confusion as I hand him the gigantic bundle of golden roses.

'Please take these to the prince's rooms,' I tell him. 'Feel free to just leave them on the floor. Or alternatively, dumping them on his bed would be a nice touch. And when he returns, tell him . . . tell him that Blaze sends her regards.'

'But – but my lady –'

'Thank you,' I say, and shut the door.

I sleep all morning. Flint and Spinner come to see me around midday, but I just pull the sheet over my head.

'I was right to be wary about Hal's intentions,' murmurs Flint. 'He must have known about this betrothal for months. What was he *thinking*?'

'Poor thing,' I hear my chaperone whisper. 'She must be heartbroken.'

But as I set off for Queen Hydra's rooms sometime later, I realize that what I actually feel is sort of . . . *good*. Like I've shed one skin and donned another, this one thicker, more difficult to bruise.

The queen is sitting waiting for me at the long golden table.

'Ah, Blaze,' she says, standing up as I curtsy low in greeting. 'Tea?' She pours me a cup, stirring in a spoonful of honey.

'Now, what is it that you would prefer to focus on today? Rain perhaps? Waves? Ice?' She smiles. 'Portals?'

An hour later I'm perched on the end of the table holding the teacup I've just lifted out of the small pool shimmering in front of me. Queen Hydra had sent the cup down the waterway from the second portal at her end, and now she wants me to try to send it back.

'Concentrate, child. Name the place you want the object to go. Hold that image in your head. Picture it with your mind's eye.'

'But what if it gets lost?' I ask.

'Then I'm afraid you would owe His Imperial Majesty one silver teacup.'

I take a breath, visualize the destination, will the cup to go there with every fibre of my being, and drop it into the pool before me. There's a prolonged, painful pause. Then the queen reaches into the pool in front of her and pulls it out.

She beams. 'Very good.'

Queen Hydra gets rid of the second portal with a wave of her hand and tells me to try to send the cup to any part of the room I choose. I do as she says, gasping in astonishment as it appears again and again, by the window, next to the door, through a section of the wall. Afterwards she has me attempt something different.

'Portals can prove excellent methods of concealment. One can use a portal to send an object to a destination, but also have it remain there, hidden. This time you don't want the cup to pass through the waterway, but for it to remain *inside* the waterway, accessible only to someone who knows exactly where to find it. Let us start off simple. Why don't you try hiding the cup here, in the portal I have drawn upon this table?'

I nod, trying to clear my mind.

The teacup hits the water with a small splash and sinks slowly beneath the surface. Closing my eyes, I will the cup to remain there, tucked away inside this secret corner of the waterway, out of sight but always within my reach.

An image swims across my vision. I see a pool – it's the training pool in the Keep. And I'm falling into it, falling *through* it, landing in a small golden room on the other side. When I look up, the ceiling is made entirely from water, suspended above me like glass.

My eyes fly open.

The pool.

The *portal*.

I feel Syla's talisman sitting cold against my chest. What if she hid it there, concealed from everyone apart from the one person she intended to discover it, who was lured there by the water whispering her name . . .

Blaze.

'Are you quite well, child?' Queen Hydra is leaning over me, concern cutting horizontal lines across her forehead.

I clear my throat. 'I'm fine, Your Majesty.'

She smiles gently. 'Good. Now, why don't you retrieve that cup.'

Mind still reeling, I plunge my hand into the portal in front of me, my fingers closing round cool metal.

42

'What do you want?'

Hal turns from where he stands by the window in my chambers. He doesn't seem to know what to do with his hands – clasping them behind his back, interlocking his fingers. Eventually he just lets them hang loosely by his sides, which makes him appear younger, more vulnerable, as he says, 'Can we talk?'

'What about?' I ask innocently. 'The fact that you've been pretending to have feelings for me?'

He takes a step towards me. 'Blaze, I –'

'Or how about the fact that you've been playing me for a complete and utter fool for *weeks* and presumably weren't ever planning on telling me the truth?'

'*Blaze.*'

'Because you weren't, were you?'

Hal swallows hard, his throat bobbing. 'Blaze, please, just listen, I –'

'I was nothing but a convenience to you. A perfect ploy to distract from what you were really doing and *who* you were really doing it with.'

My voice remains calm, even pleasant, but every word

seems to strike a match against his skin. Hal exhales in a slow, defeated way, squeezing his raven-black eyes shut and sitting down, dropping his head in his hands.

I count a full minute before either of us speaks again.

Eventually he straightens up to look at me. 'I got the roses.'

'Did you?' I nod. 'Good. I thought they'd send a clear message.'

'That message being?'

'*Piss off*, Your Imperial Highness.'

Hal looks as though I'd reached across and slapped him. He blinks several times, then, to my surprise, starts to laugh. 'I always knew I liked you, Blaze.'

Rolling my eyes, I sit down opposite him and hug a cushion to my chest. 'This had better be good.'

Hal leans forward in his chair, looking me right in the eye. 'I'm sorry. I'm sorry for using you like that and I'm sorry you had to find out the way you did. It was never my intention to hurt you. In fact, believe it or not, I actually thought I was doing you a favour.'

I stare at him. 'You thought you were doing me a *favour*?'

He shrugs. It's strange seeing him shrug. It makes him more of a boy and less of a prince.

'I figured you'd have an easier time of it here if the courts thought I was paying you special attention,' he says. 'I got the idea from your Name Day, seeing the difference in the way people acted around you after you and I danced together.'

I remember it, the way the guests' barely disguised hatred had morphed into intrigue. I had been sought out, introduced to this person and that, treated with, if not *kindness*, exactly, then something like civility. And here at the Golden Palace, Hal's company became a shield of sorts. When I was on his arm, I was untouchable.

'I didn't expect to come to care about you,' Hal continues. 'Not like this. Because I do, Blaze. I do care about you. I trust you. You're . . . you're my friend.'

I run my finger along the swirling wave pattern stitched into the cushion. 'Tell me about Elva. How did things even start between the two of you, anyway? You know, seeing as she's a serf and you're the *Crown Prince of Ostacre*.'

Hal almost smiles. 'Two years ago my father was hosting a banquet for the royal families of Thaven and Vost who were here at court discussing potential new trade routes.'

'Fascinating,' I say dryly.

'At this banquet,' he continues, 'the serfs were pouring wine during the King of Thaven's speech. I was sitting next to my cousin, Princess Lira of Vost. She had on a white dress, and this serf – he can't have been much older than eleven or twelve – he was shaking so badly that he spilled red wine all over Lira's gown, and Lira just *lost it*, screaming and shouting, demanding that the serf responsible be punished.'

I raise an eyebrow. 'She sounds delightful.'

Hal grimaces. 'She's unbearable. Anyway, during all the commotion, I noticed this girl.' His expression changes then, his voice following suit. 'A serf. I watched as she quickly swapped the tray she was carrying with the boy's jug of wine. When Lira rounded on him, the girl stepped forward. She claimed it was she who had spilled the wine, and held out the jug to prove it. She said she would take any punishment

Lira deemed appropriate.' Hal sucks in a breath. 'Elva was sentenced to twenty lashes to be carried out immediately.'

My skin grows cold.

'The next time I saw her, she could barely move without wincing. Her back ... it ...' He trails off, and for a moment I think he might cry, or stab something. 'She took the blame, took a *whipping*, all to protect that boy. After that, I found myself ... looking for her. Through every crowd, across every room, sometimes without even meaning to.' Hal's face softens. 'I've been unable to look away ever since.'

I feel a twinge inside my chest.

'The first time I worked up the courage to speak to her, she was terrified,' he continues. 'It took weeks for her to say more than a few words to me. I remember the day she told me her name. I remember the first time I saw her smile.' He smiles then, gently. 'One time I found her admiring some roses, so I left one for her in her room. She had to hide the thing under her bedroll in case she got accused of stealing from the palace gardens. But then I ... I found a way to give her a dozen roses, every day.'

I drop my gaze. All those bunches of golden roses delivered to my chambers – they weren't really for me.

'I've never felt this way before, Blaze. About anyone. And last night when I thought I might lose her ...' Hal swallows. 'I can't be without her. I can't. But I also can't *be with* her. Every time we're together, I'm putting her in danger. Fox was right about the need to be discreet, but sometimes I just feel so *useless*. If I were to do so much as insist that her duties be lessened, or saw to it that she receives more food, questions would be asked.' He shakes his head. 'Just think of what they'd say. The Crown Prince, in love with a serf.'

'Could you . . . set her free?' I ask tentatively.

'Serfs are never set free,' Hal says dully. 'I've thought about smuggling her out, but she'd only be hunted down, and how could she possibly defend herself?'

I bite my tongue. He doesn't know. He doesn't know that Elva is Fidra no longer. He doesn't know that she is now a Mage.

Hal gets to his feet, moving across to the window again. 'I can't jeopardize the treaty with Thaven,' he says. 'Wars have been started over less. As for Mirade . . . what she doesn't know won't hurt her.'

His words sting and I feel some of my bitterness return.

My voice is barely more than a whisper. 'Why did you kiss me?'

Hal takes a breath. 'Because if I hadn't, you would have wondered why.'

If guilt had a face, I'd be looking at it.

I move across to join him by the window. 'You know, if you'd just been honest from the start and asked me to play pretend with you to fool the courts, I would have.'

Hal smiles sadly. 'Remind me never to underestimate you again.'

The final week before the third trial passes at lightning speed. I train from dawn until dusk, mostly with Queen Hydra, sometimes with River. Every day I feel myself getting stronger, my reflexes faster, and every night I collapse into bed, exhausted. Yet I often lie awake, replaying that night in the Earth Cleaver's chambers over and over in my mind.

I'm not sure what to make of this peculiar new alliance between us. I'm not sure what to make of him at all.

How can a boy who ripped apart the realm, who is responsible for the deaths of thousands, who they call destruction itself, be a *Healer*, of all things? Why would the Prince of Slavers save the life of a serf? That is, if he's even a slaver at all.

I hear his voice in my head.

We all have our roles to play.

As for Elva, since coming to, she has spent the last few days recuperating, quarantined with an alleged bout of flu. Only Fox and I know the truth about her condition, since the potion he used to knock out Hal was so strong that the prince's recollection of events is hazy at best, and he doesn't appear to remember the way Elva's eyes had glowed in the darkness.

I'm still trying to wrap my head around it. That the magic of her ancestors has been returned to her. That *I* was the one who returned it, with the very talisman that took it away all those years ago. Syla's Eye – the secret weapon used to win the War of the Empires.

I graze the cool surface of the Eye with my fingers, tucking it carefully beneath the neckline of my dress.

It's now the night before the third trial, and all five courts have been summoned to the throne room, where the eight remaining Heirs are to present themselves before the Council.

Tomorrow marks the beginning of a new age, a new life. Tomorrow, I fight Marina for the Aquatori crown.

And I am completely, utterly, terrified.

Stand up straight, Blaze, I tell myself as I walk along teeming hallways and through a set of towering golden doors. *Shoulders back. Smile.*

'There they are!' Spinner exclaims, pulling me over to a crowd of familiar faces and launching herself into my brother's arms.

The very air seems to ripple with excitement as the Crowned Council sweep into the room. The emperor, gaunt as ever, the Imperial Crown glinting atop his head. Aunt Yvainne, in a red dress that flickers like candlelight. Queen Aspen, her beautiful waist-length hair threaded with flowers. Queen Hydra, dressed in a simple blue gown. And King Balen, wearing his cloak cut from morning fog, and an amused smile.

Elaith slips her arm comfortingly into mine as heads begin to turn in our direction. I feel her grow rigid as she catches sight of Cole standing a few yards away with Ember and Marina. He smirks as he leans forward and whispers something in their ears. Moments later Elaith jumps backwards in shock just as the hem of my dress catches fire.

I shriek, eyes wide with alarm as the flames begin to lick up the side of my skirts.

Disentangling himself from Spinner, Flint leaps into action, the flames shooting into his outstretched palm which he quickly clamps into a fist. With a slight hiss, the fire is extinguished. I sway on my feet, the blood rushing to my face.

And then they begin to laugh, Ember, Marina and Cole. Several others join in, and the sound of it twists something inside of me, something cold and quiet and unforgiving.

Flint is at my side, his expression anxious. Kai is restraining Elaith, while Zeph shakes his head in disgust. I catch sight of Hal among the crowd. He looks furious.

Laughter fills my head, echoing through me. I grit my teeth, glancing slowly around the room, committing this moment to memory.

For they can laugh all they like when I lose.

They won't be laughing when I win.

43

Voices fade in and out of earshot as the spectators make their way past the Heirs' tents and towards the gigantic golden amphitheatre which teeters right at the edge of Cor Caval, overlooking the Rift. The stands will soon be filled with Etheri, Fidra, foreign emissaries, courtiers from each of the Crown Courts, and various royals from neighbouring kingdoms – all of them having travelled to the Imperial Province to watch the third trial.

I've barely slept. I spent last night tossing and turning, sick with nerves, taunting laughter still ringing in my ears, thinking about the vow I made to myself in that throne room. I suppose in part it was fuelled by spite, a desire to triumph in the face of adversity. But I meant it all the same. I want to win. And for the first time I feel as though I'm in with a chance. The crown is within my grasp. I just have to be brave enough to fight for it.

Elva is still recovering in the serf quarters, which means Spinner has been tasked with making me look less like a frightened child and more like a future queen, poised and ready for battle.

'Hold *still*, Blaze. Gods, I'll never understand why anyone bothers having such long hair. I mean, look at mine,' Spinner says, gesturing to her own. 'Practical *and* stylish.' She eyes me mischievously. 'You know, I do believe I saw a pair of scissors somewh–'

'Don't even think about it,' I tell her firmly.

Spinner rolls her eyes then claps her hands briskly. 'Now, let's get rid of those *ginormous* bags under your eyes, hmm?'

Flint appears through the tent flap. 'There you are.'

'Here I am.'

He doesn't sit down, choosing instead to pace the length of the tent. There are eight tents in total, one for every Heir. Each of them contains a dressing table, several low couches, a scattering of large cushions and a selection of food. Spinner has been coaxing a bowl of broth into me for the last half-hour, but my appetite has abandoned me.

'How are you?' I ask Flint.

My brother shrugs. 'Oh, you know. Vaguely petrified. Mildly nauseous. I also can't seem to stay still without feeling as though I'm about to detonate. That sort of thing.' He opens and closes his fist as he walks, a small flame igniting and extinguishing in his palm. Eventually he comes to a stop. 'Father wrote to me.'

I feel myself stiffen.

'He wanted to wish me luck.'

'Did he?' I say in the same flat voice I always use when I talk about my father.

'He wanted me to wish you luck, too.'

It's like a punch to the throat. That even now, on the most important day of my life, my father cannot bring himself to *write*, let alone be in the same room as me. I glance at

Spinner, who's pretending not to listen as she weaves my curls into two intricate braids. My hair is my mother's hair, thick and dark. She always wore hers unbound and that's why I began braiding mine back in the weeks following her death, so as to avoid the agony in my father's eyes. But I've realized that it doesn't matter how I style my hair, nor that I am forever dressed in blue instead of red, because he will never be able to look at me and not see *her*. Just as he will never be able to look at his youngest child and not see her blood on his hands. We are painful for him, Renly and I. And I'm tired of it.

I can't help that I remind him of my mother. I can't help that I look like her. I *want* to look like her.

'Leave it down,' I say suddenly. 'My hair.'

Spinner nods, shaking my hair free from its braids until it frames my face.

Flint smiles. 'There she is,' he says, squeezing my shoulder.

The Imperial Guard are stationed around the Heirs' tents. We cannot leave to watch the trials, we must stay here until we are called for our own. I sit in my tent with Grandmother and River, not saying much, listening to the roar of the crowd. Minutes trickle by, each one stealing a part of me – my nerve, my ability to breathe, the feeling in my legs.

This time there are no beasts to defeat, no riddles to solve. The third trial is one of combat, a battle between the two remaining Heirs from each court. The battle ends only when one of the Heirs concedes, or is too incapacitated to go on.

The Ventalla are up first. Zephyr and Eriq fight for a long time, and after what feels like hours the emperor's voice booms out across the stands, freakishly amplified, announcing Zeph as the winner. I remember what Queen Hydra said about the Ventalla having a means of travel similar to water portals, only using the air. *Flitting*, she had called it. I wonder if Zeph has mastered this particular skill, whether King Balen had taught him.

It's not long before the Terrathian Heirs are called.

There's a scuffling noise over to my right and I turn to find Spinner crawling under the bottom of the tent on her stomach.

'You don't want to miss this,' she says, panting. 'Come on.'

I glance at Grandmother and River.

My trainer half smiles. 'We didn't see anything.'

'Be careful,' Grandmother adds, as I let my chaperone drag me unceremoniously underneath the tent.

'Take this,' says Spinner, draping a golden shawl over my hair like a headscarf. 'We have to stay out of sight.'

I follow her into the stands, which are so impossibly large they seem to climb high into the clouds. The base of the amphitheatre in the centre is crammed with onlookers standing shoulder to shoulder, jostling one another for a better view. Everyone seems far too preoccupied with the first Terrathian Heir's arrival to give either Spinner or me a second glance as we elbow our way through them towards the front.

Amaryllis is smiling and waving at the crowd, but I'm close enough to see that her legs are trembling. It's little wonder really, given who she's about to fight.

He takes his time. He knows how to make an entrance, I'll give him that, and when he does stride out into the amphitheatre, the crowd goes wild.

Fox smiles lazily, and it's alarming the way I can no longer find any trace of the boy who offered me a basketful of kittens for my little brother, or who so carefully tended to Elva while asking for nothing in return. No, that boy is long gone. He has been replaced with a boy I know all too well – one who is arrogant and violent and cruel.

The Earth Cleaver.

I watch as he circles Amaryllis, sizing her up. I lift my head to where Hal, his father and the Crowned Council are sitting apart from the crowd on golden thrones.

The emperor gets slowly to his feet. 'Terrathian Heirs, let the third trial begin.'

Immediately Amaryllis springs to life. She raises her arms, and small pebbles in the grass begin to grow into boulders the size of cannonballs. One by one, they launch themselves through the air directly at Fox. It's almost amusing – the careless way he sidesteps them. Amaryllis tries again and again, and each time Fox avoids the stones with ease, the crowd erupting in delight.

Abandoning the boulders, Amaryllis chooses her next weapon. The grass around Fox grows as high as his head, concealing him from sight. I gasp, convinced she's managed to entangle him, but barely a moment later the thick blades fall into a limp pile, as though somebody has sliced them in half with a scythe.

'Why isn't he fighting back?' I whisper to Spinner.

But then I realize. He's toying with her. Letting her lay all her cards out on the table in full view, waiting for the right moment to break the table in two.

Fox delicately picks a blade of grass off his shoulder and

lets it fall to the ground just as Amaryllis makes her next move. Spinner grabs hold of my arm as Fox is surrounded by an impenetrable wall of thorned branches, each one twisted and lethal.

All of a sudden the branches begin to quiver then snap. Thorns as long as my finger fly through the air and Amaryllis screams in pain as they meet their mark. Blood streams down her cheeks like tears.

Fox holds out his arms and brings them slowly upward. The crowd gasp as two gigantic trees erupt out of the earth.

For a moment Amaryllis seems paralysed, then she begins to run, a sea of nettles growing up in her wake, separating her from Fox. But it's of little use. I watch as the vines coiled round the trunks of the trees begin to unwind themselves.

Fox allows Amaryllis to run until she's almost reached the other side of the amphitheatre. Only then does he strike. His vines slither through the nettles, and Amaryllis shrieks as they find her, wrapping themselves round her wrists and ankles and dragging her back through her own small meadow of stinging plants. I grit my teeth at the pain in her cries, but I can't tear my eyes away as the vines curl themselves back round the two trees, her body suspended in the air between them like a puppet dangling from its strings.

She's in a bad way. Her hair is matted, her skin raw and bleeding. A thorn has lodged itself in her lip, which has burst, staining the front of her ripped tunic.

Fox stands below her, smiling pleasantly. 'Have you got anything else for me?'

Amaryllis gapes down at him. I will her to admit defeat, but to my horror, she throws back her head and spits out a glob of blood and saliva. It lands on Fox's boot. He peers at it then shakes his head condescendingly.

'Well, that simply won't do,' he says, turning to the crowd. 'Will it?'

He's met by a deafening roar. Fox turns back to Amaryllis. I see the shock on her face as the vines round her arms and legs begin to grow taut, tighter and tighter until they're stretching her limbs. There's a sickening *pop* as a bone is disconnected from its socket. Amaryllis screams. Fox is watching her, refusing to relent.

I stare at him, nauseated by this display of torture, yet unable to look away. And just for a split second, so brief that I'm not even sure if it really happens, he glances back at me.

The vines release Amaryllis and she falls to the ground in a heap, unconscious.

Fox turns towards the Crowned Council and bows low as his victory is announced above the roaring crowd.

44

K ing.
   The Earth Cleaver.

He's going to be *king*.

It's not like it wasn't expected. The Imperial Court had him down to win from the moment he stepped out into that arena in the first trial. Yet not once did I fully stop and think about what this would actually *mean*, and not just for the Terrathian, but for the empire. The most dangerous Etheri in the realm, who is already in possession of one of the three enchanted Eyes, now has a throne to call his own. Fox will rule the earth and control the knowledge and power of the past, and he will do it all with a crown on his head.

I remember what he said to me when we danced together. *I like winning.*

'Blaze,' Spinner hisses, tugging at me impatiently. 'We have to go. *Now*.'

Syla's Eye sits against my breastbone, tucked safely underneath my tunic. I place my hand over it, pressing it hard into my skin.

Spinner yanks on my arm. 'Blaze! Quickly! We need to get you out of here before they draw the next ring.'

But it's too late. Hal is already holding his hand aloft, a small glint of gold just visible in the sunlight. Aunt Yvainne gets to her feet. The Ignitia Heirs are next.

Spinner and I both freeze, turning to face one another as Flint's name is announced over the din, followed by Ember's.

'I'm not leaving,' I tell my chaperone.

My heart beats in time with the drums as my brother emerges from the tunnel beneath the stands. His hand moves up to shield his face from the sun's glare, but he quickly turns this motion into a wave. The crowd respond with enthusiasm, chanting his name over and over.

And then Ember is there, strutting into the centre of the amphitheatre. She comes to a stop in front of Flint and smiles sweetly.

I think about Grandmother. Today will transform everything. The outcome of this trial will change not just the future of the realm, but that of our House.

I glance at Aunt Yvainne, who is looking down at her niece and nephew with an odd expression on her face. I wonder if she's thinking about my mother. Two Harglades battling for the Ignitia throne. Alator was right – history really has repeated itself.

The emperor has started speaking but I'm not listening to what he's saying. My eyes are glued to my brother, who keeps shifting his weight from one foot to the other.

Please, I will him silently. *You have to win.*

Flint and Ember survey one another for a long time. I grip Spinner's hand tightly as Ember suddenly sends a small arc of fire in Flint's direction, which he easily deflects. He shoots one back at her and she sidesteps it neatly, still smiling. This begins a duel of sorts – a duel of fire. They appear to be sparring with one another, both flinging and blocking flames, which slowly start to increase in speed and ferocity.

'Blaze,' Spinner whispers. 'You're cutting off my circulation.'

'Sorry,' I say, letting go of her.

A moment later Flint's tunic catches fire, but no sooner have I clutched hold of Spinner again than he has extinguished it, sending a flame back at Ember, which singes a lock of her hair clean off. I watch as her smile falters, and then drops.

That was it, I realize. That is all it took for Ember to snap.

Suddenly Flint is surrounded by a wall of fire. Yet I barely have time to scream before he breaks through, sending the blazing tongues of flame rushing full force back towards Ember. But she's ready for them and flicks her wrist.

The heads of the spectators jerk up to watch the flames take to the sky, burning hotter and brighter than ever before – and then come raining down as fire bombs.

Shrieks fill the air as they hit the ground, scorching the grass, bursting outwards and engulfing one another until the entire amphitheatre seems to be devoured by flame.

'*Flint!*'

Spinner claps a hand over my mouth, her eyes wide and frightened as she takes in the scene. Then she points. 'There!'

He's standing in a small clearing, the flames around him dying down, receding at his will. But with every fire he puts out, another springs up in its place, and I can tell just by looking at his face that it's exhausting him. Sweat beads on his forehead as Ember advances, flames flickering at her fingertips, mouth curved in a triumphant smile.

I think about her rigorous training schedule. Her hatred of being overshadowed. Her compulsive need to come out on top. And I think about my brother, staying out all night, doing as he pleased, so confident in his own power as to underestimate hers. It was all just one big party to him, the Choosing Rite. He never saw Ember as a threat.

'Flint!' I scream again, but he can't hear me over the noise of the crowd.

Then Ember claps her hands together, the sound echoing around the stands. At once the flames are extinguished. All that remains is the smoking, blackened ground, and my brother, who falls to his knees upon it, his body wracked with coughs. The tears from his streaming eyes cut vertical tracks through the soot on his face. My heart clenches.

Ember skips towards him and Flint struggles to his feet, bracing himself for attack. The crowd falls silent, waiting. She's so close to him now and so tiny in comparison. It's easy to forget sometimes that she's only fifteen years old.

Ember reaches out and lays a hand on Flint's arm. 'Worry not, cousin. I accept your surrender just as I will accept your fealty.'

Flint stares down at her, his shoulders heaving as he pants.

'Though it is a pity,' Ember says with a sigh. 'It seems you're just as pathetic as your sister.'

Flint's expression changes in a split second, his eyes blazing with rage as Ember smirks, turns and walks away from him. A ball of flame forms in his outstretched palm and he hurls it with all his might at her retreating back.

I watch, helpless, horrified, as Ember spins round with impossible speed and catches the fire, as she flings it back at Flint, as it soars gracefully through the air.

And hits him in the face.

45

A pair of hands drags me through the frenzied crowd. I'm half screaming, half sobbing, trying frantically to break free, to push my way through the sea of bodies and reach my brother. But instead I'm pulled away and shoved inside a golden tent, landing on a pile of red-silk cushions.

Moments later a team of physicians bursts in. They carry a stretcher between them, but there's so many people obstructing my view that I can't see Flint properly, only an arm here, a leg there, a shock of dark curls. The physicians rifle through leather bags for supplies, soaking bandages, and shouting instructions at one another as they crowd round the limp figure on the stretcher. I dart forward, but then Grandmother and River are there, holding me back.

That's when Sheen appears beside me, his violet eyes wild. 'Is . . . is he . . .'

Spinner takes his hand. 'He'll be all right. He'll be all right, won't he?' She glances around, but nobody answers her.

I try again to get to Flint, but a physician blocks my way. 'Everybody *out*,' he demands.

Grandmother turns on him, tapping her stick angrily.

'You forget who you're speaking to, young man. I am the mother of the Fire Queen and that is *my* grands–'

Then I hear it, announced loud and clear above the din. My name.

Every bone seems to crumble to dust inside my body. I wonder at how I'm still standing and realize that River is holding me up.

'It's time,' says Grandmother gravely, beckoning me forward.

I shrink backwards, shaking my head. '*No.* I'm not going anywhere.'

'Blaze, you have no choice.'

'But Flint –'

'– Is being treated as we speak. There's nothing more you can do for him.'

River squeezes my shoulder comfortingly. I take one last desperate glance in the direction of my brother before I'm steered from the tent.

'Use your instincts, rely on your training,' River murmurs. 'Find Marina's weaknesses and target them. Do not lower your guard, even for an instant.'

Grandmother gently wipes away my tears. 'Stand up straight, my darling one.'

I nod dazedly, but inside I'm still screaming.

Two members of the Imperial Guard break away from where several knights are holding back the crowd and fall into step beside me.

'Blaze?'

I turn back. Grandmother is gripping her stick tightly, her eyes boring into mine as she seems to come to some sort of decision.

'Remember who you are,' she says.

I swallow hard, holding on to her gaze for as long as I can before the knights lead me into the belly of the stands. Blood pounds in my ears as I walk through the tunnel, emerging once more into glaring sunlight.

Only now that I'm standing in the very centre of the amphitheatre can I appreciate just how many spectators there are. Tens of thousands, maybe more, all craning to get a glimpse of me. I stand up tall, shoulders back, chin in the air. I don't smile. I don't wave.

The beating of the drums grows louder.

That's when I see Marina. She's making her way towards me from across the other side of the blackened ground, her long dark hair pinned up with those silver clips shaped like tiny fish. Her eyes meet mine and linger, her mouth curling into a smirk.

Then a silken voice slips through the din, carried on obedient streams of air. Not a request – a command. '*Silence*.'

The crowd obeys instantly. I glance upward towards the golden dais and see King Balen smiling down at me.

Beside him, the emperor rises unsteadily. 'I present the Aquatori Heirs.'

The stands erupt with cheers and applause.

I want to disappear down a portal, but I haven't yet mastered how to draw them. I want to turn and run and hide. But it's too late.

'Let the battle for the Aquatori crown begin.'

There is one brief moment of nothing. Then I am blasted backwards by a jet of water, landing hard on my back, the wind knocked out of me. The sky is a perfect blue, bright and cloudless. I see birds flying overhead.

Focus.

I scramble to my feet just in time for Marina to send another stream in my direction. I'm faster this time though, leaping out of its path.

Marina closes her eyes. I look down as the amphitheatre starts filling with water, just enough to lap at my ankles. I should act now, while she's lost in concentration. But I can't stop thinking about Flint, lying crumpled on the ground . . .

I let out a shriek of pain as the water around my feet begins to boil. It hisses and bubbles, growing hotter with every passing second. Marina whips up the simmering sea, sending a wave sloshing right at me. I dodge it, hopping from foot to foot.

I think back to the very first day of training in the Keep. She'd burned me then, too. I was defenceless and out of my depth, and she could hardly wait to show me just how unwelcome I was. I use the memory to fuel my fury, letting it pour out of me like liquid ice.

Suddenly the water around me begins to cool. I can feel it through the sodden leather of my boots. Marina snarls as small icebergs begin to form. If I can just stop her in her tracks by freezing her in place –

I gasp as I'm engulfed by steam. It's everywhere, shooting upward in great burning clouds. It takes me a moment to understand that Marina is evaporating the water. I stumble blindly, burying my face in the crook of my elbow. It's so hot that I can't breathe.

Eventually it begins to clear, and I squint through the lingering haze, my hair plastered to my face and neck.

Marina must have seen me first because when I spot her she's already running straight at me. Yet my reflexes are quicker than they once were. It's almost comical the way she slips and falls headlong on my sheet of glittering ice.

I take a small step forward as she scrabbles around, trying desperately to right herself. 'Need a hand?'

The crowd hoot with laughter.

Marina's eyes brim with resentment. Panting hard on her hands and knees, I watch as she lifts her fist into the air and slams it down on top of the ice. She does it again. And again. Her knuckles split and begin to bleed.

I stare at her in bewilderment. What is she *doing*?

Then Marina raises her hands above her head, and the frozen shards are lifted up off the ground, jagged and sharp. Letting out a savage cry, she sends them shooting towards me, enough to slice me to ribbons.

Time seems to slow as the ice comes flying through the air. I close my eyes.

And it's not a swarm of broken ice that engulfs me, but a flurry of raindrops.

Exhaling with relief, I open my eyes to find Marina on her feet, her face contorted with rage. She jerks her arm and a jet of simmering water comes shooting straight at me. I throw up a shield before it can meet its mark, the water sizzling as it hits the wall of ice.

Marina circles me, but Queen Hydra taught me well, and soon I am entirely walled in, protected from all sides. I can't see Marina any more – the ice is too thick. I'm protected, but

I'm also trapped. I've trapped *myself*. Cursing, I blast apart my wall of ice, spinning round wildly in search of my opponent.

That's when a colossal wave hits me from behind, sending me crashing to the ground.

I struggle on to my elbows, trying to pull myself up, but the first wave is followed by a second, this one so powerful I feel my head slam into the packed earth, the impact sending shock waves shooting down my neck. The pain is blinding. Stars swim across my vision and I reach out a hand to catch one.

When the wave recedes, sloshing away across the charred ground, I hear Marina laughing. Then I feel a different sort of pressure, this time on my outstretched wrist, the same one I'd broken in the first trial when Beast-Marina shoved me headlong down that mountain. The bone has healed but it's still tender, and pain lances sharp and hot along my arm as Marina grinds her foot down hard.

'Did you really think you could beat me?' she spits. 'Did you really think that whatever sadistic game the Gods are playing would end with *you* on the throne?'

I grit my teeth to keep from crying out.

'I don't know how you managed to make it this far,' Marina continues, 'but when I'm queen, I promise you, I will make you wish you had *drowned* in that storm as an infant.'

My head is still spinning, my heart hammering against my ribcage. I try to flip over but I can barely move.

'Do you know how many people died because you were born? How many great Houses lost *everything*? Their homes, their fortunes, their birthrights.'

Perhaps I'm imagining it, but there's pain in her voice, which stretches thin, threatening to break.

'And what was it all for? What have you ever done but bring misery and suffering to the very land you thought yourself worthy to rule over? You make me *sick*.'

A strangled yelp escapes my lips.

'Look at you. Ember was right. You're pathetic. *Weak*. Whatever twisted power you once had is long gone. It's like your grandmother said – the days of storms are behind us.'

The pressure on my arm lifts just long enough for Marina to slam her foot into the back of my head.

I hear my nose break before I feel it.

Then I feel it.

Marina laughs. 'So, *Storm Weaver*. Do you yield?'

I spit out a mouthful of blood, fighting to stay conscious.

'Say it,' Marina hisses. 'I want to hear you say it.'

The deafening roar of the crowd suddenly sounds far off, as though I am under water. I *feel* like water, like my limbs have been slit open and filled up with liquid. Like I could drown right here inside my own head.

The Eye digs into my chest. Round my neck sits Ostacre's greatest weapon. It called to me, this enchanted talisman. It *chose* me.

Power itself.

Any power, all power, right at my fingertips, even if I don't know how to use it yet. The old man said the Eye of the Soul gave the wielder the ability to take power, to possess it. To give it back, too. Elva proved that much. And what a beautiful thing, I think, as black spots begin to swim across my vision. To return that which was thought lost forever.

I blink.

The power to return power.

Whether forcibly taken, severed or lost, power can be restored by the golden Eye round my neck. And what did Marina just say to me?

Whatever twisted power you once had is long gone. It's like your grandmother said – the days of storms are behind us.

Slowly, I lift my head. I see myself reflected in a puddle of water at my side, my hair dripping, my nose streaming red. I look into my eyes, wide and wild. Grey, like storm clouds.

Grandmother's last words to me dive down deep into the ocean I drown in, pulling me back to the surface.

Remember who you are.

My mother named me Blaze. I am the daughter of two great Houses. I am the last Rain Singer. The beginning that brought the end. Some say I'm Gods' damned. Some say I'm a murderer, a changeling, a freak.

My entire life was shaped by that storm, by power I thought lost forever.

But what if it's not? What if I can get it back? It's not stealing. I can't steal something that's *mine*, so inherently mine that I was born with it. That it was born with me.

Remember who you are.

'Are you listening to me?' Marina snaps.

Mirrored in the water, I watch as she raises her arms to end this. But I twist round, catch hold of her ankle and tug hard. She topples over, shrieking in surprise.

Clenching my jaw, I make myself stand.

Marina lunges for me, but my spurt of water hits her square in the chest. I send a second, then a third.

Now it's my turn to carve a wave.

It rears up in front of me, ten feet tall and frothing wildly.

Marina staggers backwards, spluttering, but she barely has time to lift her hands before the wave surges forward and envelops her. I watch a moment as she thrashes, tumbled around and around.

Then I snap my fingers and the water freezes solid.

Marina is encased inside the wave, her hair suspended like a dark halo above her head, her limbs frozen at odd angles, her eyes round and terrified.

The crowd are on their feet, the Crowned Council leaning forward on their thrones.

Remember who you are.

I press a hand to the spot where Syla's Eye sits in the centre of my ribcage.

You chose me, I think. *Now it's my turn to choose you.*

The feeling starts in my chest and begins to spread. It is somehow both warm and cold, as strong as steel and yet as fragile as glass. It feels like . . . a soft tug on an innermost part of myself, one that has been asleep for a very long time.

There's another tug. Sharper this time.

Remember who you are.

Drizzle begins to fall, light and slow.

There was a time when I believed I was destined to be drizzle. Weak and inconsequential. Existing between extremes, barely there at all.

The drizzle intensifies, no longer haze but perfectly formed droplets, falling heavy and purposeful from the darkening sky.

After I learned more about my gifts and how to harness them, I thought myself rain. It's my first gift, the one that belongs only to me, which Melded itself to sadness. But I'm realizing that I am more than that. I was always meant to be more than that.

Remember who you are.

The feeling is growing stronger, like it's swallowing me whole. Rain sluices over my skin, spattering hard on the ground. I look up to find that the sun has retreated, the sky now a deep grey. Dark, swollen clouds cluster ominously above my head.

The downpour becomes a torrent. Screams pierce the air as the amphitheatre begins to flood, the water rising at an alarming rate.

Alone, I am shielded by some invisible forcefield, as though I am the very centre of everything.

The eye of the storm.

A strange sound fills my ears, faint and achingly beautiful. Tears stream down my face as I realize what it is.

Rain song.

Spreading my arms wide, I tilt my head back and let it wash over me.

Remember who you are.

It was never a question of forgetting, but of believing. And here, in this moment, I have never felt more like myself.

At last, after summoning every last drop of effort, I reach out to the storm and reel my power in. All at once, the rain stops. Clouds scatter and the sky grows lighter, a pale grey flecked with weakened sunlight. Silence descends like mist.

I stand, panting, shaking so hard my bones seem to knock together.

Remember who you are.

I am the girl who wove the storm that shook the world.

And I'm coming for my crown.

46

What happened next is a blur.

I vaguely recall the emperor saying a few words, calming the hysterical crowd and announcing me as the winner. Physicians poured into the amphitheatre, some headed towards Marina, who was lying in a sodden heap, others towards me, but I brushed them off, forcing myself to put one foot in front of the other until I was safely back inside the tunnel. Then I slumped to the ground.

I woke up some time later inside my tent. One of the physicians noticed my eyelids fluttering and murmured something I didn't catch as she tipped a vial of clear liquid down my throat.

When I eventually come to, I'm lying on my bed in the Golden Palace. It's dusk and all the candles are lit. Grandmother is leaning over me, her face tight and lined with worry. I watch it soften as she takes me in, reaching out a hand to stroke my hair.

'My darling one.'

'Grandmother,' I whisper, then inhale sharply as the pain arrives.

'They realigned the bone,' says Grandmother, gesturing

to my nose. 'The swelling should start to go down in a day or two.'

I nod, which hurts. Grandmother helps me sit up to sip some water. I almost choke on it as the memories of the trials burst through the haze of painkiller.

'Flint! Where is he?'

'Resting,' says Grandmother. 'As you should be. He's in the medical wing.'

'Is he all right?'

The slight pause before Grandmother speaks seems to clamp down on the gravity in the room. 'Your brother is doing as well as can be expected. The skin on the left side of his face was badly burned after your cousin . . .' She stops, swallows. 'They managed to save it. Except . . . except . . .' Grandmother looks away, pressing her lips tightly together.

My heart shrinks to the size of a fingernail. '*Except?*'

Grandmother cups my cheek and I'm torn between wanting to rip the answer from her mouth or clapping my hands over my ears so that I never have to hear it.

'His left eye,' she says quietly. 'It was open when . . .' She takes a long breath. 'I'm afraid he can't see out of it any more, my darling one.'

The room shifts and spins. I think I might vomit.

'You mean . . . you mean he's . . . *blind*?' The last word is no more than a whisper.

'Only in his left eye,' Grandmother says quickly.

'And there's nothing they can do?' I choke out.

Grandmother shakes her head. I bite back the sob building in my throat and swing my legs out of bed. This slight movement leaves me dizzy.

'What are you doing?'

I try to stand. 'Flint. I have to see him. I have to –'

But Grandmother pushes me gently back down. 'He's sleeping, Blaze, and you're not steady enough to go anywhere tonight. His chaperone is with him – he's not left his side. You may see your brother tomorrow once you're fit and rested, do you hear me?'

I glare at her. Then fall back against the cushions, numb.

Fury finds me first.

'*Ember*,' I breathe.

The glass of water next to the bed freezes then shatters.

Grandmother throws out an arm to shield my face. 'Blaze. *Blaze*. You must stay calm –'

But I'm wrenching myself free from the silk sheets, ice burning cold at my core as I stagger to my feet.

'River,' I hear Grandmother say.

Everything tilts sideways, but a pair of arms scoops me up before I hit the ground.

When I next open my eyes, I see moonlight filtering in through the curtains. My motions are groggy and slow, as though my muscles have been replaced with treacle. I'm desperately thirsty, but I remember that I smashed my glass of water.

Then I remember why.

I struggle into a sitting position just as a candle flickers to life beside the bed.

'I *told* you to rest,' Grandmother says with a sigh. 'Future queen or not, I would ask you to remember that I am rarely wrong, especially when it comes to you.'

She hands me another cup of water and I drain it in two gulps. That's when her words begin to permeate the remaining fog inside my head.

Future queen.

'I won,' I whisper.

Grandmother nods. 'You did.'

'And that means . . .'

'That you are about to be crowned the new Queen of the Aquatori.'

My stomach turns inside out. 'But – but the people. They'll *never* accept me.'

Grandmother places a hand over mine. 'I won't pretend that this transition is going to be easy. Many challenges lie ahead, but you must weather the storm. You must be brave. Unshakeable. Only then can you prove to the people – *your* people – that you are so much more than what they think you are.' Candlelight dances in her eyes. 'You won your crown, Blaze. Now *earn* it.'

A torrent of emotions collide into me, one after the other.

Fear, hot and suffocating, followed by that wistful pang of loss for the future I had once planned for myself. I was so focused on beating Marina, on *winning*, that I had almost forgotten winning didn't mean the end – it was just the start. What was it Grandmother had said all those weeks ago on the morning of the eclipse?

Make no mistake, the real game begins when the winners take their thrones.

Doubt burrows deep. I don't know if I have what it takes to be queen. What if I'm not brave, or unshakeable? What if

I fall flat on my face? What if the people refuse to serve me, or worse, revolt against my rule?

I rub my scar, the mottled remains of my first brandmark, my constant reminder that I am not who I was supposed to be – Ignitia. Bold and bright, a daughter of fire, another spark to stoke the legacy of House Harglade.

And yet, strangely, in this moment I find I'm glad. Because that girl couldn't have turned water to ice, or carved a wave, or called the rain. That girl isn't me. It doesn't matter who I was supposed to be, for in that amphitheatre I remembered who I am.

I wasn't born to conjure flames, but to drown them.

I feel it then, amid the fear and loss and doubt, something unfamiliar and yet almost feverish in its intensity. *Pride.*

I think of the storm, the way it felt to weave it, to control the clouds and paint the sky and watch my power rain down upon the earth. Power that is mine and mine alone.

Power that was returned to me.

Without thinking, my fingers move to brush the chain round my neck. Grandmother notices. I tense up as she reaches out and pulls Syla's talisman from beneath the collar of my nightgown.

'An eye,' she murmurs.

'It belongs to Spinner,' I lie quickly. 'She gave it to me as a good luck charm.'

Grandmother smiles gently. 'Well, then, it certainly worked, didn't it?'

I nod, then wince, lifting a hand to probe the swollen lump on my head. 'Ouch.'

'Sleep,' Grandmother orders.

'How can I possibly go to sleep after what's just happened?' I ask incredulously.

'Because, my darling one, I don't care that you're the new Aquatori Queen. I am your grandmother, and you will do as I say.'

Admitting defeat, I let her tuck me in. Something small and soft leaps on to the bed and curls up next to me, purring in my ear.

'Hello, Mouse,' I whisper, as she nuzzles into my cheek.

Despite what I said, it doesn't take long for sleep to pull me under. I dream of Flint, watching as he crumples to the ground again and again. I dream of Syla, bound in crystal chains down in the dungeons. I dream of the rain's song, pure and devastatingly beautiful.

And I dream of eyes.

Eyes and skies and storms.

47

Etheri scatter in their haste to let me pass as I make my way through the Golden Palace towards Queen Hydra's chambers.

She's sitting in her chair by the window. I am not here by invitation but it seems my visit was anticipated, as she greets me before even turning round.

'Blaze.'

I curtsy deeply. 'Your Majesty.'

'Some day soon, child, it shall be I who will bend the knee to you.'

The very idea is so absurd that I almost laugh. Clearing my throat, I rub my scar as I try desperately to think of something to say.

The queen smiles. 'It's quite all right. After nearly twenty-five years as ruler I welcome the opportunity to step down. Naturally not all of my fellow Council members share my views, but they will come to realize that when something has run its course . . .' She shakes her head. 'Well, best to let it go.'

I sink down into the chair beside her as she pours me a cup of hot sweet tea.

'And how is your brother?'

Flint still hasn't been able to utter more than a few words. The physicians think it wise to keep him dosed with painkiller. Mostly he sleeps. Sometimes his good eye shoots open frantically, then slides closed again as the drugs pull him back under.

'As well as can be expected, Your Majesty.'

Queen Hydra doesn't press me. The circlet of golden waves sparkles in the light from the late-afternoon sun.

'It feels right that I should be handing this crown over to you,' she says softly. 'I knew it was going to be yours. I knew from the moment I met you.'

Her words both touch me and terrify me in equal measure.

'I have spent the last seventeen years locked away from the world,' I say quietly. 'I've never been to the Waterlands. I don't know the people I'm supposed to rule over. I don't know the first thing about being queen. How – how am I supposed to do this?'

The queen stirs her tea, tapping the spoon delicately on the rim of the cup before replacing it on the saucer. 'If you were not daunted by the life that awaits you, I would think you unworthy of it,' she tells me.

I swallow hard. 'Will you help me?'

Queen Hydra's voice is as solemn as a vow. 'If that is what you wish.'

When I push open the door to my chambers, Elva is waiting for me. Though still beautiful, there are telltale shadows beneath her eyes, which have resumed their usual amber hue. She's gripping the back of a chair as though her legs might crumble beneath her.

'You're back,' I say bluntly.

She dips her head, butter-blonde hair spilling across her face. 'I know you must be angry with me,' she whispers. 'I . . . I never meant, I never wanted . . .'

'Elva.'

She looks up and there's fear in those eyes, real fear, and for a moment I don't see the girl standing in front of me but the girl torn from the arms of her mother and sold into serfdom, the girl who took a whipping to save a young boy from the same fate, the girl who ripped off a piece of the only garment she owns to bind my bleeding hand, and I feel any remnants of the betrayal that fuelled my anger fizzle and sputter out.

'You love him, don't you?' I say. 'Hal. You really love him?'

I see the answer in her face. I recognize it instantly. It's the same way my mother looked whenever my father walked into a room. As though she were lit up from within.

I nod, then slump into a chair, gesturing for Elva to take the seat opposite. 'How are you feeling?'

She looks stunned.

'What?' I shrug. 'Who am I to stand in the way of true love?'

She blinks then perches tentatively on the edge of the chair, hands folded in her lap. 'I feel . . . *strange*.'

'What exactly did Fox tell you?'

Elva looks suddenly terrified. 'He . . . he said that if I told anyone, he'd . . .'

'He'd what?' I raise an eyebrow.

Elva shivers, her voice barely audible. 'He said he'd kill me.'

'Not going to happen,' I assure her. 'Not on my watch, anyway. Don't let him scare you.'

She frowns. 'But . . . aren't you scared of him?'

Yes.

'No, and you shouldn't be either,' I say firmly. 'Besides, do you really think he'd go to all the trouble of saving you if he was just planning on killing you?'

She thinks about this for a moment, seemingly unconvinced.

I lean towards her. 'Do you understand, Elva? Do you understand what I – what's happened?' I catch myself just in time. Confessing that it was me who returned her magic means exposing the truth about the Eye of the Soul.

Elva shifts uncomfortably in her seat. 'He told me that I'm a . . . *Mage.*' She says the word like it burns her mouth. 'But I can't be, I –'

'It's all right,' I tell her. 'It's a lot to take in, I know.'

She buries her face in her hands.

'Elva,' I say gently. 'You do know what this means, don't you? You possess extraordinary power. You don't have to be a serf any more, you can be whatever you want, go anywhere you choose. You could . . . you could go home.'

She stills. Lifting her head ever so slightly, she whispers, 'I could go home?'

I watch in astonishment as thin tendrils of darkness begin to escape from the tips of her fingers, ribbons of shadow wrapping themselves round her.

A single tear slips down her cheek. 'What's happening to me?'

We're both startled by a knock at the door. Elva waits, panic-stricken, until the gloom dissipates, then crosses to answer it, her face flushing with guilt and delight. Hal stands on the threshold. Something in his tired eyes sparks to life as his gaze falls on Elva, and I get the feeling that she won't be going anywhere, at least not anytime soon.

I'm coming to terms with it, I am, and I've forgiven them for deceiving me, for the most part anyway, but I can't resist giving a small, pronounced cough.

'Blaze.' Hal bows his head as he moves into the room.

I rise and sink into a curtsy. 'Your Imperial Highness.'

Elva hovers uncertainly by the door.

'You can stay,' I tell her.

She shakes her head. 'I should go,' she says, then slips quietly from the room.

'So,' I venture, as the door snicks shut behind her. 'I'll bet you didn't see this coming.'

Hal sits down next to me. 'I always believed in you, Blaze. From the very beginning.'

There's a pause. I don't speak, knowing he has more to say.

Eventually he turns his head and looks me in the eye. 'Tell me I haven't lost you forever,' he says. 'Tell me we can still be friends.'

I think back to my Name Day, the way Hal held out his hand to me, and all I know is that in spite of everything, my life got a little brighter the night I met the Prince of the Dawn.

He wants to be my friend. I thought I wanted more. But I'm realizing now that maybe that's all I ever needed from him. Maybe that's all we were ever supposed to be.

'Always,' I tell him.

Hal smiles. 'I want you to know that I'm happy – no, I'm *honoured* – that you will be joining my Council.'

I smile back. 'The honour is mine.'

My brother is still asleep when I reach the medical wing, his face half obscured by bandages.

Sheen dozes in a chair next to the bed. He's barely left Flint's side since the third trial, more of a sentinel than a chaperone, guarding him with such sombre devotion that sometimes I feel as though I'm intruding. My gaze lingers on his outstretched hand lying just inches away from Flint's, my heart sinking as I take in the sight of my brother's brandmark, which no longer glows. Fresh pain rears up and threatens to choke me.

It's not just that Flint lost. It's far worse than that. It's that Ember *won*. I can barely think about her without wanting to break something. A glass. A vase. A neck.

Last night I walked in on Aunt Yvainne weeping uncontrollably in the arms of her wife, Seraphine, who was murmuring words of comfort. Our aunt has never disguised her hope that it would be Flint who would take her place upon the throne. Except now . . .

I clench my jaw, my eyes falling on Spinner. She's sleeping too, sitting propped upright on the windowsill, head tipped forward on to her chest, a single tear still dangling from her chin.

Every time I enter this room I'm torn between disappointment and relief. Disappointment because part of me longs to hear Flint's voice, to see him sitting up in bed waiting for me, and relief because the other part wants to prolong the time he spends safely tucked into oblivion, entirely unaware of what has happened to him.

He mumbles something incoherent in his sleep and I reach forward instinctively, gently pushing his thick curls back off his forehead, which is warm and damp with sweat. I cool the water in the wash bowl beside the bed, soaking a scrap of cloth and wringing it out before dabbing it lightly across the right side of his face.

A cloud of drizzle follows me all the way back to the Aquatori Wing. Yet as soon I reach my chambers my gaze lands on the eye-shaped door knocker, and I realize that there is still one person I have to visit.

I dart along the candlelit corridors to the Golden Library. My little alcove is deserted, but a small orb of light floats gently in the air beside the larger of the two armchairs.

'I know you're here,' I say into the silence. 'Show yourself.'

Suddenly the light begins to grow in both size and brightness until I'm forced to shield my eyes from the blinding glare of it. When I emerge, the old man is sitting in front of me, arranging his pale-gold robes neatly around him on the chair.

'So, girl. To what do I owe this entirely unforeseen pleasure?'

'I need answers,' I say firmly. 'And you're going to give them to me.'

He raises a bushy eyebrow. 'Am I, indeed? And what would incite me to do that?'

I don't hesitate before looping the chain over my head and dangling Syla's Eye in front of him. '*This.*'

There is a long, loaded silence.

I sink down into the armchair opposite him. 'Who are you?'

The old man smiles crookedly, age lines carving deep grooves into the skin of his face. 'The girl asks who I am. Not who I was.'

I stare at him, my mind blank.

'There was a time,' he begins, 'when I held the world in the palm of my hand. I was a force of nature, a ruler unrivalled, a God among men. I was the most powerful being on this earth. Or so I thought.'

His dark eyes are clouded with memory.

'I heard rumours,' the old man continues, 'whispers about three Magi sisters, each of whom possessed an enchanted golden Eye. The Eye of the Past, the Eye of the Future and the Eye of the Soul. I had to find out if these stories were true, and when I discovered that they were, I knew I had to act. I knew I had to take these Eyes for myself. War raged, blood spilled, and the third sister was brought to Ostacre in crystal chains.'

'Syla,' I murmur.

'Syla,' he confirms. 'Yet her elder sisters were not such obliging girls. You remember what happened to Sifa and Seera?'

I nod. 'You said they fled, that they were killed. But before they died, they hid their talismans where they would never be found.'

The old man chuckles. 'Where they *believed* they would never be found.'

'What do you mean?'

'Oh, sweet girl,' he says, shaking his head fondly. 'Do you really think I don't know that the Eye of the Past swings from your friend the Earth Cleaver's neck?'

My chest constricts, crushing my windpipe. 'I don't know what you're talking about.'

'A lie. And not a very good one either.'

I swallow hard. 'Why are you telling me this? Why did you tell me the story?'

'Because I was always going to be the one to tell it to you, girl.'

My heart beats loud and fast in my ears. 'What does that *mean*?'

'It means that I saw myself telling you this story before you were even born.'

The old man lifts a long, gnarled finger, and I realize that he's not wearing his usual pair of golden gloves. The orb of light glides closer until it hovers in the space between us, as bright as my brandmark.

'Seera tried to hide it from me, you know. And she succeeded, for many years.'

I watch, dumbstruck, as the light begins to shrink, growing dimmer and dimmer until it isn't an orb of light at all but something small and delicate, glinting gold.

'She went to her grave believing I would never find it,' he says, as the object falls into his outstretched hand. 'But I *did*.'

I'm shaking my head, refusing to believe that I am looking at the missing Eye, refusing to believe that it has been here in the old man's possession this whole time.

Fox's voice comes back to me.

The Eyes are much like their original owners. They're sisters. They like to be together.

'You . . . you have the Eye of the Future,' I whisper.

'How observant you are, girl.'

'But *how*?'

'You sound afraid. But one should not fear the future, one must seize it.'

A memory stirs. It's of those very same words spoken to me by another, someone with a voice as soft as silk.

'But perhaps you are right to be wary,' the old man continues. 'Your enemy is close, girl. If only you knew what he has in store for you.'

My hands are trembling. I clutch the arms of the chair tightly. 'Who are you?'

The old man presses the tips of his pale fingers together. 'I am many things. I was once fire, I was once water, I was once air and earth and dawn. I was the puppet master. I pulled the golden threads of life. My *name*, girl. Ask me my name.'

Another orb of light flares up next to him and I gasp. It is the Imperial Family alone who wields the gift of light, and only then, a firstborn son. An emperor.

My mind is spinning yet I am immobilized by the old man's eyes, deep black and strangely familiar. 'What is your name?' I breathe.

He holds out a hand, and on it I see a faded brandmark,

a sun enclosing an eye, and a golden signet ring engraved with a bird in flight. No, not just any bird.

A raven.

'It is a pleasure to formally make your acquaintance, Storm Weaver,' he says. 'My name is Caius Castellion.'

48

The morning of the Binding Ceremony dawns pink and gold.

I sit on my balcony, watching the sun make its slow ascent into the blush-streaked sky, my eyes aching with tiredness. Sleep has been elusive. Since the revelation in the library, I've spent most nights lying awake, turning Syla's talisman over and over in my hands.

Caius Castellion.

The old man is Caius Castellion.

Hal's grandfather. *Fox*'s grandfather. The emperor who defeated the Magi and conquered the Otherlands, who enslaved Syla, who knows that I possess the Eye of the Soul and Fox the Eye of the Past, and who himself possesses the Eye of the Future.

All this time and I didn't know. I didn't even suspect. Why would I? The old emperor is supposed to be bedridden, attended to by an army of court physicians. They say his health is poor, that his mind declines by the day. But though elderly and frail, the old man I know does not seem like someone who has been abandoned by his mental faculties. In fact he seems perfectly astute. More than astute – cunning.

Am I really expected to believe that after everything he did to possess the three enchanted Eyes, he would just sit idly by while they are wielded by another?

He's playing a game, only I don't know the rules. I didn't even know I was a player.

Heaving myself up, I go back inside in search of Mouse, but it's not my kitten waiting for me on my bed. It's a leather belt with a sheath, similar to the one River wears that holds his small silver trident, except this sheath is curved, as though it were designed just for . . .

I pick up my dagger and slot it inside. It fits perfectly. There's a note, too.

For you.

'Wake up, *Your Majesty*. It's time.' Spinner shoves a cup of well-sugared coffee into my hands. 'Drink,' she orders. 'Gods, you look *awful*.' She pushes me gently into the chair before the dressing table and examines my face in the mirror, turning it this way and that. 'Hmm,' she says eventually. 'It's not going to be easy. But I think I can make it work.'

'Glad to hear it,' I tell her.

Spinner doesn't look too well-rested herself. My guess is that she came straight from the medical wing. Like Sheen, she barely leaves. Not now that Flint's awake. A few days ago I arrived to find him sitting propped up in bed, smiling weakly.

'Well, sister mine,' he'd said, 'I hear congratulations are in order. It seems you quite literally took the third trial by storm.'

In true Flint fashion, my brother is somehow inconceivably cheerful. But I know, in the way only I can, that inside he is reeling. And when the shock eventually wears off, I worry about what might replace it.

I sit quietly while Spinner and Elva prepare me for the Ceremony, taking extra care to cover up the bruising around my nose, and by the time they're finished, I am almost unrecognizable.

'There!' Spinner claps her hands together. 'What do you think?'

'I certainly look the part,' I say.

Spinner squeezes my hand. 'You don't *look* the part, Blaze. You *are* the part.'

I walk towards the Choosing Chamber in a gown the colour of sunlit ocean – a bright, brilliant blue that glides out behind me, the material as supple and fluid as water. My hair is unbound, my eyelids dusted with a storm-grey powder. Round my neck I wear Syla's Eye, and slung over my hips I wear the leather belt complete with sheath and dagger.

The Binding takes place in a gigantic domed chamber situated at the very highest point of the palace. Here, both Crowned Councils, the old and the new, congregate to complete the Ceremony, which is presided over by the Supreme Mother of the Valla Jakartis, an ancient sisterhood of Etheri who lead modest lives devoid of riches or grandeur, never marrying, choosing instead to dedicate themselves entirely to prayer and worship.

The Ceremony comprises two parts. First, the current emperor relinquishes the powers bestowed upon him by his Crowned Council, meaning his direct line into all four gifts will be severed. Second, the new Council will step forward and the whole process will be reversed. One by one, the Heirs will be joined with the new emperor, forging the bond that will allow Hal to access and embody our powers for as long as he sits upon the Golden Throne. The coronation will take place tonight. The ensuing celebrations are said to last weeks. I only hope Flint will be well enough to attend.

I see the door up ahead, and my stomach seems to shrink at an alarming rate. I barely have time to take a breath before it's opened and I'm ushered into a small chamber.

Queen Hydra is smiling at me from the other side of the room. She's dressed in her usual simple attire, her blue eyes sparkling, long silvery-white hair spilling down her back.

'If only your mother could see you now,' she says softly. 'She would be so proud.'

Drizzle threatens to fall, but I will it away. 'Thank you, Your Majesty,' I whisper.

At that moment the door leading out into the chamber beyond swings open. I have to clench my hands into fists to stop them from trembling.

Queen Hydra crosses over to me and takes my arm. Then she says, 'Never doubt the tides of fortune, whether they break or bind.'

And with that, we step out into the beginning.

The Choosing Chamber is breathtaking, sunlight streaming in through stained glass. Curved golden pews have been erected for those important enough to witness such an event, and in the very centre of the room is a large circular pedestal. As I get closer I see that it is carved with five symbols – the Ignitia flame, Ventalla feather, Terrathian tree, Aquatori waterdrop and, in the middle of them all, the Imperial sun.

Queen Hydra and I climb the steps and take our places. Moments later there's a collective intake of breath from the onlookers, and I turn to find Queen Aspen looking beautiful in a gown of rustling leaves. Beside her walks the Earth Cleaver, his sage-green shirt billowing open slightly at his chest, exposing a few inches of golden skin and golden chain. At the sight of him my stomach flips over, and I avert my eyes as he takes his place on my left, the space between us brimming with the secrets we now share.

Another door opens on the far side of the chamber, revealing King Balen and Zephyr, both dressed in cloaks of mist-grey silk. The King of the Air comes to a stop on his nephew's other side, smiling round at the congregation.

I turn my attention towards the onlookers and spot Grandmother immediately. She's sitting with Renly, murmuring quietly in his ear. When he sees me looking, my little brother grins and waves, and I feel some of the tightness in my chest begin to loosen.

Then there's the sound of another door opening, and any solace I've found freezes solid.

Ember skips into the chamber beside Aunt Yvainne, wearing an extravagant burnt-orange gown, her lips curled in a sickly-sweet smile. I'm overcome with a sudden all-consuming urge to wipe it right off her face. The ice inside me splinters and cracks, and I take a step forward. But then, out of the corner of my eye, I see Fox give a small shake of his head, which is enough to make me hesitate just long enough for the Ignitia Queen and Heir to sweep past. I glance questioningly at him, but he's staring straight ahead, giving no indication that he's done anything to deter me. Breathing hard through my nose, I fall back into step with Queen Hydra, gazing around at the completed circle.

The onlookers fall completely silent as the final door opens and out walks the Supreme Mother of the Valla Jakartis followed by Emperor Alvar, who looks as gaunt as ever. A hereditary ailment, Fox had claimed. I wonder what it could be.

Prince Hal is last to emerge, dressed in a long ceremonial cloak of spun gold. His handsome face is pale and drawn, as though he hasn't been sleeping.

The Castellions move to stand in the centre of the pedestal. Hal seems to be trying to remain expressionless, but I notice the tremor in his hands as he folds them carefully in front of him, turning his attention to the Supreme Mother. She's a small woman, tiny really, with wispy grey hair scraped back under an imposingly tall headdress. She wears plain robes the colour of weak tea, which trail behind her as she walks slowly around the congregation.

'Today,' she begins, in a powerful, gravelly-sounding voice I was not expecting, 'is a day of great change, great promise. Today we witness the dawn of a new era.'

The Supreme Mother closes her eyes and begins to pray, the tips of her fingers pressed lightly together. My heart seems to be doing pirouettes. I concentrate very hard on my feet, then gasp with astonishment when I look up again.

Thin tendrils of gold, so fine as to resemble thread, stretch suspended in the air between the emperor and Aunt Yvainne, binding them together. Hal's eyes are wide, and Zephyr whistles quietly under his breath. I watch in raptured silence as yet more threads of power spring forth from the emperor and glide towards Queen Hydra.

The Supreme Mother's voice rises from a mutter to a

chant, her pale robes whispering across the pedestal as the emperor is joined with all three queens.

Just then, Fox, who has been watching the proceedings with only mild interest, turns rigid. I can see the muscles twitching in his jaw, the stiffness of his shoulders, the sparks of intensity in his green eyes as he stares into the depths of something I cannot see.

I glance around at the others, but no one else seems to have noticed.

Hesitantly, I reach out and touch his arm. And suddenly I am no longer in the Choosing Chamber. I am somewhere else entirely.

A large room, filled to bursting with flowers. There's a rocking horse in the corner, and in the centre, a bed. There's a child sleeping in it, her long auburn hair spilling over the pillows. It's the little girl from Fox's first trial. His sister.

Freya.

The vision turns slightly blurry, but I make out a figure approaching the bed – a man, tall and dark and dressed in robes of steel grey.

I hear the echo of a voice.

To break the world, you must first break his heart.

The man strokes a long, pale finger down Freya's cheek, and all of a sudden her leaf-green eyes fly open. She begins to choke, convulsing as if her air supply has been cut off.

I look on, helpless and frozen, as her small body goes limp.

The man turns round, and I see his face.

I let go of Fox's arm and the Choosing Chamber swims back into view. His expression is awash with such an amalgamation of emotions that I can't quite disentangle them. But as he steps forward into the circle, I see one that I recognize.

Raw, blinding rage.

'You,' he breathes, pointing a finger straight at his uncle.

Every pair of eyes in the room snaps to King Balen, who merely raises an eyebrow. The Supreme Mother trails off mid-sentence, turning to survey the scene.

Fox is vibrating with fury. 'It was you,' he says. 'All this time.'

The Supreme Mother bristles. 'You dare to disrupt –'

But the emperor holds up a hand, silencing her. The golden tendrils still gleam, connecting him to the members of his Council – all but one.

King Balen steps in front of his brother, his gaze locked on Fox. 'My dear nephew,' he says silkily, 'are you quite well?'

That's when the ground begins to quake. The onlookers scream, gripping tightly to the golden pews, clutching one another in fear.

During this brief moment of panic, Fox slides my dagger from the sheath at my hip. He advances towards King Balen, still standing protectively in front of the emperor, who seems unable to move, tethered as he is on all sides by unbreakable threads of power.

Fox draws the knife back and lunges for his uncle. Yet the Ventalla King only smiles widely before flitting into thin air, and I watch, horrified, as my dagger is buried deep in the emperor's heart.

49

Blood blooms across the emperor's chest.

He tries to stem the flow with his hands but already his cloak is stained scarlet. The dagger clatters to the floor as he falls to his knees.

Everyone is screaming.

And that's when I realize – the emperor is not the only one bleeding.

Time seems to slow as I take in the rest of the Crowned Council. Queen Yvainne, Queen Aspen and Queen Hydra are all drenched in blood, each of them clutching the spot over their heart. One by one, they all collapse to the ground, which has ceased its shaking.

Some of the guests have fled the chamber, while others are seemingly immobilized with shock. I can just make out a terrified Renly in Kai's arms as he and Elaith disappear through the towering golden doors.

A team of physicians swarms into the chamber just as River reaches me. His presence seems to jolt me awake and I rip the sleeves from my dress, which he uses to staunch the flow of blood still bubbling up through the deep gash in Queen Hydra's chest.

This can't be happening. How are the Council bleeding out before my eyes?

My gaze falls on the tendrils of power tethering the queens to the emperor. I hear Caius Castellion's voice in my head.

I was the puppet master. I pulled the golden threads of life.

Even as I watch, the tendrils flicker slightly then begin to fade.

Of course. Because that's what they did, the Council – pledge their lives and their power to him who reigns over us all. And in that moment, as they were linked together as one, Fox had stabbed his father through the heart.

An agonized scream rises above the others. Kestrel Calloway is hunched over the emperor, tears splashing on to his face as she holds it in her hands. Hal is crouched next to her, his entire body shaking. I whip my head round, looking for Fox. He's standing motionless, clutching the Eye of the Past round his neck.

And I understand. Sifa's talisman – it gave him a vision.

Freya didn't die of the sweating sickness. She was killed in cold blood all because of a prophesy – murdered by her uncle, King Balen.

Fox's eyes are wild with shock, his features twisted with pain.

To break the world, you must first break his heart.

The Cleaving . . . The Rift . . .

The boy who broke the world.

Realization floods through me just as an awful keening sound fills the chamber. Grandmother kneels beside Aunt Yvainne while a wailing Seraphine rocks her body back and forth.

Then – silence.

Complete and utter silence, as though the very air is holding its breath. It's only when I hear the soft chuckle that I realize why.

King Balen has emerged from nothingness into the centre of the pedestal. He glances around at the bodies of his fellow Council members and tuts. 'Such a waste.'

All around me mouths are opening and closing, but no sound is forthcoming, because sound is carried on the air, and the air belongs to King Balen.

The king walks the circumference of the pedestal, stepping daintily over his brother's legs and coming to a stop in front of Fox. 'Oh, nephew. Just look at what you've done.'

Fox lunges forward, but King Balen has evidently placed a barrier of dense air between them and Fox is unable to touch him. I watch his gaze dart towards where my dagger lies discarded near the emperor's body. King Balen notices too. With a delicate flick of his wrist, he sends the weapon flying across the chamber. Then, an invisible stream of air pulls forth Sifa's Eye from where it sits tucked beneath Fox's shirt. I let out a silent gasp of horror as the talisman hovers gently a few inches above his chest.

King Balen beams. 'I knew it. Oh, you clever, clever boy. The Eye of the Past. How long I have searched for it.'

Roots sprout up across the pedestal, spreading out towards King Balen, but he just makes another careless gesture and the golden chain begins to tighten round Fox's neck.

'Such a prize.' The king reaches out to stroke the Eye, just as he stroked Freya's cheek. 'I thank you, nephew, most ardently, for finding it for me.'

The roots slow their progress, twisting in on themselves. '*You*,' Fox chokes, his hands scrabbling at the tightening chain. 'You killed my sister –'

'I did.' King Balen brings his foot down on a now-immobilized root, causing the wood to splinter and snap through the thick silence. 'A necessary sacrifice, I'm afraid, given the prophesy. But that's a story for another time, for I believe there is yet another prize in our midst. And I think I know exactly who wields it.' The king's black eyes glitter. 'Isn't that right, little dove?'

My heart seems to judder to a halt.

The next moment I'm lifted into the air by a powerful gust of wind. I dangle, suspended in place, struggling desperately as King Balen advances towards me. Gritting my teeth, I send a blast of ice straight at his face, but he deflects it.

Suddenly the room is filled with blinding light. Hal is on his feet, arms raised. He stares from Fox, to me, to his uncle, as if unsure who to attack and who to defend.

The king's change in focus appears to be enough for the onlookers to regain their voices.

I watch as Grandmother pushes through the team of physicians, a ball of flame growing in her palm and reflected in her eyes. When she speaks, her voice burns with death-like rage. 'Stay *away* from my granddaughter.'

River tears his gaze from a fading Queen Hydra and moves to stand beside her. I hear the unmistakable sound of footsteps coming from outside the Choosing Chamber, but King Balen points lazily at the doors, which slam shut. There are several terrified shrieks. Kestrel Calloway is still sobbing uncontrollably upon the emperor's chest.

'Oh, *enough* already,' says King Balen with a sigh. 'I can barely hear myself think.' He raises a hand and almost everyone in the room is lifted a few feet into the air then hurled against the walls. Hal's crown is thrown from his head and rolls across the ground.

Silence descends once more.

'There,' King Balen says happily. 'Much better, don't you think, Lady Harglade? And please allow me to be the first to offer my condolences on the death of Queen Yvainne. That's two daughters you've lost now. That must require some carelessness.'

The sound that rips itself from Grandmother's mouth is one of pure fury – a battle cry. Her ruby-encrusted stick falls to the ground. She plants her feet, squares her shoulders, and for a moment I don't see an old woman, stooped with age and grief, but Leda Flameslinger.

Descendant of the Fire Goddess, Vesta. Head of House Harglade.

A *warrior*.

She begins to launch flame after flame at King Balen, while River follows suit with shards of ice and boiling jets. My eyes widen as I take in the two of them, fire and water, fighting together in tandem. It's instinctive, the way they move. Like a dance, rhythmic and fluid, one they seem to have learned the steps to a long time ago. Twice King Balen is almost knocked off his feet. Yet already I can see Grandmother and River beginning to tire as age catches up with them, while the Ventalla King holds fast, countering each attack.

'Grandmother!' I shriek as she stumbles, but River is there to steady her.

That's when King Balen sweeps his arms forward, sending a violent squall in their direction, which blasts them backwards as if they were no more than the feathers adorning his gleaming golden crown.

I scream as Grandmother and River collide with one of the golden doors and slump in a heap next to Hal and the Supreme Mother, who lies with her neck bent at an odd angle.

King Balen beams up at me. 'Now, where were we?'

At that moment there's a clattering sound behind him.

Fox is panting, his broken chain dangling from one hand while Sifa's Eye skitters across the pedestal, causing King Balen to hesitate just long enough for the vines snaking round Fox's wrists to launch themselves at him, wrapping round his ankles and sending him crashing to the ground.

As the king is brought down, his command over my invisible tethers loosens and I feel myself falling through the air. I cry out, bracing for impact.

But Fox gets there just in time, catching me in his arms.

His jaw is clenched and he sets me down, eyes blazing. I hold on to his gaze for one fleeting moment before turning and racing towards Grandmother. But before I can reach her, the air around me thins.

I can't breathe.

I can't breathe, and nor, it appears, can Fox.

King Balen, now back on his feet, stoops down and picks up Sifa's Eye from where it rests a few paces away from the emperor's cooling body. Fox falls to the floor, gasping, clutching at his throat just like Freya had in his vision. I watch as he mouths one single word.

Run.

But I don't. I stagger forward, sending a weak wave towards King Balen. He deflects it with an amused chuckle, causing the water to slosh over the floor next to where Queen Hydra lies, the life draining out of her. I try again, but already I can feel myself becoming light-headed. Dark spots crowd my vision and I collapse to my knees.

'Finally,' says King Balen. 'Some manners.'

He claps his hands and air comes flooding back in. I heave great, ragged breaths, watching as Fox does the same.

'I find I grow tired of our games today, little dove. I wish for us to be friends. And one does not steal from one's friends.'

'Steal?' I choke out, my fist closing round Syla's Eye. 'It doesn't belong to *you*.'

'Incorrect, sweet one. What with my brother's untimely death, as the Eye was once my father's, it is now mine by right. So be a good girl and hand it over.'

I shake my head.

King Balen clicks his tongue. 'Stubborn little thing. I could take it from you, you know. I could rip it from your neck. But I would so much prefer it if you were to offer me it willingly. After all, if you are to be my queen we must learn to trust one another.'

Your enemy is close, girl. If only you knew what he has in store for you.

My throat tightens. 'What do you mean *your* queen?'

'You didn't really think I would let my nephew take the Imperial Crown, did you? Dear Haldyn is too much like his father to ever be a true leader. Too soft. Too easily distracted by pretty things. No, that burden should fall to one who is truly worthy of it. And, with power itself in my possession, who would dare challenge me?'

Fox gets to his feet, but he's blasted backwards by a gust of air before he can take so much as a step towards us, landing with a dull thud next to Queen Hydra. The blood from her wound has mingled with the water on the floor, the remnants of my fallen waves. She held on longer than the other Council members but she's dead now, I'm sure of it.

'Just think,' King Balen continues. 'Just think of what we could achieve together. The world we could create, the kingdoms we could raze to the ground.'

Perhaps I'm imagining it, but I could have sworn that Queen Hydra's arm just twitched.

The Ventalla King holds out a hand. 'The Eye, little dove.'

My mind spins, my fingers skimming the chain round my neck.

'No,' Fox whispers, his voice hoarse.

Slowly, I pull the chain over my head.

'That's right,' croons King Balen. 'Now, give it to me.'

Behind him, Queen Hydra's eyes flicker open. I watch in astonishment as her hand begins to move jerkily through the water.

My gaze snaps back to the king. 'If I give you what you want, do I have your word that no one else dies?'

King Balen inclines his head. 'Oh, sweet one. You have my solemn vow.'

Queen Hydra's hand is still moving. Beside her, Fox's eyes are trained on me.

'You and I, little dove,' King Balen says softly, leaning forward. 'You and I will conquer all.'

444

I look down at the talisman in my palm. Power itself. Power that should never belong to someone like King Balen, who would take it by force and use it to exploit others for his own gain. And if he were to get his hands on all three . . .

The king moves closer. His voice is as silky smooth as ever, but I can hear the note of impatience in it. 'Give me the Eye.'

I get to my feet. 'Fine.'

'*No*,' snarls Fox.

King Balen smiles. 'I knew you'd make the right choice.'

'Yes,' I tell him. 'So did I.'

I draw back my arm and throw the Eye with all my might towards Queen Hydra. I watch as it flies through the air in a great soaring arc and falls through the portal she has drawn in the blood-soaked water, disappearing from sight. The portal closes behind it and the Aquatori Queen's eyes flutter shut for the final time.

An enraged scream tears apart the room. King Balen turns on me, his face contorted with fury. But at that moment the doors around the Choosing Chamber burst open and in pours the Imperial Guard.

As the knights advance, King Balen's raven eyes meet mine. Then he is gone, vanished into thin air. But his words remain, the whisper of a promise.

'This is only the beginning, little dove.'

50

We sit on the roof of Harglade Hall, watching the sun set over Valburn.

'Back where it all began,' says Flint, tossing me a peach.

I catch the fruit and take a bite. The day has been uncomfortably hot, with not even the slightest breath of breeze to alleviate the closeness of the air. It's been the same for weeks – bright hot days, cold dark nights, reports of wildfires, crops dying, monstrous waves.

The Gods are angry, the natural order has been thrown into chaos, and the elements are out of control.

'What do you think of this one?' Flint asks, gesturing to the patch over his eye.

'I like it,' I tell him, but that's not quite true. The truth is that it unsettles me. Horrifies me, even. Because I'm not used to seeing Flint like this – damaged.

He takes a swig from a dusty bottle of wine. 'Spinner sent me a crate full of patches. She and Elaith reckon they can turn them into a fashion statement, said they'll have everyone wearing one by Dawnday.'

I try to smile. 'I don't doubt it.'

Renly mutters something in his sleep, shifting his head in

my lap. Since watching the emperor being stabbed through the heart, he's been suffering from nightmares, and he's not the only one. I can still smell the blood, can still see the three queens lying dead around me.

After the Binding Ceremony, many called for the Earth Cleaver's execution, demanding the deaths of the old Council be avenged. The people don't know what really transpired in that chamber. They don't know what I know. About King Balen, about the prophesy. But regardless, killing an Heir is forbidden. It is our most ancient, most sacred law.

So, Fox wasn't executed – he was exiled.

It was Hal's first decree as emperor.

Hal, who has spent these last few weeks tailed by an incessant deluge of advisers and emissaries, who has had to step into his new role under the worst possible circumstances, and who lost a father and banished a brother in the space of a few days, all while waiting for his uncle to make his next move for the throne.

King Balen could be anywhere, biding his time, gathering his supporters. But one thing is for certain – he will return.

In light of this, much like the last seventeen years, I have been placed under heavy guard, unable to venture out anywhere on my own, and I have accepted it with the grace and dignity of a future queen. Or at least, that's what they think.

I knew I had to tell Flint about the three enchanted Eyes. He didn't believe me at first, and just made a joke about needing a new eye himself. But I persisted.

'So what you're saying is,' my brother began slowly after I'd finished explaining, 'King Balen has the Eye that once belonged to . . .'

'Sifa.'

'Sifa. And that with it he has the ability to see the past?'

I nodded.

'And you have – *had* – the one belonging to . . .'

'*Syla.*'

'Which gave you the power to summon that storm in your third trial and return the gifts of your Obsidian serf girl?'

'Precisely.'

'And King Balen wants it?'

'Badly.'

'But you chucked it through a portal to . . . *where*, exactly?'

'Well, that's just it,' I said. 'I don't know. The only thing going through my mind when I did it was that I wanted to get the Eye as far away from King Balen as possible. Wherever it is, it was sent there by some remnant of my subconscious.'

Flint grimaced. 'So it could be *anywhere*?'

'In theory.'

'Well, that certainly gives us a lot to go on. And the old man in the library, the one who told you the story, the one who turned out to be *Caius Castellion*. He has the last Eye. The one belonging to . . . to . . .'

'Seera.'

'Yes, her. Where do you suppose he's taken it?'

I shook my head. 'Your guess is as good as mine.'

Caius disappeared straight after the Ceremony. For all I know, he could have been in league with King Balen this whole time. But somehow I don't believe it. And if I'm right, and he has an agenda of his own, then my list of enemies has doubled. So, with King Balen in possession of the Eye of the Past and Caius Castellion in possession of the Eye of the Future, it is imperative that the Eye of the Soul be found, and fast. If I found it before, I can find it again. I *must* find it again. Because if it falls into the wrong hands, we are all lost.

When I first proposed my plan to Flint, he told me that I was foolish, reckless and out of my mind. That I was an Heir, soon to be crowned queen. That I couldn't just go gallivanting off in search of an enchanted talisman with the power to destroy the world. But I ground him down. It has to be me, I told him. I was the one called to the Keep, I was the one who sent the Eye through the portal.

'I'm coming with you, you know,' Flint says, now lying back on the roof with his arms folded under his head.

I frown. 'Don't be ridiculous. You're still in recovery.'

'Oh, *I'm* ridiculous? That's rich coming from the girl who's lived the best part of her life under house arrest deciding to just wander merrily out into the big bad world.'

I roll my eyes.

'Besides,' Flint continues. 'What do you want me to do? Stay here? With Grandmother unable to string a sentence together, and Spinner sending me different samples of the silk she's considering for your coronation gown? I'll pass.'

'You could always stay at the palace,' I suggest.

'Oh, because the atmosphere is *so* much better over there? Seriously, Blaze, I can't take much more of this doom and gloom. I've endured weeks of it already.'

'So that's it, then? You've made up your mind? You're coming with me?'

My brother nods.

'You said yourself it'll be dangerous.'

'Sister, danger is my middle name.'

'Strange. I always thought it was Percival.'

Flint grins at me.

I gaze out at the Creek, watching the sunlight sparkle off the water, thinking about the crown of golden waves waiting in the throne room. Not inherited – won. Yet still to be earned.

Queen Hydra's last words come back to me, and I hold them close.

Never doubt the tides of fortune, whether they break or bind.

Acknowledgements

I want to start by thanking my agent, Catherine Cho of Paper Literary. You are the wisest and most insightful person I know, and the fiercest champion of this story. Thank you for believing in me – and Blaze – from the very beginning.

Thank you to my editors, Carmen McCullough, Kate Meltzer and Emilia Sowersby. I am forever grateful for your sharp eyes, excellent advice, and endless encouragement.

None of this would have been possible without the incredible team at Penguin. Thank you, Alice Todd, Tom Rubira, Awo Ibrahim, Alicia Ingram, Shreeta Shah, Libby Thornton, Millie Street, Sarah Doyle, Adam Webling, Katherine Whelan, Chessanie Vincent, Lottie Chesterman, Rachael Hughes, Alice Grigg, Susanne Evans, Beth Fennell, Millie Lovett, Maeve Banham, Magdalena Morris, Clare Braganza, Ellie Williamson, Stella Dodwell, Rosie Pinder, Aisling O'Toole, Cande Rivero, Chloe Traynor and Faith Young.

Thank you to the brilliant team at Roaring Brook – Connie Hsu, Allison Verost, Julia Bianchi, Samira Iravani, Kathy Wielgosz, Jennifer Healey, Celeste Cass and Tatiana

Merced-Zarou. I'm beyond thrilled that the Storm Weaver series has such a tremendous US home.

Thank you to my international publishers and translators for taking such good care of this book, and for your dedication to championing stories all around the world.

Thank you, Melissa Pimentel, for your stellar editorial insight pre-submission.

Thank you to every librarian, bookseller and blogger who has supported *Heir of Storms*. I'm so grateful for all that you do for readers and for writers.

Thank you to the many wonderful teachers I've had over the years at Buckstone Primary School, Boroughmuir High School, the University of Stirling, and the University of Edinburgh. Your kindness and encouragement was truly invaluable to me.

To the Hamiltons –

Thank you to my mum. Because of you, I've always believed that I could do anything I set my mind to. You are my safe place, my biggest supporter, and my favourite person in the world. Nan and Bubba, my earliest memories are of you reading to me. Thank you for everything. I'll never be able to put into words how much you mean to me. I love you forever. Nisey, you are the best auntie and a true soulmate. My life is infinitely better because you're in it.

To the Murrays –

Thank you to my dad, for always listening, for making me laugh, for keeping every story I've ever written, and for being someone I can talk to about anything. Granny and Grandad, you have seen many different versions of this book, but your enthusiasm has been never-ending. Your selflessness and compassion inspire me every single day. Rebecca, thank you for all the wise counsel and heart-to-hearts. I feel very lucky to be your little sister.

Emma Wadee, thank you for a lifetime of love and guidance, and for always being there no matter what. Amber Wadee, you are the sun in human form. To all the Wadees – I'm so grateful I got to grow up with you.

Gill and John Wright, thank you for being my second parents. Sam Wright, thank you for twenty years of friendship, and for once telling me, *Whatever happens, your book will always have one reader.* Beth Wright, I'm sorry for locking you in that cupboard when we were younger. I hope I've made it up to you since.

Kirsty Sutherland, my day one, I don't know what I'd do without you. Amy Niven, my angel, you make everything brighter. Mhairi McDougall, my rock, I'm very glad we decided to stop being enemies. Tia Fitzgerald, Emma Anderson, Emily Rigg, Eilidh Robertson and Aimee Vincent – I adore you all.

Hayley, Keith and Karis Mackie, where have you been all my life?

Jess, Hux and Ziggy, thank you for being the best dogs in the whole wide world.

And finally, to my brother, Sam – thank you for being my built-in best friend, and for being so flatteringly unsurprised by the news of my book deal. You are the reason I was able to put the love Blaze has for Flint and Renly into words.

It's a real privilege to write for young adults. I never needed books more than during adolescence. Being a teenager is tough. It's a state of constant emotional whiplash. Blaze learning how to Meld was something I found very healing to explore. I wanted to create a way in which pain could become power, so I wrote a story about a girl who can turn sadness into magic. I hope you enjoyed reading it as much as I loved writing it.

LAURYN HAMILTON MURRAY

grew up in Scotland writing stories about
sad girls, secrets and storms. She holds
a BA Hons in English Literature from the
University of Stirling and a Masters in
Creative Writing from the University of
Edinburgh. She is happiest when reading
in the sun and hiking with her dogs,
Huxley and Ziggy.